Elaine,

Thank-you for your
hospitality & support

Gisela

KILOWATT

A NOVEL BY

JOE MCHUGH

Calling Crane

Kilowatt
by Joe McHugh
Published by Calling Crane
Copyright © 2007 by Joe McHugh
www.callingcrane.com

ISBN 978-0-9619943-4-7

Library of Congress Control Number 2007902321

Printed in the United States of America
by Sheridan Books, Inc., a member of the Green Press Initiative.
May 2007

1 2 3 4 5 6 7 8 9 10

Disclaimer

KVMR-FM is a real radio station located in the real town of
Nevada City, California. The incidents and characters, however,
described in this novel are entirely fictitious and bear no relationship
in any way to any person, corporation, or organization. Really.

For my wife Paula,
for her help, love, and patience.

ACKNOWLEDGMENTS

I would like to thank the following individuals: Dr. Louis Bloomfield, Professor of Physics at the University of Virginia, and his son Aaron, a high school senior who shares his father's passion for scientific inquiry; David Warren, government relations director for the Washington Public Utility Districts and former director of the Washington State Energy Policy; Petr Merkulov, retired colonel with Special Forces for the Russian Army, and Dr. Patricia Krafic, professor of Russian Language and Literature at Evergreen State College.

I wish to also thank my daughter Anna McHugh for her invaluable help as editor.

I owe a huge debt of gratitude to the staff and congregation of the First Christian Church of Olympia, Washington, who provided me with a writing office and much needed encouragement and affection.

Others I would like to thank include Emily, Patrick, and Clara McHugh who each contributed ideas and encouragement, Lucy Winter, the best of mother-in-laws, Joanna Robinson, Steve Baker, Drew Batchelder, Dr. James Grimes, Will Sherlin, Jim Hightower, John Vanek, Susan Sanders, Ted Beedy, Kaye Connors, Skip Houser, Ted Andrews, Kathy Yeates Peck, Georganna Carey Galateau, Dr. Joe Pellicer, Clint Sullivan, Christopher Carey, Hilary Lien-Beye, Aileen Denton Setter, Doris Scarborough, Martha Jackson, Deb Ross, Joel Steever, and my good friends at the Timberland Library and Otto's Bakery in Olympia, Washington.

For additional help I would like to thank Tyson Slocum with the consumer advocacy group Public Citizen, Dan York with the American Council for an Energy-Efficient Economy, and James Bushnell, research director for the University of California Energy Institute.

KILOWATT

"If everybody minded their own business,"
the Duchess said in a hoarse growl,
"the world would go round a deal faster than it does."

"Which would not be an advantage," said Alice

Lewis Carroll

PROLOGUE

On July 3, 1989, an article appeared on page nine of the Soviet military newspaper Red Star *reporting that the Soviet Navy had deployed a Poseidon-class submersible to the Barents Sea as part of a marine environmental research project. Two days later* Pravda *reported the tragic loss of seventy-three sailors in an airplane crash in a remote region of the Ural Mountains. The sailors, according to the article, were being transferred from the Northern Fleet at Severomorsk to the Pacific Ocean Fleet at Vladivostok. When questioned by a reporter from Reuters, V.I. Volkov, Chief of the Soviet Navy Political Directorate, denied that any relationship existed between these two incidents. He was lying.*

THE DAWN MIST drifted in ghost-like columns across the still surface of the lake. In the shallows near the shore a heron stood motionless besides a fallen tree; farther out the dark head of a beaver glided past trailing a strand of water lilies. For Admiral Dmitri Nikolaevich Rastakov. these moments of beauty and unhurried solitude were rare and cherished—especially now with his nation in crisis and Gorbachëv leading them all to perdition.

He made another cast and watched the lure arc and drop with a soft splash. With a flick of the wrist he set the spinner and began reeling it in. Perhaps it was time to retire, he thought. Get out before the pressures of the job killed him. He could just make out the bright flash of the spinner as it ran in toward the boat. He had two perch caught already and would use them for his famous *ukhá*, the fish soup his grandmother had taught him how to make. Pulling his line from the water, he reached into the tackle box for another lure and was startled by the sudden trilling of the mobile telephone. A large, cumbersome device encased in military steel and powered by nickel-cadmium batteries, it connected him to the Ministry of Defense and went with him everywhere, like a personal demon.

For a brief moment he was tempted to pitch the accursed thing overboard. Instead he lifted the black receiver.

"Yes?"

"Comrade Admiral, I have been trying to reach you for many hours."

"The reception is seldom good here, Comrade Captain. What do you want?"

"We have a situation, very serious. I am on my way to you now and will arrive shortly."

Rastakov returned the receiver to its cradle. The caller was Vasili Pushkin, a descendent of the noted Russian poet and his chief of staff. Mobile phones were not secure so Pushkin could say nothing more. The serious situation must have something to do with the sea trials for the *Tigron*, the new BARS-class attack submarine taking place in the Barents Sea four hundred miles to the north. Why else had Pushkin dared disturb him during his jealously guarded once-a-year fishing trip? A foreboding like dark winter clouds gathered in his mind as he retrieved his fish and laid them in the bottom of the boat. He cursed as he yanked the oil-stained rope and the outboard motor surged to life. He pushed the throttle arm and the boat swept around, the bow lifting, as it headed toward the shore, the waves fanning out in velvet undulations behind him

So, he thought to himself, it *was* too good to be true. Despite the long years of suffering and sacrifice, Russia was quickly falling into irrelevance. A second-class world power. Everything broken. But *if* the new technology had succeeded, what then? The Russian Bear would play its tune and the rest of the world would dance— the United States, Western Europe, China.

The rising sun was beginning to illuminate the upper branches of the white birches along the western shore of the lake as he cut the motor and allowed the wake to push him up to the dock. In the silence, he heard the KA-29 Helix helicopter approaching from the northeast, the urgent thumping of its six long blades cutting through the morning air, growing steadily louder and more commanding. An eagle resting on a tree limb near the bank took wing in protest, swooping low over the water.

Rastakov tied up to the dock and, forgetting the perch, hurried up the long narrow steps to the *dacha*. He called to his wife. He only had a few minutes to tell her he was leaving and to gather his things. Their vacation was over; she would have to close up on her own.

ON THE FLIGHT back to the Northern Fleet Naval Command Center, Pushkin briefed him. What he said confirmed Rastakov's worst fears.

"The *Tigron* performed flawlessly for the first twelve hours of her underwater high-speed trial," Pushkin shouted over the high-pitched whine of the helicopter's two turboshaft engines. "Then we received a broken up transmission; the signal was unintelligible. After that, only silence."

"What steps have you taken to locate her?" Rastakov asked.

"The destroyer *Druzhni* and sub-tender *Pechora* were on station monitoring the tests. They have located the emergency buoy. The *Tigron* is on the sea bed at a depth of four hundred feet."

"Any surface debris?"

"None, Comrade Admiral."

So it was possible the *Tigron's* hull remained intact. Perhaps it was only a power failure, serious but not necessarily fatal. Rastakov forced himself to concentrate. Why had the sailors made no attempt to escape? The submarine's conning tower was equipped with a VKS pod. It was designed to accommodate most of the crew, and once detached, would float to the surface and serve as a lifeboat until rescuers arrived. But there was no VKS.

He looked out the side window. The sun was nearing its zenith and a whitish haze obscured much of the earth below. He rubbed his face and reminded himself to shave when they landed. He leaned back against the headrest, closed his eyes, and tried to imagine what the sailors inside the *Tigron* were going through. He had served sixteen years aboard submarines and knew the constant unspoken dread that lurked in the back of each submariner's mind—the dread of being trapped inside a stricken vessel deep beneath the surface of the ocean. It took a special kind of courage to overcome this fear and he often wondered what led young men to volunteer for such hazardous service. For some, no doubt, it was the desire to protect their beloved Mother Russia from her enemies; for others, little more than a restless young man's need to escape the crushing boredom and alcoholism of some village out on the steppe, doomed to discover in time that he has merely traded one kind of claustrophobia for another.

"Comrade Admiral?" Captain Pushkin was awaiting orders. To save the men inside the *Tigron*, Rastakov knew he must refuse to think of them. Instead he must focus on basics: currents and weather conditions, battery life and fuel requirements.

He felt confined and unbuckled his safety harness. "Do we have a rescue submersible ready for service?"

"Yes, at the base in Severodvinsk. It is being loaded onto a freighter now."

"When will it be ready to sail?"

"Within two hours."

Seventy-three men and the most important ship in the Soviet Navy lost at sea. A catastrophe.

"Do you have the weather forecast?"

Pushkin handed him a printout that called for clear skies through the next day, then clouds and scattered showers for the remainder of the week.

"Do the Americans suspect a problem?"

Pushkin gave a shrug. "We have detected no increase in their signal activity."

"Good, we must proceed with great caution."

A cover story was needed to explain away the use of the mini-sub; nothing went unnoticed by the American satellites. An article in *Red Star* about a marine research project should suffice. He would ask Pushkin to write it. He came from a literary family. They might yet fool the Americans.

Twenty-two hours later, radio communication from the search and rescue team in the mini-sub was patched through to the Command Center. Because everything about the *Tigron* and its prototype technology was ultra-top secret, the signal was not broadcast over the public address system. Instead it was routed to only two sets of headphones, those of Admiral Rastakov and his chief of staff.

The submarine was lying on the sea floor, and the captain of the mini-sub reported no visible damage to the hull. He moved the sub into position over the forward emergency escape hatch.

"We are docking now."

There was a long pause broken by intermittent static.

"Docking is complete," the voice returned. "We are opening the escape hatch into the fourth compartment."

More static. Rastakov glanced over at Pushkin. The man's face was impenetrable as stone, but the dark circles under his eyes testified to his lack of sleep.

"The hatch is open," the captain's voice was efficient, brisk. "Lieutenants Voronin and Biryukov are entering the vessel."

For the next hour, disembodied voices of the rescue team came from the dark void of the sea into the Admiral's headphones. They spoke of grotesque scenes of death and destruction. Several times the men vomited, fouling their breathing masks. Twice they requested permission to turn back but were ordered to continue, documenting what they found with underwater cameras. They paid a high price for completing the work—within a month Lieutenant Voronin would resign his commission, while Lieutenant Biryukov would spend the next two years in and out of a psychiatric hospital. They would be the only ones ever to go inside the ill-fated *Tigron*.

*   *   *

SHORTLY AFTERWARDS, Naval High Command sent Rastakov orders to attach magnetic charges to the hull of the submarine and blow her up. There was to be no formal investigation. No final report. No evidence whatsoever that a submarine called the *Tigron* had ever existed—except for the bones of seventy-three sailors scattered across the sea floor awaiting the end of time.

Then came the decision by the Kremlin to terminate the Svarog Project, the name given to the prototype technology being tested aboard the *Tigron*. Rastakov couldn't understand. What had happened was most unfortunate, yes, but the new technology could be Russia's salvation. All that was needed was time to work through the problems.

"Time and lots of rubles, Nikolaevich, which we do not have," said Commissar Volkov, chief of the Soviet Navy Political Directorate. He had at last agreed to see Rastakov after repeated requests from the admiral. Spread out on the desktop between the two men were the photographs taken inside the *Tigron*. Volkov, a notorious chain smoker, lit a fresh cigarette.

"And there is something more I must tell you, Comrade Admiral. Anatoly Kryuchkov is dead."

The news stunned Rastakov. Kryuchkov was the scientist responsible for the Svarog Project; the man and the project were one and the same.

"Dead? How?" Rastakov said, trying to gather his wits.

Volkov tilted back in his chair exhaling blue smoke into the air. "The KGB screwed up big time, that is how. They had Kryuchkov under surveillance, but a week after the *Tigron* accident, he slipped away. They found his clothes folded neatly on the bank of the Moscow River. Two days later the body washed up down river. Most of his flesh had been eaten away."

"Do they know for certain it was Kryuchkov?"

"He was wearing a medical necklace."

Rastakov waited as the Volkov took another puff on his cigarette.

"They checked his dental records. A positive match."

"It could have been an accident, not suicide."

"There was a note."

"What did it say?"

"That he was responsible for the accident and the death of so many men, could not live with the burden of guilt, that sort of thing. Kryuchkov was most upset that his discovery was being used by the military. He objected vigorously." Here Volkov waved his hand as ashes fell on the carpet. "But none of us has the luxury to please only himself. Is that not so, Comrade Admiral? We serve for the good of the state."

Rastakov had spoken with Kryuchkov in person only twice, but he had heard through the grapevine that the scientist was unhappy working for the military.

"Certainly we can continue without him," he said.

"I am afraid not." The knell of fatalism in his superior's voice was unmistakable.

"Why not?"

"Because our little inventor destroyed critical project data. Again the KGB cannot say how he gained access to the computer files and drawings, but he did, and they are gone."

What incompetence! What waste! He pleaded with Volkov to resurrect the Svarog Project but was reminded that the project, like its inventor, was dead. End of story.

As for the Communists, Rastakov knew it would not be long until they were finished as well. In time the organized criminal gangs would take control of Mother Russia, aided and abetted by corrupt officials like Volkov. Well, as far as he was concerned, they could have her. He would go back to his fishing.

1

REB DID HIS best to ignore the ticking of the wall clock as Dr. Yoon studied the readout from the tonometer, a marvel of twenty-first century medical technology that shot puffs of air against the eyeball to measure the intraocular pressure. Like most Americans, Reb hated waiting, especially this doctor kind of waiting. For him it was a club people joined as they got older, whether they wanted to or not; a sort of bargain-basement Club Med where, instead of lolling away pleasant hours under the Caribbean sun drinking Pink Flamingos, its members sat glumly in examination rooms under the indifferent glare of florescent lights, or paced nervously back and forth at home waiting for the telephone to ring with test results that would foretell their fate. Good news and life went on pretty much as it had; bad news—and judging by the ophthalmologist's somber expression the news was bad—then what? Keep his chin up and play the dutiful patient? Get a second opinion? And what about the cost? Would Blue Shield live up to its commitments, or would the ravenous appetite of the medical industrial complex devour his life savings, as it had so many others? Reb tried to think of a joke to drive these depressing thoughts from his mind. There was the one about the Irishman who was dying of cancer but told his friends it was AIDS, because he didn't want any of them sleeping with his wife after he was dead. Or the patient who had both his feet amputated and—

He was interrupted by the sound of Dr. Yoon's voice.

"Your pressures are increasing," the doctor said, holding out the strip of paper in the way a detective at a murder scene might offer a spent shell casing to his partner. Reb made no effort to take it.

"What about the eye drops?" he asked.

Dr. Yoon shook his head. "They no longer seem to be effective. Your right eye is forty; your left eye is thirty-eight. And there appears to be damage to the optical nerve."

"Permanent damage?"

"I'm afraid so."

Reb thought about his grandmother Libby who went blind from glaucoma in her eighties and had to be put in a nursing home. He would bring her audio books from the library and sometimes he read to her. Now here *he* was, only fifty-three, and already doing the glaucoma shuffle.

"What's the next step?" he asked.

"Laser surgery."

"What will that do?"

"Open up the small filtering area in the eyeball. That will allow the fluid to drain, which should reduce the pressure."

"Will it keep me from going blind?"

Concern softened the ophthalmologist's features.

"We've made great strides in treating glaucoma in recent years, Mr. Morgan, but your condition is unusually aggressive. The medicated drops should have helped, but they haven't. Surgery is the next step." A slight pause as he searched for words. "Unfortunately, we will have no way of knowing for sure whether it will lower the pressures until after the procedure. You should prepare yourself."

Right, Reb thought. Prepare myself.

THE SKY WAS dark with waiting rain as he made his way out to the parking lot—dark and brooding like his mood. A woman pulling a crying child by the arm hurried past as he unlocked the door to his car and felt the first sprinkles on the back of his hand. Five minutes later he was on Business I-80 heading west

toward Sacramento, the rain so heavy it was like driving through
a car wash at fifty-miles-an-hour. He strained to see ahead, the
wipers of his 1967 Volvo 800S unable to keep up with the deluge.
He considered pulling over and sitting out the downpour, but
he wanted to get home. He had a lot to think about. The last
three years had been a disaster. First there was the break up of his
marriage. He and Kate had been married a long time and raised
a child together. Brendan was now in graduate school in Virginia
and would receive his doctorate soon. Once a week they talked on
the telephone and discussed basketball or the latest article in the
New Yorker; the divorce was never mentioned.

Then the early morning phone call from Mrs. Throckton in
New Jersey. His father was in the hospital, she told him. He'd
had a massive stroke and the doctors didn't expect him to last
long. This was followed by a hurried flight to Newark and a cab
ride to the hospital where they said their good-byes with Reb
doing all the talking, and his father, unable to speak, clutching
his son's hand and peering over the edge of oblivion with moist,
tired eyes.

And now, if Dr. Yoon was to be believed, his glaucoma was out
of control confirming the old adage that troubles came in threes.
Reb turned the defroster fan knob up to full but still had to wipe
the inside of the windshield repeatedly with an old undershirt he
kept under the seat. The taillights in front glittered through the
rain like fairy jewels, flashing now and again as someone touched
a brake pedal. He took several long breaths to center himself and
calm his emotions. Trouble was a mountain canyon, dark and
steep, and time was the river that ran through it, bumping and
churning among the boulders. But eventually time would find its
way out again into open country and sunshine. The trick was to
keep the heart in the center of the current, otherwise it could
circle back into eddies of anger and regret. He'd known his share
of hearts trapped in those eddies, or worse, sucked into everlast-
ing holes of despair. That wasn't for him; he would trust time to
carry him safely through.

The traffic eased as the rain let up, and he found himself stuck behind a UPS semi-trailer. He checked the lane to his left and pulled out to pass. A car horn blasted in his ear and he had to jerk the car back behind the truck again, his heart pounding, as a silver BMW swept past, the driver shaking his head with disgust.

Suddenly the full impact of recent events came crashing down on him. He hadn't seen the car. Was it the rain or was his peripheral vision going to hell? If the latter, then he was a menace to others as well as himself. He would have to give up driving. What would he do then? Take public transportation? Get a Seeing-Eye dog? A white-tipped cane?

He felt the challenges piling up in front of him, the first of which was how he would make a living. Photography had been his passion and career since leaving college. Not only did it nurture his creative imagination, it allowed him to work for himself. Given his problematic relationship with authority over the years, this was probably a good thing. But photography was also a cobbled-together livelihood. There were art shows and galleries for his fine art photographs and weddings and portraits when money was tight, with the occasional assignment for the local newspaper thrown in if the regular photographer was on vacation or out sick. That would all end, of course, if his eyes went south on him. Beethoven had managed to continue composing even after he lost his hearing, but a blind photographer? Reb didn't think he had the genius to pull it off.

"You need cheering up, son," he said out loud and switched on KVMR-FM in Nevada City. KVMR was a non-commercial, community radio station located in the Sierra foothills and the only one he listened to anymore. They featured a wide range of music including reggae, folk, rhythm and blues, jazz, and women's music. They also broadcast left-of-center call-in talk shows, astrology readings, political debates, lectures by leading progressives, live reports from environmental conferences, and a community swap shop. Program directors at mainstream public radio stations called it "patchwork programming," a pejorative term because, to their way of thinking, such eclectic programming hurt station "branding." Reb enjoyed the variety. He also appreciated the fact that the DJs were all unpaid volunteers. They would come in at two in the morning just so they could share their favorite Ani DiFranco CD or bootleg recording of the Grateful Dead.

He caught the end of Amy Goodman's *Democracy Now* as he took the Midtown-J Street exit. He had moved into a one bedroom apartment on the top floor of an older home soon after the divorce. He liked the neighborhood's mix of ethnic restaurants and shops. He was particularly fond of the art-house movie theater and late-night cafe over on Broadway.

The local news had an extended piece about the upcoming election in Nevada County and how outside Republican operatives were once again pouring buckets of campaign money into the county to gain control of the Board of Supervisors.

What is it with these Republicans? Reb thought to himself as he pulled into his driveway. They drape themselves in the mantle of small town American virtues, and then they play the pimp for every developer and multinational corporation that comes along looking for a good time. Whatever happened to the party of Lincoln and La Follette. He was about to switch off the engine when the station's program manager interrupted his thoughts.

"Have you ever dreamed about working in radio as a news reporter? Well, here's your chance. KVMR is hiring three interns for our news department. These are full-time paid positions where you will learn how to cover local and regional news as part of a great team of dedicated news hounds. For job description and application call 530-555-KVMR, or visit our web site at KVMR. org. KVMR is an equal opportunity employer."

Reb switched off the car but didn't get out. Radio. He let the word ramble about awhile inside his head until it began to kick up the dust of memory. Soon after arriving at college he had joined the radio club. There were only a dozen or so members and he was given his own Thursday evening music show. He played a lot of Jefferson Airplane and Joni Mitchell. Dylan and the Band too.

The memory was bittersweet because being part of the radio club meant a great deal to him. But then sometime during his sophomore year, his thoughts shifted away from college to the streets where the anti-war movement was coming into its own and the hippies were stirring up their own kind of trouble. College suddenly felt like a prison, and so he left and never looked back.

He got out of the car and climbed the stairs to his apartment. He grabbed a yogurt and a package of smoked salmon from the refrigerator. He thought about calling Brendan with the news about his eyes but decided to wait. Instead, he dialed the number for KVMR.

2

MARTY HAMILTON BACKED his rented Jaguar into a one-hour parking space on 12th Street. He expected his meeting to take more than an hour but he was running late and didn't have time to drive around looking for a longer-term space or a lot that wasn't full.

"Stop worrying," he told himself as he switched off the engine. "With your salary, you can afford a hundred parking tickets."

He tucked his Oakley sunglasses with titanium frames into their case and tossed the case onto the passenger seat. His colleagues in the marketing department at EnerTex liked to put on airs. They called themselves "deal originators." Not Marty. He knew who he was. A salesman, plain and simple. And what made being a salesman special was the happy fact that he was selling the one thing everyone wanted. Not sex. Better than sex. Energy. Electricity. Kilowatts. The power to run coffee makers and air conditioners, to run everything that made modern living modern. He liked the sound of that last part; it had a ring to it. "Everything that makes modern living modern." He pulled out his palm pilot and jotted down a reminder to work the phrase into a presentation someday.

Two blocks away he entered a recently renovated office building on K Street and rode the elevator to the tenth floor. The velvety notes of orchestral music wafting out of hidden speakers helped settle his youthful nerves and focus his attention on the meeting ahead. He straightened his tie and examined his finger-nails. He considered a short line of coke to bolster his confidence but convinced himself he could do without. "They need you more than you need them," he told himself.

Stepping out of the elevator, he followed the hallway to the offices of Margaret Greer, Special Assistant to the Governor. He opened the door and went in. On the wall behind the reception-ist's desk hung the Great Seal of the State of California. I *do* love this job, he thought as approached the attractive young brunette.

"Hi, I'm Martin Hamilton," he said as he handed her his card. He was tempted to add, "but you can call me the 'Tin Man.'" It was a nickname he'd picked up in college from a character in a movie about two aluminum siding salesmen in Baltimore during the 1960s. Instead he glanced at his Cartier TANK watch.

"I have a two o'clock appointment to see Ms. Greer."

"Please go right in, Mr. Hamilton. They're expecting you," the young woman said and he thought he detected a dash of come-hither warmth in her smile. Trimmed out in his dark blue $2,900 Domenico Vacca suit, Marty Hamilton was an eyeful and he knew it.

The office was spacious and elegant, with floor-to-ceiling windows that looked out over the Sacramento River glittering in the afternoon sunlight. To the right of the polished mahogany desk, four chairs were arranged around a low table upon which rested a crystal vase of fresh-cut flowers, their soft fragrance permeating the air. Marty recognized the vase. It was Waterford. His mother collected Irish crystal and he had developed a keen eye for it over the years. The carpet under the table and chairs was hand-knotted Persian with a preponderance of deep reds.

There's real money to be made in this room, Marty said to himself. And the Tin Man is just the clever boy to make it.

A woman and two men sat around the table and they stood as their visitor entered. The woman took charge of the introductions.

"I'm Maggie Greer, Mr. Hamilton. This is Tony Seriafi and Bob Hunt. Tony is with the California Energy Commission and

Bob works with the legislature." The men shook hands like fellow Rotarians, everyone smiling. It put Marty in mind of his grandfather, the owner of the Oldsmobile dealership in Kalamazoo, Michigan, during the Second World War. For more than four years no one could buy a new car. None were being made. It was all tanks, trucks, and airplanes for the war effort. Then in '46, automobiles started coming back on the market again and people lined up to buy them. In fact, they were so hot to get their hands on a new Olds that his grandfather liked to brag that he didn't need salesmen on the floor anymore—just "order writers." It was that way now for Marty thanks to EnerTex. No real, honest-to-God selling; just writing down orders.

"Would you like some coffee or tea?" Maggie asked after they were seated.

"Sure, coffee would be great."

She picked up the telephone on the table.

"Susan, please bring coffee in for everyone."

Polite with the hired help. He liked that.

"Well, Mr. Hamilton, we're eager to hear what you have to say," Maggie said.

Marty opened his briefcase and drew out three glossy, full color booklets which he distributed.

"I don't need to remind you of the fix California got itself into during the energy crisis of 2001," he began. "Rolling blackouts. Utilities going broke. The state pressuring its neighbors for additional supply. It cost the governor his job." He paused a moment as if the memory was painful for him; the others waited.

"It's true electricity prices have come down since then," he went on, "but what about the future? It is estimated that by the year 2030, California's population will grow to well over *fifty* million. That's an increase of *fourteen* million from what it is today. This means the state will need a minimum of 92 gigawatts of electricity to meet its needs. Currently, the state has 66 gigawatts of supply on hand, but 32.1 gigawatts of that supply is generated by older fossil fuel plants that will be retired before 2030. Add to that loss another 5.4 gigawatts from retired nuclear plants and the state will have to come up with 55 gigawatts of new supply at the very least. Quite a challenge no matter how you look at it."

Too many numbers perhaps, but he wanted them to appreciate the fact that he'd done his homework. He could also tell by the way Hunt and Seriafi shifted uneasily in their chairs that the recitation was having the desired effect. California was facing some hard choices. Electricity was essential to nearly every aspect of life in the Golden State. Hospitals, agricultural irrigation, manufacturing, telephones, waste treatment plants—even the fabled cable cars of San Francisco—would all grind to a halt if the electricity ran out. So where was the state going to get the additional juice? One scheme involved shipping dirty coal-generated electricity over the border from Mexico. But that would require building new high-load transmission lines. Who would build them and how long would it take? Fossil fuel power plants could be thrown up relatively quickly, but it took a minimum of ten years to site and build a transmission line.

Tony Seriafi was the first to respond. "We've initiated a program to install solar panels on a million homes by the year 2018, Mr. Hamilton."

"Yes, I've heard," Marty said, "but the most that will get you is 3,000 megawatts, if you're lucky. Solar is an immature technology at best."

He wanted to say more, but checked himself. No good would be served by playing the scold. All the same, the energy outlook for California, as it was for the rest of the country, was bleak and the sooner they faced the truth the better. So many factors played a part. Even small technological developments could effect future energy needs in surprising ways. The growing popularity of widescreen televisions and plasma computer monitors was a case in point. A typical plasma screen consumed roughly 1,000 kilowatt-hours a year, compared with the older cathode ray tube which used 233 kilowatt-hours. Thus, if half the 12.7 million households in California replaced their CRTs with plasma displays, the state's annual electrical usage would grow by 7.6 billion kilowatt-hours, an increase of nearly 1.3 percent. And this from just one electrical appliance. What would happen if there was a sudden spike in the price of natural gas, or a couple of years of below average rainfall, or a terrorist attack on a major power plant? The state would be forced to ration energy again, leading to economic and political instability.

Hunt looked at his watch and then at Maggie Greer, his impatience ill-masked, and Marty realized it was time to buck up the natives.

"But I didn't come here to peddle doom and gloom," he said with a smile. "Quite the opposite. Like your governor,"—he turned and looked at the life-size framed photograph of the charismatic governor that hung on the wall. The strong jawline, the flinty blue eyes, the slightly goofy grin, it was a face he'd known and loved since childhood. The only thing missing was the signature machine gun. He turned back and discovered that everyone was watching him. He felt a stab of embarrassment.

"Like your governor," he repeated himself, "I believe California has a bright and promising future. Granted, energy deregulation has created difficulties. It wasn't thought out properly; it should have been done in stages. Still, it's a proven fact that government-regulated markets do not work. Only free, competitive markets lead to the innovations that solve real world problems."

"Look Mr. Hamilton—" Hunt tried to interrupt.

"What you're about to say, Mr. Hunt, is that the energy market is different from other markets. It's a market of scarcity because the natural resources we use to generate electricity are finite. Furthermore, most come with negative environmental consequences. Well, that might have been true in the past. But today there's an exciting new technology on the horizon, a technology that will revolutionize how electrical energy is generated and consumed in this country and eventually around the world."

He leaned forward and put his hands on his knees. "The alchemists of the Middle Ages searched in vain for a way to turn lead into gold." This was a riff he'd picked during a lecture on European history while at Vanderbilt. "The Philosopher's Stone" was the name they gave the mysterious and elusive substance they believed could bring about this magical transformation. Well, I can say now with complete confidence that the EnerTex Corporation of Texas has discovered the Philosopher's Stone for our modern age, an entirely new generation technology that will provide Americans with an unlimited supply of affordable, non-polluting electrical energy. If you would now please turn to page three of the prospectus. . ."

He sat back and waited as they turned their attention to the booklets they held in their hands.

"On page three you will find a photograph of our Ranger 1 power plant. It's located in west Texas near a town called Birdstar. The plant went into service a year and a half ago and has a maximum output of 850 megawatts. It's the first of its kind to use ATG technology."

"What does ATG stand for?" Seriafi asked.

"Active Transdimensional Generation. If you turn now to page ten, there is a table with price-per-kilowatt comparisons."

Again he paused.

"As you can see, when compared with coal, natural gas, and nuclear, our new ATG generation process provides electricity at substantially lower cost. And the best part is that EnerTex is able to lock in these low prices over the long term. That means guaranteed, rock steady pricing for the next ten to twenty years. You'll be able to plan your economy knowing in advance precisely what your energy costs will be."

Like a skilled magician waving his wand, young Marty Hamilton had swept away their impatience and anxiety and replaced it with a glorious vision of hope and happy tomorrows. He hadn't learned that trick going to Wharton. No, when it came to selling, the Tin Man was a natural.

There was silence for several minutes as the state officials pored over the prospectus.

"Okay, I give up," Hunt said, "what's the fuel source?"

"I'm afraid I'm not at liberty to say, Mr. Hunt. The information has been classified top-secret."

"Classified? Who classified it?"

"The feds," Tony Seriafi said. "I sent you an email about it, Bob. The technology's so new the government doesn't want it falling into the wrong hands."

"Well, I've heard some crazy schemes in my time but this one takes the cake," Bob said shaking his head and frowning. "You can't go around building power plants without letting people know how they work, what fuel they use, or if they're safe or not!"

It was Maggie's turn to join the conversation. "Two years ago a special six member board was set up to oversee these new power plants and to make sure they pose no threat to public health or the environment. The board is part of the Federal Energy Regulatory Commission and has sole regulatory oversight."

"The legislation establishing the board was passed by Congress," Seriafi added, "and signed into law by the president."

"So the federal government can come into California and do whatever it wants when it comes to regulating electrical generation," Hunt said, his face coloring. It was huge sore point the way more and more state laws were being superseded by federal laws. This included regulations protecting the environment and food safety and labeling standards. Even the voter-approved use of medical marijuana had been trumped by Washington.

"Look, Bob, there's more to this than just reducing the cost of electricity," Maggie said. "It's about reducing global warming. Isn't that right, Mr. Hamilton?"

"The ATG process produces zero emissions of carbon dioxide which is why EnerTex plans to build—"

"If your power plants are as good as you say they are and can help solve the problem of global warming," Hunt said, "then why keep the technology secret? Why not give it away. Post it on the internet. Encourage nations big and small to replace their older polluting plants with these new ATG power plants because global warming is the most serious problem to ever confront mankind and we better do something about it, and do it damn quick."

Marty was speechless; it was the first time anyone had made such a suggestion. What officials usually wanted to know was how EnerTex came up with the technology in the first place, and whether the federal government had helped in its development. It required some fancy footwork to field that particular question since he didn't really know the answer. He assumed some genius at EnerTex had invented the ATG process but the higher-ups would never confirm or deny. Not surprisingly, this gave rise to a variety of rumors; one making the rounds even mentioned the CIA. None of this, of course, had anything to do with him. He was just a salesman, a lowly cog in the machinery of capitalism. But one thing he *was* sure of: capitalists don't *give away* valuable technology. Not even the mighty Bill Gates, who gave his money away but never the operating system.

Fortunately Marty was spared having to respond to Hunt by the arrival of the secretary who entered the room carrying a tray of cups and saucers. She moved around opposite Marty so that she could catch his eye as she set the tray down. This excited him and made him feel important, just what he needed to hold his own with a bunch of California politicos. She left the room before anyone spoke again.

"You must understand our concerns, Mr. Hamilton," Seriafi said in an obvious effort to steer the conversation back to the land of the possible. "What you are saying, if I understand you, is that EnerTex is willing to build its new power plants here in California, but for national security reasons, the citizens of our state will play no part in inspecting or regulating these facilities?"

"That's correct. The federal government would assume full responsibility, not the state."

Marty reached down and picked up his coffee. "Furthermore, before we begin the siting process, we will require that you pass legislation exempting EnerTex from state regulatory oversight."

"That's impossible." Bob Hunt said. "The legislature won't stand for it."

Marty sat back cradling his cup and shrugged his shoulders.

"Then I guess EnerTex will have no choice but to build its power plants elsewhere."

The first rule Marty had learned in a seminar on negotiating was to care, but not too much. If California wasn't interested in getting its energy house in order, then so be it. It was no skin off his nose.

"The state governments of Arkansas, Mississippi, and Maine are willing to meet this legislative requirement," he said. "I'm sure more states will follow when they see how significantly our new plants will cut their electrical energy costs."

"But the political landscape in California is different than it is in those other states," Seriafi said.

"I realize this," Marty said, "but it is precisely the way you run your politics that's caused the mess you're in." Time to call a spade a spade. It gave him a kick to lecture people who were at the top of their game and more than twice his age.

"Not without the help of some pretty damn dishonest Texas corporations," Hunt was quick to add.

"Bob, please," This from Maggie Greer who long ago had accepted the fact that ninety percent of her job was unruffling feathers. She turned to Marty. "Mr. Hamilton, isn't there *some* way we can deal with this problem short of passing special legislation?" She already knew the answer because she had been on the phone earlier that morning with Marty's boss, the CEO and president of EnerTex, Avery Axton.

"There may be a way," Marty said, pausing to sip his coffee. Give a little to get a lot, he told himself. "I believe the people in Nevada might be willing to help."

"Nevada? How's that?" Hunt asked.

"The governor and several key officials have indicated a willingness to allow EnerTex to build two or three power plants in their state and then send the electricity generated by the plants to California. That way the regulatory responsibilities will fall upon their shoulders, not yours, and they are only too happy to pass those responsibilities along to the appropriate officials in Washington."

"Would that result in higher electricity prices for California consumers?" Seriafi asked.

"Of course," Marty said, "but the savings over what Californians currently pay for electricity would still be substantial."

"But two or three plants in Nevada can't hope to meet California's electrical energy needs." Hunt was trying to work out the math, balancing megawatts and votes.

"You're right," Marty said. "In time, we will need to build plants inside California, but by then perhaps the citizens of your state will have learned to trust our company and agree with our position on regulatory oversight."

Marty looked at his watch as if to say, "Well, now that we've dealt with the bigger issues, can we wind this up? How many megawatts did you have in mind this afternoon, Madame? A thousand? Five thousand? Perhaps you'd be interested in a vacuum cleaner or a set of encyclopedias while we're at it."

Writing orders, not selling, that's what he was doing. And he might get it all done before his parking meter ran out. Anything was possible for the Tin Man these days.

3

THE DRIVE FROM Sacramento to Nevada City took Reb an hour and ten minutes since the rain had stopped. The week before he'd had the Volvo's engine tuned and it navigated the winding roads of the Sierra Foothills with hydrocarbon-intoxicated enthusiasm. His own enthusiasm was in high gear as well although he was slightly embarrassed by the Walter Mitty-like fantasies coursing through his head. He was going to be another Edward R. Murrow—cigarette in one hand, microphone in the other—reporting from the rooftops of London. Or Charles Collingwood sending his radio dispatches back from the blood-stained beaches of Normandy. These men were before his time, but he was old enough to know who they were and how their work shaped the early days of electronic journalism. Perhaps an opportunity would come his way to make a contribution, to report on a story of real importance. Stranger things had happened.

Taking the downtown exit off Highway 49, he turned onto Broad Street. Isolated patches of blue in the sky overhead brought with them the promise of better weather and he rolled down the window to let in the invigorating scent of ponderosa pine. He enjoyed visiting Nevada City with its quaint Victorian architecture and small town feel. Christened "Queen of the Northern Mines" during the Gold Rush, it was one of the oldest towns in the Golden State and a favorite with tourists from the Bay Area. It was also a magnet for New Agers, a catch-all phrase that included psychic channelers, aroma therapists, astrologers, and other seekers of spiritual understanding, both frivolous and sincere.

He crossed Deer Creek and parked in front of the stately, if frayed-at-the-cuffs, National Hotel where the upper crust of Nevada County congregated in the 1800s and made their deals for gold mines and water rights. It was rumored the hotel was haunted and that guests were regularly awakened in the middle of the night by the sound of doors opening and closing and disembodied footsteps in the hallway. For Reb that notion only added to the hotel's charm, and he once suggested to Kate that they celebrate their anniversary there. Kate, however, wasn't big on ghosts and they wound up renting a bungalow for the weekend in Half Moon Bay.

The offices for KVMR were on Spring Street across the street from the Miner's Foundry Cultural Center and as Reb entered he was met by a middle-aged woman sitting behind a desk. She had white wavy hair and she wore a large turquoise and silver necklace.

"Can I help you?" she asked.

"I'm here to see Phil Cook," Reb said. "We talked on the phone this morning. It's about a job with the news department."

"Phil just stepped out; he'll be back in a minute. You can wait for him here if you want."

She pointed to a chair that was hemmed in by boxes of music CDs, discarded computers, and bins full of mail.

"My name is Mattie," she said with a friendly smile.

"I'm Reb, Reb Morgan."

"Where are you from?"

"Sacramento."

She shook her head. "The valley's too hot for me."

"Have you worked here long?" Reb asked.

"I volunteer twice a week answering the telephone. I'm a midwife the rest of the time."

"My son Brendan was delivered by a midwife. Well, that was the plan, but after eighteen hours of labor, the midwife told us to go to the hospital. That's where he was born, by C-section."

They were interrupted by the arrival of the program manager, a large man with sandy hair and a slightly disheveled appearance, who was carrying a paper bag and large container of coffee.

"Lunch," he said holding up the items by way of an apology for not shaking hands as Mattie made the introductions.

"Why don't I give you a quick tour of the station before we talk," he said.

They walked through the outer office past a cluster of desks into another room that was filled from floor to ceiling with shelves full of CDs.

"This is the music library," Phil said. "The CDs are sorted with colored tape on the spine by genre—red is for rock, green for folk, black and orange is for international."

The CD shelves ran down the middle of the room and along two walls. The older vinyl albums, the kind Reb grew up with, were stacked endwise on shelves that spanned the remaining two walls. Reb noticed a *Traffic* album he had once owned and pulled it out. The ink on the jacket cover was faded, much like his memories of those times.

From the library Phil led him down a short hallway with two doors on the left and a wall of mail cubbyholes at the end. The first door had a glass window and a glowing red "ON-AIR" sign above it. Inside Reb could see two people. One was a stocky man wearing a flowered Hawaiian shirt. He had salt-and-pepper hair tied back in a long pony tail and was sitting behind the control board. The other man was shorter, with close-cut, tight curly hair. He was perched on a high stool with a microphone on an extension arm in front of him. Both were wearing headphones.

"This is our on-air studio," Phil said. "Broadcaster are required to take a class and get certified before they can apply for their own shows."

"Is it hard to get a show?" Reb asked.

"That all depends."

"On what?"

"On the time of day, mostly. There's stiff competition for the morning and early evening shows."

"Who decides who gets a show?"

"The program committee. It's made up of broadcasters and community members."

They walked to the next door which Phil opened so Reb could look inside.

"This is the main production studio. The news department has its own studio upstairs. It's quite a bit smaller but the equipment is state-of-the-art."

Five minutes later they were seated in Phil's office. Reb had thought the front office cluttered, but it ran a poor second to the profusion of padded envelopes, broadcast trade journals, newspapers, empty jewel cases, cassette tapes, and assorted correspondence that were heaped upon the program director's desk. Creativity and chaos were often bedfellows.

"Ever worked in radio before?" Phil asked, leaning back in a cracked vinyl swivel chair that looked as if it had been with the station since it got its license in 1978.

Was this part of the interview? Reb wondered. He wanted to make a good impression; he'd never been formally interviewed before.

"The college I went to in New Hampshire had its own radio station. I hosted a weekly music show my first two semesters. It was a lot of fun."

"Why did you stop?"

"I left college."

Phil popped the lid off his coffee and the dark aroma filled the room.

"Ever go back? To college, I mean?"

"I went to photography school in San Francisco for two years. I've been doing photography ever since."

"Well let me tell you about what's going on here." Phil said and then sipped his coffee. "A board member has given the station a sizable donation to build a first-rate news department. His name is Brent Abrams. He believes the establishment sources of news in this country are seriously screwed up."

"Where did Abrams get his money?"

"Made it in Silicon Valley. Cashed out just before the high-tech bubble went bust and moved up here to retire. He came on the board a year ago because he said he enjoyed listening to the station. We could use the money for more important things than a news department, such as buying our own building so we don't have to rent anymore, but it's a restrictive gift, so news it is."

He took another sip of his coffee but left the bag with his lunch unopened

"Until now," he said, "all we've had is a part-time news director. That's Alice Carpenter. The other reporters are volunteers. Last February we added a daily five-minute local news segment to follow the BBC World News feed. Now, thanks to the gift, we can make her job full time and train three new reporters."

"How many people do you think will apply?" It was the question foremost in Reb's mind. He wanted to gauge the competition.

"Hard to say," Phil shrugged. The telephone on his desk began ringing but he ignored it. "Intern might not be the right word, but we didn't know what else to call it. It's a learning position, but it comes with a salary. Do you want to know what it pays?"

Reb nodded.

"Twenty-six thousand dollars a year with benefits. For community radio, it's all we can offer but you'll get on-the-job training too."

Twenty-six thousand was at the bottom of the pay scale given the cost of living in California. Still, money matters seldom made it to the top of Reb's priority list. Why that was, he couldn't say. He liked money, got a rush whenever he sold a large framed photograph at an art show, but he didn't think about it very much. Doing the books and paying the bills had been Kate's bailiwick, and the fact that she earned a good salary as a hospital administrator had meant that he could continue with his photography. Then his father died and he inherited a legacy which he invested in bonds and bank CDs so that he now could almost get by on the interest. Besides, he *wanted* the job. One benefit of the glaucoma was that it had added a sense of urgency to his life. No more playing it safe; he didn't have the time.

"So how do I apply?" he asked.

"You want the job?"

"I do."

"Can I ask you why?"

Reb took a moment to consider his answer. If he told Phil that he might be going blind, the program director would understandably be reluctant to give him the job. Age was already a factor working against him; a *blind* old guy would be too much.

But would it be *lying* to conceal the fact? Dr. Yoon said the laser surgery might fix everything and then he would have thrown away a great opportunity for nothing.

"I guess I'm looking for a change." Reb said. The truth about his glaucoma would have to wait. "And I'm something of news junkie." Which was true. He made a point of reading the San Francisco *Chronicle* and Sacramento *Bee* from cover to cover every day, and he had subscriptions to the *New Yorker*, the *Atlantic Monthly*, and the *Economist*. His biggest addiction was C-Span, which he often preferred to watching a movie or reading a book.

Phil was looking at him so that he felt compelled to go on.

"I guess the real reason," he said, "is that the world is pretty messed up right now. There's global warming, which is no joke, and more and more countries are getting nuclear weapons. The Middle East is a wreck, so is much of Africa. Like most people I don't feel like there's anything I can do to make things better, but I want to try. I'm not good looking or thick-skinned enough to go into politics, nor do I have the necessary degrees to work for the government or an NGO. I'm not rich or a celebrity, so what can I do?"

"Work for community radio?" Phil said.

Reb shrugged. "Sacramento is the capitol of the seventh largest economy in the world. There's got to be a lot to report on here."

He could have said more about how being a photographer was lonely work and that he missed being around other people. Besides he was beginning to lose his interest in photography—perhaps in life itself, like the lyrics of the Grateful Dead song, his tears turning to stone. It had been different before the divorce and his father's death. An old woman in a worn coat sitting on a park bench watching lovers walk past hand in hand. Reb once saw the meaning of existence in that single image. Or a child on a tricycle, or a policeman polishing his buttons before the Saint Patrick's Day parade. Now he didn't care all that much if he ever shot another photograph. It *was* time for a change. Either that or go the medication route, Prozac, Zoloft, Lexapro, the whole mélange of corporately manufactured molecules whose corollary function was to keep a drugged-out populace from the realization that the self-same corporations were a major source of the problem.

"I should warn you that community radio stations like KVMR are not the most functional organizations to work for," Phil said putting down his coffee and rummaging around inside his desk for an application form.

"What do you mean?"

"Bloated egos, petty rivalries, feuds over money, marital infidelities, you name it, you'll likely find it here. The station would make a fine setting for a soap opera."

Reb didn't know if Phil was exaggerating or not.

"Why do *you* do it then?" he asked the program director.

"For the money, why else?"

They both laughed as Phil withdrew a piece of paper from a drawer with the triumphant smile of someone who had caught a hare in a thicket with his bare hands. Taking a pen from his shirt pocket, he handed the paper and pen to Reb who took them over to a nearby table. He made room by shoving aside a half-filled box of stale donuts and began filling out the form. Whatever else was going wrong in his life, this, at least, felt right.

4

WHERE DID THE time go? Valdez wondered as she glanced over at the display on the microwave. She had been up since six; it was now eight-forty and the children had missed their bus. She would have to drive them to school before making the fifty mile commute to work. Sandra was executive director of the Family Resource Center in Lubbock, which was fortunate because that made her the boss and not likely to get fired for arriving late. It would be the fourth time this month.

"Luis, Maria, hurry up and get in the car. We don't have all day."

"I can't find my homework, Mama."

"Never mind your homework; tell your teacher you will bring it in tomorrow. And put the milk back in the refrigerator."

She knew they were making a racket and hoped it wouldn't wake her husband. Ernesto worked the graveyard shift as a security guard at the new power plant west of town and he needed his sleep. They had been trying for months to get him on the day shift without success. She hated this arrangement because they seldom got to spend time with each other. He was asleep when she left in the morning, and by the time she got home, he was getting ready to go to work at the plant. Dinner was the only meal the family shared together during the week, and even that failed to happen on the evenings when she had to remain in Lubbock for meetings.

She grabbed her purse and briefcase and hustled the kids out the back door and down the steps toward the car, nearly tripping over the cat as she did so.

"Mary in heaven help us," she muttered under her breath.

Five minutes later she dropped the kids off at St. Theresa's Elementary School and from there she drove through Birdstar past the courthouse, turning east on Waller Road. As she swung onto the northbound ramp of Interstate 23, she switched on the radio and Lyle Workman's folksy voice filled the car.

"Earlier this week Senator Jim Starling of Pennsylvania announced a proposal to charge a two-percent "user's fee" on all political donations. The money would go into a special fund so local election officials could purchase additional voting machines and not keep people waiting for hours out in the rain and cold to cast their vote. The money could also be used to make sure that results from computer voting machines are verifiable by requiring that the computers print paper receipts. Airline passengers pay a user fee to make sure airports and the air traffic control system work efficiently. Well, those who donate to political candidates should want the same thing too—a system that's both efficient and fair. A good idea, right? Wrong, according NAFE, the National Association for Free Enterprise. They claim the user fee is just another tax and they're against taxes. Well, I did some research and this is what I found out. NAFE is funded almost exclusively by one of the largest broadcasters in this country. And is that any surprise? Where do most political donations go now? I tell you where: right into the pockets of the big broadcasters to pay for expensive campaign commercials. Is it really too much then to ask them to give up a small percentage of their large profits so the citizens of this country can maintain a healthy democracy? After all, the airwaves belong to the people; the broadcasters are just borrowing 'em, and for free too.

And while we're talking about elections, Congress. . ."

She listened to the five-minute commentary which came on every weekday morning at 9:10 following the national and local news. Then, as was her custom, she switched off the radio so she could mentally organize her day. But she never missed Workman if she could help it. They had met and become friends while he was Texas Commissioner of Agriculture under a former Democratic governor back in what she regarded as the "good old days." A colorful and uniquely Texan sort of character, Workman was opinionated, witty, and a natural-born storyteller. He billed himself as "a friend of America's working man and woman," a citizen-activist with the guts and determination to speak up for the little guy, and if he stomped on some right-wing Republican toes now and then while doing it, that was okay with Sandra. Somebody sure needed to straighten those birds out.

But mostly what Workman did was lift her spirits by making her laugh. She needed that now more than ever. Everyday it seemed there were new budget cuts which meant laying off Center staff and reducing services. Her agency had once been the darling of the system. Agencies from all over Texas had looked to them for inspiration and guidance on how best to deliver effective community-based social services to children and families. Articles about the Lubbock Family Resource Center showed up regularly in national magazines and she had once been invited to testify before Congress. Now she could barely keep the doors open and the lights on. It made Sandra angry when she wasn't busy being depressed.

Pulling into her reserved space behind the Center, she opened the door and stepped out. The temperature was already eighty-five degrees and the forecast called for another scorcher, the tenth in a row. She felt sorry for the low-income families her agency served since many of them lived without air conditioning, some without refrigerators. People went a little crazy when it got so hot; they did stupid things like beat their children or stab a neighbor.

"Ms. Valdez, there's a man waiting to see you. He's in your office." Rita was the Center's receptionist. She had come to the agency through AmeriCorps. A bright girl with a flare for organization.

"I don't have any appointments this morning," Sandra said, momentarily confused. "Who is he?"

Rita shrugged. "A government official I think. I've never seen him before."

"What's he doing in my office?"

Rita looked unhappy. "I couldn't stop him."

Sandra didn't have the heart to give her a lecture; the poor girl was overworked as it was.

Entering her office, Sandra found a man in a dark suit seated in the chair opposite her desk. He was typing on a laptop that he had open on his knees and he stopped and looked at her without getting up.

"Sandra Valdez?" he said.

Cop energy, Sandra decided. She could tell by the way the question used the voice, as if it owned it—a dead giveaway.

She dumped her purse and briefcase on her desk but remained standing.

The detective, or agent, or whoever he was, snapped his computer closed, leaned over, and slid it into its case next to the chair. He straightened up unsmiling.

"I'm Special Agent Brewer," he said pulling out a leather wallet and flipping it open to reveal a badge and identification card. "I'm with Homeland Security."

The name of the agency had always sounded to Sandra like the name of a bank and she was tempted to say, "Can I have the toaster if I open a new checking account?" but thought better of it. These people needed to be taken seriously; they were gaining power and could hurt people in more ways than Sandra wanted to think about.

"What do you want?" she asked.

"I'm here about your husband, Ernesto," he said putting away the wallet.

She was surprised. She had assumed he was checking up on an immigrant client, they had a number on their service roster, but her husband? What had he done? He was back home in bed as far as she knew.

"It's just a routine inquiry, Ms. Valdez," he said. "No need to worry. I just want to ask you a few questions." On their own these words were pleasant and reassuring, but to Sandra they lacked any relationship to the hard, perfunctory tone of voice uttering them. That voice was all police business.

She began to fume. Who did he think he was barging his way into her office without an appointment and setting up shop with his little computer and then prying into her personal life? It called to mind the stories her father used to tell her. As a young man in Arizona during the Second World War, he helped build one of the camps used to intern Japanese-Americans. He talked about watching the trucks arrive day after day filled with men and women, young and old, and how they would clamber down awkwardly from the tailgates clutching their flimsy cardboard suitcases and stand in the glare of the desert sunlight looking dazed and lost. He felt sorry for them.

For Sandra, a healthy dose of caution was in order whenever the government got paranoid and started snooping into people's lives.

"How long has your husband worked at the Ranger 1 power plant?" Agent Brewer asked. Through some sleight of hand he had produced a small tape recorder and placed it on the desktop between them.

"Since they built it."

"Why did he apply for work there?"

Sandra shifted her weight from one leg to the other.

"This is west Texas if you haven't noticed, and there aren't many good jobs, especially for Latinos."

"Why did you husband pick security?"

"He served as an MP in the army. Can I ask where this is going?"

Brewer ignored the question. "Has your husband been complaining about health problems lately?"

"Health problems? No," she said.

"Are you sure?"

"He has a bad back that acts up sometimes, but he disclosed that on his application."

"Yes, I know. We have a copy of the application."

"Then why are you asking me when he went to work at the plant? Apparently you already have that information."

"Yes, but we like to cross check the answers we receive."

"To see if one of us is lying, you mean?"

"No, we're just trying to be accurate. I only have a few more questions."

He looked down at his tape recorder as Sandra struggled to contain her rising irritation. She sat down. "Continue," she told him.

"Has your husband complained about not feeling well? I don't mean his back, but other things?"

"Such as?" Her mind was in a turmoil trying to make sense of what was going on.

"Aching joints, muscles?"

"Sometimes."

"Trouble with his eyes?"

"No."

"His hearing?"

"No."

"Chest pains, shortness of breath?"

"No." She picked up a pen and began tapping the edge of the desk; she had other, more important things to do.

"Difficulty controlling his bladder?"

"Look, what is this about? I need to—"

"What about chronic fatigue? Temporary forgetfulness?" He paused and then added, "Diminished sexual desire or function?"

If there was a line, Brewer had just crossed it. She wanted him out of her office, pronto.

"None of these things," she said, her voice flat and business like. "You can leave now."

"Are you sure?"

"Sure that I want you to leave? Yes, I'm quite sure."

He remained seated, studying her, and she was determined to give him nothing more. A tense silence hung heavy in the room. The telephone in the outer office rang once and Rita answered it. The aquarium bubbled softly next to the filing cabinet.

"Are we done?" Sandra said.

"For now." He stood up.

"Perhaps you can tell me something." Despite herself, emotion was crowding its way back into her voice. "What has the Department of Homeland Security to do with my husband's job at the power plant? It's not a government facility."

"Power plants are prime targets for terrorists and fall under the authority of Homeland Security."

"But what's my husband's health got to do with terrorists?"

"It's relevant."

"How?"

"I can only say it's relevant."

"Then why talk to me? He's the one you should talk to."

Brewer switched off the tape recorder and dropped it into the side pocket of his jacket.

"Do you know what I think?" she said. Her temper blazed, the flames obscuring out her better judgment.

"I don't think this has anything to do with terrorists. This is about the EnerTex Corporation and their big-shot buddies in Washington and they've got you out dealing with some nickel and dime lawsuit over health insurance—or is it workmen's compensation?"

The agent said nothing but reached out and took a piece of candy from a bowl that Sandra kept on her desk. She watched him in a state of dumb bewilderment. Rather than put the candy in his mouth, he dropped it into his shirt pocket and smiled at her. It was creepy. He was telling her that he had the power to do or take anything he wanted. She wanted to slap him. They faced each other a second or two longer; then he turned and walked out of the office. She took a deep breath. It saddened her to realize how much she had grown to mistrust her own government in recent years.

5

THE NEWS PRODUCTION studio at KVMR was little more than a walk-in closet and crammed with so many pieces of high-end audio gear, their green and orange power lights glowing in the semi-darkness, that scant space remained for carbon-based organisms such as Reb Morgan and Alice Carpenter. Today, the sixth day of Reb's training, they were working their way through the plug-ins for the station's audio editing and mixing software. Alice enjoyed teaching news production and she was impressed with Reb's progress. Relieved too. Twenty-eight people had applied for the intern positions, and it had been her job as head of the news department to select the final three. She had found the process daunting especially since she knew many of the people who applied; Nevada City was a small town and opportunities of the sort KVMR was offering were rare—one woman in her yoga class was now giving her the cold shoulder because she hadn't been picked. Despite this, Dan and Vicki had been relatively easy choices to make. They were both in their twenties, and for the station to survive, Alice believed, they had to involve more young people. The fact that Vicki was both Asian-American and a woman accorded with the KVMR's goal to increase diversity.

Then why had she gone with Reb Morgan? He was intelligent and enthusiastic, but so was everyone else who applied, and most were younger. One contributing factor was his skill as photographer; the station was exploring ways of providing additional content over the internet, which included visual content. But perhaps the real reason was that she wanted to work with someone her own age, someone who politically and culturally shared similar points of reference. If she happened to mention the name Senator Sam Irvin, for instance, or Agent 86, he would know who she was talking about. And he wasn't full of himself; he didn't try too hard to impress. Above all, she liked his laugh.

"Let's go over how to use the de-esser plug-in," she said as Vicki and Dan came crowding into the studio.

"How long are you two going to be?" Vicki asked. "We're putting together a story about the raw sewage that spilled into Lake Wildwood yesterday. We have some interviews to edit and want to get it on tonight's news."

Alice looked at Reb who shrugged. "I'm in no hurry," he said.

"How long do you need?" Alice asked looking at her watch. It was quarter to six.

"An hour, maybe two," Dan said.

"Do you want to get something to eat?" she asked Reb.

They walked over to Scanno's Restaurant on Broad Street and were seated at a table near the back by the hostess who took their drink orders.

"Have you eaten here before?" Alice asked.

"No," Reb said, "it's my first time."

"Look over there," she said pointing to the ornately carved black walnut bar. "It was brought by sailing ship around the Horn to San Francisco during the Gold Rush. They then loaded it onto a wagon and hauled it up here to Nevada City.

The bartender, a sturdy man with thick arms and a full red beard, was leaning over the bar talking to a female patron. Reb could easily imagine him arriving with the bar in the 1850s.

"Can I ask you something?" Reb said. "Why news? I mean, why not host a music program like most of the other DJs?"

"I used to have my own Saturday morning music show, but then Redwood Summer came along and I started doing news."

"You were part of Redwood Summer?" Reb asked.

"We were trying to stop the Maxxam Corporation from cutting down one of the last stands of old-growth redwoods on the planet."

"Isn't Maxxam Charles Hurwtiz's company?"

"He used junk bonds to buy Pacific Lumber and then had to triple the timber cut just to service the debt. It was a disaster for the redwoods."

"Yeah, I know. Hurwitz is part of that wrecking crew coming out of Texas these days."

Alice nodded in agreement. The trouble began with the savings and loan fiasco back in the eighties when the American taxpayers bailed out Hurwitz to the tune of 1.6 billion dollars. Dozens of other high-flyers got bailed out as well, most of them from Texas. But was it fair to blame a place for the bad things people did? People were people and greed was greed pretty much anywhere you went. Still, so many powerful corporations and politicians called Texas home, it did make a body wonder.

The waitress showed up with a bottle of Cabernet and Reb poured them both a glass.

"I went just to protest at first," she picked up the story, "but then Phil asked if I'd file some news stories for KVMR. He gave me a tape recorder and a microphone and I started interviewing the organizers, protesters, and families of the loggers. I've been doing news ever since."

"Do you like it?"

"Most of the time, but I miss my music show."

"Why keep doing it then?'

"Why do we do anything in life?" she said. "A job needs to be done, someone asks you to do it, and so you do it."

"There's got to be more to it than that," Reb said.

She laughed. "Of course there is. For one thing, I'm good at managing people, even thought it isn't easy at a place like KVMR, where everybody has an independent streak. I also need the income."

Reb took a sip of wine.

"And there's the big picture to consider," she said.

"Which is?"

"The community radio movement is under a lot of pressure these days from commercial and religious broadcasters who have more money and political clout. There's even competition from the big NPR stations."

"And doing news can help?"

"If it's done right; if you can provide your listeners with information that they value and can't get anywhere else."

Their meals arrived, and while they ate, Alice talked about growing up in south Florida where her father had been a pilot who flew B-52s armed with nuclear bombs during the Cold War.

"Is he a conservative?"

"You bet."

"What's he think of your liberal views?"

"We don't discuss politics."

"And your mom?"

"She's always voted Republican but she doesn't buy all of it. She thinks going to war in Iraq was a colossal mistake and she's also for a woman's right to choose."

"Why does she hang with Republican then?"

"Habit. Loyalty. She says she doesn't trust the Democrats."

"Do your parents still live in Florida?"

"Too many hurricanes; they moved to San Diego four years ago. What about your parents? Are they still alive?"

"No, my dad passed away last year. He was an insurance investigator. He ran his own shop until the day he died."

"Was he a good investigator?"

"Very good."

"What about your mom?"

"She died when I was fifteen. She was hit a by a car while she was crossing the street to get the mail."

"Were you close to your mom?"

"Yeah, we were close."

She wanted to know more but she didn't feel it was her place to ask—it was hard to imagine losing a parent at such a young age.

"Phil tells me you're separated from your husband," Reb said, wanting to change the subject. "How long has that been going on?"

"About six months."

"Do you think you'll get back together again?"

"We'll wait and see," she said.

"My wife and I were divorced two years ago," he said. "She now lives in Lake Tahoe with an investment consultant."

"What's her name?"

"Katherine. Kate. We met at a commune in upstate New York. We later moved to San Francisco where I went to photography school. That's where our son Brendan was born."

"Any other children?"

"No."

"Where is Brendan now?"

"In grad school at the University of Virginia."

Alice talked about her own children. Jason was the oldest and worked for an environmental engineering firm in Hawaii, while Beth was finishing her last year at UCLA.

"For a couple of ex-hippies, our kids have done okay in the world," Reb said, and she smiled.

They finished their meal and split the check. Walking up Broad Street, they didn't speak and Alice's mind kept returning to the question of her marriage. The trial separation gave every sign of becoming permanent. Alice held the Sacramento law firm of Hitchens, Dunn and Mackleroy to blame. Wayne had jumped at the chance when they offered him the job. After eleven years with the Public Defender's Office in Nevada County, he felt "used up." Now he earned four times his previous salary and would make partner in a few years—not bad for an attorney going into private practice so late in the game. She fully supported his decision to switch jobs at the time; the extra money was a big help with college expenses. But Wayne changed after he started working in Sacramento and that eventually drove them apart. He seemed to care more about impressing big clients and hobnobbing with the

power brokers in state government and their corporate lobby-
ists than he did about helping some single mom on welfare. And
then he had an affair with another attorney in the firm, a young
redhead just three years out of law school. It lasted six months.
When Alice found out, Wayne broke it off.

They reached the station and Alice found herself depressed.
"Do you mind if we call it quits for today?" she said.

Reb drove down to Sacramento listening to Marie Dooley's
Celtic music show on the radio. He sensed a sadness in Alice that
matched the sadness in his own heart. She understood.

6

PROPPED UP IN bed inside room 117 of the Airporter Motel, the drone of traffic only partially drowned out by the wheeze and rattle of the exhausted air conditioner, Dr. Walter Easler raised his glass and took another swallow. On the night stand shone a lamp with a soiled shade and next to it was a near empty bottle of Kutskova vodka.

"It is time to leave," he said aloud in slurred English to the solitary image in the mirror that stared back at him from across room. "If I stay, I shall be as guilty as they are."

He frowned at his crumpled clothes and considered undressing. Instead he took another swallow of vodka.

"But where can I go?" he said addressing the image again. "I have no home to return to. No family. No friends. I am cursed. I have become the Flying Dutchman." He smiled without pleasure at the aptness of the allusion. "Yes, the Flying Dutchman."

The clock radio read 12:42 in the morning. He must act. The memory of the last six months oppressed him so that he could barely breathe. The trouble started soon after the power plant came on-line. He had been confident up until then that he had solved the problem with the containment force field. But slowly he realized that it was still there. He thought about the *Tigron* and the government cover-up. They lied to the families of the sailors, telling them that their loved ones had died in an airplane crash in the mountains instead of at the bottom of the sea. The lying had angered him and he called Pauli, the American engineer who had become his friend. He told Pauli everything, and Pauli said he knew people who could help. Three days passed and they arrived in Moscow and got him away from his KGB handlers. They provided the corpse for the staged suicide and the truck that smuggled him out of the country, first to West Berlin and the house near Planckstrasse, then by private airplane to Lisbon and the hotel by the sea. That is where he met Samantha. Lovely, capable Samantha. She gave him a new identity, a new life—passport, driver's license, even Mastercard and Visa. He was no longer Anatoly Kryuchkov; he was now Dr. Walter Easler. And he had a new job as director of research for an energy company in Texas called EnerTex.

Another swallow as he recalled the seven long years of research followed by the building of the Ranger 1 power plant. They were hot, windy days, living in a trailer as he supervised the construction of the ATG reactor.

The next swallow drained the glass which he dropped onto the bed as he licked the edge of his shirt sleeve, an old Russian custom. Vodka was meant to be drunk with food, but when there was no food, you licked the sleeve.

A car alarm sounded in the parking lot and Walter, his eyes heavy-lidded from the alcohol, waited for someone to turn it off. He remembered brimming with enthusiasm the day the EnerTex plant went operational. Unlimited electrical energy without pollution or greenhouse gases. No toxic waste. It was the solution to one of mankind's most perplexing problems. It all seemed possible until he read the results from the tests he had run and saw that the acceleration effect was still there—much less than with the submarine, but irrefutably there.

The alarm was silenced, the murmur of a man's voice, a woman laughing.

Walter seldom drank for he had seen what it had done to his father. But he was sick at heart; the failure of the force field meant that the EnerTex workers were in danger. And even those who lived in the town nearby.

He swung his legs clumsily over the side of the bed and reached for his cane which was wedged between the mattress and the night stand. He stood up and waited until he was sure of his balance. Stress made the effects of his polio worse and the vodka compounded the problem. He moved slowly, using the cane to steady himself. The bathroom reeked of cheap air freshener and the cold fluorescent light hurt his eyes. The ventilation fan rattled even more than the air conditioner. He relieved himself and returned to sit on the edge of the bed, then rubbed his forehead and picked up the telephone. He took a slip of paper from his shirt pocket and dialed a number. He pressed more numbers on the key pad as he cycled through the automated options. At last a real human voice came on the line.

"This is Karen. How can I help you?"

"I want to book a flight."

"What is your destination and date of travel?"

"Chicago. I wish to go to Chicago. Tomorrow."

"From what city will you be departing?"

"Houston."

"What time of day do you wish to travel?"

"It does not matter. Middle of the day."

"What class of service do you require?"

"Economy." Traveling first-class or staying in a luxury hotel was too risky; he might run into someone from EnerTex. He must be cautious now, very cautious and clever.

"Can I have your name, please?"

"Dr. Walter Easler."

"Can you please spell your last name for me?"

"E-A-S-L-E-R. Dr. Walter Easler."

He finished making the reservation and set the clock radio for 7 a.m. He laid back on the bed again, pillows pushed up against the wall, his legs stretched out toward the image in the mirror.

"You are a handsome fellow and you do not interrupt," he said with courteous nod. "I like that."

He retrieved his glass and reached for the bottle but accidentally knocked it off the night stand with the side of his hand. It dropped down next to the bed with a thump, the vodka spilling out and soaking the carpet. He left it there.

"I have drunk too much," he said. Somewhere the flushing of a toilet made water rush through a pipe in the wall near his head. He was growing sleepy and could barely keep his eyes open.

Walter had gone to his boss Avery Axton and begged him to shut down the power plant. They quarreled. EnerTex had already spent too much on Ranger 1, Axton said. Fix the problem, tell us what you want and we will get it for you. Walter knew it would be the *Tigron* all over again, only now it would happen more slowly and only a few would know the truth. He had to get away. He would play no part in the deception, the tragedy. . .

He at last trailed off to sleep, with the light burning yellow next to the bed and the slumped figure in the mirror quiet and still.

THE NEXT MORNING Walter arrived at Bush International Airport and made his way to the gate. He was struck by the curious notion that the busy terminal was a grand stage upon which three simultaneous plays were being performed; what distinguished each from the others was the element of *time*.

In play number one, the actors had too little time. They had overslept or gotten stuck in traffic. Perhaps their originating flight arrived late and they hurried down the concourse, roller cases bouncing crazily from side to side behind them as they ran, stricken with fear that their airplanes would fly away without them.

The actors of play number two inhabited ordinary time. They were the passengers who could afford a moment to read a section of the newspaper or get a bite to eat before boarding their flight. These were also the shop and service employees who straightened the magazine racks and cleaned the bathrooms— and the gate attendants who assigned emergency-row aisle seats to the fortunate few. These non-passengers worked their eight-hour shifts and went home to their families, each day more or less the same as the next.

Then there was play number three, the time-drags-on-forever play. The performers in this peculiar farce slumped uncomfortably in chairs designed to deny them comfort. They gazed dejectedly at departure screens, wandered the concourses aimlessly, depleted cell phone minutes talking to spouses or giving endless instructions to corporate underlings. They got drunk in the airport bars and flirted with indifferent, foot-weary waitresses. All the while their sorrowful frustration rose and swirled through the great building like a noxious contaminating miasma that could inspire the pen of a Dante.

A man with a protruding stomach and his front shirt tail sticking out plopped down next to Walter. He was perspiring, his inflated balloon of a face flushed with exertion and annoyance.

"It took me more than twenty minutes to get through security," he said between breaths. "They pulled me aside and had me take off my shoes and my belt. Why hassle me? I don't look like no A-rab, do I?"

The man gave no indication of expecting a verbal response so Walter just nodded. How childlike some Americans could be, he thought. So narrow-minded and self-absorbed, even after 9/11. They wanted oil for their SUVs and lawn mowers and electricity to power their consumer electronic goods. But they also expected to be left alone.

And yet Walter had grown to love America. He loved their silly movies full of car chases and beautiful women. He loved country western music. He ate at truck stops and bought stuffed armadillos. He feared he was going crazy, loving America the way he did, and began to doubt his resolve to leave her behind. Where would he go? Chicago was only the first stop in his flight from EnerTex and the life he had known in Texas. From Chicago he would fly to Canada, from there to Malaysia. Where he would go after that, he could not say. Money was not a worry. He was sixty-three and had enough to last the years that were left to him. But a man without important work to do in the world, alas, was a man whose life had no meaning. He hadn't always believed this.

America had taught him that it was not enough to be kind and cultured, a lover of beauty, an intellectual. All that truly mattered in this place called America was that a man's talents be valued and wanted by society. It was no longer God, but the corporate CEO, who handed out the coveted titles—director of research, vice president for product development, sales manager for North America. EnerTex had given him a new identity, and he now felt an emptiness inside as he prepared to turn his back on it. Would he always be the Flying Dutchman, a man alone in the world with never a safe harbor in sight? Life isn't perfect, he told himself. If a few must suffer for the benefit of the many who was he to shake his fist at the heavens? Was he honestly to blame for what had happened to those inside the *Tigron*, or for what was happening now to those who worked at the power plant? Someone had to pay the price for new technologies, even if they did so unwittingly.

"This is a pre-boarding announcement for United Airlines Flight 1182 to Chicago-O'Hare." A woman's voice came through the ceiling speakers drowning out CNN on the overhead television monitor two rows of seats away. "Passengers traveling first-class and those needing extra assistance, or who are traveling with small children under the age of five, are invited to board at this time. Please have your boarding pass ready. Thank you."

Walter watched a mother with two children move toward the gate. She was followed by a half dozen well-dressed businessmen. Each in turn handed the attendant a boarding pass and disappeared down the jetway. Walter stood. He leaned on his cane with his right hand and pulled the handle out of his rolling suitcase with the other. More people crowded toward the gate in preparation for the general boarding announcement, including the unhappy man who sat next to him. Walter stood motionless for several seconds watching them, and then he turned and began walking down the busy concourse away from his flight and a life of uncertainty and idleness. He would show up for work at EnerTex tomorrow. He would make up an excuse about being sick. Mr. Axton said they still needed him and perhaps, in the end, that was enough.

7

"How are you feeling today, Ernesto?"

The Valdez family had just finished dinner and the children were in their rooms doing homework. Sandra was running water for the dishes while her husband cleared the table.

"I feel okay," Ernesto said coming into the kitchen. Sandra turned off the water but did not turn to face him for fear her eyes would betray her.

"How are your hands? Are they still hurting you?"

Sandra had not mentioned her meeting with Agent Brewer. The man had upset her and she wanted to understand his game first. Amarillo was the nearest city with a Homeland Security office. Why would he make the one hundred and twenty mile trip from Amarillo to Lubbock if it wasn't important? Did he have other business in the area? No one drove around West Texas for the sake of the scenery. The agent asked if her husband was having trouble with aching muscles or joints. Ernesto *had* been complaining about aches and pains, especially in his hands. He was afraid it might be arthritis, even though he was only thirty-four. And there were lines and dark patches under his eyes. Maybe they had been there all along and she hadn't noticed them. You live with someone for years, go to work every day, raise children, you can't be expected to notice all the subtle changes that take place over time. Was she only observing these changes now because

Agent Brewer had planted the idea in her mind with his ridiculous questions? It was making her *loca*.

"My hands feel better today," he said as he scraped the left over food into the compost bucket on the counter, "but I'm tired. It must be this night shift they've got me on. Maybe I should try some vitamins."

Yes, that must be it, Sandra tried to convince herself as she slid the plates into the hot, soapy water. It's hard to sleep during the day. Still, the worry lingered on for the rest of the evening after Ernesto had gone to work.

THE NEXT DAY was Saturday and Sandra drove over to see her friend Hazel Pendergast. Hazel worked at the Cut and Curl Beauty Salon three days a week; the rest of her time she spent looking after her three kids. Her husband Mike was part of the maintenance crew at the EnerTex power plant. Sandra was very fond of Hazel but envied her also because her husband worked days.

"Have you and Mike been having any trouble in your sex life?" Sandra asked as she spooned Coffeemate into her cup. The question took Hazel by surprise but not because she found talking about sex awkward. Quite the opposite. An important part of her job at the Cut and Curl as she saw it was dispensing sexual advice to her clients. It was cheaper than going to a therapist and they loved her for it. Besides, there weren't any therapists in Birdstar.

"Why do you ask?"

"Ernesto and I are very lucky," Sandra said. "We both enjoy sex."

"Congratulations. You'd be surprised how many couples don't."

"You and Mike?"

"We like sex just fine. I'm talking about some of the women who come into the salon. When they start complaining about how their husbands ignore them, I tell them to give their husbands more vitamin F."

Sandra laughed but Hazel could tell something was bothering her friend.

"What's this all about?" she asked. "Has Ernesto become uninterested? Have you become uninterested?"

"No, it's not like that. He's. . . he's just not as enthusiastic as he used to be," she said and took a sip of her coffee. "He used to be the one to start things off, but lately it's me. I don't mind so much but it's different. And he takes longer to, you know. . ."

Hazel was tempted to offer her friend a sample of her famous advice. "Rent a dirty movie and see if that helps." Or, "they have these internet sites where you can buy things to spice things up." But some intuition held her back, a shadow of doubt stealing over her own heart.

"Do you suspect he's having an affair?" she asked.

"No," Sandra shook her head. "You know Ernesto; he's not like that."

Sometimes women friends saw something in a husband that a wife couldn't, or wouldn't. But when it came to Ernesto, she couldn't imagine him making the midnight creep to cheat on his wife. It just wasn't in his makeup.

"So you want to know if I'm having the same kind of trouble with Mike?" Hazel said. "Is that it?"

Sandra nodded.

"Well the truth is, we *are* having some problems in that department, though I haven't told anyone about it. Mike says it's not because he's falling out of love with me. He says he just feels different. Physically, I mean. The desire is there, but he can't do it as much as he used to. I think it's making him depressed, and of course once you start down that road things only get worse. So much of sex is what goes on inside your head. We've even talked about going to a doctor."

"You have?" Sandra said. "What can a doctor do?"

"There are drugs. And they can do things to a man's anatomy."

Sandra then told her friend about Brewer's visit to her office and about the questions he asked.

"He wanted to know if we were having trouble with our sexual relationship, if Ernesto had changed in that way."

"He did?"

"What's bugging me is how did he know? How would someone from Homeland Security have that kind of information?"

"I just remembered," Hazel said touching her forehead. "A guy came by the salon on Tuesday. He said he was conducting a health survey for the EnerTex Corporation and he wanted to ask me some questions about Mike. Well, you know how it is on Tuesdays; I was busier than a hummingbird on diet pills. So I told him I couldn't possibly answer any questions."

"What did he do?"

"He said he'd come back later, but I could tell he was pissed. I was afraid I might have made things difficult for Mike at work."

"Did he come back?"

"No, it was only a couple of days ago."

Sandra felt a surge of relief; she wasn't just being paranoid. Something must be wrong at the power plant, otherwise why would have sent someone to talk to Hazel too? And why was Homeland Security mixed up in it? Was it even Homeland Security? She had read newspaper accounts about people using fake police IDs. She could see his face so clearly in her mind. Agent Brewer. Maybe that wasn't his real name. She was going to get to the bottom of what was going on. Of that much she was sure.

8

THE FIRST NINE months at KVMR so monopolized Reb's time
and energy that little was left over for worry. The laser surgery
had gone off without hitch but the results were discouraging.
True, the pressures had stopped charging upward, no small bless-
ing there, but neither had they retreated, which meant that every
six weeks he had to return to Dr. Yoon's office to stare at a red dot
in the center of what looked like a huge white salad bowl set on its
side. The nurse would darken the room and then tiny pin-pricks
of light would flash on and off randomly inside the bowl. Reb's
job was to press a button on a hand-held device every time he saw
a flash. Click. Click. . . Click. Click. He knew the pauses meant
he had failed to detect one of the little lights at the far edge of the
bowl and the experience invariably cast him into a melancholic,
end-of-the-world kind of mood, as if the stars in the heavens were
slowly winking out, one after another.

And the burden of his illness was made greater still because he
was facing it alone. If he were a church-going kind of person, he
might talk to his pastor. But Reb's spiritual faith was not of the
organized variety. When pressed, he described himself as a cross
between a Dorothy Day Catholic Worker type of Christian and a
Taoist of the Chuang-Tzu persuasion. He knew what this meant
even if few others did.

Once or twice he considered engaging the services of a therapist but never made the call. Cost was partly to blame; given

his modest community radio salary, eighty dollars a session was nothing to sneeze at. But perhaps the real reason was that no one in his family had ever gone to a shrink. Irrational or not, he didn't want to be the first. So that left sharing his troubles with a woman. Increasingly he wished the woman was Alice. They had spent so much time together during the early days of his radio training, alone walking the streets of Nevada City talking over story ideas, interviewing people, and staying late in the news studio editing and mixing audio. Afterwards, driving back to Sacramento he would recall the scent of her auburn hair and it would stir up a turmoil of suppressed desire.

But as the months passed, they saw less and less of each other—news team meetings twice a week and occasionally hosting the bar together at some KVMR event. He thought about asking her out, but then reminded himself that Alice was married and she'd probably go back to Wayne in the end. There were plenty of other women in the world, he told himself; he just needed to make more of an effort to find one who was available.

In Sacramento, he often stopped by the Riverland Brewery on Capitol Boulevard on his way home from the station. Every Thursday a group of women came in, grabbed a large table in the back, and ordered pitchers of beer. They would talk and laugh and he tried to imagine himself taking one of them out. Maybe they would go to a movie, take salsa dancing lessons together, or do whatever it was that dating couples did these days. Then he'd think, Christ, I'm too old for this, and would turn his attention to the Kings' game on the television above the bar.

The news stories he produced during this period ran the gamut from a three-part series on the dilapidated system of levees along the Sacramento River—another New Orleans waiting to happen according to the scientists he interviewed—to a profile of the founders of the *Teddy Bear Convention*, an annual event that drew thousands of people to Nevada City from all over the world. The assignment, however, that most excited his interest was a white-water raft trip he took down the South Fork of the American River. Each year a rafting company called Alpha

Adventures donated a trip to a charity in San Francisco that ran a
residential treatment and vocational training center for hard-core
drug addicts. Marshall House's policies were strict but its success
rate was impressive. To be admitted into the program, addicts
had to agree to sever all connections with family members for
the first eighteen months. After that, they were permitted to see
their spouse or child only once a month, provided they had made
adequate progress in their treatment program. That's where the
raft trip came in. It took place on Father's Day and two dozen
Marshall House residents got to see their children again for the
first time.

Reb showed up at the river put-in near the town of Coloma
two hours east of Sacramento. It was early morning. The sky
was clear and blue with temperatures expected to reach the mid-
eighties, ideal weather for June. He was placed in a raft guided
by a young, no-nonsense woman named Carrie who stowed his
microphone, headphones, and digital recorder in the raft's dry
bag. Besides himself and the guide, there were three men in the
raft with their children. Soon the canyon walls closed in around
them as their brave company of rafts swept downriver. Boulders
jutted up out of the water and deer could be seen along the banks.
As they approached the first rapid, the passengers, young and
old alike, grew pensive and quiet. It was their first white-water
rafting experience, and for most, the first time they truly had
been out in nature. Reb realized it was as alien an environment
for them as it would be for him to race camels on the plains of
Mongolia. This emotion of unfamiliarity seemed to thicken the
air about them. Then they hit their first white-water, a class-
two rapid called "Barking Dog." The men screamed, the kids
screamed, and from that moment on they couldn't get enough
of it. Their enthusiasm was so intoxicating, in fact, that Reb
chanced damaging his equipment by pulling it out of the dry bag
and recording the whoops and hollers as they shot through the
next two rapids. He positioned himself in the center of the raft
just before they dropped into the seething, raging water, pulled
the headphones down tightly over his ears, and hung on with one

hand while holding the microphone aloft with the other. It was a comical sight that only added to everyone's enjoyment.

At the lunch take-out, Reb interviewed the fathers and kids individually. He found the fathers remarkably eloquent about their struggles and hopes. But it was the children who knocked him out. Each began by talking about the water, how cold it was and how scary it was going through the rapids. But then the intensity of their eyes changed and deepened, and their smiles moved from enthusiasm to joy as they talked about how much they had missed their dads and how happy they were to be with them again. To Reb, they got at the very heart of what it meant to love someone.

Which also made it radio of the first order; he couldn't imagine anyone listening to the sounds of laughter and splashing water, the words of the children as they talked about their fathers, or the cry of the lone red tail hawk soaring above the river canyon and not sense the magic of what had taken place that day.

Reb also began to regard river guides in a different light. His first impression, mixed with a tinge of envy, was that they were just hedonistic, sun-tanned young people blowing off the summer having a bit of fun. There was that, of course, but there was something holy in the way they went about their work too. In fact, this sense of holiness so lingered with him for days afterwards that he went back several times to interview guides at their base camp on the river. The theory he came up with and managed to weave into the story was that river guides constituted a kind of religious order all their own. They lived simply, often communally, and were free of the greed and hunger for fame that goaded and tormented so many of their contemporaries. Many came from the upper ranks of society and had enjoyed every advantage that money and position could provide. And yet, like Franciscans of old, they had turned their backs on the world and its vanities. In much the same way that monks and nuns in other parts of the world served as keepers of sacred temples, raft guides kept the living rivers upon which they spent their days, temples whose names were the American, the Keweah, and the Salmon. Each raft was a sort of floating chapel in which differences in social rank and privilege quickly and naturally fell away. The banker and corporate CEO paddled along with the school custodian and taxi driver in a common purpose which was to stay alive and find a measure of spiritual renewal by absorbing the beauty, pulse, and non-humanness of the ancient river canyons. Reb observed first-hand how the experience transformed people. He watched the way they slowed down and became protective of others who only hours before had been complete strangers. For some, just escaping the tyranny of the clock was enough.

It took Reb a number of sessions in the studio to mold the piece into what he wanted. He worked mostly at night and at one point seriously considered taking the training to become a raft guide himself. That way he could guide on weekends. Radio work was intellectually and creatively challenging but sitting in front of computer screen for hours on end was also a kind of slow murder—not to mention the strain it put on his eyes. Oh yes, the glaucoma. He'd become so absorbed in the editing, he almost forgot about it. Best to give raft guiding a pass. Many of the guides had nicknames. What would his be? Charon, after the blind boatman of Greek mythology who ferried dead souls across the River Styx? That should go down well with the raft company's marketing department. No, better to buy a gym membership, or maybe take up jogging.

SEVERAL MONTHS AFTER the rafting story aired, Reb received an e-mail from the station manager. The message read: "Come see me as soon as you get in." So he went upstairs and knocked on Kevin's door.

"Come in."

Reb entered the office and had to step over Kevin's black Labrador to reach a chair.

"I have some pretty exciting news," Kevin said, all smiles. "You know that piece you did on the Father's Day white-water raft trip? What was the name of the organization?"

"Marshall House."

"Well, Phil sent a copy of it to the NFCB and they called me this morning. Your piece has been nominated for a Golden Reel Award for best local public affairs documentary. If you win, KVMR gets a Golden Reel too because the documentary was produced here at the station."

Kevin's grin was infectious even though Reb felt slightly embarrassed by his ignorance. "What's a Golden Reel?" he asked.

"Only the top honor from the National Federation of Community Broadcasters. It's like the Oscars of public radio, up there with the Peabody. We won a Golden Reel a couple of years ago for a piece a high school student did on the Public Defender's office here in Nevada County. The award normally goes to the big stations in New York or LA. It'd be a real coup to win another one."

"What happens next?"

"We'll send you to the NFCB conference to get your award."

"If I win, you mean?"

"You get to go either way. They announce the winners at the banquet on the last night of the conference."

"Where's the conference held?"

"This year it's at the Hilton in New York City."

"Can the station afford it, sending me to New York, I mean?" He didn't want to sound negative but he knew the station was far from flush, and from what he'd heard the prices for hotel rooms in New York were out-of-sight.

"Not to worry. Brent Abrams is picking up the tab. He's paying for Alice to go too since she's head of the news department."

This last bit of information cheered Reb even more than being nominated for an award. He had just learned from Phil that Alice had filed for divorce. They were now both free, white, and twenty-one. And if the old movies were right, the Big Apple was a great town for falling in love. Bad eyes or not, life was looking up for Reb Morgan.

9

THREE TOURS OF duty in Afghanistan as an intelligence officer with special forces convinced Colonel Viktor Degtyar it was time to quit. His unit's job was to hunt down and interrogate suspected Mujahidin. Torture was an everyday duty and the stench of blood, urine, and fear still clung to him and kept him awake at night. So he resigned his commission and returned home to a country that was starkly different from the one he had left, a Russia reordering herself along criminal lines under the euphemism of privatization. The emerging strong men pursued power ruthlessly. Valentin Gromonov was one such man.

Viktor met Gromonov at a party in Moscow for the kick-off of the world concert tour of the mega rock band *Aquarium*. Gromonov's huge, meaty head moved in quick jerks atop a compact, muscular body held aloft by short, sturdy legs—a wrestler's body.

"You were with the Spetsnaz in Afghanistan," he said to Viktor, his mouth full of Osetra caviar, as the two men moved side by side along the buffet line. "You are a specialist?"

"We are all specialists," Viktor said.

"Yes, this is true. But you are very good at finding people from what I hear. Very skilled. Very thorough. These are admirable traits. I think the leaders of the Mujahidin were smart to be frightened of you."

Gromonov. Viktor had seen his name and face many times in the newspapers and on television. He was the head of a syndicate, one of a handful of super-wealthy oligarchs who sprang up after the collapse of the Communist regime. A man to watch. A man with protected interests. Was this how Gromonov knew so much about the career of a retired army officer?

"I hear they tried to send you to Chechnya," Gromonov said, "but you refused."

"I am no longer interested in the army."

"An ugly business, Chechnya. You were wise not to go."

Viktor shrugged; the conversation bored him.

"I hear also you consult on security issues for a Swiss company," Gromonov said, "but that they pay you little."

From compliment to insult, Viktor thought, and he turned to walk away.

"No please, hear me out," Gromonov said in an apologetic tone. "Your business is your own, Colonel, but I am looking for a man such as you. A man whose talents are, what should I say, under appreciated? You should call me."

Placing his plate down next to the rasstegai, Gromonov produced a business card from his vest pocket which he handed to Viktor, leaving a spot of grease on it with his thumb.

"You can reach me at this number. You will not be sorry."

A government official, sotted with drink, came up behind Gromonov and began slapping the large-headed man on the back repeatedly in an exaggerated demonstration of affection.

"Valentin, my excellent friend. How good it is to see you!"

Gromonov struggled to swallow without choking as he spun about, his eyes hard and dark, to see who was touching him. Then he smiled, flashing several gold teeth and his voice boomed out, "Yegor, my good friend. You are looking well."

His eyes, however, were unchanged. Viktor, who had noted the same predatory look often enough among fellow officers in basement interrogation rooms in Kabul, instinctively stepped back. Gromonov was not a man to know pity or doubt and any attempt to dupe him would be to play a very dangerous game; Viktor suspected the Moscow River had swallowed its share of weighted corpses of those who had tried and failed.

He set his plate down and moved away from the buffet line while Gromonov continued his chat with the government official. He was no longer hungry. Crossing the ballroom in the direction of the exit, he wondered if he could work for a man like Gromonov. He told himself he would go home and sleep on it. What else did he have to occupy his time? Gromonov was correct about his Swiss employers. They were misers and dull as ditch water. With what little they paid him and his military pension, he had barely enough to purchase vodka and the occasional services of a prostitute. Perhaps he *would* give Gromonov a call.

A noisy rush of people came surging toward him. In the center were the guests of honor, the band members of *Aquarium*. They were surrounded by a jostling, animated entourage of adoring fans and the air crackled with excitement as the pheromones of hungry young bodies swirled around him. A girl with raven black hair, older than the rest, in matching purple velvet jacket and slacks brushed up against him. She glanced at him and laughed. Her eyes were thick with mascara; a tattoo of twisting briars wound itself around her white neck. Viktor put aside his plans to leave the party and instead followed the girl and the band back into the ballroom. He wanted vodka. He wanted the girl. He wanted to forget.

"THIS IS AN odd country these days, don't you think?" Gromonov tossed a rust-covered bayonet and several green tarnished brass belt buckles onto the desk for Viktor to inspect. It was midmorning and they were in an office at the far end of an aging warehouse next to the rail yards. A kerosene stove vented through the wall heated the space. It was Gromonov's working office, not his show office.

"They were dug up near Voronezh," Gromonov said. "They are Italian and are worth money. People in the West are crazy for such things."

Viktor was aware that one of the newer scams in Russia was a very old one. Grave robbing. Five million Germans and their allies had met their end on the Eastern Front and had been tossed and bulldozed into mass graves along with their Iron crosses, battalion pins, and SS belt buckles. A few of the bigger gangs were equipping teams of "black trackers" to scour the countryside for these desirable trinkets.

"We use computer-enhanced battle charts and metal detectors to find the graves, but it can be dangerous work. There is much unexploded ordinance."

Viktor suddenly feared he was being recruited to find war souvenirs, but Gromonov read his expression and laughed.

"No my friend, I need you for the living, not for old bones and lost glories. Have you heard of a scientist named Anatoly Kryuchkov?"

"No," Viktor said.

"I am not surprised. Kryuchkov's father was a brilliant physicist who worked on the hydrogen bomb after the war, but he went insane and died in a nut house. Anatoly was his only son and smart, like his father. He made something that was kept very secret—a new way of making electricity. The process does not require hydrocarbon or nuclear fuel. Nor does it rely on the sun, the wind, or geothermal heat. The Kremlin believed this technology would transform the world and they put Kryuchkov in charge of developing it. It was called the Svarog Project in honor of the ancient Slavic God of fire."

"So what happened?"

"In 1989 an attack submarine called the *Tigron* was outfitted with an experimental power plant using the new technology. But there was an accident, a terrible accident, and the submarine was lost at sea with all hands."

"I heard of no accident involving a submarine." Retired or not, Viktor paid close attention to the military news.

"Perhaps you remember a Navy transport airplane that crashed in the Ural Mountains during a storm?" Gromonov said. "Seventy-three sailors were killed. The government said they were being transferred to the Pacific Fleet in Vladivostok. It was reported in the newspapers and on the television."

"The wreckage was never found," Viktor said, "the bodies of the men were never recovered."

"A fabrication," Gromonov said, slapping the desk with the palm of his hand. "Those men lost their lives onboard the *Tigron*. It was a huge disaster and the government covered it up. Kryuch-kov blamed himself for the death of so many sailors and commit-ted suicide. That is what they say, anyway. The government, the KGB, everybody. One night, they say, Kryuchkov went to a place high above the river. He took off his clothes and jumped in. He left a note. Very sad, don't you think?"

Gromonov paused as he lifted a pot from an electric burner and poured two cups of black tea.

"Would you like to know what I think?" he said after handing one of the cups to Viktor.

"I think our Anatoly, maybe he never drowns in the Moscow river. Instead, I think he is smuggled out of the country and sent to America to work for an energy company. It takes him eight, ten years, but he solves the problem that destroyed the *Tigron*. Do you see? And this American company will soon become rich selling Russian electricity to the entire world."

Gromonov sipped his tea.

"Did the authorities find Kryuchkov's body?" Viktor asked.

"Some days later. It was badly decomposed. Unrecognizable. They used dental records for official identification."

"And?"

"I have learned in life, Colonel, that anything is possible if you have enough money. And the Americans have money. So I think, what if the dental records were falsified? It is not so difficult, with a bribe, to have one set of x-rays replaced with another."

"Who else believes Kryuchkov might still be alive?" Viktor asked. He had little doubt that Gromonov knew all about falsify-ing death records.

"An associate of mine who works in one of the ministries. He is a clever man. He believes the CIA was involved, and that

Kryuchkov is now living in the United States. He thinks Kryuchkov works for a company called EnerTex. This company is in Houston. Have you heard of it?"

Viktor shook his head.

"It is run by a man named Avery Axton who is a close personal friend of a former president of the United States. Now do you understand?"

"Your associate believes that the CIA, acting under orders from the president, handed Kryuchkov over to this company in Texas, is that what you are saying?"

"He is guessing; he does not know this for certain."

Viktor leaned back in his chair and sipped his tea.

"EnerTex is a small company," Gromonov said, "but it will soon become a very large company because they have stolen our technology for making electricity. My associate says they have already built one power plant and will build more. The United States government has special arrangements with Mr. Axton and EnerTex—very secret and unusual arrangements, from what he hears."

"And he believes there is a connection between this new technology and the Svarog Project?" Viktor said.

Gromonov nodded. "As I said, he is clever when it comes to these things. Not like me." Gromonov gave a shrug and smile of innocence that Viktor found annoying.

"So how does Kryuchkov fit into all this?" Viktor asked.

"Without Kryuchkov, there is no new process, no Svarog Project. My associate wants to investigate but the Kremlin will not allow him to. They are very definite. Kryuchkov is dead, they say. But Valentin Gromonov does not work for the Kremlin. He works for himself. So I think I will investigate. Perhaps I am wasting my time and money. Perhaps Kryuchkov is as dead as the owner of this old bayonet." He picked up the weapon, looked at it briefly, and then put it down again. "But I have what the Americans call a *hunch*."

There was loud thump on the door and Gromonov got up to open it with a look of impatience. A heavy-set man wearing boots, a cigarette dangling from his mouth, began to enter the room holding a large cardboard carton that Viktor guessed held more war relics.

"Not now," Gromonov snapped, shoving the box and the man backwards out of the room and slamming the door. He returned to the desk and sat down.

"I have all the strong men I need, Comrade Colonel. Accountants too. What I need is a man like you, a man who can find someone who doesn't want to be found. I have read your file and know much about you. You have courage. You speak very good English. I will pay you to go to America and find out if Anatoly Kryuchkov is alive or dead. I have people in Texas to help you.

"The Americans will have given him a new identity."

"Of course."

"And if I do not find him?"

"Then I will know he is dead and the Americans have invented this technology on their own. But if he is alive, then I want you to bring him back to Russia. He should give this wonderful invention to his own people, not the Americans."

And make you rich, Viktor thought. Gromonov was unlike his fellow oligarchs. Most had been managers of Soviet factories and made their fortunes by buying up stock in their own companies when industry was privatized. Gromonov, however, had worked his way up from the streets running prostitutes and selling drugs. His real break came in the late 1980s when Gorbachëv regulated the sale of vodka. There was too much alcoholism, the president said. It was like America in the 1920s; underground syndicates, one run by Gromonov, began siphoning off vodka from state-owned plants and selling it on the black market for rubles, which they then converted into dollars. The dollars Gromonov invested in other profitable ventures, some legal, some not. While Viktor was in Afghanistan risking his life hunting down and killing terrorists, Gromonov, safely back in Moscow, was importing opium by the kilo from the same country and processing it into heroin, which he then smuggled into Europe and the United States. Viktor did not hold it against him. People did what they had to do.

Still, Viktor had "associates" of his own with access to information, and from them he learned that Gromonov had invested heavily in oil wells near the Caspian Sea. Pipelines had to be built so the precious oil from this remote region could reach customers in the West, customers who would pay in dollars and euros, not worthless rubles. And these pipelines had to be protected because there were bad people who wished to blow them up—ethnic separatists, religious extremists, competing gangs. So Gromonov invested more money. He purchased security, costly but necessary. Should a new energy technology now replace oil, Gromonov faced ruin.

That was why he needed to get his hands on Anatoly Kryuchkov, if the physicist still existed. He could then either exploit the new technology or get rid of the inventor and keep the world hooked on oil. It was how Gromonov had grown rich and powerful. He understood the mechanics of addiction.

"America is a very big place," Viktor said. "It will be difficult to find this man, if he is still alive."

"Begin in Texas," Gromonov said standing. He went over to a safe in the corner of the room. He leaned over and worked the dial. Pushing down the handle, there was a satisfying click and the door swung open. He reached inside and withdrew a large envelope and handed it to Viktor.

"Here is what little information exists about Anatoly Kryuchkov. It cost me more than you can imagine."

Viktor withdrew several pieces of paper and a black and white photograph. It showed a man of small stature in profile crossing a city street. He had a cane in his right hand and appeared to be supporting his weight with it. Viktor looked up at Gromonov.

"Kryuchkov was stricken with polio as a child," Gromonov said. "It was a mild case and he recovered, but it came back when he was forty. To walk, he must use a cane.

"It is difficult to make out his face, he is too far away. Where was this taken?"

"In St. Petersburg. Twenty years ago. He was attending a conference."

"There are no other photographs of him?"

"The government has more, I am sure, but this is the only one I was able to get."

"I am surprised."

Gromonov lifted his eyebrows but said nothing.

Viktor then scanned the sheets of paper. They pertained to the energy company in Houston, Texas, called EnerTex. Included was a short bio and a picture of the company's president, Avery Axton.

"EnerTex built its first power plant near a village called Birdstar in western Texas," Gromonov said. "It went on-line eighteen months ago and produces eight-hundred and fifty megawatts of power. The company will not reveal how the electricity is generated or what fuel is used. The United States government is shielding them. It is quite extraordinary."

Viktor waited for more information but received none.

"And if I find Kryuchkov and he refuses to come back with me, what then?" he asked.

"You will kill him."

Neither man spoke for the span of a half a minute. The colonel looked at the photograph while Gromonov sipped his tea.

"My friend, " Gromonov said, "some men need a reason to kill. Others need only an excuse. Some cannot be kept from killing, they enjoy it too much. You are of the first sort, I think. So here is your reason. The United States has grown conceited and stupid. They break treaties at will and invade poor defenseless country whenever they want. They are like a spoiled child whose toys can destroy us all if we are not careful."

With his palms on the desk, Gromonov leaned forward. "Now it is possible that a Russian scientist has turned over to them the means of dominating the world's economy far into the future. Energy, Colonel. The wars of our age have all been fought over energy. So I ask you, should Russia, like the rest of the world, become America's lap dog because one of our own has betrayed us?" He shook his head slowly. "If Kryuchkov will not help us, then we must prevent him from helping our enemies."

For the next half-hour the two men discussed money and logistics. Gromonov would pay Viktor thirty thousand dollars and his expenses; he would give Viktor an additional forty thousand should he find Kryuchkov and bring him back to Russia.

"And if I must kill him?" Viktor asked.

Gromonov's dark pig-like eyes shone with mischief. "Kill him only if you must; he would be useful to me."

"But if I must kill him?"

"There will be a bonus, of course."

"I want the money in euros, not dollars," Viktor said. Gromonov considered the request, his expression saturnine. Euros would cost him more but he wasn't surprised. Many involved in illicit trade around the globe were moving from dollars to euros, one more sign of America's decline.

"Euros, yes, agreed, in euros," Gromonov said standing up. Viktor stood also and they shook hands.

Viktor had known from the moment he entered the office that he would take the job; he just wanted to be sure everything was spelled out beforehand. Misunderstandings with a man like Valentin Gromonov could be fatal.

And should this gangster who violated the graves of soldiers underestimate a former colonel of the Spetsnaz and attempt a double-cross, it would cost him dearly.

10

SANDRA SLID THE video through the after hours slot at the Movies To Go store before crossing the street to the Family Resource Center. With Ernesto working nights, they seldom went out to the movies, nor did they watch them at home except on rare occasions. But she was determined more than ever to figure out what was going on at the power plant and Hazel recommended she watch *Erin Brockovich* starring Julia Roberts.

"It's about an ordinary woman who goes up against a big corporation and wins," Hazel told her. "And it's a true story."

So Sandra watched it and then had a long talk with Ernesto. She told him about Agent Brewer, and on the drive to work that morning, she formulated a plan which included talking to as many of the wives of power plant employees as possible. She spent practically every second of her spare time over the next five days on the telephone and the stories she heard sounded eerily familiar—husbands suffering from aching joints and muscles and chronic fatigue. Others complained about blurry vision or forgetfulness. She could recite the litany of symptoms in her sleep. One woman told her that her husband had lost two teeth in the last six months.

"First time it happened," the woman said, "Ed was eating his supper. He bit down on something hard and spat his tooth onto the plate. Three weeks later another fell out while he was brushing his teeth."

"What did the dentist say?" Sandra asked.

"He didn't know what to say, and that worries me. Ed's been using snuff since he was a teenager competing in rodeos. It could be cancer."

Sandra couldn't escape the nagging fear that Ernesto and his fellow workers were being poisoned by some kind of radiation. Her friend Betty Mae, however, who worked for the Dalton County sheriff's office in Birdstar assured her that there were no radioactive materials at the plant.

"Look hon, if they had anything hot out there, we'd know it. State and federal emergency planning requires we be informed."

SANDRA ENTERED THE Resource Center and found Laura Andrews waiting for her. Laura, a tall, slender woman in her late forties with wheat colored hair, was a family physician who donated her services one day a week to the Center.

"You said you wanted to see me, so here I am," Laura said smiling. She was always upbeat, a trait Sandra appreciated.

"Rita, please hold my calls," Sandra told her secretary and then turned to Laura. "Let's go in my office."

Once behind the closed door Sandra told Laura about Ernesto and the others.

"We could test for Lyme Disease," the doctor said, "that would match some of these symptoms."

"Lyme Disease? I didn't know we had that in Texas."

"It's found wherever there are deer ticks. It's a nasty bacteria, similar to syphilis."

The mention of the word syphilis connected with someone in her family threatened to stampede Sandra's emotions and it showed.

"It's a spirochete that effects the brain and nervous system like syphilis," Laura hastened to clarify. "But Lyme has nothing to do with sex."

"You can't get it by having sex?" Sandra asked.

"Not as far as anyone knows. Look, Sandra, I don't know much about Lyme Disease. Most general practitioners don't."

"I don't remember Ernesto getting a tick bite," Sandra said. "Besides, why would a bunch of people who all work at the same place suddenly come down with Lyme disease? It doesn't make sense."

"Are there many deer inside the power plant property?" Laura asked.

Sandra shrugged. "I don't know. Ernesto says the area around the plant is restricted."

"Then they probably don't allow hunting and the deer might be congregating there. Animals are smart about figuring out where they're safe. Do you know of anyone else in Birdstar who's having these kinds of health problems, someone who doesn't work at the power plant?"

Sandra shook her head.

"You could check with the schools; they'll know if any of the children are presenting symptoms. Meanwhile, I'll do some research. I'll want to draw blood from Ernesto and the others. Can you arrange for them to come up to my office?"

"How long will this take?"

"That's hard to say. It's a process of elimination."

"But the workers at the plant are in danger now."

"I'll do what I can to speed things up, Sandra, but it will take time. I'll need those blood samples first."

Sandra could feel her impatience pulling her apart inside like a malevolent spirit. Laura's words, "it will take time" stung her ears and she wanted to yell at her friend, "tell me *now*, not later." What was happening to her? Why did she feel so anxious and keyed up all the time? It wasn't her normal self, she knew that. Her temperament had been much like her mother's, a child of Mexican immigrants who survived the worst of the Great Depression and the Second World War—she lost a brother on Iwo Jima—and yet never lost her emotional equilibrium and infectious optimism. Sandra tried to identify when the change began to take place inside her. It was before Agent Brewer's visit, she knew that. A year ago? Maybe two, not longer. Perhaps she was suffering the onset of premature menopause.

"Is there something else that's bothering you?" Laura said softly, breaking the silence.

"No, I'm sorry. I *do* appreciate your help."

"What will you do if we find out what's making Ernesto and others sick?"

"Complain to the county; get them to investigate."

"And if they won't listen? You know EnerTex slings a lot of weight around this part of the state."

"Then I'll go to the press, or organize protests. I'll think of something."

"Well then, all I can say is, go for it, girl!"

The two women smiled and felt slightly dangerous.

TEN DAYS LATER Laura called back with the test results.

"I wish I could give you a definitive answer, Sandra, but I can't. Whatever it is, it's not Lyme disease, West Nile virus, Legionnaire's, or any of the usual suspects. It could be a chemical toxin we don't know how to test for. That's my guess. I'm going to a conference next month where I can talk to some folks from the CDC. Maybe they'll have some ideas. I'm sorry I can't be more help than that."

"You *do* believe me, Laura, that something is wrong at the power plant?"

A slight pause and then, "I believe that *you* believe it."

Hearing these guarded words, Sandra felt an enormous frustration dragging her down. If a woman she'd known and worked with for years didn't believe her, then who would? The word "hysteria" had not been mentioned, but it was certainly in the air. A suggestion or two by a government agent and Sandra Valdez was letting her fears run away with her. The pressure at work over the last six months had been brutal. Maybe she was losing perspective.

She hung up the phone and went over and sprinkled food into the fish tank.

No, she told herself, something bad is going on. Call it woman's intuition. It was the same feeling she got when one of her kids was about to come down with a fever, or was being bullied at school—a knowing deep down in her bones. She would try to convince Ernesto to quit his job. It would be tight financially with the children and the mortgage and everything but health was more important than money. She returned to her desk and looked at his photograph. He was good man, but she knew he would not quit his job no matter what she said, and this only added to the preponderance of her frustration. She would have to produce concrete evidence, but how?

Sandra stepped into the outer office.

"Rita," she said, "I'll be taking a few days off. I might stop in to check my e-mail, but as far as anyone is concerned, I'm not here. Can you handle things for awhile?"

"I'll do my best, Mrs. Valdez," Rita said, forcing a smile through her worry. She could sense that something was wrong with her boss. For weeks Mrs. Valdez hadn't been acting herself. Then there was the closed door meeting with Dr. Andrews. Did Sandra have breast cancer? A bad heart? Maybe she was suffering from excessive stress, social work burnout. Rita reached under her desk for her purse and cigarettes. What would happen to the agency? For many in the city it was the last strand in a social safety net that was being ripped to pieces by the political sharks of the conservative right. She stood up to go outside, but the phone rang and she picked it up.

"Family Resource Center."

An official sounding voice, a man's, said, "Let me speak to Sandra Valdez."

"I'm sorry, she's out of the office for several days. Can I take a message?"

A click and then silence.

"Asshole," she muttered as she hung up the phone and went outside for a smoke.

11

"I'LL HAVE THE short stack of blueberry pancakes and two eggs over medium." They were in the Marketplace Restaurant on the ground floor of the Hilton New York Hotel and Reb was in high spirits because he had made love to Alice for the first time that evening. It started with a decision to take a taxi downtown to a club in the West Village to see a popular Zydeco band. They danced, sweated, drank too much, and when it was time to say goodnight, she invited him into her room.

And when did Alice first suspect that they would become lovers? Probably that night at Scanno's when they first had dinner together. All the same, the intervening months had seen them going off in different directions. For Reb, it was radio work, morning, noon, and night. For her, it was dealing with the divorce and keeping the news department on track.

She and Wayne hoped the divorce would be amicable but quickly realized they seldom are. Property issues needed to be sorted out, the classic who gets the Rolling Stones' *Let it Bleed* album and silver tea service from Aunt Gertrude—not to mention the house. Their salvation was hiring a skilled mediator instead of lawyers so that only a few barns got burned and cattle slaughtered by the time the divorce decree was granted and Alice became a single woman again.

"Would you like some fresh-squeezed orange juice?" The waitress' eyes sparkled as if sensing their love-making in the air.

"A large, please," he said.

"Do you have a copy of the program schedule?" he asked Alice as the waitress walked away.

She took hers out of her purse and Reb began going over it, occasionally marking it with a pen. Alice watched him. Vicki and Eric had made great strides as radio reporters but Reb's work stood head and shoulders above anything they had produced. The Golden Reel nomination was proof of that. What was it, though, that gave his work that extra lift? A sense of urgency was the closest she could come to naming it; the impression that every second counts. One of the more striking peculiarities of human nature, as she saw it, was that people knew they were going to die and yet went along as if they had all the time in the world. She had heard of an order of monks during the Middle Ages who slept in coffins to remind themselves that life was transitory and that it should be lived to the fullest. Reb was like that; he didn't take time for granted. He was always pushing himself to do better and sometimes it irritated her. Why couldn't he relax, slow down once in a while? Now she knew the reason. He had told her his secret after they had made love. He had glaucoma and was afraid he was going blind.

"The Media Island folks are putting on a workshop this afternoon," Reb said looking up from the program.

"I'd like to go to that," Alice said, momentarily pulled out of her thoughts. "When is it?"

"Two-thirty."

He went back to reading the program while she looked about the restaurant. It was awash with the sights, sounds, and smells of public life, people talking and laughing, the aroma of coffee and fried eggs, the waitresses moving deftly among the tables like dancers performing to an orchestra of clattering breakfast dishes and clinking of silverware.

Reb had asked for her forgiveness for withholding the truth about his condition when he applied for the job at the station. He told her about the laser surgery, how inconclusive the results had been. He was on a new medication and it seemed to be working—better than the last batch of eye drops, he assured her. She turned to look at Reb again with a divided heart. A part of her had no wish to commit to a long term relationship so soon after the divorce, while another longed for just such a relationship with Reb and no one else—even if he wound up disabled and she had to take care of him. She could feel Old Man Confusion trying to force his way into her bliss, lugging along his tattered satchel of worries and unanswerable questions. But for now, she would bar the door.

A bright laugh from somewhere across the large room made her turn her head again. The restaurant was packed with bleary-eyed community radio people from all over the country, with some Federal Communications Commission and Corporation for Public Broadcasting officials thrown in for good measure. A motley group all in all, she thought, given the posh milieu. She then noticed a short, slender man in a pearl gray Stetson making his way through the room. He moved uncertainly as if looking for someone.

"Do you know who that is?" Alice said.

Reb looked up.

"In the cowboy hat," she said. "That's Lyle Workman."

Reb was excited by this news. KVMR aired Workman's audio essays and he was a dedicated fan. As the Texan came by their table Reb stood up.

"You can join us if you'd care to, Mr. Workman," he said gesturing toward one of two empty chairs.

"I was supposed to meet up with some folks for breakfast, but I don't see them anywhere," the Texan said with a boyish grin.

"Then please join us," Alice said, "we'd be honored."

"Well, don't mind if I do."

He sat down and hung his hat on the remaining chair while Reb looked about for the waitress to bring another menu.

"We've already ordered," Alice said. "I'm Alice Carpenter and this is Reb Morgan. We're with KVMR in Nevada City, California."

"We broadcast your commentaries," Reb said.

"I know," Workman said. "I get a lot of e-mails from your neck of the woods. By the way, I heard your work in the listening salon last evening. It was a top-notch piece of reporting. I always wanted to go white-water rafting, but I never got the opportunity."

"Give me a call next time you visit northern California and I'll see if it can be arranged," Reb said as he pulled out his wallet and handed Workman a business card; he had befriended the owners of Alpha Adventures while working on the story.

"I just might do that," Workman said. "You know, it may be a good thing I ran into you folks—"

The waitress arrived with a menu and Reb's orange juice.

"I already know what I want, miss," Workman said looking up at the young woman. "A bowl of oatmeal with sliced bananas and two percent milk."

"Coffee or juice?"

"Just water, thank you."

She walked away and Workman joked, "I act more like Wilford Brimley every day because I travel so much and have to pay extra attention to my diet. But as I was saying, there's a woman who keeps calling me about a power plant where her husband works. It's owned by a company called EnerTex and she thinks the plant is making her husband sick."

"Where does she live?" Alice asked.

"In a town called Birdstar about an hour south of Lubbock."

"That's a pretty name for a town," she said.

"I think so too. Anyway, EnerTex has come up with some new-fangled way to generate electricity. It's very hush-hush but it's supposed to be entirely clean and real cheap to make."

"What's the woman's name?" Reb asked.

"Sandra Valdez. I've known her for years. She's good people."

"And she's convinced it's the power plant that's making her husband sick?" Alice asked.

"Not just her husband, but some of the other men who work there too."

"What's the company have to say about it?" Reb asked.

"They don't seem much interested in talking about it."

Workman then listed the different ailments. "But they can't tell from the blood tests what's causing the trouble."

"What does Ms. Valdez want you to do?" Alice asked.

"To look into it for her but that's not exactly my line of work. Mostly I write books and produce radio commentaries. I pitched the story to a reporter with the American-Statesman in Austin but he sort of let it drop."

"Why?" Reb asked.

"Too busy, I guess, like most people. Maybe you two should take a shot at it. I know it's far from home, but California has been roughed up pretty good by the Texas power boys and your listeners might find it interesting."

Reb looked at Alice.

"This is the sort of thing Abrams wants us to do," he said. "He wants to give NPR and PRI a run for their money, doesn't he? Well, it takes a national story to do that."

"And you think this is a national story?"

"It could be."

Alice could see Reb was itching to take Workman up on the idea but the travel costs alone would likely bust the budget. She would have to talk to Kevin and Phil and they would have to convince Abrams to pony up the additional funds. . . She just didn't see it happening.

Workman broke in as if reading her thoughts. "Tell you what I'll do. I'll pay all your expenses if you'll come to Texas and meet Mrs. Valdez and some of the plant workers. Root around a little and see if you don't turn up with an acorn or two."

Reb saw his chance. "What do you say, Alice? Are you up for an adventure?"

She sipped of her coffee, reluctant to commit one way or the other. The sounds of the restaurant pressed in on them; she felt compelled to say something.

"Maybe you should investigate the story on your own, Reb," she said. "I've got the news department to run."

He wanted to argue, tell her it would be more fun working on the story together, but he could see that she found the situation awkward with Workman looking on.

"We'll talk about it later," he said with an easy smile. He turned to the Texan. "Can we get back to you later about your offer?"

It was Workman's turn to give Reb his card. "Take as much time as you need. I'm sure Sandra will appreciate any help you can give her."

Just then a man with a bulging briefcase full of sample program CDs and brochures came up to their table.

"There you are, Lyle," he said. "We're out in the lobby. The wait for a table large enough for all of us was too long so we decided to go to the Astro Diner. It's around the corner on Sixth and 54th Street."

"Okay," Workman said, "I'll join you as soon as I finish up here. I've already ordered my breakfast. You all know each other?"

Reb and Alice introduced themselves.

"KVMR is great station," the man said. "I'm Bill Chevy. I'm with the KAOS folks from Olympia."

He leaned across the table and shook their hands with the cheerful enthusiasm of a Baptist preacher greeting the faithful after worship service.

"How did you get into radio?" Reb asked Workman when they were alone again.

"It was my Great Aunt Oleta," Workman said. "Her family purchased the first radio set in the little town where they lived in East Texas. She said the neighbors would come over in the evening and sit in the yard, adults, kids, everybody, and her father would set the radio up on the window sill in the kitchen so they could all listen. It was my Aunt Oleta who convinced me that telling stories on the radio was the best way to inform and persuade people."

"Was she a good storyteller herself?" Reb asked.

"A splendid storyteller, and chock full of old-time country sayings like 'most of his religion was done in his wife's name' and 'he didn't have sense enough to spit downwind.' I've used many of them in my own stuff." He laughed.

"Ever broadcast a commentary you wish you hadn't?" Reb asked. Workman appeared as surprised by the question as Reb was for asking it.

"Just once," he said after a slight pause, his expression now serious. "It was about a congressman who was blocking a bill to raise the minimum wage. He came from a rich family and never had to worry about money a day in his life. His attitude towards working people really got under my skin. So I went to town on him and maybe he deserved it, but the day after it aired he announced that he was giving up his seat because he had cancer. Six months later he was dead. He never wrote to me—I'm not sure he ever heard the commentary—but I felt bad about it. Some folks say politics isn't personal, but it is."

THE WINNERS OF the Golden Reels were announced that night at the banquet. Reb, however, was not among the small group of excited producers who stepped onto the platform to receive their awards and the accolades of their peers. He was actually relieved.

"I don't want to peak too soon," he said half-jokingly as he and Alice made their way to the hotel bar.

"What are you talking about?" she shot back.

"I've only been doing radio news for what, ten months? The woman who won in my category, she's been at it for years. She's paid her dues and deserves to win."

"Give me a break," Alice said, unexpectedly annoyed by his blasé attitude. "It's not about putting in ten months or ten years. It's about talent and drive, both of which you have in spades."

"I appreciate your confidence, I really do, but a person needs luck too," he said. "No matter how potentially great a story is, if you don't get the right interview, well, it's just that, a potential. The guy who wins the big award in photojournalism wins because he was at the right spot at the right time, and that takes luck as well as skill."

"Some people make their luck," Alice said.

Reb shrugged. "I'm sure they do, but it also takes time."

While they looked around the crowded bar for a table, Reb wondered why he wasn't more disappointed. He said he didn't want to peak too soon. But he had to wonder if he ever *would* peak. He was fifty-four, and other than fathering a son, he didn't think he'd made much of a mark in the world. Did that make him "a slow starter"? A "late bloomer"? It was an important question if he had but one life to live. But what if the soul experienced multiple lives, and that gains made in one lifetime, no matter how modest, were carried over into the next? That was what the Hindus believed. Reb found this view of time preferable to the notion that people only got to go around once. It comforted him to think that earnest efforts served some purpose and were not wholly in vain. His mother died when he was fifteen. She possessed a fine mind and read constantly. Not just mysteries, of which she was inordinately fond, but histories and books of essays and poetry. She listened faithfully to the Texaco-sponsored radio broadcasts of the Metropolitan Opera and, just as faithfully, followed the fate of her beloved Mets as they slugged it out each year in the National League. For her, intellectual and cultural improvement was as necessary as breathing. Was it all lost then when she died? She was still a young woman, and except for a few letters, she left no tangible record of her thoughts and wisdom. Waste of that sort was an affront to Reb's fundamental belief in cosmic justice. Even though his mother laid aside her physical body, her soul, he believed, continued its journey. And who knows? They might even meet again someday. He fervently hoped so.

12

THE PHONE CALL was from Ron Jarrell, chairman of Republican National Committee and concerned a young charismatic two-term Congressman from California who was running for a seat in the Senate.

"Avery, we need one of your jets," Jarrell said, his voice full of energy. "California is a large state and Congressman Lainey has a lot of real estate to cover. The jet would be a real asset."

Avery Axton accepted that this was part of the deal—access had its price—but he was confused.

"I thought Congress outlawed the use of corporate jets for its members."

"Clean, honest government, yeah I know, but Lainey is giving up his seat so he can campaign full time."

"Giving up his seat; what if he loses?"

"Don't worry, we'll find something for him to do. He's an up-and-comer. So what do you say about lending us a jet?"

"Tell me more about your man," Avery said. "I haven't heard much about him."

"He comes from an old California ranching family. Served eight years in the Marines. He's smart, handsome, and his wife is Isabel Moreno."

Avery remembered reading somewhere that the popular actress was married to a Congressman.

"That should help you with the Latino vote," he said.

"We're going to win this race, Avery. Can I count on you for the jet?"

Avery liked Jarrell. He was a no-nonsense political operative who didn't muck up his work with a bunch of bull about the need for less government in people's lives. If the truth be known, what corporate contributors wanted was more government, not less. Big pharma wanted taxpayer funded research and the extension of patent rights. They also wanted the government to keep cheap Canadian meds out of the American bloodstream, while the agro/chemical industry wanted government to pressure other countries into accepting genetically engineered foods and terminator seeds. Then there were the defense contractors. All they wanted was the government to build bigger and better wars.

A large part of Ron's job was to make sure the merry-go-round of corporate largess in exchange for government favors remained sufficiently lubricated with cash so it didn't squeak and wake the sleeping public. Luckily, the citizenry would have to hear it over the drone of their televisions sets, which Avery didn't think was likely.

"When do you need the jet?" he asked.

"Sometime next month."

"Give me an exact date, Ron; I've got a company to run here and we've been known to use our jets from time to time."

"Wait a minute and I'll find out. Let me put you on hold."

When dealing with politicos it never hurt to apply a dose of marketplace discipline, Avery believed. He looked at the framed photograph on the wall behind his desk. It showed him standing between the president and vice-president of the United States. All three were smiling and it gave him a warm feeling. He sincerely believed in what the opposition like to call "crony capitalism." It made sense that the country's most successful corporations should direct national affairs. They had the experience and know-how, after all. The alternative was that tender, sappy hero of Frank Capra's imagination, the *public*. But was the taxi driver in Cleveland, the pipe fitter in Montgomery, or the special ed teacher in Duluth capable of mastering the multifaceted realities of the global economy? Of course not. The dance of market forces that created jobs, stimulated consumer spending, and kept the oil flowing was a step only corporate leaders knew. And Fate had decreed that America lead the world into a new millennium and the efficiently run corporation was her shining gift to the world.

Which was one more reason why he liked Jarrell. Ron wasn't a nay-sayer, a complainer, a Chicken Little. He was a realist who played his part in the great drama of world history with vigor and determination. Both men shared a faith in America's noble destiny.

Ron came back on the line. "Sorry it took so long, Avery," he said, "We need the plane by the 20th."

"You know, Ron, it could hurt your candidate's chances if it gets out that EnerTex is helping him."

"No way. By the time the election rolls around, the good people of California will see EnerTex as their savior, the specter of rolling blackouts banished forever. Isn't that what you're promising them?"

"And we'll deliver on that promise too."

"I'm sure you will. Hell, Avery, you could get elected senator or governor yourself if you ever decided to run."

"That's not my style, Ron. I prefer making money to hustling votes."

"They go together, my friend. Always have and always will. We'll talk soon."

Avery hung up the phone, got up from his desk, and walked over to the windows that looked out upon the city. The ever-present smog obscured Houston's outlying areas, so he lowered his gaze to the traffic making its way along Smith Street. A man in a motorized wheelchair navigated the busy sidewalk while another man, briefcase in hand, stepped out into the rush of cars to hail a cab. Two blocks away he could see the glittering towers of the Enron building standing tall in all their tarnished glory. The ol' Crooked E. He then noticed a helicopter approaching from the south. It swept over the EnerTex building and in a moment swung back into sight again. Avery watched it skirt the tops of several tall buildings until it hovered above one owned by a multi-national oil company. Lowering itself onto the rooftop helipad, it sat, engine running, blades turning, like a dragonfly impatient to be airborne again. A man climbed out wearing the white robes of a Saudi sheik. Clutching his attaché case in one hand and his robes that threatened to billow out in the wash of the rotating blades in the other, he hurried, stooped over, across the tarmac toward the entrance. The helicopter lifted into the sky, tail first, nose down, and then banked sharply and headed back the way it had come. Avery frowned. He didn't like Saudis. They were Arabs with too much money and power. New York had its Jews, Houston its Arabs.

He glanced at his Rolex SUBMARINER. The date was June 6th, his brother's birthday. The realization unsettled him. Maybe he should send Elliot a card or give him a call. He decided to do nothing. It was only a birthday and he doubted Elliot would even notice. Standing by the window on the thirty-sixth floor of the EnerTex building, Avery suddenly felt oddly alone in the world.

He glanced at his watch again. 1:58 p.m. He returned to his desk, picked up the remote control, and switched on the LCD television mounted against the wall so he could catch the news headlines at the top of the hour. The CNBC newscaster was reporting on a suicide bomb attack accompanied by images of mangled bodies and ambulance workers, while a continuous stream of stock quotes moved across the bottom of the screen. Avery noticed that two stocks in which he had strong positions were trending upward and this brightened his mood. The truth was that few men in the world understood the subtle and complex intricacies of modern business as well as Avery Jordan Axton. Accelerated depreciation, index warrants, beta equations, capital-ization ratios. The more arcane, the better. At his core, however, where the true man resided, complexity gave way to simplicity. There a single force animated his will and gave meaning to his life: the desire for money and power. Others might regard this fixation as little more than naked greed, but not Avery. He saw it as his *virtue*, by which, however, he did not presume to imply some sort of moral authority. Instead, he employed the word in its ancient, classical sense as it referred to the *nature* of a thing. A knife cut by virtue of its sharpness. Water cleansed by virtue of its wetness. Avery Axton made money by virtue of his wanting it so much. Money didn't make him happy, he accepted that, but it did provide him with a sense of *rightness*. In terms of physics, money was much like mass: the more of it there was, the more gravity it exerted upon its surroundings, so that all things naturally bent toward it. Conversely, not making money felt wrong to him, even though he had money enough to last ten lifetimes. It was this simplicity of purpose that lent power to Avery's actions. He was always on task and single-minded in the manner of a Samurai warrior, his energies never dissipated by momentary distractions and irrelevant considerations.

In this, as in most everything else, he was the exact opposite of his brother. Two years younger, Elliot was the poet and dreamer of the family who had grown up to become a doctor and who now operated a non-profit clinic for low-income patients in one of Houston's more blighted neighborhoods. Elliot regarded money in a wholly different light than his CEO brother and they used to argue about it.

"Money isn't something to be hoarded," Elliot continued. "It should be shared openly and fairly with everyone in society the same way blood runs through the arteries and veins to the different parts of the body. You know what happens when a body dies?"

Avery had little patience with rhetorical questions.

"The blood pools," Elliot would continue. "It no longer flows. That's what's happening in America today. The enormous fortunes being made by a handful of individuals is not the sign of a healthy, vibrant society, but of one that is dying—if not dead already."

Avery considered this a pile of happy horseshit and said so.

"Money has done more to improve the lot of humankind on this stinking planet than anything else. It motivates people to get off their duffs and invent a better water wheel or breed of dairy cow. Without it, we would still be living like Indians, trading beads with each other and chasing down buffaloes, if and when we could find them."

"Money is more insidious than that," his brother countered. "It's a kind of slavery."

"What are you talking about?"

"When you get down to it, human labor is what gives money its value. If you own a portfolio of stocks and bonds and bank CDs and receive interest every month on these investments, then you are living off someone else's sweat; someone is creating the wealth you enjoy. The fact that you don't *see* the African-American woman who is holding down three jobs, or the Mexican family out in the fields picking the vegetables that show up on your dinner table doesn't change the equation. They are working for you. Have you ever read Tolstoy?"

Avery seldom read fiction, something his brother knew, so he let the question pass.

"Well, Tolstoy put it in terms of gambling. You go to the casino and you're exceptionally lucky at the blackjack table and stuff your pockets full of chips. But for you to win this money, it follows that someone else must have lost it. It's unlikely you'll know who that person was or ever meet him. You certainly won't see him later in his room frantically trying to figure out how to get out of the jam he's in. He wrings his hands. He's wracked by remorse. He considers suicide."

"Please, let's go easy on the *pathos*."

"But it's true! Your winnings are the cause of someone else's suffering and the glitz and glamour of the casino only exists to hide the more squalid aspects of what's really taking place."

"That's where you're wrong," Avery shot back. "I didn't force the poor slob to plunk down his chips and gamble away his rent money. He did that all on his own, and if I should then benefit, what sin have I committed? I took my chances, same as he did."

"But with money," Elliot countered, "the game is rigged; someone always has the advantage. One guy has more brains than the next guy, or has the right skin color. Or he speaks the right language, or belongs to the right club. Maybe he's inherited enough money to put him ahead. Then the squeeze is on, and instead of chains and whips like in the old days of African slavery, we have debt to keep people in line and toiling away so their betters can live it up in Fat City. You know what I'm talking about. Look at credit card companies; they're our modern-day overseers. Many working people can't earn enough money to get by on so they rack up credit card debt. Then they're hit with sky-high interest rates and late fees that prevent them from ever paying down the principle."

"Is this supposed to bother me?" Avery's laugh was calculated to nettle his brother. "If it's a choice between the *haves* and *have-nots*, Elliot, I'll take the *haves* every time. They're my friends. They wash and wear clean clothes. They invite me to dinner parties and send me lovely cards at Christmas. We are members of the same tribe. Am I a monster because I'm ambivalent about the *have-nots* because they're too ignorant or lazy to read the fine print on a credit card application? Give me a break. Poor people don't care what happens to me. They don't lay awake at night worrying because I might have prostate cancer or a bad heart. So why should I worry about them?"

Here Avery would adopt his sincere, world-weary older brother manner. "Forget all this warmed-over Tolstoy malarkey, Elliot. You claim people work like dogs their entire lives and never get ahead. But you know what? They *do* get ahead; on average they see their lives improve—if not *their* lives, then those of their children, and their children's children. Look around you. Our lives are infinitely better now than they used to be. Only a couple of generations ago people worked twelve to fourteen hours a day, six days a week. They cooked meals over an open fire and slaughtered whales to light their homes. Their hair was infested with lice, they got syphilis and went crazy; their teeth rotted and fell out. Old men suffered from hernias and gout, women hemorrhaged and died during childbirth. And what makes the difference between then and now? Money. Money and it's twice-blessed child, capitalism. That's what built the hospitals and the schools and the public water systems. And if a few individuals become rich in the bargain, I say all the better, since the rest of mankind benefits mightily as well."

"A rising tide lifts all ships," his brother said, anticipating what was coming next.

"Just because it's a cliché, Elliot, doesn't make it any less true."

"But can't you see how our obsessive behavior toward money corrupts the mind and soul? We greet the world as children with awe and wonder, our hearts free and joyful. Then the ways of money take over. We learn to be anxious, to scheme. We begin to see everything as a commodity, each with an assigned value, even people. These apples cost fifty-nine cents a pound, while these other apples cost ninety-five cents a pound. This man's time is worth seven dollars an hour, while across town, another man's time is worth four hundred dollars an hour. We are led into captivity by business. Sitting in our cubicles on the twenty-second floor of some office building or strung out along an assembly line, we forget that we are made of stardust. Instead we have allowed ourselves to become little more than trained hamsters. We wake at night and worry about bills and insurance policies and the cost of college tuition for our children. We no longer trust Medicare and Social Security to take care of us in our old age, so we frantically put aside money, never knowing how much will be enough. Gold has become our idol, Avery. It no longer serves us, but we it. And more's the shame on us for doing so."

These conversations used to interest Avery, but lately he found them tedious. Both men had inherited a sizable fortune from their father who had founded EnerTex just after the war. While many of his army buddies were taking advantage of the G.I. Bill to go to college, Archibald Axton—except for the IRS, everyone called him Archie—had set his sights on becoming an oil baron. He had noted the essential role oil had played in the war and so he packed his bags for west Texas and set up a small oil exploration and drilling company that wound up finding more natural gas than oil. One thing led to another, and by the time he passed away in 1989, he had assembled an impressive list of holdings in energy-related businesses. Avery joined the firm straight out of college and took over as president and CEO when his father died.

Elliot, meanwhile, finished his medical training and started a clinic. He also joined a popular swing band called the *Texas Wonderboys*. Avery thought it smacked of hypocrisy for his younger brother to talk so disparagingly about having money when he never had to hustle to get it in the first place. It was that way with most people. They complained about how wealthy people were too rich, how they cheated and perverted the system. But every time he walked into a restaurant or an art show opening, they were all over him, their mouths filled with cloying flattery.

"How are you, Mr. Axton? My husband and I have always wanted to meet you. I must say what you've done with EnerTex is simply amazing!"

The truth was they wanted money as much as he did, because to be rich in America was to be visible, while to be poor was to be invisible. Maybe if his brother was sixty and unemployed with no health insurance or savings, he'd view things differently. Avery found the greatest benefit of money was that it enabled him to preserve his dignity. If you had enough money, you didn't have to take shit from anybody, and that was saying something.

Switching off the newscast, Avery turned his thoughts to the demands of the present. Leaning forward in his black Italian leather executive chair, he pushed the call button on the intercom to summon his secretary.

"Brenda, tell Jim Logan to get one of the jets ready for Congressman Lainey's people. They'll pick it up on the 20th of next month. Make sure not to give them the new Gulfstream. Also send a birthday card to my brother. You have the information. Did that Homeland Security report show up yet?"

"FedEx just delivered it, sir. I'll bring it in. And Mr. Hamilton is here to see you."

"Good. Send him in too."

Avery closed his eyes. He'd been listening to audio tapes on Zen meditation on the drive to and from work. He needed to clear his mind so he could figure out what to do about the power plant. There was potentially a serious problem at Ranger 1 but it could be managed if everyone kept their heads. He'd sort it out; making the big money wasn't always easy.

The tall mahogany door to his office suite opened and Brenda entered carrying a FedEx envelope. As always she was dressed to the nines in an Albert Nipon tweed three-piece suit, her dark auburn hair pulled smartly back and held by an antique tortoise shell clip. Gold hoops swung from her ear lobes. Behind her walked a young man. Avery smiled warmly as he welcomed him.

"Marty, good to see you," he said, directing his employee to a chair. "How's it going with the California crowd?"

"They're sharpening their pencils, sir. I expect we'll have a signed contract by the end of the week."

While this exchange was taking place, Brenda unobtrusively placed the report on Avery's desk and withdrew. All that remained was the seductive presence of her Chanel perfume.

"How long have you been with us, Marty?"

"Just under two years, sir." Marty said fighting the temptation to look around; it was the first time he'd been invited into his boss' office.

"Do you like the work?"

"It's the best."

"Don McBride speaks highly of you." McBride was Sales Manager for North America. If he was talking Marty up, it meant better things to come. Marty just hoped he wasn't blushing.

"I give it the old college try, sir."

"And what college was that?"

"Vanderbilt, sir. I got my MBA at the University of Pennsylvania."

"I gave a lecture at Wharton last year," Avery said as he stood up and walked over to a cabinet against the wall. He swung a door open to reveal a fully stocked bar.

"I didn't know that, sir."

"Gave it to 'em straight, like a Texan. They weren't ready for that." He chuckled. "Can I get you a drink? Scotch? Bourbon?"

Marty experienced a moment's indecision. Should he accept or not? It was the middle of the day and Marty was on company time. What would a *regular guy* in Avery's world do under the circumstances? He intensely wanted his boss to see him as a *regular guy*. "I'll take a bourbon on the rocks, sir, if you have it."

Avery dropped a couple of ice cubes into a cut-crystal glass and filled it nearly full from a bottle of Jack Daniel's Black Label. He didn't fix a drink for himself and Marty cringed for making the wrong call. Avery handed the glass to Marty and then stepped back and leaned against the front edge of his desk so that Marty had to look up at him.

"You strike me as a man who doesn't let the grass grow under his feet," Avery said.

"Not if there's an opportunity on the horizon, sir."

"And what opportunities do you see for a young man like yourself here at EnerTex?"

"The sky's the limit, sir. The energy sector is long overdue for innovation, not just in technology, but in how energy is bought and sold."

"So I take it you're a fan of deregulation?"

"If done correctly, sir, yes."

"Uneven track record so far."

"It's the scouts, sir, like the guys at Enron, who get shot full of arrows. The settlers who come along later are the ones who reap the rewards."

"So you see us as *settlers* here at EnerTex?" Avery said with a bemused smile.

Wrong image, Marty thought to himself. Too sedentary.

"No, not exactly, sir," he said. "Our electrical generation technology is as new as it gets, but we've learned from past mistakes when it comes to valuing and negotiating long-term contracts with transmission companies and our large institutional custom-ers. What I mean, sir, is that the industry has finally figured out how to successfully manage risk."

"Have we now?" Avery made sure not to raise his eyebrows though the urge to do so was there. "Tell me about it."

The Tin Man felt a surge of enthusiasm ripple through him. The president and CEO of EnerTex was asking for his opinion about the most exciting development in business practices in the last hundred years, as far as Marty was concerned. He wanted to jump up out of his chair and pace back and forth as he talked, but he controlled himself. The next few minutes could make or break his career; it was best to come across as mature and restrained.

"I believe it is now possible, sir," he said, his voice measured and authoritative, "through the intelligent use of sophisticated information technology to accurately evaluate every conceivable eventuality that might adversely impact a particular market—in EnerTex's case, the electricity market—and to offer our long-term customers innovative financial instruments that remove any possible liability."

"Derivatives? You're talking about derivatives?" Avery said.

"That is only one approach, sir. I believe there are other avenues to explore as well."

Avery looked down at the young man in the expensive suit and shoes, with his soft hands and clean fingernails, and doubted Marty had ever come within ten miles of an oil rig. What did he know about risk? It took a Texan with some years under his belt to truly appreciate danger and uncertainty. The state's short, troubled history was full of risk. Tornadoes, blizzards, lightning storms, dust clouds, hail, wind, and drought, and that was just the weather. Add to that hostile Indians, war, poisonous snakes and insects, outlaws, carpetbaggers, Mexican rustlers, busted banks, land swindlers, gas well explosions, and oil rig fires, and it was hard to believe some thirty-year old hotshot with a Dell laptop and a spreadsheet could make it all go away by manipulating a couple of mathematical equations so that each risk was given a value—a plus 4.9 here, a negative 13.8 there. These new leaders of corporate America, the wunderkinds from Harvard, Stanford, and the University of Pennsylvania, had no interest in playing by the old rules. They didn't work their way slowly up through the organization from job to job. Instead, they expected to go straight to the head of the line, all the while preaching the gospel of *paradigm shift* and providing those with lesser intellectual ability a glorious vision of how business would be conducted in the twenty-first century.

Hubris, Avery thought to himself. *Hubris*. An interesting word. He looked it up once. It originally came from the Greeks, but in Old English it referred to the offspring of a wild boar and a domestic pig. He found the allusion instructive. It meant that hubris wasn't simple pride. If a man was favored by fate to do great things and was duly proud and confident of that fact, all well and good. Hubris referred rather to someone seduced by arrogance or guile into stepping outside his assigned destiny. By doing so, he became an abomination, like the beast that was neither boar or pig. And *hubris*, by its very nature, conjured up *nemesis* to destroy the beast, because of its failure to conform to the established order.

Hadn't these young bucks learned anything from the Enron fiasco? Old "Kenny Boy" had really given them their heads. Hired them by the cartload and set them up in that brace of mirrored towers just up the street. People who worked there called it the *Death Star*. They were out to rule the universe. And they very nearly pulled it off until a few inconvenient details slipped out regarding off-shore partnerships and a billion plus dollars of hidden debt. It was like when Luke Skywalker put his photon torpedo down the reactor's exhaust shaft in the first *Star Wars* movie. It blew Enron all to hell, and there were bleeding and dead commodity traders, deal originators, and accountants strewn from coast to coast. But mostly in Texas, where the stench of rotting careers up and down Smith Street was nearly unbearable.

All the same, Avery had his reasons to thank Enron. For one, with all the media hype and Wall Street wet dreams going on during their spectacular rise, insignificant little EnerTex was able to pursue its goals unnoticed and unmolested. State and federal energy regulators could be cajoled in private and, when expedient, pressured by the White House. They could even be bribed when absolutely necessary, just so long as nothing slowed down the construction of the Ranger 1 power plant in Dalton County with its new, untested generation technology. Environmental impact requirements were set aside since, from the wartime administration's point of view, the need for increased energy production trumped all other concerns. In the end what should have taken ten to fifteen years to accomplish was done in less than two. It was the magician's art of misdirection. Step right up, ladies and gentlemen, and make sure to keep your eyes on Enron while the man behind the curtain gets some real work done.

And Enron should be thanked for luring a so many financial geniuses away from Wall Street and bringing them to Houston. This was no mean accomplishment since the city—hot, humid, and buggy—was one of the most unpleasant places on the face of the earth. Pollution from the many oil refineries and chemical plants made the air practically unbreathable. Traffic was horrendous and, because the city had no building codes, it was an architectural nightmare. The joke went that Houston wasn't hell, but it was only a local call away.

Avery took a moment longer to regard the young man before him. Perhaps he was being too harsh. McBride claimed Hamilton had promise, that he was clever and hungry enough to make a name for himself, provided he was given the right kind of encouragement. The company was going to expand dramatically in the next couple of years and they needed leaders. The choice was to either bring them in from outside or grow them from within. Avery preferred the latter option because he valued loyalty above all. Hamilton was full of himself but what young man wasn't? In an odd sort of way, Avery saw something of himself in the younger man. There was a reckless, belligerent streak beneath the carefully groomed exterior. His own son was a fuck-up; maybe he should take a chance on Marty. But first he would give him a test, see how he managed, and go from there.

"I have a personal favor to ask, Marty," Avery said.

Marty sat forward in his chair.

"Sometimes a public relations situation comes up that we prefer to keep in the family, if you know what I mean," Avery said.

Marty nodded even though he didn't know what Avery was talking about.

"Well, just such a situation concerns a radio journalist from California who has been hounding us for weeks with requests for information. He has it in his head that there's some kind of worker safety problem at the Ranger 1 plant and he wants to meet with our engineers and the plant foreman. He even wants to interview me, which of course is out of the question."

This only deepened Marty's confusion. A radio journalist? Worker safety? What did this have to do with him? He was a salesman, and although his part of the deal with the state officials in California and Nevada was pretty much over with, he had been expecting any day to be sent to another state or country. He needed clarification but wasn't exactly sure how best to ask for it. He took a pull on his drink without thinking.

"But there are no worker safety concerns at the plant, are there, sir?" he asked.

"None whatsoever. An allegation was made by the wife of an employee some months ago and we promptly conducted a thorough investigation that proved that nothing was wrong. But you know how it is with these media people, Marty, they're all out to make a name for themselves."

"But if there's no story, sir," Marty said, "then why waste time on him?" He regretted the comment as soon as he'd made it; it wasn't his place to second-guess the president of the EnerTex Corporation. Luckily, however, Avery gave no indication of annoyance.

"These things have a way of taking on a life of their own. An unsubstantiated rumor begins to circulate and very quickly enough people believe it to make a difference."

Avery thought about Ron Jarrell. There was a man who understood how half-truths and outright lies could be skillfully employed to sway public opinion at the just the right moment, such as before an important election. Nor did it matter if the falsehoods were later discredited since the damage was done and the preferred candidate safely in office. The public's memory, Avery knew, wasn't much longer than that of a goldfish.

Marty meanwhile made his own mental calculations. The word on the street was that EnerTex would soon go public. The company needed a massive infusion of capital if it hoped to start building power plants everywhere and the period just before an Initial Public Offering was crucial because any negative publicity, warranted or not, could hammer the stock price. Marty saw the connection and understood Avery's concern.

"What radio station does this reporter work for?" Marty asked. "Perhaps the station management can be reasoned with." He hoped they were dealing with one of the big radio chains like Clear Channel headquartered out of nearby San Antonio. Marty was sure they could be counted upon to keep America's corporate interests uppermost in their considerations.

Avery shook his head with disgust. "He's a nobody. Works for some hole-in-the-wall outfit in a little town in northern California." Avery reached around and retrieved a slip of paper from his desk.

"The station is called KVMR. It's in Nevada City, California."

"That's near Sacramento. I know the town." Marty said, happy to contribute something tangible to the conversation. "It's a touristy sort of place on the way to Lake Tahoe. What's the reporter's name?"

Avery glanced again at the paper. "Reb Morgan."

"What do you want me to do about him?"

"Whatever it takes. Didn't you take some corporate communications classes in school?"

"Yes, sir. I considered a career in PR but I'm glad now I didn't."

Avery thought to himself, You're right there, Mr. Hamilton. You don't get a coveted place next to the Money River working in the PR office; you just see to it that no outsider finds it, or better yet, ever learns about its existence."

"You handle this Morgan guy without raising a fuss, Marty, and I'll make it right with you." Avery said. "You have my word on it."

"What about my sales work, sir?"

"We're scaling back our marketing efforts for the time being. We couldn't handle any more customers if we had them."

This was news to Marty and he didn't know what to say.

"I'll have Joe Brennerman handle your accounts in the meantime." Avery was about to say something else but read a flicker of suspicion in the younger man's eyes.

"This isn't a demotion, Marty," Avery said with a warm, reassuring smile. "You're the best deal originator we have and I think you know it. Your work will be waiting for you. There may even be a promotion."

"How far do you want me to go getting rid of this guy?"

"Let's just say I'll leave that to you. We're committed to results here at EnerTex, Marty. Those who produce results can expect to rise quickly in the company."

The two men regarded each other for a brief moment and Marty stood up without waiting to be told. Avery reached out and shook his hand while placing his left hand on the young man's shoulder and gently steering him toward the door.

"Stay in touch with Brenda, my executive assistant. She'll provide you with all the pertinent information. Let her know if you need anything. And here, take this."

The CEO produced a business card. "Special Agent Arnold Brewer is with the Department of Homeland Security. He's sort of on loan to us for the time being. He is a valuable source of information. I recommend you take advantage of him."

Marty slipped the card into his pocket and left the office to talk to Brenda.

Avery turned his attention to the report from Homeland Security that sat on his desk. Access, he thought with satisfaction. The name of the game was access, and Avery Axton had access up the wazoo.

13

IT WAS EASY getting Brenda to go to bed with him. Frankly Marty had expected more of a challenge. For starters she was older than he was. And married. Her husband, a pilot for FedEx, commuted twice a month from Houston to the company's hub at Subic Bay in the Philippines. This meant he was away much of the time, which was how Brenda liked it.

The Tin Man's interest, however, in this particular romantic conquest was not entirely carnal. He sought information. He was curious to find out why the great Avery Axton had chosen him of all people to deal with a troublesome journalist. He didn't buy the "keeping it in the family" explanation. Any job in the globalized corporate economy could be outsourced—even murder.

"It's because you know how to get what you want," Brenda said in a teasing voice. They'd just had sex for the second time and she was propped up in bed smoking a cigarette.

"Why didn't Avery assign someone from the PR department?" he asked. "Am I being eased out?"

"Put out to stud? Is that what you mean?"

Marty did not find the analogy amusing.

"Here, have a cigarette," she said holding out her pack of Virginia Slims. "It'll help you relax."

Marty shook his head. It already took all his will power to keep his lust for alcohol and cocaine under control; another addiction was out of the question.

"Avery is very thorough with his background checks," Brenda continued, the playfulness dropping out of her voice. "He gets personally involved when it comes to his top hires. He uses a company out of Dallas called Infoseek Associates. Ever hear of them?"

"No."

"Well, they're good; they don't miss much. It seems your creative efforts on behalf of your fraternity didn't go unnoticed."

A prickly, burning sensation traveled up his neck to the tips of his ears. It wasn't shame, a bothersome condition for which he had developed a strong immunity over the years; but a reaction to being found out. He felt suddenly exposed and vulnerable.

"Then why did Avery hire me to work for EnerTex if he knew about it?"

Brenda laughed. "You are young, aren't you?" The conversation was not going the way he wanted. He was the one who was supposed to be in charge. Brenda stubbed out her cigarette, got up, and went into the bathroom and he heard the shower come on. As he lounged in bed, he thought about his last year at Vanderbilt. He had been president of his fraternity and they had hosted a party, a Class-A blowout with students crammed into all four floors of the frat house and spilling out into the street. The weather in Nashville was unusually warm for late autumn and a lunatic moon beamed down at the revelers from a purple sky. Despite repeated complaints from the neighbors, the police could do little to tone things down short of arresting everybody and that would require way too much paperwork. So the party roared on and shape-shifted over the course of several hours into a hungry, restless creature. Even by Marty's jaded standards, the consumption of alcohol and drugs was, quite literally, staggering. Then sometime during the night, two of his fraternity brothers lured a young woman upstairs and raped her. It was not date rape but outright sexual assault. The girl, a freshman, never saw it coming. Luckily for the perpetrators charges were never filed—the girl apparently was too ashamed to come forward—and it appeared the whole incident would blow over. But then a college newspaper caught wind of the story and began asking questions. The paper wasn't the *Hustler*, the university's official conservative newspaper, but a twelve-page weekly rag started by an extra-bright journalism student named Bert Nichols whose father was an editor for the New York *Times*.

This placed Marty in a predicament. He had to expel the offending brothers from the fraternity—never an easy task—but more than that, he had to protect the brotherhood's reputation. Their relationship with the university was already strained by earlier infractions, and if the story about the rape got out, there was a very good chance their charter would be revoked. As president, he was determined this would not happen on his watch. He considered phoning his father for advice but decided against it.

Warren Camden Hamilton III was a lawyer and lobbyist for the National Rifle Association who operated out of their Washington office, where he was on intimate terms with most of the power brokers in the nation's capitol. Whenever some fifty-five year-old white guy in Topeka slipped down into his basement den late at night to stroke his AK-47, he had Warren C. Hamilton to thank for helping convince Congress to rescind its prohibition on assault weapons.

Marty respected his father's success but there was little warmth between them, and so he decided to look to his own devices. He was young and believed he could charm his way out of the situation. He invited Nichols to lunch to see if the editor could be reasoned with. This turned out badly since all Nichols did was assail him with questions that he had no intention of answering. Several times Marty was tempted to reach across the table and smack the little shit. So much for mollification; Marty's next step was to see to it that two of the newspaper's student reporters got knocked around late one night after a football game. He also hired a geek with the on-line handle "Dark Angel" to hack into the paper's computers and steal their files. This turned out better than Marty expected because the stolen data contained a confidential list of the paper's sources, including the names of a dozen faculty members, some not yet tenured, who fed information to the paper on the sly about a variety of questionable dealings on the part of the university administration. It was hot stuff and likely to place the unfortunate professors' careers in jeopardy should their names get out. Thanks to Marty, that's exactly what happened several days later.

But still the editor came on, a regular Clark Kent, compelling Marty to withdraw five hundred dollars from the fraternity's slush fund to engage the services of a sorority sister named Amanda. A tall slender Nordic blond with exquisite green eyes, she started volunteering at the newspaper and it wasn't long before she had Nichols on a string. Pot was smoked, sexual favors exchanged, photographs taken. After which Nichols folded up his tent and went away. It was a shabby business all in all, and though Marty wasn't particularly proud of what he'd done, he enjoyed every minute of it. He even convinced himself that he'd done Nichols a favor.

"Now the little prick knows how the real world works and how easily a journalist can be compromised."

Lying in Brenda's bed, the satin sheets in a heap to one side, the smell of her cigarettes in his hair, Marty began to realize what Avery wanted. He wanted this Reb Morgan to fold up his tent and go away, just like Bert Nichols. Okay, the Tin Man could hang with that. Hell, it might even be fun. He'd start by Googling the son-of-a-bitch. It was amazing how much you could learn about somebody using the internet. One thing was for sure, some old hippie radio guy from California was no match for Martin Hamilton, the future CEO of the EnerTex Corporation.

Brenda's voice called out to him from the shower. "Marty, come join me."

He did.

14

THE CELL PHONE vibrated like some mutant insect inside his jacket pocket as he made his way from the Amarillo Federal Building to the parking lot. He took it out but didn't recognize the caller ID.

"Yeah?" he said.

"Is this Special Agent Brewer?"

"To whom am I speaking?"

"Marty Hamilton. Mr. Axton told you I'd be calling."

"Oh yeah, you're the guy from EnerTex. What do you want?"

He had reached his car but delayed opening the door knowing it would be an oven inside until he got the AC on.

"I need some information about a radio journalist. His name is Paul Andrew Morgan." Marty had the tech staff at Google to thank for Reb's Christian names. "He lives in Sacramento, California, and works for a small radio station called KVMR. We believe he'll be traveling here to Texas soon."

"What do you want to know about him?"

"His travel itinerary. His airline and arrival time. Car rental company? Anything you can give me."

"Could take some time."

"I can't wait around on this, Agent Brewer."

The heat radiating up from the sunbaked asphalt was making Brewer cross.

"You know, we have more important things to do than run errands for EnerTex, Mr. Hamilton."

"Then you'd better take it up with your supervisor." Marty wasn't about to take guff from a government gumshoe. He knew the order to give aid and comfort had come down from on high.

"Yeah, right," Brewer said with an audible sigh of capitulation. "Give me a number where I can reach you."

Marty gave Brewer his cell number. Step one accomplished. Now to call his good buddy Dean Wakefield and score some weed. Dean was a day-trader who lived in Houston, but the bulk of his income came from a pot growing operation he had going with a farmer in Indiana. Marty knew from experience that his friend grew and distributed some of the finest cannabis on the planet. In time Mr. Wakefield would become a very wealthy man. It paid to cultivate the right connections.

SIX DAYS LATER Marty walked into the rental car return area at the Lubbock International Airport. The day before he made friends with a twenty-four year old loser named Gill who cleaned cars for Avis. Better yet, Gill was hooked up with Krystle, who worked the Avis counter. It didn't take Marty long to strike a deal.

"Which car is it?" he asked Gill, who had just finished vacuuming out an Oldsmobile Alero.

"The red Chevrolet Cavalier in stall B-24." Gill pointed.

"Are you sure this is the car your friend will give them?"

"It's no big deal. She'll tell 'em it's the only car available."

Marty looked at his watch. He needed to hurry; Morgan's flight would arrive soon. He glanced around to see if he was being observed and then the thought struck him: what if the little fuck informed on me? He stared at Gill and decided the acne-scarred youth lacked the imagination for anything that creative.

"Is the car locked?" he asked.

"No."

Marty strode over to the Cavalier. Not far away, a couple was arguing loudly because neither had remembered to fill the gas tank. Marty opened the door of the car, slipped inside, and placed his attaché case on the passenger seat. He popped it open and withdrew two thick envelopes, a roll of duct tape, and a magnetic radio transmitter. He attached the transmitter—a special global positioning satellite beacon—up under the dashboard and then ripped off a length of tape and stuck one of the envelopes to the bottom of the driver's seat. The whole operation took less than thirty seconds. As he walked past Gill on the way out, he slipped the car cleaner the other envelope.

"Thanks, man," he said.

"Anytime," Gill grinned back.

SOUTHWEST FLIGHT 1228 arrived twenty minutes late. Reb and Alice were among the first to deplane and they found the airport nearly empty.

"I guess they don't handle many flights on Saturdays," Alice said as they walked down the concourse toward the baggage claim area. Reb had a black nylon bag slung over his shoulder that held his recording gear. He had a slight headache and the whine of the jet engines had left a ringing in his ears.

"People in Texas think they live in another country," Reb said. "They talk about having *borders* instead of state lines."

"Well, Texas was its own country for a short while," Alice said.

"To be honest, I wish they'd stayed that way."

They arrived at the baggage claim area along with a dozen or so passengers from their flight.

"What do you have against Texas?" Alice said.

"Do you want a list? How about slavery, the Civil War, Joe McCarthy, the Kennedy assassination, Johnson and Vietnam, Enron, Halliburton, the Bush family, Tom Delay—"

"What has Joe McCarthy got to do with Texas?" Alice interrupted. "Wasn't he from Wisconsin?"

"Yeah, but it was the big oil, ultra right-wing nut jobs from Texas who bankrolled him and got him elected. They used to call

McCarthy Texas' third senator. Any way you look at it, the state has given America an impressive string of scoundrels."

"Other states produce scoundrels too."

"Sure, but name me one good thing that's come out of Texas in recent memory?"

"Willie Nelson. The Dixie Chicks. Larry McMurtry. They're all from Texas. Lyle Workman too."

"So was Molly Ivins. I stand corrected." Reb knew the headache was coloring his mood. He stared at the baggage carousel and willed it to begin turning. Alice meanwhile was wondering why she was defending Texas all of a sudden, since she didn't care much for the state either. Her reasons, however, were more personal than political.

His name was Clint Worthington and they met while at UC-Santa Barbara. She found the whole idea of him being a Texan very romantic—this was during what she afterwards referred to as her "cowboy phase"—and she liked to imagine Clint galloping across the open prairie with John Wayne and Henry Fonda, his bed roll tied to his saddle, the wind in his hair. But then Clint took her home to Dallas to meet his parents over Christmas break. It was quite the let-down because she discovered that Worthingtons were full-blooded suburbanites. They lived in air conditioned ease in a split-level house in a development called Trinity Oaks. John Worthington was an electrical engineer at Texas Instruments while Clint's mother, Doris, was District Chairwoman of the Daughters of the American Revolution, a woman who got her hair done up into a bouffant every Friday and drank like a fish the rest of the week. The Worthingtons owned a pet monkey named Skeeter, and they dressed the poor creature in a tight red suit and round flat cap like a bell hop at a fancy hotel and tipped him with a bright new penny anytime he did something that they regarded as extra cute. The worst experience during the visit was Christmas Day supper. There were just the five of them: Alice, Clint, his parents, and the monkey, who squirmed about in his little highchair and pulled compulsively at the strap holding his

cap on. The conversation was sluggish at best and steered clear of
any and all sensitive topics including the war in Vietnam, the Civil
Rights movement, music, movies, and California. What remained
were comments such as "the last three weeks have been dry, we
could use some rain," and "I don't think this ham is as tender as
the one we had last year, dear."

Alice wanted to scream; she felt as if she had been dropped into
a 1950s science fiction movie where everything on the surface was
deadpan politeness, while out in the backyard, in a rabbit warren of
subterranean passageways, long armed Martians were implanting
control devices into the brains of captured humans like her hosts.
She went to sleep that night to the muffled sounds of Lawrence
Welk on the TV downstairs, and by the end of January, Clint was
history and Alice had no desire to ever visit Texas again.

The bags at last came up the ramp and dropped onto the
turning carousel. Reb and Alice collected theirs and went to the
Avis counter to see about the car they had reserved. The girl
handed them a set of keys to a red Chevy Cavalier in stall B-24.
They went outside, found the car, and loaded their bags into the
trunk.

"You know you're right," Reb said as he closed the trunk, "I
should improve my attitude. I've some interviews coming up and
people can tell when you've got a chip on your shoulder."

"This kind of heat can put anybody on edge," Alice said
looking up at the sun-burned sky and shielding her eyes.

"Do you want to drive?" he asked.

"No, I'll drive later."

As they pulled down the aisle toward the exit, they passed
an Avis employee in an orange jump suit who was removing old
newspapers from the back seat of a car. He straightened up as they
drove past and waved at them, smiling. Reb thought to himself,
they sure are friendly down here. I'll give them that.

15

HIS TWO CLOSEST friends cleared out of West Texas as soon as they could afford the bus fare. Billy Underwood was now a union carpenter in Memphis and Bobby Ray White worked as a welder on the docks in Seattle. Mike Pendergast couldn't blame them. Work was scarce around Birdstar and the social life had little to recommend it, unless your idea of a good time was knocking back a six pack of Lone Star beer, cranking up Waylon Jennings on the pickup's stereo, and shooting prairie dogs by moonlight. Still, there was Hazel. She was a woman a man couldn't help but notice and Mike had noticed hard and decided to stay put.

His Uncle Ferris, who like to refer to himself as a big wheel in the Dalton County Democratic Party, found Mike a job driving a grader for the Texas Department of Transportation. It wasn't the best job in the world, but it enabled Mike to marry Hazel and purchase a modest three-bedroom house with ten percent down and an FHA guaranteed loan. Then the kids started coming. Melissa, Jennifer, and little Mikie. Everything was going along, as Uncle Ferris would say, "easy as a hoss-fly ridin' in a mule's ear" until a Republican got himself elected governor and Mike was suddenly out of a job. Hazel went to fixing hair but Mike couldn't find permanent work—just odd jobs here and there—nor could he pack up and leave like Billy and Bobby Ray had done. He had a family to support. Then the new power plant came to town and Mike snagged a job on the maintenance crew.

Only now Sandra Valdez had got it in her head that something at the plant was making people sick. Hazel was concerned too, but he felt fine. Well not exactly fine, but he wasn't sick, just tired most of the time. And he kept getting his kids' names all mixed up, something his granny used to do in her later years. She'd yell, "Willie, Mike, Davy, stop chucking rocks against the garage," even though only one boy was doing the chucking. They called it her "shotgun address." Say the name of each and every grandson in quick succession and she was bound to hit with one of them.

Now Mike was doing the same thing. He put it down to information overload. It seemed folks in America were so crammed full of information that they couldn't keep their facts straight. Newspapers and magazines, television shows, radio commercials, movies on DVD, and now these little Ipods that could store and play a thousand songs or more; was it any surprise then that as one more thing came into a person's head, another had to pop out just to make room? Maybe that helped explain how a moron got elected president of the United States, even if he was from Texas. But then again, anything was better than the jerk who'd held the job before him. On that point Mike Pendergast lined up shoulder to shoulder with the Republicans, even if they *had* cost him his highway job.

"I mean, if you're going to get a blow job in the Oval Office," he remarked to his neighbor Luther one day soon after the news came out, "then at least do it with somebody who can keep her mouth shut." Neither of them caught the joke.

"HURRY UP, MIKE," Hazel yelled over her shoulder as she went out the back door. "We're supposed to be at the Resource Center by three." She was wearing her tight-fitting zebra-striped pants with an orange tank top. How she managed to keep the same sexy shape she'd had back in high school after three kids was a mystery to Mike. He didn't know much about human anatomy but he had watched what happened to other women after they'd popped out a baby or two. Fat city and bad hair. Their husbands did even worse. Fat city and no hair. He blamed it on west Texas; there just wasn't sufficient motivation to keep up appearances after a certain point. Yet he had to hand it to Hazel. She was all business when it came to how she looked and he reckoned he'd follow her into a nest of angry hornets if she asked him to.

"I think this reporter nonsense is just a big waste of time," he grumbled as he walked around to open the driver's side door of their Dodge Ram 4 X 4. "Ain't nobody ever going to listen to what they have to say anyway."

"You don't know that," Hazel said. "They just might get EnerTex to deal with what's going on."

They climbed into the truck and Mike started up the 320 Horsepower Cummins Turbo Diesel. "And can you tell me exactly *what* that something is supposed to be? Sandra's got you seeing bug-a-bears where there ain't any." He backed out of the driveway.

"Well, what about what you told me?" Hazel said. "You know, how every time the bosses from Houston show up, they shut the reactor down before they come around and don't turn it on again until after they're gone? That sure doesn't sound right to me."

He wanted to come back at her with something clever but couldn't think of anything. He pushed the truck into gear and started down the street. She was right; it was peculiar. A person would think that EnerTex's head technicians would want to see the reactor and turbines operating while they were there, but they never did. In the beginning, right after the plant went operational, it was different. The managers and technicians lived in Birdstar and worked at the plant every day. One guy, a foreigner who walked with a cane, lived on site in a trailer twenty-four/seven. He was an odd duck and mostly kept to himself. He went in and out of the reactor building at least twenty times a day carrying a device that looked like an old-fashioned bread box. Mike assumed it was some kind of testing equipment. A co-worker started calling the man "Dr. Strangelove" behind his back and the name stuck. Then one day, out of the blue, EnerTex gathered up everybody, except for the security detail and a skeleton maintenance crew of which Mike was a part, and shipped them all off to Houston.

The company said they could run the whole shooting match from there using computers and specially dedicated telephone lines. It seemed to work. The plant had been operating at close to one hundred percent capacity for over eighteen months with only six site visits from the higher-ups in all that time.

They arrived at the Lubbock Family Resource Center at a quarter after three. The Center closed at three on Saturdays and they walked around to the back door and knocked. Sandra opened it and they stepped inside.

"Everyone's in the conference room," Sandra said, taking a quick furtive look outside before closing the door. Her behavior made Mike feel sneaky. She then gave Hazel a hug and led them down a hallway into a room with a table placed at one end. The blinds were drawn and the sunshine streamed through in knife edges. Mike saw a man in a chair wearing a denim short sleeve shirt, khaki shorts, and purple nylon-strap sandals. He decided it must be one of the reporters from California. Next to him sat Ernesto. Working different shifts the way they did, Mike seldom saw Sandra's husband. They used to be close friends.

"Hey Ernesto, how goes?" Mike said.

"Not bad," Ernesto answered with a weak smile. Mike thought he looked tired, like someone just getting over the flu.

He then noticed another woman in the room, middle-aged, slim, wearing shorts and a white, embroidered Mexican blouse. She must be the other reporter.

Sandra made introductions.

"Lyle Workman asked us to look into this story," Reb said, "and that's why we're here."

"Who's Lyle Workman?" Mike asked.

"He's on the radio," Sandra answered. "He's from Texas."

"I don't care if he's from Mars," Mike said. "What's he got to do with us?" This elicited a sharp glance from Hazel with the unspoken text, "Don't be an asshole, Michael."

Sandra didn't seem to notice. "Mr. Workman contacted these people in California on my behalf. They've agreed to investigate why the workers at the plant are getting sick."

Mike was going to object to the word sick, but one look at Ernesto made him pause. Instead he said, "Why not just ask EnerTex?"

"I have," Sandra said. "Repeatedly. But they won't respond."

"I called EnerTex a number of times myself," Reb said. "I emailed and faxed them too. It wasn't until yesterday that they finally got back to me. They left a message at the station saying that if we're willing to drive to Houston, someone from the public relations department would talk to us."

"Are you going to go to Houston?" Sandra asked.

"That's the plan, but I don't expect to get much out of them."

"There's a woman with an energy watchdog group in the city who has also agreed to meet with us," Alice added. "She might know something useful."

Mike glanced over at Ernesto. "You okay with this?" he asked.

Ernesto nodded.

"I appreciate you coming today," Reb said, "and I don't want to keep you here any longer than is necessary. Let's get started."

He placed a black bag on the table, unzipped it, and began pulling out pieces of recording equipment and assembling them. It made Mike nervous. He wasn't sure the interview was such a good idea.

"Look," he said, "I'd like to help and all, but I don't want to lose my job."

"There are laws to protect whistle blowers," Alice said.

Rather than reassuring him, the "whistle blower" label set off alarms inside Mike's head and he stiffened.

"We signed a contract, you know," he said, "all of us did who work at the plant. They made us sign it when they hired us. It says we can't talk about our work to anyone. It says we can be prosecuted and thrown in jail if we do."

"They can't do that," Alice said.

"They can and will." Mike said looking her squarely in the eye. He wanted her to understand that he knew what he was talking about. "It's national security. No more power, no more country. Think about it. What would happen if a terrorist figured out how to sneak into the plant and blow it up? That's why we can't talk about our work. National security."

"I can respect that," Reb said, wanting to calm Mike's fears. "We'll do this off the record. But you do need to tell me as much as possible about how things work out there at the plant if we're to be of any help. It's your call."

His appeal was directed to Sandra, Ernesto, and Hazel as well and he looked at each of them in turn, waiting for a reply. The room felt warm and stuffy. Sandra stepped over and overrode the settings of the climate controls. In a few seconds a current of cool air began flowing into the room from vents in the ceiling.

"What do you mean by 'off the record?'" Mike asked.

"I'll record the interview for my use only," Reb said. "It's more accurate than taking notes. But I won't broadcast any part of the recording without your permission. I give you my word on it. A journalist's first responsibility is to protect his sources."

"You mean you won't put it on the radio unless I say it's okay?"

"Exactly."

"And if they put you in jail, you still won't tell them that we talked?" Mike had seen news stories on television about the government throwing reporters in jail for refusing to reveal their sources.

"As I said, you have my word on it."

Mike shifted his weight back onto his right leg and rested his hands on his hips as he considered the situation. Media people were scum bags—well, maybe not Tom Brokaw, but most of the others. He hated the way they stuck microphones in some poor woman's face just after she'd lost her husband or child in an accident and say, "And how does this tragedy make you feel, Mrs. Jones?"

He wanted to open the blinds and let the light in; the cloak and dagger stuff was making him crazy.

"You know your word doesn't mean much to me," he said.

"Sandra trusts them, Mike," Hazel said. "I think we should too."

He wished he was at home watching the game on TV instead of being forced to make a decision that could wreck his life. Did Hazel realize what was at stake? He would be the one going to jail, not her. And Ernesto.

"What do you say, Ernesto?"

"I'm willing to trust these people."

Mike looked at Hazel, read the determination in her eyes. Ah, what the hell, he said to himself. If I don't cooperate, I'll never hear the end of it from Hazel. And there'll be no sweet thing if Hazel gets upset, not for a long time.

"Okay, I'll answer your questions but don't let the tape get out of your hands. Where do you want me?"

Reb indicated a chair and Mike sat down.

"What do you want to know?" Mike asked after making himself comfortable. Reb slid the microphone stand across the table in front of him and turned on the recorder.

"Tell me about the power plant called Ranger 1" Reb said."

"I've heard they're going to name all the plants that way. Ranger 2, Ranger 3, like that."

"How does the plant function? What source of energy does it use to generate electricity?" Reb asked.

"That's the big secret. Nobody knows."

"You're saying you don't know how it works?" Alice said.

Mike didn't answer but looked at Reb as if to say, "Who's conducting this interview anyhow?"

"I've been to the EnerTex web site," Reb said, "and there's not a word about the energy source or how the electricity is generated."

"Like I said," Mike smiled. "Nobody knows—no one I work with, that's for sure."

"What Mike says is true," Ernesto said.

"But somebody must know," Again it was Alice and this time Mike turned to her.

"They do in Houston. I mean, they would have to, right?"

Reb paused while he considered his next question but Mike jumped in ahead of him. "You want me to describe the plant, physically I mean?"

Reb nodded. Sometimes it was best to shut up and let the other person do the talking.

"The reactor containment building is square and about half the size of a football field, about a hundred and fifty feet on each side. Inside the walls, the ceiling, even the floor are made out of some kind of titanium alloy."

"How do you know it's titanium?" Reb asked.

"One of the engineers told me. You can tell it's not steel or aluminum."

"Isn't titanium alloy expensive?"

"Fucking A."

There was an uncomfortable pause as Mike stared at the microphone and made a mental note to watch his language. Hazel looked disgusted with him.

"As I was saying, the inside of the building, the walls, ceiling, and floor are covered with thousands of transistors; each about the size of a postage stamp. The transistors are spaced six inches apart. It's like being inside one huge circuit board."

"What do the transistors do?" Reb asked.

"They generate some kind of force field. If you put your hand up close to one of the walls, it pushes back. It's really strange. The reactor is in the middle of the containment building."

"Why do you call it a reactor?" Reb asked. "It's not a nuclear plant, is it?"

"No, it's not nuclear but everybody calls it a reactor—the supervisors, the technicians, everybody."

"Go on."

"The reactor is a cube about the size of a, I don't know, a shipping container only it's square, like the containment building."

"How many feet on a side?" Reb asked.

"Forty feet give or take, I never measure it, and the surface is so smooth and black that it reflects the lights that run along the top of the containment building. It's beautiful really, but the engineer couldn't tell me what it's made of."

"Why couldn't he tell you?" Reb asked.

"He said he didn't know. My guess is it's a weird kind of metal, or maybe stone, like marble."

To Reb the whole setup sounded like something out of a Terry Gilliam movie. "What else can you tell us?" he said.

"A single thirty-six-inch pipe goes in one side of the reactor, and there are two eighteen-inch pipes coming out the other side."

"What's in the pipes?"

"Water."

"Where does the water come from? A well?"

"The water doesn't come from anywhere; it's a closed system."

"I don't understand."

"Half the water gets superheated inside the reactor. Then it goes to another building in one of the eighteen-inch pipes, where it turns a steam turbine that makes the electricity."

"It still sounds like a nuclear power plant to me," Reb said.

"I've already told you, it's not nuclear." Reb might be trustworthy, Mike thought, but he wondered how bright he was.

"Are there cooling towers?" Reb asked. He was thinking of the massive concrete structures whose hour-glass shapes had been burned forever into his consciousness after the accident at Three-Mile Island.

"No, there are no cooling towers," Mike said.

"Then how do they cool the superheated water?"

"That's what the other eighteen-inch pipe does. It's full of supercooled water. The water cools the turbine so there's no net increase in temperature."

"So the hot and cold water cancel each other out?"

Mike nodded.

"And then the water is sent back into the reactor again?"

"Through the thirty-six inch pipe. It's a closed system, like I said."

Reb was doing his best to imagine the process but he couldn't understand how a reactor, whatever kind it was, could superheat and supercool water at the same time.

"Do you ever go inside the containment building?" Alice asked.

"All the time. It's part of my job. You can't walk on the floor because of the transistors, so they built a series of suspended catwalks."

"Do you wear any kind of protective clothing?" she asked.

"No, but you can't have any metal on you. One of the first things the company did before I went to work was to pay a dentist to take out all my old mercury fillings and replace them with acrylic. The only trouble is, I miss the radio reception." Mike grinned boyishly at his joke until he caught Hazel's stony look.

"Do you test for radiation?" Reb asked.

"You mean like use a Geiger counter? No."

"So what kind of fuel does the reactor use?"

"Company secret. You tell me."

"The government must know," Alice said. "Power companies are regulated. Do inspectors ever show up at the plant?"

"None that I've ever seen." Mike turned to Ernesto. "You ever see any inspectors?" he asked.

Ernesto shook his head.

"They leave us pretty much alone out there," Mike said.

Just then there was a knock on the back door and Mike nearly jumped out of his skin. It surprised him just how keyed up he was. As Sandra went to see who it was, an atmosphere of suspense filled the room. No one spoke.

Sandra returned in a moment, accompanied by a woman carrying a large envelope. "This is Laura Andrews," she said introducing the doctor to Reb and Alice.

"I'm sorry I'm late," Laura said. "I'm on call this weekend and a little boy fell off an outdoor play set and broke his wrist."

She sat down and Sandra said, "Laura's a doctor. She examined Mike and Ernesto and some of the other men who work at the plant. She ran tests to find out what might be wrong with them."

"What did you find out, Doctor?" Reb asked.

"Nothing definitive I'm sorry to say. I brought copies of the results with me. I can let you have them if no one objects."

Reb looked at Mike and Ernesto who both shrugged their agreement.

"That would be great," Reb said and the doctor handed him the folder which he laid on the table next to the recorder.

"When I'm finish interviewing Mike and Ernesto," Reb said, "I'd like to go over the medical reports with you."

"From what I understand," Alice said turning her attention to Mike again, "only men work at the power plant, is that right?"

Mike looked at her not knowing what to say.

"This is the twenty-first century," she continued, "there must have been some female applicants for the plant jobs."

Mike hated this sort of gender stuff and didn't know what to say.

"I've been asking myself that same question," Sandra stepped in. "I called the EnerTex employment office and all they told me was that it was company policy."

"What policy?" Reb asked.

"Only men area are allowed to work at the power plant."

"Wal-Mart tried that routine and got their asses sued," Hazel put in. She had never thought about why women didn't work at the plant.

"They said they employ women at their headquarters in Houston," Sandra said, "but not at Ranger 1."

"What reason did they give?" Hazel asked.

"They didn't give a reason," Sandra said.

"But there are laws," Hazel's blood was heating up and her face was beginning to redden. "It's not right."

Reb decided to calm things down. The more he learned about the power plant, the less sense he could make of it.

"Tell me what it's like working at the plant, Mike," he said.

Mike shrugged. "It's a job. There are parts you like and parts you don't." He looked at Hazel and could tell by the distracted way she was tapping her right foot that she was still upset.

"I'm on the maintenance crew, but the way they've got the place designed there's not much to do—replace a light fixture, mop the floor, run tests on the electrical circuits. They mostly want us there in case something goes wrong. There are red emergency phones everywhere that are connected to the control operators in Houston. But the part I like best is sitting inside the containment building during my lunch break watching the reactor. There's something about it, I don't know, it's kinda. . . fascinating."

"How is it fascinating?" Alice said.

"Well, the water makes this constant whooshing sound as it flows through the pipes. It's restful and you can imagine the turbine turning and the electricity singing in the transmission lines, going to where some kid is getting lemonade out of the refrigerator, or maybe a farmer's setting up his milking machine. It makes you feel good to be part of it all."

Amazement replaced anger as Hazel stared at her husband. She had never heard him speak poetically before and she found the phrase "singing in the lines" particularly fetching.

"Have you noticed anything unusual while working at the plant?" Reb asked.

"Like what?"

"Tell him how they shut the plant down when the big wigs come to visit," Hazel said. Mike obliged and talked at length about how the reactor was taken off-line whenever the management team from Houston showed up.

"Look, we're not fancy people," Hazel said when he was done, "and we're not important people. But we're the kind of people who do the work that keeps this country going. And I think it stinks when some big-ass corporation like EnerTex comes along and takes advantage of ordinary folks like us just to so they can make a quick buck. Their first responsibility should be to the health and welfare of their employees."

"But what are we dealing with here?" Alice asked. "If people are getting sick, then what's causing it?"

"Asbestos or PCBs or some crap like that," Hazel said looking expectantly over at Dr. Andrews for confirmation.

The doctor shrugged. "We haven't been able to identify the toxin, if that's what it is."

"Can't or won't?" Hazel said.

Sandra was surprised by her friend's hostile manner and she felt obliged to set her straight. "Laura isn't protecting EnerTex, Hazel. She's donating her time and expertise; it's not her fault she can't tell us what's wrong."

"I'm sorry," Hazel said looking sheepish. "My daddy used to say I should mix shoe polish in with my toothpaste. That way I could shine my shoes while I'm putting my foot in my mouth."

Mike burst out laughing and everyone joined in. Reb suddenly realized he genuinely liked these people; he only wished he could help them.

"What about EMF syndrome?" he said turning to Dr. Andrews. "Could that be causing the problems?"

"What the heck is EMF?" Hazel asked.

"Electromagnetic Field Syndrome," Laura said. "It's a condition that some people believe is caused by the magnetic fields that emanate from the high voltage lines that pass near people's homes."

"A woman whose hair I do is a real estate agent in Lubbock," Hazel said. "She says it's nearly impossible to sell a house that has one of them big power lines running overhead because people think it'll make them sick."

"How does it make them sick?" Mike asked.

Laura looked doubtful. "Some researchers claim low-level EMFs from power lines can cause childhood leukemia, but the evidence remains equivocal and contradictory. In fact, the federal government investigated EMFs back in the early 90s but they found no evidence of negative health effects associated with power lines."

"So it's not true?" Mike said.

"And when did you start trusting the government?" Hazel snapped.

Mike shrugged and decided to stay out of the conversation. He had already told them all he knew about the power plant.

"There's a condition called Electromagnetic Hypersensitivity or EHS," Laura continued. "It's caused by exposure to household appliances, cell phones, and television sets, pretty much anything that generates an electromagnetic field. Some people claim they're so severely afflicted by EHS that they have to quit their jobs and change their lifestyle entirely."

"What can people do to protect themselves from electromagnetic fields?" Sandra asked.

"I've heard some people sleep under aluminum blankets," Laura said.

That was it, Mike had a stomach full of this nonsense. Aluminum blankets. No one was going to make him sleep under an aluminum blanket. He wanted to go home and he looked over at Hazel, but she was ignoring him.

"We don't know what kind of electromagnetic field the power plant puts out," Hazel said, "but Mike says you can feel it with your hand. That's got to be pretty strong."

"What kind of ailments do people get with EHS?" Alice asked.

"Mostly nervous disorders," Laura said, "Fatigue, stress, trouble sleeping. Others complain about aching muscles, burning eyes, and digestive disorders."

Hazel shot a quick glance over at Sandra before asking the next question.

"Do electromagnetic fields make people forgetful, or have sexual kinds of problems?"

"Not that I've heard," Laura said, "but this is an area where there's a lot of controversy. I could make a few phone calls and see what I can find out."

"That would be helpful," Reb said.

Hazel and Sandra nodded in agreement.

Mike thought there'd be no living with Hazel now.

A light flashed inside Alice's head. "I know why," she said abruptly. Everyone looked at her. "It's because they don't want to be responsible for causing birth defects."

"Who doesn't?" Reb said.

"EnerTex. That's why they won't let women work at the power plant. Either it's all those electromagnetic fields, or despite what they say, they've got radioactive materials out there. If a woman got pregnant, it could effect the fetus, and they certainly don't want a lawsuit like that on their hands."

Reb reached down and turned off the recorder. So many ideas were flying around he felt thick-headed. He stood up. "Let's take a break for five minutes, and then I'll interview you, Ernesto, if your ready," he said.

Mike was relieved his part was over. "Can we go home now?" he whispered to Hazel. She looked dissatisfied but nodded her head in agreement.

"It was nice meeting you," she said to Reb and Alice as Mike stepped over to say goodbye to Ernesto. "We appreciate all your effort," she said.

"I only hope we can help," Reb said.

As Mike walked down the hallway he held a troubling picture of his friend in his mind. A Texas way of describing Ernesto was to say "he was rode hard and put away wet." Maybe Hazel wasn't crazy and something really was wrong out at the plant. EnerTex. What were those guys up to? Suddenly he wanted answers too.

16

REB AND ALICE walked out of the Family Resource Center into the dusty light of a warm Texas evening. Reb had the two mini-disks containing the interviews in his shirt pocket and knew he had to keep them safe for Mike and Ernesto's sakes. He wondered about the legality of the confidentiality contracts they had signed. This was new ground for him, and for Alice too he suspected. Maybe they should talk to a lawyer.

As they approached the rental car, Reb saw a metallic gray Porsche 911 with its signature rear-flared wheel wells parked about three-quarters of the way up the block on the far side of the street. It was a hot little number that struck him as oddly out of place given the neighborhood. The side windows were tinted but he could see through the front windshield that someone was in the car. He suddenly got the creeps; they were being watched. They opened the doors of the Cavalier and were nearly bowled over by the rush of energized molecules from the commercial-grade car deodorizer that had baked too long in the Texas heat.

"Let it air out for a minute or two," Alice said turning her head and stepping back from the car.

"Not a good idea," Reb said as he forced himself into the car.

"What's wrong?" she said following his lead.

He started the engine, opened his window, and turned the air conditioning to full power. He then took the minidisks out of his pocket and began looking around.

"What are you doing?" Alice asked.

"I want to stash these someplace safe."

"I can put them in my purse."

"No, I don't want them on us."

"Why not?"

"I don't want someone to take them if we get mugged."

"What makes you think we might get *mugged*?" Alice almost laughed, the idea so surprised her.

Reb opened the glove compartment, considered a moment, and then closed it. "These people are trusting us with their lives, Alice," he said, "and I just think we should take some precautions."

"But I still don't see what's that's got to do with us getting mugged."

"I think there's a chance we're being followed," he said. "EnerTex might have hired someone."

He closed the window. The smell had dissipated somewhat, and they began driving slowly down the street. Reb checked the rear view mirror repeatedly to see if the Porsche followed them, but it stayed where it was. Turning left at the first intersection, they drove two more blocks and turned left again. They were now in a district of low warehouses, and after driving several more blocks, he pulled over. They sat for a several minutes not talking, the engine idling, the AC blowing frosted air into their faces. Reb turned his head. There were no cars on the street in either direction. He opened his door and stepped out.

"Where are you going?" Alice asked. They hadn't checked into the hotel yet and she was exhausted and wanted to take a shower.

"Nowhere."

He squatted down so he could peer under the driver's seat. His plan was to wedge the minidisks up underneath somehow. Instead he found a thick envelope attached to the bottom of the seat with duct tape. He tried to tell himself that Avis had put it there, that it probably contained copies of repair records, and yet an unsettling sensation stole over him. It was as if the envelope possessed telepathic powers and was saying, "I don't belong here, can't you see that?"

He waited several seconds before tearing the envelope loose and hopping back in the car, closing the door after him.

"What's that?" Alice said as Reb held up what looked like a crude paper doll with two dangling arms made of wide strips of tape.

"We're about to find out," he said.

He ripped the end off the envelope and pulled out a plastic baggie filled with marijuana. He shot a glance at Alice and then lifted the bag in the palm of his hand to judge the weight; somewhere between two and three ounces, he guessed. He opened the baggie and held it up to his nose; the sweet aroma of cannabis was unmistakable. Again he looked at Alice as adrenaline shot through his system, accelerated his heart rate, and threw open the flood gates of paranoia.

"It's a set-up," he said. "Someone's out to get us busted. Feel under your seat, Alice."

Alice reached her hand down. "What am I looking for?"

"More pot."

After several seconds she shook her head.

"We've got to get rid of this," Reb said. He scanned the area and noticed a dumpster nearby. He got out and hurried over to it, checking all the while that no one was around. He lifted the heavy lid, tossed the marijuana inside, and lowered it again slowly to prevent it from clanging. In a moment they were driving away.

Reb asked Alice to get out the city map Avis had given them. "I want the scenic route to the hotel, you know, with lots of unnecessary turns and some doubling back."

She gave directions while he kept his eyes glued to the rear view mirror. He saw nothing of the gray Porsche or any indication they were being shadowed.

As a child, and even later as an adult, Alice couldn't stand the kind of movies where someone would say, "Oh, don't worry, it's probably nothing," when it obviously *was* something, and something terrible too. Sometimes she got so anxious and frustrated that she'd walk out of the movie theater, or turn off the video player if she was at home, unable to watch what was about to happen next. Now, in real life, she wasn't going to be the one to say, "Oh, don't worry, dear, it's probably nothing." She hoped it was nothing. She hoped there was a plausible explanation for why a bag of marijuana was under the seat of the car. It probably belonged to the previous renter who had simply forgot to take it along when he turned the car in. She had left things in rental cars before, an umbrella, a sweater, even a digital camera that she never got back. But she wasn't about to offer Reb this or any other explanation. From what she knew about Texas, it was the worst kind of place to get busted for drugs. She imagined themselves standing before a "good ol' boy" judge in the courthouse in Lubbock. Two aging California hippies. That would go down well.

"And what are you two doing in Texas? the judge would ask and they'd reply, "Oh, just trying to get the dirt on a highly respected corporate citizen of your state who helps fund your schools and little league teams." Alice knew the phrase "Don't mess with Texas" wasn't just a cute slogan dreamt up by the state department of tourism. It was the psychic grunt of a xenophobic mentality fired by too much heat and bad history. She suddenly remembered how much she disliked Texas.

17

REB WAS SCHEDULED to host the evening news but he had overslept. Anxiety pressed in on him. A round wind-up clock, the kind with a pair of bells on top, looked over at him accusingly from the top of the dresser as he hurried to pull on his clothes. He was in the bedroom of a large house very much like the one his aunt used to own in San Francisco. It took forever to get his shirt on, he kept fumbling with the buttons. The telephone on the table next to the bed started to ring. Once, twice, three times. He didn't have time to answer it. Dead air. KVMR would be broadcasting dead air because he wasn't there. The FCC would yank their license. It would be his fault. The phone stopped ringing. He couldn't find his shoes. He looked under the bed, in the closet. The door bell chimed. It sounded far away. More painful frustration. Who was it now? He went to the top of the stairs and looked down at the front door. The stairs were narrow and steep and they began to telescope. He felt dizzy and decided not to go down and answer the door; he had to find his shoes and get to the radio station. But then the door swung open and a man, dressed all in black, his features hidden under the shadow of a wide brimmed hat, stood motionless in the doorway. A paralyzing fear gripped Reb. He knew with cold certainty that the figure in the doorway was Death. He also sensed in some other part of his mind that he was dreaming. He tried to call out but his teeth felt as if they were welded shut. He struggled to break free of the dream. Then he heard the strained yelping of a wounded animal and recognized the sound as his own voice. He forced his eyes open as the dream loosened its grip. He was in the hotel room in Lubbock and Alice was gently shaking him.

"Wake up. You're having a nightmare. It's okay."

Her voice, kind and reassuring, helped drive the phantoms back into the inner recesses of his mind. He was badly shaken; his pajamas were soaked with sweat. His teeth were sore; he had been grinding them.

"Are you all right?" she asked as she turned on the light.

He seldom had nightmares even though he was an inveterate dreamer. Every night his mind played host to a parade of strange visitations and disjointed occurrences so that he often awoke feeling exhausted, as if unable to pass beyond the dream state into that deeper realm of true, restorative sleep. Kate once suggested he visit a sleep clinic. There might be a drug he could take, she told him; there were special machines for breathing. But dreaming was such an integral part of his personality and experience of life that he rejected the idea. As a child he walked in his sleep almost every night, which drove his poor parents crazy. His father would get up to go to the bathroom and discover his son wandering from room to room in a trance. Sometimes his mother would awaken to find him standing next to her bed, looking down at her. She would ask what he wanted and he would just stand there, mute. Then she'd realize he was asleep and she would gently guide him back to his own bed, only to be awakened three hours later, the ritual repeated. It wasn't until Reb's teenage years that the sleep walking mercifully stopped. But not the dreaming.

"What time is it?" he asked Alice.

"6:40."

"Can you go back to sleep?"

"What were you dreaming about?"

He told her about the dream. She had a dream interpretation book at home and she wished she had brought it with her. Clearly, the appearance of Death in Reb's dream was a warning. But a warning of what?

They managed another hour of light sleep before getting up and going down to the restaurant for breakfast. Afterwards they planned to drive south to Birdstar and nose around a little, talk to the townspeople, and ask some questions. Reb had toyed with the idea of driving out to the plant and applying for a job. At least that way he could size up the place. But as they were leaving the Family Resource Center, Ernesto had told him that all the interviewing and hiring was done off-site at the Sundowner Motel out by the interstate.

"How often do they accept applications?" Reb asked.

"Every four months."

"Why in Birdstar? Why not at the plant?"

"It's a high security, no-go zone," Ernesto said. "Here, look at this." He pushed up his shirt sleeve and Reb expected to see a tattoo. Instead he saw an area about the size of a dime up near the shoulder where the skin was slightly raised and translucent.

"It's an identity implant," Ernesto said. "A computer chip tells EnerTex the location of every employee at the plant every second of the day."

"Does Mike have one?" Reb asked.

"Everyone who works there does; it's how EnerTex keeps track of your time. We don't punch a time clock like in the old days."

"Does it hurt having that thing put under your skin?" Alice asked.

"No," he shrugged indifferently, "they numb up the area before implanting it. You forget it's there after awhile."

Reb wondered if the chip could track people anywhere they went, not just around the plant. If so, then they would have a record of Ernesto and Mike's visit to Sandra's office in Lubbock. Would they suspect them of talking to the press? Reb decided to keep this concern to himself; there was enough anxiety to go around as it was.

What Ernesto's demonstration did accomplish, however, was to knock down his hopes of getting inside the plant. That left a walkabout in Birdstar as their only option. He felt like such an amateur. They had no real plan; they was just making it up as they went along, hoping to get lucky. What they needed was a "deep throat," someone who could point them in the right direction. Maybe if worked for the *Washington Post* it would be different. But working for KVMR? Who was he kidding?

On the way out of Lubbock, they stopped at the post office and Reb dropped the minidisks with the interviews into a priority envelope that he insured and mailed back to himself at KVMR. Just to be safe, he told Alice.

The journey to Birdstar took fifty minutes. The town was the seat of Dalton County, which had been hit hard by the dust storms of the 1930s. Conditions got so bad, in fact, that many of the county's residents sold out and headed west on Route 66 to California where they acquired the moniker "dust bowl immigrants." Those who remained hunkered down and did the best they could. Some entrepreneuring souls prospected for oil and gas but with so little success that seventy years later, the county was still just barely holding its own.

Reb and Alice took the Waller Street exit off the interstate and drove into Birdstar. In the center of town was the courthouse square replete with restful, squirrel-friendly benches and agreeable walkways watched over by a brotherhood of venerable oaks. The only flaw in this Norman Rockwellian tableau was the courthouse itself, which squatted like a dumb brute in the center of the square. Constructed in 1880 out of native Texas granite and red sandstone, the building was crowned with an ill-proportioned dome that sometime during the last fifty years had been painted an unbecoming flat black. It was such a thoroughly unpleasant looking structure that Reb half expected to see the words "Abandon All Hope Ye Who Enter Here" inscribed above the entrance.

On the southeastern corner of the square, next to a pharmacy, was Lucy's Bluebonnet Cafe. Reb parked in front of the restaurant and they went inside. It was as if they had stepped back in time. Behind the counter, which ran the length of the dining room, were machines for making coffee and milk shakes and a large chalkboard touting the daily specials. Framed photographs of the town during its horse-and-buggy days adorned the other walls with several faded photographs showing the courthouse under construction.

It was eleven-ten in the morning, and except for an elderly man at the counter smoking a cigarette, the place was empty. Reb and Alice took a table by the front window that was covered with a red-checkered vinyl tablecloth. A middle-aged woman with a mound of black hair piled up on top of her head came over with their menus.

"Y'all both want coffee?" She looked and sounded tired.

They nodded and Reb said, "You've got a nice town here."

"We think so. Just passing through?"

"Sort of," Alice said.

"Where're you from?"

"California," Reb said.

"Always wanted to visit California," the woman said wistfully looking out the window as if California were just down the street and around the corner. "My Uncle Odell settled out there after the Korean War. He did his basic training at Fort Ord. Said he couldn't live no other place else on earth."

"Does your town have a newspaper?" Reb asked.

"Sure does. It's called *The Bird Call*. Comes out twice a week. Their offices are over yonder on the other side of the square." She walked over to the counter, picked up a newspaper, and brought it back. She left to get their coffee and Reb began looking through the newspaper.

Unlike the restaurant, the news was sadly up-to-date. The lead story concerned the ground-breaking ceremony for the new county jail. Below it was an article about a couple who got busted with a meth lab in their mobile home. Along with the paraphernalia and manufacturing gear and several handguns, the police found a sixteen-month-old crawling around on the floor amongst all the toxic chemicals and dirty needles. An article on page two talked about reductions in block grants from the state and federal governments and what that would do to county services. Except for a couple of wedding announcements, the paper was slim on happy news.

"Who's the editor?" Alice asked.

Reb looked on the back of the front page. "Marvin Spooner, publisher and editor."

"Great name," Alice smiled. "He could be a good contact."

The waitress came back with two heavy white ceramic cups. After setting them on the table, she deftly produced an order pad from her apron pocket with one hand and a pencil from her hair with the other. "So what will y'all have?" she said.

"I'll take the tuna fish sandwich on wheat," Reb said.

"With fries?"

"Sure."

"And you, miss?"

"I'll have the same, but can I have fruit instead of fries?"

"We have apple sauce."

"Do you have any fresh fruit?"

"Can't keep it."

"Why not?"

"Spoils too fast. Must be the weather around here. Bananas are the worst. They turn black before the day is out."

"Has it always been like that?" Alice said.

"No, just the last year or two. Maybe it's got to do with that climate change thing everybody's talking about."

"Global warming," Reb said. Corporate strategists and the politicians they bankrolled adopted the word "climate change" after testing it out on focus groups. It sounded less threatening than "global warming," and implied that somehow humans weren't to blame. The same went for replacing "estate tax" with "death tax." Same tax, but different reaction from the electorate.

The waitress ignored the correction.

"Canned fruit does okay," she said to Alice. "I might could find some fruit cocktail in the back. You want me to look?"

"No, apple sauce will be fine. Thank you."

As the waitress walked away, Reb looked out the window and eyed the square. No gray Porsche; he turned back to Alice.

"What do you think of Ernesto and Mike?" he asked.

"In what way?" Alice said.

"Do you think they're telling us the truth? They could be lying."

"Is that what you think?" The possibility had never crossed her mind.

"We don't know much about them, do we?" Reb said. "Maybe it's all part of an elaborate scheme to sue EnerTex. They could be using us."

"How?"

"To build up public sympathy in case they wind up taking EnerTex to court. You know, a heartless corporation poisoning its own workers. It's not out of the question."

"Ernesto and Mike sounded pretty believable to me."

Reb gazed out the window again and tried to remember what his father had taught him about investigative work. It was a subject Earl Morgan loved to talk about.

He turned back to Alice. "Did you know that the average human being loses two hundred hairs a day, and that a single hair follicle can reveal a suspect's race, gender, and hair coloring? It can also reveal drug use and vitamin deficiencies."

"Can't say I did."

"It's true. And you can lift a fingerprint from almost any surface, even the human body, using Super Glue."

"Why are we talking about Super Glue?" Alice asked.

"I told you my father was an insurance investigator. He used to tell me this stuff. He was also big on figuring out if someone was lying or not, like if some guy claimed an electrical short was responsible for burning down his business when the truth was he'd hired "Moe the Match" to do the job for him. My dad said a liar will give himself away in all kinds of subtle ways."

"Such as?" Alice said.

"A classic give-away is when someone touches his nose."

"You mean like Pinocchio?" Alice said.

"Don't laugh. My dad took me with him to traffic court once—I must have been around eleven—and we sat in the back of the courtroom and watched the people who'd been given tickets go before the judge to give their side of the story. And every time somebody would say something that was pretty hard to believe, he'd touch his nose."

"That's wild."

"It's called 'deception leakage.' Have you ever heard the old saying, 'he's a stinking liar?'"

Alice nodded.

"Well, when someone is under pressure and starts lying, his body secretes a unique odor. My dad was so good he could sometimes smell it."

"I heard someplace that you can tell if people are telling the truth or lying by how they move their eyes," Alice said.

"That's correct," Reb said. "Most people look up and to the left when retrieving a memory, and they look up and to the right when making something up. But you can't always be sure; some people do it in reverse."

"Then it doesn't help much."

"No it can help, but first you have to establish which way a person moves his eyes. You do it by asking a couple of innocent questions."

"Like what?"

"Well. . . what was the color of your first car?"

Alice waited.

"Go ahead," Reb said, "what color was it?"

"My first car? Green. It was a Volkswagen."

"And what do you think of the United Nations?"

"A flawed but necessary organization."

"I agree but when I asked you for a *fact*, the color of your car, you looked up to the left. Then when I asked you to formulate an *opinion*, you looked up to the right. So now that I know how you use your eyes, I can ask the questions I really want answered."

Alice experienced a sudden distaste for what Reb was doing. With only two questions he had managed to get inside her head. It was fascinating but it also bothered her. Reb sensed her discomfort.

"I know these things because of my dad but I hardly ever use them—even when I should, like yesterday," he said.

"So you didn't check Mike and Ernesto out to see if they were lying?" Alice said while making a conscious effort not to move her eyes in any direction.

"I should have, but I never think of it until it's too late."

The waitress arrived with their sandwiches and they began to eat. After a few minutes Reb said, "My dad was an investigator. He used his eyes to figure people out. It's what he loved to do. I became a photographer instead because I fell in love with light, how it's always changing and how it can make things so beautiful, like now, the way it's coming through the window and shining on your face. I would miss that more than you can imagine."

Alice realized he was talking about going blind and she felt a sense of powerlessness well up within her.

"So what about Ernesto and Mike?" she said wanting to get his mind off the glaucoma, "Are they lying or telling the truth?"

"I think they're telling the truth. Either that or they're two of the best liars I've ever met."

They finished their sandwiches in silence and the waitress returned to their table.

"Either of you fancy dessert?" she said gathering up the plates. "We have some fresh dried apricot pie?"

Reb was a great pie lover, and even though he'd never eaten one made from dried apricots—he would ignore the apparent oxymoron, fresh dried—he would give it a try.

"How is it?" Alice asked after his third bite.

"Not half bad," he said trying to smile and chew at the same time. "Tastes like. . . Texas. Want some?"

She was about to say yes but a closer look at the dark orange gelatinous filling dissuaded her.

Their meal finished, Reb and Alice paid the check and went in search of Marvin Spooner. The sun was doing its best to melt the asphalt as they hurried across the street and entered the square and the welcoming shade of its gracious trees. They passed two women sitting on a bench silently smoking cigarettes. Farther away a man drove a mowing machine between the trees and Reb paused to take in the scent of the fresh-cut grass, a smell that always conjured up pleasant childhood memories. This time, however, he was surprised when it failed to do so. His mood in fact moved in the opposite direction. He felt *too* grown up, like a weary traveler who, having crossed the Great Divide of life, finds the ground falling away steadily beneath his feet. This image, coming as it did so abruptly and unexpectedly, cast him against his will into a peculiar kind of melancholy.

"What's wrong?" Alice asked him.

"I don't know," he said. "It's just a feeling."

Luminous spears of sunlight penetrated the canopy of leaves overhead and he became aware of another emotion active within him, a sensation just below the naming of his conscious mind, intimating that something about the town was *wrong* despite its quaint charm. He thought he might be going a little crazy; it happened now and again but never in this way. Maybe it had to do with his early morning dream.

Alice felt her own spirits falling and suspected that Reb's mood was infecting her own. It was unbearably hot and yet a sudden chill raced through her body and she reached over and took hold of his arm. The women on the bench were watching them suspiciously so they resumed walking. They skirted the courthouse entrance and did not stop again until they reemerged into full sunlight on the far side of the square. They waited for a cement truck belching diesel exhaust to rumble past and then crossed the street.

The offices of the *Bird Call*, like the restaurant, hearkened back to an earlier time. A reception room with a twelve-foot ceiling and a long counter sheathed in oak wainscoting greeted visitors as they came in from the street. The air in the room was old and dusty and permeated with the scent of printer's ink.

Reb and Alice approached the counter where a young woman was busy sorting coupons. A stack of newspapers sat next to a computer keyboard and monitor where customers could compose their own classified ads.

"Excuse me," Reb said, "we're looking for Marvin Spooner."

"That's my dad," the girl said. "He's in the back."

She turned around and called though an open door down a hallway. "Daddy, there's some people here to see you."

In a moment, a man of medium height appeared. He was rather pear-shaped and wore a crown of rusty curls. Reb took him to be in his late fifties. He had intelligent eyes, an abundance of freckles, and an easy, cheerful manner.

"What can I do for you?" Marvin asked.

"My name is Reb Morgan, and this is my colleague, Alice Carpenter. We're radio journalists from California."

"Are you now?" The editor's features noticeably brightened. "I'm from Huntington Beach myself. My daughter Kaye"—he nodded toward the young woman—"was born there."

Kaye looked up from her coupon sorting and smiled.

The situation suddenly struck Reb as humorous. He had expected the quintessential rural Texan whose ancestors were a mix of hardy pioneers and cowboys. Instead he found a former southern Californian suburbanite and his daughter.

"I worked for the Orange County Register for twenty years," Marvin continued. "Ended up as managing editor. Then my arteries plugged up and I had to have an angioplasty. My doctor said the cause was excessive stress and air pollution; forced me to reevaluate my priorities, you might say. I'd always wanted to run a small town newspaper, so I shopped around and found this one up for sale. Pulled my savings out of the bank and bought it. Never looked back. Best decision I ever made."

"What do you like about it?" Alice asked. Marvin's jocundity was doing wonders for her mood.

"You know everybody. They come up to you in the bank and the supermarket. They tell you what they think of the column you wrote, even when they don't agree. You see, you're the one telling their story. You put in print the day they're born, win the little league championship, graduate from high school, and get married. You write their obituaries too. The whole package from cradle to grave. That makes you an important part of their lives. You're needed. Heck, in California, I was just a worker bee in a hive of millions. Here I get to do it all: cover news; shoot photo-graphs; sell advertising; and write the occasional column. Once a year the Rotary Club even feeds me lunch. I say pretty much the same thing every year, but who else are they going to get? So tell me, what can I do for you?"

"We're investigating the EnerTex power plant," Reb said. "There are allegations that the plant is injuring the workers."

"Did Sandra Valdez put you up to this?" Marvin asked as a gallon or two of good naturedness drained out of his manner.

"It's because of Ms. Valdez that we decided to investigate," Alice said. "Are you aware of her concerns?"

"I am." His tone was guarded.

"So you don't think there's anything to the story?" Reb asked.

"Don't get me wrong. Sandra's a fine woman and respected by everyone here in Birdstar, including me. It's just, well. . . let's take this into my office. The power plant is a touchy topic around here and I'd prefer to discuss it in private."

Just then, as if cued by an unseen director, an elderly woman came in from the street to purchase a newspaper.

Reb and Alice followed the editor down a hallway into small, cramped office, made even smaller by the presence of a massive roll top desk and a cardboard box for a laser printer on the floor.

"Would you mind helping me with this?" the editor asked Reb putting his hand on the box. "It needs to go out front."

Reb lifted one end while Marvin took the other; the box was cumbersome but not particularly heavy.

"Used to be I could carry a box like this by myself, no problem," Marvin said. "Guess I'm just getting old."

When they reached the front counter Marvin said, "Just set it down here." His face was flush with the effort. "The UPS driver will pick it up later. It has to go back to the company we bought it from."

"What's wrong with it?" Reb asked.

"It's the fourth printer I've ordered this year. Just can't seem to get one that works properly."

"Have you tried a different brand?"

"That's what's so frustrating. We've tried Xerox, HP, and Canon and none of them work."

"What's wrong with them?" Reb asked as they walked back to the editor's office.

"They print great and then all of a sudden the prints get fuzzy, or some of the dots drop out."

Reb had little experience with laser printers and no useful advice to offer. As they entered the office again, Marvin slapped his hand down on the roll-top desk and said, "Nothing broken here. Works as good as it ever did."

"Did it come with the paper?" Reb asked feeling certain it had; it fit the place so well.

"The man who started the *Birdcall* brought it out with him by train from Philadelphia in 1884. He wrote stories on it about bank robbers and cattle rustlers. At least, that's what I like to tell myself. Lends a dash of romance to the job, don't you think?"

The editor motioned his guests to two straight back chairs while he settled into an old oak desk chair that negotiated the worn wood floor on a set of metal rollers that cried out for oil.

"Do you mind if my daughter joins us? She's a journalism student at Pepperdine University. She lives with her mother in Malibu but took a semester off to get her feet wet and help her old dad out."

He yelled for Kaye to join them.

"If someone comes in for a paper, they'll just leave the money on the counter," he assured them. "Money's a bit tight around here these days but Birdstarians are an honest lot."

Reb thought the editor was troweling on the "ah shucks" Mayberry routine a mite too thick. If the local residents were so honest, then why the new jail?

Kaye came in but she remained standing because there were no more chairs. Reb offered her his but she declined.

"You said money is tight," Alice said, "but what about the power plant? Doesn't that help?"

"Not like it used to," Marvin said. "When they were building the plant there was all kinds of money around town. The motels were full up with construction workers and engineers and you could hardly get a table in any of the restaurants. They even built a new housing development just west of town for the technicians and managers to live in. But then all but a handful left and took their jobs and their paychecks with them."

"We were told the plant is run from Houston," Reb said. "Isn't that kind of strange?"

"Not really," Marvin said leaning back and scratching the back of his head. "I used to shop at the K-Mart in Huntington Beach and it was always too cold and once or twice I complained and they told me that the air conditioning wasn't controlled from inside the store but by a computer someplace in Utah, or Ohio, I can't remember. It's the way the world is going these days; no use fighting it."

"Do you have any ideas about what might be happening to the workers at the power plant?" Reb said.

"On or off the record?"

"You sound like a government official," Alice said.

"Reckon I do at that," Marvin said, "but everything I have in the world is tied up in this place. It may not look like much, but it's mine, and EnerTex is a power to be reckoned with in Dalton County, if you can forgive the pun. I just don't want the paper's name associated someone doing a hatchet job on EnerTex."

Alice stiffened. "Why do you think we'll do a *hatchet job*, as you put it?"

"I'm not saying you will, but I don't know anything about either of you, do I?"

"You know Sandra Valdez," Reb said.

"Yes, and like I said, she's a fine woman and an upstanding citizen of Birdstar."

"Did she come to you with her concerns about the plant?" Reb asked.

"Not at first."

"How do you mean?" Alice asked.

"She tried to interest some of the big city newspapers first, and when they ignored her, she contacted the paper in Lubbock."

"And they ignored her too?" Reb said.

"Yep, even though she works up there and is a known quantity."

"Then she came to us," Kaye Spooner said. "She had some medical reports, but they weren't conclusive. My dad asked me to look into it."

"And did you?" Alice said.

"I called the EnerTex office in Houston," Kaye continued, "and told them I wanted to do a feature about the power plant's two-year anniversary which is coming up soon. I asked if they would give me a tour of the facility."

"How did they respond?" Reb asked.

"A Mr. Vernachek met me at the plant. He was very pleasant but he wouldn't let me bring my camera inside for security reasons."

"Did you find anything suspicious?" Alice asked.

"No. . . not on the surface."

"What do you mean 'not on the surface?'" Alice said but Reb interrupted before the young woman could answer.

"Was the plant operating while you were there?" he asked. He was thinking about what Mike had told them.

"As far as I could tell it was," Kaye said.

"What about Mr. Vernachek?" Reb said, "What was he like?"

"Hard to say. We weren't there very long. He had me in and out in no time."

"Did that seem suspicious to you?" Alice asked.

"He said he had a meeting to get back to in Houston. He flew out on one of the company's jets to meet me."

"That's a lot to go through for a small town newspaper," Alice said.

"We may be small," Marvin said, "but we've got big plans." Reb turned to the editor to see if he was joking. "Let's just say

EnerTex pays very close attention to what goes on in Birdstar," Marvin said, his expression serious.

"Did you get to talk to any of the workers?" Alice kept her focus on Kaye Spooner.

"A couple, but I was so hurried I couldn't ask the questions I wanted to. It's when I got back home that I began to suspect that something wasn't right."

"Now don't start that again, Kaye," Marvin said and Reb could sense the tension between father and daughter.

"What did you suspect?" Alice asked.

"Well, I felt. . . I don't know, kind of yucky after being at the plant."

"I had her go to the doctor and he said there was absolutely nothing wrong with her," Marvin said.

"No he didn't, Daddy."

It was obvious Marvin would prefer to let the matter drop but his daughter would have her say.

"You see, I've been having health problems since I moved back here to Birdstar four months ago. Nothing major. Little things. I'm tired a lot and I get headaches and bad cramps. They come on suddenly and then go away. The doctor can't say for sure what's wrong with me. He thinks it might be an allergy, but I spent a year living here with my dad in 1996 and I was fine then."

"Why did you go back to California?" Alice said. It wasn't any of her business but she wanted to know. Kaye didn't seem to mind.

"I missed my mom, and the schools are a lot better there."

Despite his tendency toward boosterism, Reb noted that Marvin made no attempt to defend the public education system in his adopted state—former governors could spin that fiction if they wanted to.

"Can you describe how you felt after returning from the plant?" Reb asked.

"Exhausted, wrung out."

"Was it something at the plant that made you feel that way?" Alice asked.

She shook her head. "I can't say. It could've just been one of my spells. That's what they're like."

Reb was trying to put the pieces together in his mind when the elusive sensation that had been nagging him suddenly took form.

"The birds," he said, "where have all the birds gone?"

Alice looked at him uncomprehendingly.

"We don't know," the editor said, his features sagging.

"What are you talking about?" Alice said.

"Birdstar," Reb turned to her. "The town is called Birdstar but there aren't any birds. Didn't you notice? When we walked through the square. There weren't any birds singing. I just realized that's what was wrong."

"No one knows what's happened to 'em," Marvin said. "Experts from Texas A & M were here a half dozen times but they can't figure it out. Nor can the state Audubon Society."

"Have there always been birds around town?" Alice asked.

"Always. Finches, robins, orioles—mockingbirds too. This is the first year there haven't been any, not even in the countryside. It's got people worried."

"I'm not surprised," Reb said. "Have any other towns in Texas lost their song birds?"

"There've been declines in the number of birds in some places," Kaye said, "but nothing like what's going on here."

The desk bell on the front counter chimed. It was an old-fashioned sound.

"Go see who that is, Kaye," her father said and she left the office.

"What's going to happen to the insect population without birds to control it?" Reb said.

"The governor is scheduled to visit us next week," Marvin said, "Everyone is hoping its just a temporary sort of thing."

Kaye came back into the office. "It's Mr. Gallagher, Dad. He has the proofs for the new ads he wants to show you."

"Excuse me," Marvin said getting up from his chair. "This will only take a moment."

Reb thought they had taken up enough of the editor's time and was getting up to leave when Kaye handed him a CD in a black jewel case.

"Here are copies of the photographs I took when I was at the plant," she said.

"I thought you said Mr, ah,—"

"Vernachek,"

"Right, Vernachek. I thought he wouldn't let you bring your camera into the plant."

"I left the D50 in the car but I have one of those tiny new digital cameras. It's about the size of a credit card. I bought it on eBay and keep it in my purse."

Alice detected a mischievous glint in the young woman's eyes and felt a surge of affection for her.

"You can keep the CD if you want," Kaye said. "I have copies of the photos on my hard drive. Just don't mention it to my dad. He worries too much about me."

"Thank you," Alice said with a smile as she touched Kaye gently on the arm.

18

THEY SAW THE car as they came out of the newspaper office. A metallic gray Porsche 911. It was parked diagonally in front of a vacant store on the west side of the square. Was it the one they'd seen in Lubbock? Reb decided it had to be and he made a snap decision.

"Go back to the car," he said to Alice. "I have to take care of something."

"What's going on?"

"I need to find out who is following us, and why." He nodded in the direction of the Porsche.

Alice watched him march away and then headed back to the rental car. She was confused and apprehensive. What if Reb got into a fight? Got himself arrested? Again the fear of being dragged into a Texas courtroom returned like a tedious relative. She felt vulnerable—and was angry too. What right had Reb to bark orders at her? It was something Wayne used to do. Everything would be going along right as rain when suddenly he'd flair up and it was impossible to reason with him. It might be another driver cutting him off, or a player crowding him during a basketball game. Once at a party an attorney from his office started hitting on her and the way Wayne reacted was frightening. He acted as if he would kill the guy, and she understood at close quarters why this volatile and unpredictable aspect of the male psyche was responsible for more than its share of the world's miseries.

It was why she was attracted to Reb. He wasn't competitive; he was easy going. So why the Clint Eastwood routine all of a sudden?

She reached the car only to discover that Reb had the keys and she couldn't unlock the door. This made her even madder and she refused to watch what was happening, refused to admit that her anger was a ploy to suppress a deeper emotion. She cared very much for Reb and feared for his safety.

Reb, meanwhile, was running flat out on instinct and adrenaline. As he approached the Porsche he saw that the engine was running. He had already rejected the idea that the driver was a cop. The government didn't purchase sixty thousand dollar automobiles for its employees to tool around in. This was private sector cash.

Reb rapped twice on the tinted window with his knuckles. No response. He rapped again, and this time the electric window slid down with a barely discernible hum and a sturdily built man in his late twenties or early thirties wearing a salmon-colored Ralph Lauren polo shirt looked up at him through a pair of expensive sunglasses. The taunt muscles of the face betrayed no emotion whatsoever.

"Excuse me," Reb began his act with the *bon-ami* of the social director aboard a Norwegian cruise ship. "I was wondering if you live around here?"

Reb could sense the gears turning inside the man's head as he took several seconds to respond.

"Just passing through," he said, the voice a monotone.

"Where're you from then?" Reb kept the smile in place while noticing how the man's index finger kept tapping the button that operated the electric window.

"Dallas," he said.

Reb leaned down so his face came level with the stranger. His father called this the "knee-to-knee" method of interrogation. For white American middle class males, the ideal distance between interrogator and interrogatee is twenty-seven inches. Any closer, Earl Morgan told his son, and the suspect becomes uncomfortable. Any farther away and it's easy to miss the important but subtle clues in facial expression. The interrogator also doesn't want any object like a chair or a desk acting as a barrier. Reb had the car door, that couldn't be helped, but he judged his distance to be roughly twenty-seven inches. He could now fully appreciate the sports car's ivory colored leather upholstery and ultra-modern instrumentation. There was a laptop sitting open on the passenger seat connected by a USB to a device Reb had never seen before. It was the size of a pack of playing cards with a ten-inch antenna protruding upwards from the side.

"I'm doing an article for Texas Journey Magazine about why people visit west Texas," Reb said. "Are you here in Birdstar on pleasure or business?"

"Look, I don't want to—"

"This will only take a minute," Reb cut in, "and I'll send you a copy of the magazine if I quote you in the article."

For all his "hail fellow, well met" shtick, Reb could see the man wasn't having any of it. A more primal, non-verbal communication was taking place between the two men, one that relied upon posture, eye contact, and the release of specific chemicals to get its meaning across. Translated, Reb's message read, "I've made you, you son-of-a-bitch. I know you're following us, and I've a pretty good idea who sent you."

Marty Hamilton's message was also clear. "You keep on with this bullshit and I'll get out of the car and clean the fucking street with you."

At fifty-four, Reb still had fast reflexes but he doubted he could go many rounds with the youthful gym rat confronting him. And there was the fact that KVMR didn't provide a dental plan, a consideration that enabled Reb's cerebral cortex to commandeer a sufficient number of neural pathways to override the prompting of his lizard brain.

"Well, I can see you're busy, sir. Thanks for your time." Reb stepped back as the tinted window slid back up and the Porsche reversed abruptly away from the curb, changed gears, and accelerated away down the street. Reb smiled as he watch the car go.

Had its owner wished to project the fiction that he was merely waiting for someone, he would have stayed where he was. Reb always felt better when things were out in the open.

He started back toward Alice, pleased with what he'd accomplished but then noticed that his hands were trembling. He rubbed them together and shook his arms to release the tension. He could see Alice standing by the rental car watching him with what looked like a scowl. He touched his pocket and realized he had he had the keys and felt stupid.

"Sorry," he said unlocking her door before going around to unlock his own. He started the engine; the interior still reeked of air freshener.

"Well, what did you find out?"

"It was a guy. I'm sure he's the one I saw in Lubbock," Reb said.

"Did he admit it?" Alice asked.

"No, but I could tell. And there's something else."

"What?"

"He had some kind of transmitter or receiver in his car."

"What does that mean?"

"I'm not sure. If it's a transmitter, then he's probably in touch with someone else who's also following us."

"But why use a transmitter? Why not use a cell phone?"

"I know. That's what I think. If it's a receiver, then they've probably put a bug in our car."

First we find dope, Alice thought, and now Reb thinks there's a listening device in the car. When did they put it in the car? At the Resource Center? At the motel last night? The idea that some sneaky bastard bugged their car while they were inside the motel making love added a panicky quality to her anxiety.

"Have they been listening to everything we've said?" she asked.

"I could try and look for the bug, but I doubt I'll find it," Reb said.

"Why not?" Alice was for any action that might relieve the growing sense of menace.

"It could be anywhere in the car," Reb said. "Sometimes they're so small, you need special scanners to find them."

"Then what are we going to do?"

"I'll call Avis and arrange to switch cars at one of their agencies. That should take care of the problem, if there is one."

"Great, we just told them what we're going to do," Alice said.

Reb turned off the engine and they both got out of the car without saying another word. They crossed the street to the courthouse square where they found a vacant bench in the shade. Reb caught himself turning his head constantly from side to side looking for the Porsche; he needed to calm down and think things through.

"So who's following us, the government?" Alice asked.

"No, I think its EnerTex."

"Then we've got to do something," she said. She could hear her own voice slipping the reins and rising in pitch. "Maybe they'll try some other scheme to get us arrested."

They stood and began walking. Reb said, "Let's go back to the newspaper office."

"Why?"

"I think its high time we got ourselves some insurance."

They found Marvin Spooner in his office working on an editorial and Reb asked him if he could recommend a good lawyer in town.

"Why do you need a lawyer?" Marvin asked.

"We need one who's on a first-name basis with the powers that be in Dalton County—the sheriff, the district attorney, and the judges," Reb said.

"You still haven't said why you need a lawyer."

"Let's just say we think someone might be trying to cause us trouble," Reb said.

Marvin glanced briefly at Alice and then back to Reb. "I'd go see Willard Stompings. His law office is around the corner. He's president of the local Rotary Club, and all those people you just mentioned are members too."

Reb and Alice thanked him and turned to go.

"Willard's an honest man," Marvin said, getting up from his old chair to walk them out. "People trust him. Tell him I sent you."

As they reached the front office, Marvin said, "You know, I was thinking after you left that maybe you should check out the housing development I told you about, the one they built while the power plant was under construction. Nobody lives there now."

Reb regarded the editor with renewed interest. Was Marvin giving them an important tip? Maybe Birdstar was another Love Canal.

"What's so interesting about the development?" Reb said.

"You can get a *really* good deal on a new house; they're desperate to sell them."

Neither Reb or Alice knew what to say.

"Birdstar is a great place to retire," Marvin went on, "you and your lady friend might consider moving here."

Had they not both been so winged out by the guy in the Porsche, they might have laughed. As it was, they said goodbye and went to see the lawyer.

19

THE PRACTICE OF law in Dalton County was not by any stretch of the imagination a glamorous occupation. As if to emphasize the point, Willard Stompings' law office was achingly ordinary. Home Depot economy-grade luan paneling covered the walls and the green acrylic carpeting was worn and stained in places. All in all, the place exuded an air of dreariness that matched the emotional state of the people who found themselves, for one unhappy reason or another, seeking Mr. Stompings' legal advice. His secretary, a thin angular woman who must have decided to postpone retirement a decade or two past, spoke with a pleasant Texas drawl.

"Mr. Stompings is in court right now, but I expect him shortly. Y'all can wait if you like."

They waited. A clock encased in a rectangular oak cabinet hung on the wall, its short swinging pendulum visible through an etched glass window underneath. The clock's function, Reb surmised, was to remind anyone who should glance at it that the law was a slow, steady, organized process that marched forward to the resolution of conflict with each ponderous tick of its internal mechanism.

Reb turned to say something to Alice and found her tapping the face of her watch.

"What are you doing?" he asked.

"It's not working right. That clock says it's ten minutes after two, but my watch says it's one-fifty-five."

"So?" he said.

"My watch was five minutes *faster* than the clock in the restaurant. The battery must be dying."

While Alice reset her watch, Reb mentally reran the encounter with the man in the Porsche. He wondered if he could accurately describe the man if he had to. What color was his hair? Light brown. His eyes? He was wearing sunglasses. What kind of computer was he using? A PC but he couldn't tell what brand. License plate number? He wanted to kick himself for being so lame. Why hadn't he thought to write it down? Some hotshot reporter. There's more to the news business than doing interviews, he scolded himself. You better start using your eyes, while you still can.

Reb was interrupted from this internal self-flagellation by the arrival of the lawyer. At six foot six, everything about Willard Stompings was over-sized, from his eight-inch hat and fifty-inch chest, to his size eighteen double-E feet. Looking him up and down, Reb wondered if growth factors in gold fish—how the size of the container determines the size of the fish—might not apply to human beings also. Growing up in New Jersey, Reb topped out at five-foot nine. There was no mistaking what state Willard Stompings did his growing up in.

Alternating back and forth, Reb and Alice told their story to the lawyer.

"So what do you want me to do for you?" Stompings said when they were finished.

"Have you had any dealings with the EnerTex Corporation?" Reb asked. "Ever represented them in a legal action?"

The attorney laughed. "They don't need a hick lawyer like me to do their dirty work; they've got their own stable of over-paid attorneys in Houston for that."

"Why do you call it "dirty work"?" Alice asked.

"Isn't that what most big corporations want their attorneys to do for them?"

Reb warmed to Stompings. He wasn't keen on lawyers to start with, but he found the man's forthright manner refreshing.

"I don't personally have anything against EnerTex, you understand," Stompings continued, "I just don't like it when some big outfit comes to town and starts throwing its weight around. They scared some local land owners into selling them their property."

"How did they do that?" Reb asked.

"By convincing the county supervisors to set up a special development board with the power of eminent domain. That way the county could condemn the land and hand it over to EnerTex, if the owners refused to sell." He gave a light shrug. "I'm not sure it would have made it through the courts, but nobody wanted to risk it. So they took EnerTex's offer and that was that."

"Wouldn't property owners be happy to sell their land to EnerTex for a power plant?" Reb asked. "I mean, there doesn't seem to be a big demand for rural real estate around here."

"It wasn't just for the power plant," Stompings said. "EnerTex also needed land at the edge of town for a new housing development for their employees. Let's just say their initial offers for the properties were far from generous. It made people angry. But jobs are jobs," he shrugged again. "That's how the politicians saw it and they did their best to be accommodating."

"That being the case," Reb said, picking his words carefully, "would you say everything's on the up-and-up in Dalton County when it comes to the law?"

Willard Stompings leaned back in his chair as a smile spread across on his broad face. "Is the law in EnerTex's pocket, is that what you're asking?"

Reb nodded.

"Well, some pretty dumb things go on around here from time to time. Maybe a relative of the judge gets a break the next guy doesn't, but that's in the nature of rural justice—it's not what you know, but who you know. But as for out-and-out corruption, you don't have anything to worry about in Dalton County."

"Then if something were to happen, would you be willing to represent us?" Reb asked.

"I charge $120 an hour. I'd charge more, but I wouldn't have many clients."

Reb and Alice thanked him, took his card, and left. Reb wasn't sure how capable Willard Stompings was as a lawyer, but it was reassuring just having a guy as big as him on their side.

BEFORE CLIMBING BACK into the car, Reb and Alice discussed their plans. They would drive south to Midland—that was the location of the nearest Avis agency—and spend the night. The next morning they would exchange cars and head to Houston for their meetings with EnerTex and Sheila Kennedy. Reb could tell Alice wasn't thrilled about driving five hundred and sixty-eight miles across Texas in a single day during the hottest part of the summer. Any hopes he had entertained about the trip being a romantic getaway were long gone.

As they passed the high school at the southern edge of town, a yellow dog darted out in front of them. Reb yanked the wheel and the car swerved onto the shoulder, spraying gravel into a four-foot ditch that ran alongside the road. Another inch or two, Reb realized, and they would have gone into the ditch as well. He eased the car back onto the blacktop again.

"That was close," he said.

"They don't like it when you kill their dogs," Alice said. There was a pause and then she said, "Just get us out of this town, Reb." She had had enough of Birdstar and all the crazy shit that was going on. The man in the Porsche, the chance they were being listened to, the missing birds. . .

"Are you all right?" Reb asked.

She wanted to yell at him, no I'm not all right. Can't you feel it? There's something seriously weird about this town. Her mind wanted to name it but couldn't. It wasn't evil, she had experienced that before. Twice. Evil was brutally cold and barren. It sucked the joy out of life. No, this was different—a diffuse anxiety spreading invisibly through the molecular fabric of the town like a disquieted spirit. She had felt it most palpably while crossing the courthouse square, but even here, at the outskirts of the town, it clung to her as if unwilling to let her go. You've got to stay rational, girl, she told herself and stared out the window as the countryside swept past. They had a long journey in front of them. After several minutes she looked at the dashboard clock and then at her watch.

"It's off again," she said.

"What's off?"

"My watch. It's fast. By seven minutes."

Reb hummed the *Twilight Zone* theme softly.

"It's not funny," she said and meant it.

Reb stopped singing. "The place got to me too," he said.

"Why do you think all the birds left?" she said.

"I don't know. Birds are funny that way."

"What do you mean?"

"I've heard that when there's an extra big berry crop someplace, suddenly millions of birds will show up from all over. There's no way they can communicate physically with each other over such large distances, but somehow they just know."

"I think they left because of the power plant," Alice said. "The timing is consistent."

"It could be a coincidence."

"But what if it's not? Wouldn't the canary leave the mine if it could?"

Reb looked down at the speedometer. As eager as he was to be free of the town, the last thing he wanted was a speeding ticket.

"Let me ask you something," he said.

"What?"

"Did it seem to you that we were stuck in Birdstar longer than we actually were?"

"We're under a lot of stress," she said as she reset her watch.

"Yeah I know, but—" he remembered to look in the rear view mirror for the Porsche and was relieved to see an empty road behind them.

"Why don't you get out the travel guide and find us a motel in Midland for tonight," he said.

Alice touched her finger to her ear to remind Reb to watch what he said. He nodded his head and glanced in the mirror again. This time a police car was fifty yards behind them. Where the hell had he come from? His mouth went dry. They continued on for two more miles and then the flashing lights came on.

"Shit," Reb said.

Alice turned and looked out the back window as Reb pulled the car over to the side of the road. He shut off the engine and waited. Nothing happened for several agonizing seconds. Maybe it's true, Alice thought, the town won't let us go.

"Why's he just sitting there?" Alice said.

"He's calling us in first, checking us out."

"Were you speeding?"

"No."

"Are you sure?"

Reb stared up at the rear view mirror; this trip to Texas was getting funkier by the minute.

A deputy sheriff got out of the cruiser and strode up to the Cavalier with his hand on his service automatic, which made Reb speculate on what kind of tough hombres they had in this part of Texas. He opened the window.

The policeman stopped a foot short of the window so that Reb, with his declining peripheral vision, had to turn nearly a hundred-and-eighty degrees to see him clearly. Reb knew this was standard police procedure for a traffic stop because it afforded the officer enough time to react should the driver attempt to pull a weapon. Modern police work revolved around increasing reaction time in potentially dangerous situations. Even a few milliseconds could mean the difference between a good or bad decision. Conversely, compressed time, turbocharged by fear and an elevated heart rate, dramatically increased the likelihood that someone would get hurt. Reb was all for the first option and it heartened him to see that the officer was a professional and doing it by the book.

"May I see your license and registration please?"

Reb complied. "What seems to be the matter, officer?" The stock phrase was meant to inject as much normalcy into the situation as possible.

"Please remain in the vehicle," the officer said and then walked back to his cruiser and called in the particulars. While he was doing this, another patrol car approached rapidly from the other direction and pulled over on the far side of the road, lights flashing. An officer got out and walked over to the first police car. Within a minute, a third car arrived on the scene. This last belonged to the Texas Highway Patrol. Reb knew by now that this was no routine traffic stop. He forced a smile. "We just need to stay cool. It'll work out."

Alice wasn't so sure. She was already contemplating how she would use her one phone call. Would she call Kevin at the radio station? Her parents? Wayne?

After several minutes, all three policemen approached the rental car. Deputy Lane, identified by the black plastic tag pinned to his shirt above his star, took the lead. "Would you both please step out of the vehicle?" he said.

Reb looked over at Alice and shrugged fatalistically. They got out of the car and were directed to stand on the side of the road while the two deputies and the state trooper began searching the car. Given recent events, the situation bordered on the surreal, and try as he might, Reb couldn't dispel the image, part *Take the Money and Run*, part *Oh Brother Where Art Thou*, of being sentenced to a Texas chain gang for the remainder of his life.

Not surprisingly, the first place the officers looked was under the driver's seat. Reb was tempted to yell, "I threw it away," but kept silent. Finding nothing, the police searched under the front passenger seat and the glove compartment. By the time they reached the trunk, their enthusiasm for the project had waned and they gave it little more than a perfunctory glance. Meanwhile, remorse had superseded the fear of chain gangs in Reb's mind. Why had he dragged Alice into this mess? Naive and irresponsible were the indictments that came most readily to hand. Of course, if Alice had known what he was thinking, she would have probably slugged him. She had been a radio journalist long before Reb came on the scene and had agreed to help cover the EnerTex story with her eyes wide open. Come what may, she told herself, they were in this together.

The search was finally called off and Deputy Lane came over to where Reb and Alice stood.

"Y'all are free to leave," he said. The two other officers had already returned to their cruisers.

Reb wanted to ask Deputy Lane if he had a search warrant or probable cause for what he'd just done, but again he kept his mouth shut. He and Alice got back into the rental car as Deputy Lane walked back to his, turned off its flashing lights, and sped away. Reb's emotions were equally balanced between relief and anger. He needed to think before he spoke. Alice was quiet too, but more from a concern that the car was bugged. Reb pulled back onto Rte. 385 and they continued south.

They spent the night at the La Quinta Inn in Midland and exchanged the Cavalier for a Chevy Malibu at Avis early the next morning. Reb then called Willard Stompings on their cell phone and told him what happened.

"You say you were stopped and searched just south of Birdstar?" Despite the fact that the digital connection kept cutting in and out, Reb detected a note of incredulity in the attorney's voice.

"I'm telling you, they knew exactly where to look. They were obviously tipped off."

"That's a tad hard to swallow," the lawyer said. "These Dalton County boys may not be the brightest bulbs in the law enforcement chandelier, but I can't see them going off half-cocked on account of an anonymous tip."

"What makes you think it was anonymous?" Reb asked.

"So what you're saying is that some functionary at EnerTex called the sheriff and said, 'Hey by the way, Sheriff, there's a couple of hippies driving around your jurisdiction with drugs stashed under the driver's seat of their car. Why don't you go out and arrest them?' It just doesn't work that way."

Reb tried to see it from the lawyer's point of view. He also noted the use of the word hippies. They might as well be Peter Fonda and Dennis Hopper for all the added harm it would do them. Still, it *was* a stretch to think a simple phone call from

Houston could jump-start the entire law enforcement establishment of Dalton County. Unless, of course, the law was bought
and paid for by EnerTex which Stompings refused to believe. The
fact they had been stopped and searched could not be denied; nor
that the cops knew exactly where to look. If Reb by sheer dumb
luck hadn't found the pot and gotten rid of it, Alice and he would
be in a world of hurt right now.

Reb asked the lawyer find out how the authorities were tipped
off to the marijuana. Maybe the sheriff wasn't exactly thrilled
about being sent off on a snipe hunt and would share his frustra-
tions with a fellow Rotarian. The attorney said he would look
into it. Reb knew he was getting ahead of himself in terms of who
would pay the legal fees. He would ask Alice to talk to Kevin.
Maybe Workman would pick up a portion. Worst case scenario,
he'd pay Stompings' fee himself. Whatever happened, he had to
know what was going on.

After giving the lawyer their cell number, they continued their
journey. Both slept badly the night before, and the worry and
uncertainty were taking their toll. Reb's eyes were red and sore;
he hoped it was an allergic reaction to something in the Texas air,
a weed or an oil refinery, and not caused by the high pressures of
his glaucoma.

Texas was the West in all its unending glory and the West, as
the old-time cowboy wrote in his diary, "was a place where a man
could walk himself to death and not get anywhere." That's how it
felt to Reb as they worked their way, hour after hour, across the
state. Were they being followed? He got to where he didn't care
all that much, so long as a soft bed and a cold beer awaited him at
the end of the journey.

Then twenty miles east of San Antonio they ran into a cluster
of thunderstorms. The blackened sky across the broad horizon
to the east came alive with lightning strikes. The bright flashes
came so rapidly, one upon the other, that they created an eerie
strobe effect with the beating of the windshield wipers, befitting a
frenzied pantomime performed by demons.

Reb took it as a sign that they were entering the heart of the darkness. Houston was a city that represented much that was truly wrong with America. There the powerful gods of power and greed entwined in a lover's embrace that knew nothing of shame or restraint. The whole corrupt Enron crowd had called Houston their home. As did the corporate raider Charles Hurwitz and his Maxxam Corporation whose mission it seemed was to cut down every last stand of old-growth trees in North America. Add to that the corporate headquarters for Halliburton, El Paso Energy, and Waste Management. And here comes EnerTex, the new kid on the block and soon-to-be darling of Wall Street. EnerTex. The name itself was full of sharp edges and raw ambition.

Meanwhile, Alice wrestled with her own dark internal emotions as they pushed through the storm. She wanted to go home. Now. Today. This very moment. Several times while going around San Antonio she considered asking Reb to drive her to the airport. She couldn't remember ever feeling so out-of-place, unless it was during a bad acid trip she once had at a Black Sabbath concert. The show had been held inside a professional hockey rink, and all night she could feel a deadly cold seeping up through the retractable floor that covered the ice. By comparison, Nevada City was her safe haven, an island of relative sanity in the maelstrom that was modern America. How much longer this would last was difficult to gauge. Nevada City was changing. The shops and restaurants were going upscale and real estate prices were skyrocketing, as more and more wealthy people picked the area as a place to retire. One serious side-effect of all this was that the political leadership of the county was moving steadily to the conservative right. An old story. The artists and eccentrics discover a sleepy town someplace off the beaten path, a town imbued with it a unique kind of funkiness, and they move there and fix up some of the old properties. They open a bookstore with a cafe in back, a natural food co-op, and a Waldorf school. Then one day the town's name appears in a national magazine's list of great places to live and it's not long until the rich and bored move in, displacing the very people who made the town desirable. In the end what remains is a pseudo-artsy town like Carmel or Sedona, a town in which the artists are forced to either become real estate agents or move away.

They drove past a rest area that was crowded with vehicles waiting out the storm and Alice tried to imagine what the people inside the cars and trucks and RVs were doing. Some she guessed were sleeping. Others were listening to the radio or playing cards with their kids. Where were they going? Houston? New Orleans? Florida? Did any of them feel as out-of-place as she did? She chided herself for wanting to run away from Texas so much. How could she hope to learn anything, grow socially and psychologically, if she didn't leave the comforting reassurances of a place like Nevada City now and again? Here in the heartland of her nation she had the opportunity to interact with all kinds of people, most of them quite different than herself. Ernesto and Sandra. Hazel and Mike. Dr. Andrews. These were good, solid people who tried, each in his or her own way, to make the world a better place. Even a West Coast transplant like Marvin Spooner, full of romantic notions about small town America, could plop himself down in west Texas and make a life for himself. She respected that kind of flexibility and determination and wished she was more open to new experiences, especially those that challenged her everyday assumptions and beliefs. Nevada City was like an old sweater, warm and familiar. But sometimes it could be a velvet coffin too.

"What do you say we use the 'little gray cells?'" she said turning to Reb, her voice breaking the hypnotic trance induced by the motion of the wiper blades and the lightning.

"Little gray cells?"

She tapped her forehead with her finger. "The *lee-teal* gray cells." She had fallen in love with the books of Agatha Christie when she was fourteen, especially those about the diminutive Belgium detective, Hercule Poirot, who boasts of his superior brain filled with many thriving gray cells.

"Okay," Reb said, "where do we start?"

"One, what do we know to be true? Two, what do we merely suspect is true? And three, what should we do next?"

"We're in Texas," he said. "That's a fact, so it goes in category one, what we know to be true."

"Right. And why are we here?" she asked.

"Because Lyle Workman bought us a couple of airline tickets."

"And he did this because. . . ?"

"Because he was concerned about workers getting sick at a power plant."

"But could there be another motive behind Workman's encouragement?"

"Such as?"

"Maybe he has a personal ax to grind with EnerTex. Or it's a Republican-Democrat thing. They *do* take their politics seriously down here." She recalled a news story about a bunch of Texas lawmakers, all Democrats, who hid out in a Holiday Inn in Oklahoma for weeks on end to avoid a Republican sponsored vote on redistricting.

"I don't think he'd lie to us just to gain some political advantage." Reb said.

"But we're not absolutely sure," Alice said. "You brought up the fact that Ernesto and Mike might be lying to us."

"I thought we decided they weren't."

"Then maybe something else is making the workers sick, not the power plant?"

"To be honest, everything else goes in the second category; things we only think are true." He appreciated good process, the methodical laying out of facts. Anything else was just kids rolling around on the ground. But the ambiguity surrounding the EnerTex story was making him thick-headed and ill-tempered.

"What about the man in the Porsche?" Alice said. "Was he following us or not?"

"I'm sure they planted the dope in the car to get us arrested," Reb said. "I watched those cops; they went right to where it was supposed to be. That's conclusive evidence as far as I'm concerned."

"So it belongs in the first category," Alice said. "There must be a story here if someone is trying so hard to get us out of the way."

"You sound like you're trying to convince yourself," Reb said.

"Maybe I am."

"Do you think we're wasting our time?"

"I won't lie to you. I've had it with Texas. I want to go home."

They drove on in silence for a mile or two, the lightning all around them.

"I'm glad you're here," Reb said. "I really am."

A bolt of lightning struck so close it illuminated the interior of the car and Reb felt his taut nerves tighten even more.

"What's your gut tell you about this whole EnerTex thing?" Alice asked.

"My gut? Hard to say."

"Are you frightened?"

"A little, I guess. What about you?"

"I am but not for myself."

It hadn't come out the way she intended.

He waited.

"I've been thinking about your dream," she said.

He glanced over but she had her head turned and was staring out the passenger window at the lightning.

The nightmare had been about death. Metaphorical or literal, he couldn't say; the hour, the minute, the very second of that event was kept secret from everyone. Had his mother expected to die that morning? She was always the first one up in the family. She fixed the lunches for school and fed the dog and the cats. She then made coffee and its aroma floated upstairs into the bedrooms to arouse the rest of the family. After that, still in her robe and slippers, she stepped outside and probably idled for a moment on the porch by the kitchen door breathing in the crisp morning air, listening to the birds chattering in the trees. Then she started across the street to get the newspaper from the blue plastic container below the mailbox. And that was her moment, etched into the stone of destiny since before time itself. There was an old country hymn with the line, "I'm ready when You call me, Lord, but give me just a little more time." Was his dream merely a warning to tread carefully, or was it a non-negotiable notice sent down from the head office of an impending transfer to another state of being? Reb took his hand from the steering wheel and rubbed his eyes as the lightning flashed against the dark sky like white veins pulsing with amphetamines.

"Do you want me to drive?" Alice asked.

"No, I'm fine."

She opened her purse and took out a container of bilberry capsules and handed one to Reb along with the water bottle. She did this six times a day for his eyes because she'd read that pilots during the Second World War ate wild bilberries to improve their night vision. Perhaps it would help his glaucoma. She also carried fresh carrots around with her and other vitamins. She suggested once that he smoke marijuana because it was supposed to lower the pressures inside the eyeball, but Reb said marijuana made him think too much. An odd choice, she mused; think too much or go blind.

Another five miles and the lightning began to die away as the rain splattered in increasingly heavier drops against the windshield. Reb could feel the tension, both inside and outside the car, lessen and he reached down and switched on the radio. He looked for an Austin FM station because the city was famous for its music scene. Suddenly the voice of Hank Williams came out of the speakers.

"Hey good lookin'. What you got cookin'? How about cookin' something up with me?"

Suddenly it was 1951 and America was a very different place. They both began to sing along and the storm clouds of anxiety lifted for a time.

20

LIKE A DRUNK skier going over a cliff, the situation for Marty Hamilton had deteriorated quickly. It started with Morgan confronting him in Birdstar; he had been caught off guard and lost his temper—and with it his better judgment. He wanted to fuck with the guy, shut him down, so he called Brewer who then called the Dalton County sheriff and the rest was history. No drugs, no arrest, everybody standing around with dogshit on their shoes.

"Listen, Hamilton," Brewer said when he called a short while later on his cell phone. "I don't care who you work for, don't ever make me look the fool again. Understand, asshole?"

Marty understood that he needed to call Avery before Brewer did. He would explain that the marijuana was under the seat when Morgan and his girlfriend picked up the car. He had put it there himself. Or maybe the little prick who worked for Avis ripped him off after all and kept the dope for himself. Marty would kill the motherfucker if he had.

Then he heard his boss' voice in his head. "What marijuana? What's this all about, Marty?"

No, maybe talking to Avery wasn't such a bright idea. The whole reason he'd been given the task of dealing with Morgan was because Avery didn't want to be involved.

Marty pondered what to do next as he splashed cold water on his face. He was in the washroom of a McDonalds on the east side of Midland. He had spent the morning and most of the afternoon driving around town. After the fiasco with the police and the disappearing marijuana, he followed Morgan and the girl south to Midland where they had taken a room at the La Quinta Inn out by the interstate. Marty decided to sleep in his car in the parking lot of a truck stop down the street but a rattling compressor on a reefer truck kept him awake most of the night. Then he forgot to set the alarm on his watch and overslept. It was just after eight when he drove past the motel and discovered that the red Cavalier was gone. He powered up the GPS tracking software on his laptop and located the vehicle in downtown Midland. He drove to the address and found an Avis rental agency where the red Chevy Cavalier was already being cleaned for the next customer. As for Morgan and the girl, they were long gone.

He pulled a paper towel from the dispenser and patted his face. He needed a shave but didn't want to waste the time. The last six hours had been a confused blur. He had gone with the only actionable assumption, which was that Morgan was meeting with someone in town. Fortunately he was able to wheedle the make and model of the car Morgan was now driving out of the agent—a middle-aged divorcee named Doreen—along with the license plate number. So he combed the streets looking for a white Chevy Malibu, and whenever he saw one parked in front of a restaurant, a radio station, or an office building, he slowed down to check the plate number.

He studied himself in the mirror above the sink—not the best of times for the Tin Man—and then he went out and ordered a Big Mac and a chocolate shake. Back in the Porsche he picked up his cell phone. He couldn't put off calling EnerTex any longer.

"Hey, it's Marty. What's up?"

"Same old, same old," Brenda said. "Where are you?"

"West Texas, just outside Midland."

"What are you doing there? Your buddy from California just called to confirm his appointment here tomorrow morning with Chuck Hathaway."

"You mean Morgan?"

"None other."

"What's he doing going to Houston?"

"It was Avery's idea. You know Hathaway. He can charm the diamonds off a rattlesnake."

"It would help to know these things."

There was an uncomfortable pause and then Brenda said, "Avery's been asking about you."

"What did you tell him?"

"That you do it like a stallion."

"No, really."

"What could I tell him? I haven't heard from you. He thinks you might be dropping the ball on this one, Marty."

He was battered by fear and anger —fear of blowing the best shot he'd probably ever get at a big promotion, and anger for being asked to do the impossible.

"What does Avery want me to do, kill the son-of-a-bitch?"

"Take it easy," Brenda said, suddenly alarmed. Security was constantly warning EnerTex employees to be careful about what they said on the telephone; someone might be listening. It didn't have to be the feds; it could be a competitor or a foreign government. Only yesterday a team had swept the entire thirty-sixth floor for bugs. She thought Hamilton had enough sense not to blow it.

"He just wants to know what you've been up to," she said. "Use encrypted e-mail next time. It's more secure."

"Right." He realized he needed to chill out; west Texas was getting to him.

"See you soon," he said.

"I'm looking forward to it."

The truth, however, was that she was ambivalent about ever seeing Marty again. He had a strong, fully formed man's body, but inside he was just a boy. She knew the type. In the corporate world they were legion. They did deals and made gobs of money. They married attractive, bulimic women and sired children. Then came the office affairs and expensive divorces. They drank too much. Most did drugs. Sometimes they got caught with their hand in the cookie jar and were carted off to jail. In the end, they went to their graves having never grown up or taken responsibility for much of anything. They weren't wicked; that required imagination and nerve. They were just children who played at life.

Well, that wasn't for her. She grew up in Texarkana in a family who'd known its share of hard knocks. Her father, who worked for the railroad, was an alcoholic. He could be sweet as pie one minute and a raging, abusive terror the next. Worse yet, he was always investing the family's money in schemes his drinking buddies got him into—schemes that inevitably failed. Her mother was the one who kept it together. Velma Luanne Foster was a rock. For over twenty years she operated a bread slicing machine for a commercial bakery, never earning much over minimum wage in all that time. She raised five kids—Brenda was the second to the youngest—and only once in her life owned a new store-bought dress. The rest of her clothes, and those of her children, she sewed herself. She seldom laughed, never took a vacation, and suffered from varicose veins and migraines.

Brenda had made other plans for her life. She scraped and saved to get through two years of community college and then got a job with a regional natural gas company in Houston. The company eventually became Enron and it was the perfect place for a woman with an opportunistic streak to begin her climb. One reason was that many of the top executives where in the habit of cheating on their wives. If, for instance, Brenda wanted a positive score from the all-important Performance Review Committee, all she needed to know was whose ego—and other parts—needed stroking. Somewhere in all this she met Larry Stevers, a pilot for FedEx, and they got hitched. She was never exactly sure why. Maybe she just wanted to wear a pretty white dress and have a party. But it *did* give her a useful kind of leverage in the arena of office sexual politics. She could now turn down a suitor with the excuse that she was married. Or not. It was her decision. As for Larry, she assumed he was pursuing his own erotic adventures, especially during his frequent lay-overs in Bangkok. The city teemed with prostitutes and her only fear was that he would pick up a disease and pass it on to her. She was careful to take precautions. And she planned to divorce him when the time was right.

Then Enron ran into trouble. A lucky few saw it coming and Brenda was one of them. She wasted no time cashing out her stock options before handing in her notice. EnerTex, the company that hired her, was working on a new technology for making electricity. The CEO was Avery Jordan Axton. He came from an old Houston family who had made its pile in the oil and gas exploration and drilling business. Avery wasn't Big Rich by Houston standards but he had done everything right—gone to the right schools and joined the right clubs. He then served four years in the Air Force and married Elizabeth "Bea" Rhineholt, the daughter of Herman Rhineholt, who owned the largest outdoor advertising business in Texas. Bea had money of her own and was willing to help bankroll Avery's new electricity venture.

Suffice it to say, there was no boy in Avery Axton. He could be charming and considerate when it suited him, but when it came to promoting the interests of EnerTex and making money, he exhibited an animal ruthlessness that turned Brenda on. He was going to be her ticket to the up-market lifestyle she coveted. The signs were already there. The more successful EnerTex became, the more she sensed Avery growing bored and restless. Sometimes he discussed his private life with her. What should he do about his son who had been kicked out of boarding school for stealing? How could he get out of going to Hilton Head for the holidays with his wife's family? Brenda of course was more than willing to play the role of trusted confidant, and it didn't hurt that Bea Rhineholt was rapidly going to seed; too many charity banquets and luncheons for the Friends of the Library had layered on the soft fleshy pounds. Giving birth to three children had taken care of the hips. It was just about time for Avery to trade in the old model for a newer one. Then Brenda would get her multi-million dollar house in River Oaks, diamond jewelry from Tiffany and Cartier, and a vacation villa on the French Riviera. Not only would she learn to rub shoulders with the Big Shots, she would become a Big Shot herself. She would serve on the board of the art museum and United Way—maybe she would organize a fund-raiser for the local Republican Party. Brenda Sue Axton from little ol' Texarkana. A year, two at the outside, and it would all be hers. She felt certain of it. That's why she had to be cautious with the likes of Marty Hamilton. She could have her fun but there needed to be room on her card when Avery asked her to dance.

MARTY PUSHED THE red button on his cell phone and tossed it on the seat next to him. He reached over and pulled a map from the glove compartment. He would have to drive all night, but he could conceivably make it to Houston in time to pick up Morgan and his girlfriend again.

What was this radio dickhead up to anyhow? So he met with a couple of employees and their wives. Former employees was more like it. Marty took their photographs with his digital camera and a 300mm telephoto lens as they left the Family Resource Center. He would e-mail the photos to Brenda, along with the one of the tall woman who drove the blue Volvo station wagon. He had written down her license plate number and then called a friend who worked for an insurance company in Dallas. The woman's name was Laura Andrews and she was a doctor. Marty didn't know what was said during the meeting but he doubted it could hurt EnerTex in any serious way. Then again, there was no way of knowing since Avery was keeping him in the dark. All his boss had said was that it had something to do with worker safety. The Tin Man was a deal maker and a deal maker needed all the facts. Garbage in, garbage out, one of his professors like to say. Faulty data in, bad deal out. That's why Marty had opted for the extra insurance of having Morgan and the girl arrested. But he had acted too soon. The smug bastard with his "I'm writing an article for Texas Journey Magazine" had made it personal, and now he had burned his bridges with Agent Brewer.

Marty turned the key and his Porsche vroomed to life. It was five hundred and eighty miles to Houston. He removed a thin packet of coke from his wallet. He would need it if he intended to drive all night. He pushed the CD tray selection button until *Guns n' Roses* came slamming out of each of the fourteen speakers of the Porsche's 350-watt Bose Cabin Surround™ Sound system. Pulling onto the interstate, he settled into a groove and began thinking. He had all night to come up with plan B.

21

"I HAVE A meeting with a reporter from the *Wall Street Journal* at eleven-thirty so we'll have to make this short." The baritone voice belonged to Charles Hathaway, vice president for communications and public relations for the EnerTex Corporation. Reb and Alice had been waiting for him at the front reception desk for the last twenty minutes, watched over by two stone-faced security guards. On the wall behind the desk hung the company logo: two parallel lightning bolts of polished chrome passing through the word *ENERTEX*—nothing organic, old-fashioned, or inefficient about Houston's newest and most promising energy company.

Hathaway handed Reb and Alice each a large plastic VISITOR badge and then he led them down a corridor past a bank of elevators to a windowless conference room. As they entered, Hathaway checked the time on the cell phone clipped to his belt. The gesture reinforced Reb's impression that Hathaway was a busy man for whom time was a stern taskmaster.

"Nice place you've got here," Reb said as he placed his equipment bag on a table and unzipped it. "It'll just take me a minute or two to set up my recording equipment."

Hathaway gave a lame smile but said nothing.

"We passed through quite a thunderstorm last night," Reb said taking the microphone from its padded bag and inserting the AA battery which powered the condenser element inside. "I've never seen anything like it."

Hathaway checked the time on his cell phone again and said, "I'll be back when you're ready." He left the room without another word and Reb looked over at Alice and shook his head with an air of disgust as if to say, *impatient bastard.*

What was it about busy people that irritated him so much? Perhaps it because they were part of an emerging new social hierarchy that determined a person's position in the pecking order by how busy he or she was? For to be busy meant one had important things to do. Nor did it seem to matter very much what urgent tasks the very busy person was doing, so long as he was busy. Busy people were always "cutting things short," "penciling in" appointments, and requiring subordinates to reduce information to "bullet points." They claimed the right to these shorthand relationships because they were, well, so *busy.*

This, of course, was the very opposite of what was considered desirable and noteworthy only a couple of generations ago. Back then, leisure defined the upper class; to be seen as busy, especially with trade, diminished one's social status. Rich and powerful people didn't need to run around frantically; they could slow down and enjoy life. Visit the ancient ruins of Egypt. Design a garden. Take in a weekend of fox hunting in the country. And they were envied by those of the lower orders for possessing such a luxurious surfeit of time.

Not in the twenty-first century. Now to be busy was to be happy and on top, while to be idle, truly idle, was the worst condition of all. Those unfortunate souls had few options when it came to covering up the poverty of their non-busyness. They could pretend to have found enlightenment and go live in an *ashram* in India, or they might tell their friends they were writing a novel. It was worrisome, Reb thought, that busyness for busyness' sake should so dominate human affairs. The Taoist masters of old had a proverb that went "action without reflection leads to the evil of bewilderment." That was contemporary America in a nutshell.

The night before, after the long drive from Midland, he and Alice checked into the hotel only to find that they were so charged with positive ions they couldn't fall asleep. Alice suggested they turn on the television and they caught the last twenty minutes of the movie *Back to the Future.* They then changed into their bathing suits and complimentary bathrobes and went down to enjoy the hot tub.

"I don't think there is just one kind of time," Reb said as he settled into the Jacuzzi next to Alice; he was still thinking about the movie.

"How many kinds of time are there then?" she asked. They were alone, and their voices echoed off the hard tile surfaces, as the swirling water coaxed the fatigue from their bunched up muscles.

"There are two kinds," Reb said. "I call one "tic-toc" time, or *logos* time. It's the kind of time that's expressed in abstract numbers, by factory whistles and airline schedules. It's what most people these days think of when they talk about time."

"Scientific time."

"Yes, a kind of *sanitized* time."

"What's the other kind of time then?"

Reb settled lower into the tub so one of the jets could massage the back of his neck.

"I call it *mythos* time. It's a fluid kind of time. Flexible. Always expanding and contracting. Logos time never expands or contracts. A logos second is always a second, a logos minute is always a minute."

"Is mythos time what happens when we dream?" she asked. "The kind of time that stretches and gets all distorted?"

"But it happens when we're awake too. You know how it is. One day you're able to get everything accomplished right on schedule; you're productive and very much in control. But then the next day, no matter how hard you try, you can't seem to get anything done."

Alice smiled. "I know the experience well."

"So do most people. But do we ever think to hold the nature of time responsible for what's going on? Do we say, oh well, time went faster today than it did yesterday? No, of course not. Instead, we think there's something wrong with us; it's somehow our fault. We believe that if we were only more disciplined, more organized, everything would be different. We go out and pick up another book on time management or buy a digital organizer. But if we only came to see that *time* itself is the culprit, then we'd learn to relax and go with the flow. We wouldn't fight it nearly so much.

"Sometimes when I'm having a particularly frustrating day—the kind of day when I feel I should have just stayed in bed—I make a point of asking other people if they're experiencing the same kind of frustration."

"And what do they say?"

"More often than not, they say they are, and that makes me think it's *time* that does the changing, not me."

"When did you develop this big interest in time?"

Reb had to think. "My last year in high school; I hated the whole time regimentation drill—you know, bells telling you to change classes and all that. Before clocks came along, people's relationship to time was determined by natural rhythms. They got up with the sun and went to bed with the sun. The days got longer, then shorter. Nowadays, everything goes 24/7. It's all logos time now."

"I once worked with a Lakota Sioux woman who talked about *Indian* time," Alice said. "She said an Indian would make an appointment for, say, two o'clock and have every intention of being there on time, but if something came up unexpectedly that she felt was more important, maybe someone needed her help or wanted to visit, she'd deal with that first, even if that meant being late for her other appointment. She was on *Indian* time, not *white man's* time."

"In Argentina," Reb said, "the government is trying to get everybody to work on time. They say the economy suffers because so many people show up late. The government and business interests want more logos time and less mythos time."

"I can't stand the whole atomic clock thing," Alice said. "My sister gave me one for Christmas last year. It uses a radio signal to synchronize itself to the master clock at the US Naval Observatory. That's way too freaky for me."

Reb laughed. "For me too. What did you do with it?"

"I sold it on eBay. I mean, why would anyone, except maybe a pilot, need to know the time down to the nanosecond? Most people I know set their clocks ahead on purpose. The clock next to my bed and the one in my car are both set ten minutes ahead. I like the luxury of having a few extra minutes in case I'm having trouble waking up or I'm running late for a meeting."

"I read somewhere that the big touring circuses experienced a marked increase in the number of accidents in recent years," Reb said. "Do you know why?"

Alice shrugged. "They're trying more dangerous stunts? The performers are not as well trained?"

"Actually it's the music. To save money, the owners have replaced the live bands that used to travel with the circuses with recorded music. The trouble is that many circus acts are choreographed to the music. That's how it works. The trapeze artist lets go of the bar at a specific musical cue so her partner, who's also timing his actions to the music, can catch her."

"And sometimes they get a ahead of themselves, or fall behind," Alice said.

"Exactly. The conductor of the live band who's paying close attention can speed up or slow down the music when necessary, but recorded music plays on at the same tempo no matter what's happening, and the consequences can be devastating."

"Did you know that in India they used to tell time by burning very long sticks of incense?" Alice said. "There were various scents along the stick for different times of the day, so you didn't have to look at it like you would a notched candle. So if you smelled sandalwood, then you knew it was mid-morning, but if you smelled lavender, then you knew it was early evening."

"I wonder if animals tell time by smell?" Reb said. It was a possibility he'd never considered before. "I suspect plants give off specific chemical aromas at different times of day."

"I think women are more comfortable with mythos time, as you call it, than men are," Alice said. "They have more natural dynamic rhythms going on inside their bodies than men do."

"Creative people too," Reb said.

"How do you mean?"

"When I'm in the studio at KVMR working on a news story, I get so caught up in what I'm doing that the time just flies by. The same thing used to happen when I was in my dark room developing photographs. Compare that to how time drags when you're waiting for a delayed flight at the airport."

"But that refutes your theory about time," Alice said. "If time expands and contracts, like you said, then it shouldn't matter what you're doing. I mean, if time speeds up when you're doing something you enjoy, but then inches along when you're bored, then it's you, and not time, that's the variable."

"Yes and no," Reb said.

Alice waited.

"It depends on which kind of time you've *entered into*." Reb said. "The way I see it, logos time and mythos time happen simultaneously."

"That doesn't make sense. You don't enter into time."

"But you do. We're in time now."

Alice gave him a skeptical look.

"You know the story about Rip Van Winkle?"

Alice nodded.

"Well, it's only one of many folktales that deal with the difference between *mythos* and *logos* time. When I was a kid, my mother used to tell me a story about a Scottish fiddler who travels to Inverness to find work and gets hired by a short man in funny clothes to play his fiddle at a party. Only he doesn't realize the little man is a fairy. So he goes to the party and has a grand old time. The fairies fill his stomach with venison and whiskey and his purse with gold coins. But come the first light of morning, he discovers that an entire year has passed. I like the idea that time can be one thing and something else as well. It helps me approach time with an attitude of respect."

The conversation was interrupted by the water jets turning off and Reb had to climb out of the tub and rotate the timer knob to start them again.

"What did you mean about approaching time with an attitude of respect?" Alice said as he slipped back into the water.

"We know we should be treating the earth with greater affection and reverence," Reb said. "We should stop polluting the air, cutting down the trees, and dumping our poisons into rivers and oceans. The earth is our mother. She's all we have. We should love and care for her, the way she does for us."

Alice nodded her agreement. "Okay?"

"Well, I think we should try and have the same relationship with time, a relationship of respect and affection. The old myths tell us that *time* is our father. Well if that's the case, then we should honor our father instead of constantly fighting with him. We "beat the clock." We "kill time." We act like spoiled teenagers who resent the limits our father places on us. We feel victimized by time."

Victimized was a word Alice had never associated with time. She tried to imagine consciously changing her relationship to time; what would that feel like?

"Hurry sickness is a very real condition in America today," Reb went on, "and in other industrialized countries as well. People are so pushed along by the demands of modern life that they feel like they're always on the edge, always trying to catch up. It gets so they can't digest their food properly, or fall asleep when they want to. And hurry sickness makes people unwell in other ways; they get ulcers and high blood pressure and migraines."

"Maybe it's because people drink too much caffeine," Alice said half-seriously. She'd read in the Houston *Chronicle* that morning that there was so much caffeine in the waters of Puget Sound near Seattle that scientists were worried about its effect on marine life.

"I think drinking caffeine is more a coping mechanism than the source of the problem," Reb said. "The same goes with methamphetamine use. A woman with four kids and very little money doesn't get strung out on meth because she wants to party. She uses meth to help her keep up with all the demands in her life, kids, laundry, getting the car fixed."

"The same goes for a lot of business executives from what I hear," Alice said. "If it's not meth, it's cocaine. Everybody's under pressure to perform."

They sat for awhile without speaking. Alice had her eyes closed and her head tilted back so that her hair swam seductively about in the moving water, and Reb found his attention drifting in the direction of *Eros* time. He moved closer and took her hand in his. She turned and opened her eyes and he was about to kiss her when an elderly man entered the room. He stripped off his robe, doused himself under the shower, and dove into the pool, where he began swimming laps.

"Maybe we should go back to the room," Alice said and they both climbed out of the tub and toweled off.

"Can I tell you one of my greatest desires?" Reb said.

"Right now?" she said.

He smiled. "No, after that."

"What?"

"To become friends with time."

Friendship was another concept Alice had never associated with time and she wasn't sure what to say.

"I mean, what's the all big hurry about?" Reb continued. "Eternity isn't something that's going to happen later. It's happening now. We're in eternity. You, me, and that guy over there; there's no reason to be anxious."

"That sounds like a statement of faith."

Reb laughed. "I believe in Time: Time the Father; Time the Son; and Time the Holy Ghost. . . yes, I see what you mean. But it's the only sane response to mortality I know. We've talked about how time steals away our peace of mind. It's not really time that's doing it, it's the realization that we're going to die someday. We're driven to get as much in before the closure fairy with the scythe on his shoulder shows up at our door. Eat, drink, and be merry, but whatever you do, never accept the passage of time without a fight. Cling to your youth. Get a face lift, a boob job, hair implants, and dose yourself with Viagra. It seems, I don't know, so desperate and pathetic."

"But the other response isn't much better," Alice said as she carried her wet towel over to box and dropped it in.

"What do you mean?"

"Sitting around moping and feeling sorry for yourself because you're getting old and you're going to die soon."

They made their way to the elevator and pushed the button.

"To become friends with time," she said wrapping her hand around his arm. "You know, that's a lot harder than it sounds."

"I know."

THAT WAS LAST night. Today they were inside the heart of the corporate beast where everything was about logos time.

"Do you think Hathaway's ever coming back?" Reb asked Alice. Twenty minutes had passed and he was tired of waiting.

"Eventually," she said.

"Well, I hope so. I'm getting hungry."

The door opened as Reb said these words and Hathaway entered. He carried a large envelope which he handed to Alice.

"Here are some materials about our company," he said and his features flooded with sudden pleasantness as if he'd thrown a switch. He turned with a smile to Reb.

"Are we ready?"

"Ready when you are," Reb said as he powered up the recorder. The PR man sat down and ran the tips of his fingers through his gray-tipped hair. Alice moved around the table to sit next to Reb. She laid the envelope unopened in front of her on the table.

"You said you're with a radio station in California?" Hathaway said.

"Yes, KVMR," Alice said.

"I'm sorry but I never heard of it."

"We have a large and loyal following," Reb said.

"I'm sure you have." If there was a pin drop of sarcasm in this remark, Reb couldn't hear it.

"Please start by stating your name and position," he said.

"I'm Charles Hathaway, vice president for communications and public relations."

"How long have you been with EnerTex?"

"Six years."

"And before EnerTex?"

"I was director of governmental relations for Focus Armaments."

"From what we understand," Reb said, "the Ranger 1 power station came on-line a year and a half ago. What is its current output?"

"850 megawatts."

"Would that be considered a significant amount of generation?"

"Yes."

"Do you sell your electricity to utilities in other states?" Alice asked.

"No."

"Why not?" Reb asked.

"Texas is unique in that its power grid is self-contained. It's essentially an island.

"Is there a market in Texas then for this much additional electricity?" Reb asked.

"The demand for electricity in Texas is growing, as it in most parts of the country. Not only is Ranger 1 helping meet that demand but it is providing that electricity at a *much* lower cost."

"But won't that eventually force other power plants to shut down?" Reb asked.

"That is the likely scenario."

Official spokespeople loved the word "scenario," Alice thought.

"I can't imagine the competition will be happy about having to close their plants," Reb said.

"It will cause hardship, I understand, but that's the price of progress. You see, traditional power generation, whether from coal, oil, natural gas, or nuclear, comes with a number of social and environmental negatives. Ranger 1 has none of these. It is one hundred percent clean."

"So is solar-generated power," Alice said. "How does your technology compare with solar?"

"Solar is clean, but it is not financially viable. In fact, it takes more energy to manufacture a solar panel than it produces. Did you know that?"

She didn't, nor was she sure she believed it.

"But if people were willing to pay a little more for their electrical power," Alice said, "then more money could be invested in the kind of R and D that would make solar power profitable."

"Perhaps. I'm not an expert on the future of solar power," he said. "But I can tell you this. With our new ATG technology, EnerTex is able to compete successfully in the marketplace as it exists *today*, and by doing so, significantly improve the quality of life for everyone. What could be more desirable than that?"

"Can you tell us how the ATG process works? What is the fuel source, for example?"

"EnerTex has developed a revolutionary process for generating electrical power, and Ranger 1 is the first commercial facility to use this process. We envision a time, in the not too distant future, when EnerTex will provide ultra-affordable, clean power to some of the world's poorest countries. They will be able to use this power to modernize industry, desalinate and purify water, and provide their people with expanded public transportation, health care, and communication networks."

Reb knew the first rule officials adhered to when being interviewed was: always answer the question you *wish* you had been asked, not the question you actually *were* asked. It drove him nuts how often reporters let them get away with it.

"I understand, Mr. Hathaway, but what we want to know, and by '*we*' I mean our listeners and the citizens of northern California, is what *fuel* does the Ranger 1 power plant use to generate this electricity?"

With a light sigh a tolerant but tired adult might use to address a precocious child, Hathaway replied, "EnerTex believes that it is vital to the national security of our country that this information remain classified. The United States government concurs and has passed special legislation to that effect. I cannot say any more."

"Is ATG some kind of cold fusion process?" Alice asked.

"I really cannot say."

"Perhaps then," Reb said fighting to push down his rising irritation, "can you respond to recent allegations that the workers at the Ranger 1 plant are experiencing a variety of job-related health problems?"

"We have no knowledge of such problems, nor have we received any complaints from our employees."

Reb knew this was a lie and was tempted to say so. Sandra Valdez had told him that she had sent half a dozen letters to EnerTex—to protect her husband's job, she had rented a box at the post office and sent the letters under an alias. So even if EnerTex had decided not to respond to the letters, they had to at least know something was up.

"What about Homeland Security?" Reb asked. "If there's no problem as you say, then why are they investigating the health of EnerTex employees?"

The PR man's features were immutable as polished marble.

"I don't know anything about an investigation by Homeland Security or anyone else. I'm sure the materials I gave you will answer any other questions you might have."

Alice studied Hathaway intently. He was every inch the public relations professional—confident, friendly, and utterly trustworthy. And undeniably handsome, even though she guessed his age was not far south of 60. Why then did she dislike him, a dislike that bordered on revulsion? It had something to do with his vibe. You could dress up a vibe, give it a couple of coats of nice-guy paint, but it was always there below the surface, beaming its signature wave out into the cosmos like a pulsar. She thought his name should be "Hasaway" as in, "Chuck has a way of getting you to believe his brand of bullshit."

"Now, if you will excuse me," he said pushing his chair back from the table and standing up. "I have another meeting."

"Is there a chance we can interview Mr. Axton?" Reb said. "We understand EnerTex will soon expand its operations into California and I'm sure the people in our state would be very interested in learning more about him and hearing his views."

"We're fielding requests for interviews from a number of California newspapers and television stations and I'll be happy to put you on the list, if you wish."

And hell will freeze over before you let us play with the Big Boys, Reb thought with equal measures anger and shame. The reality of his powerlessness struck him to the core. To EnerTex, he and Alice were no more than a couple of bothersome centipedes to be brushed aside with the flick of the hand. It had been that way for the great mass of humanity since earliest time—used, abused, or ignored depending on the momentary inclinations of a small group of their fellow creatures. Rarely were these elites pulled down from their elevated positions. Even when they were they quickly returned, or others just like them. Would it always be that way, he wondered?

Hathaway's cell phone chimed and the man unholstered the device and put it to his ear with the fluid motion of an experienced gunfighter.

"Hathaway here." A long pause. "Yes, get the figures from Ron; I'm just about done here." He returned the phone to its holster. "I'm sorry but we really do need to wrap this up."

"Just a question or two more," Reb said not certain where to go next with the interview but wanting to slow down the efficient turning of the corporate machinery at EnerTex, if only for a few moments longer.

"Does a Mr. Vernachek work for EnerTex?" he asked.

"Yes, Mr. Vernachek is a member of our communications team here in Houston." Hathaway looked at the door as if to say, "Mustn't keep the Wall Street Journal waiting."

"Not long ago Mr. Vernachek gave a reporter from the *Birdcall* a tour of the power plant. The reporter's name is Kaye Spooner. She's the daughter of the publisher and she had the distinct impression that Mr. Vernachek was hurrying her through the facility. So I was wondering, why the big rush after making the trip all the way from Houston? Was Mr. Vernachek trying to prevent her from speaking to any of the employees?"

"I'm sure Pete had other pressing commitments that day; I'm not in charge of his schedule. The very fact that he made the effort to give Ms. Spooner a tour should demonstrate that EnerTex is willing to accommodate the press whenever possible, provided the requests are made through appropriate channels." The shell of friendliness was quickly dissolving.

"Does EnerTex employ its own security people?" Reb asked.

"Security issues are confidential."

"Are your security people following us?"

He had intended the question to sound more professional, more dignified. He should have said *under surveillance* instead of *following us* which made him sound slightly paranoid—which he'd readily admit to.

Hathaway's eyes receded back into his head and grew hard as flint. "This interview is over." He stepped over to the door, opened it, and stood there waiting. The tension in the room was palpable. Reb began packing up his equipment, slowly, methodically—one last pinch of sand in the corporate gears.

"I have a question," Alice said, getting up and walking around the table. "Why doesn't EnerTex allow women to work at the Ranger 1 power plant?"

Reb who was wrapping the cord around the headphones looked up; he had forgotten about the gender employment issue.

Hathaway remained silent but Reb detected a flicker of doubt in his manner. The man was evidently working out in his mind what to say; it was probably the first time anyone from the media had broached the subject.

"Legally, you know, you can't exclude women," Alice continued, "there are laws."

"EnerTex does not participate in discriminatory hiring practices," Hathaway said, his voice acquiring a robot-like cadence.

"Then how do you explain the fact that the only people working at the power plant are men? Mere coincidence? Or perhaps the only thing Texas women want to do is to is stay home and have babies."

"I didn't say that."

"I'm glad to hear it," she said stepping closer, crowding him slightly. "So do you, or do you not allow women to work at the power plant?"

Instead of answering, he took a step backwards grabbing his cell phone as he did so. He pushed a button.

"Hathaway," he barked. "Send security."

Alice was so startled she laughed. She was suddenly inside a Michael Moore movie and was about to be forcibly shown the door. She turned around and picked up her purse, anger supplanting her surprise. Rudeness of any sort infuriated her. What did Hathaway think she was going to do, physically attack him? Well, if they wanted a fight, she'd give them one.

As they walked back to the car along Smith Street, Alice checked the cell phone for messages—she had switched it off during the interview. There was one from Kevin back at KVMR. She dialed the number, still fuming.

"We're having trouble on this end," Kevin began.

"What kind of trouble?"

"A Texas law firm sent the station a threatening letter. They advised us, in no uncertain terms, to stop harassing their client or they'll be forced to take legal action."

"Don't tell me, EnerTex is their client."

"One and the same."

"The last time I checked, we still had a First Amendment."

"It's more complicated than that, Alice, and you know it. I've called a special meeting of the Executive Committee for tonight. I'll let you know how it turns out."

"Well, don't run scared, Kevin. Just tell EnerTex to go to the devil."

"They *are* the devil," Kevin said.

Alice was reduced to silence as the meaning of Kevin's words swirled about in the digital ethers.

"Are you still there?" he asked.

"Yes."

"Look, I'll call you after the meeting if you want," Kevin said. "That should be around midnight your time."

"Yeah, okay, we'll want to know if we're wasting our time or not."

"How are you two getting along? Making any headway with the story?"

"Not enough."

"So why is EnerTex being so defensive?"

"That's what I'd like to know. We're living in the age of preemptive strikes, Kevin. Do you want to talk to Reb?"

"No, just tell him what's up and keep working on the story until you hear otherwise."

They reached the parking garage. "I wish I could be at that meeting," she said to Reb. "I'd give them a piece of my mind."

"What piece is that?"

"Don't be cute."

"The axle turns a little, the big wheel turns a lot," he said.

"What the hell is that supposed to mean?"

"Attend to what's directly before you and the rest will take care of itself."

"That's easy for you to say, Mr. Reporter, but I'm the news director. Since when does KVMR cave in to pressure on a story?"

"We better hurry if we want to get something to eat before our next appointment."

It was hard to argue with someone who kept changing the subject. And she was hungry too.

22

THE AEROFLOT FLIGHT from Moscow to New York was exhausting. A buxom woman smelling of boiled cabbage occupied the seat next to him and was determined to relate her life's story from beginning when she was a little girl in Togliatti near the banks of the Volga and her father was a manager at Avtovaz, the largest car manufacturer in Russia. "He was a good man, an honest man, but the Communists were always trying to—"

Viktor cut her off. He was sick of stories about Russia in the old days. She pouted for the remainder of the flight and he found it difficult to sleep. The only consolation was the food which was delicious. Given Aeroflot's dismal safety record, the joke went that passengers ran a good chance of getting killed, but at least their last meal would be excellent.

From New York he took an American Airlines flight to Houston where he was met at the airport by a young man wearing a Houston Astros ball cap. His name was Uri Gryaznov. He was slim, in his mid-twenties, outgoing and energetic. He worked for the local Russian syndicate; Gromonov had sent him to pick Viktor up.

"I am to take you to the hotel, Colonel," Uri greeted him in Russian. "Let me carry your luggage. The car is waiting outside."

They emerged from the terminal into the glare of sunshine and the aroma of burning tobacco. A late model blue Toyota

Camry stood idling by the curb, a policeman leaning over talking to the driver on the far side. Uri opened the trunk and dropped the bags inside. He then opened the rear door for Viktor. The driver was a woman, also in her twenties.

"This is my sister," Uri said as he climbed into the backseat next to Viktor. "Her name is Tatyana." She turned around, gave a small nod, and put the car into gear without looking at the policeman who had to jerk his head back from the window with an expression of surprise and disappointment.

It was Friday afternoon and limousines with darkened windows swooped in and away from the terminal like a flock of hungry blackbirds, doors opening and closing like flapping wings, as travel-weary alpha males climbed inside and were whisked away to their palatial homes and dry martinis. Peering over her shoulder, Tatyana found an opening and eased the Camry into the flow of traffic. Soon they were clear of the congestion and headed toward downtown Houston on the freeway.

"We have been briefed about your mission," Uri said.

"I require a helper," Viktor said.

"It is all arranged," Uri replied smiling.

"I have other needs as well."

"Tell me what they are and we will get them for you. Do you smoke?" Uri pulled out a pack of Marlboros but Viktor ignored the offer and instead turned to stare out the window at the city that sprawled out flat and mindless as far as the eye could see. How could anyone hope to find a lone individual in such a place? He needed sleep. He faced forward and noticed a pair of dark eyes regarding him in the rear view mirror.

"Were you born here or in Russia?" he asked his guides.

"In Magnitogorsk," Tatyana said from the front seat, her gaze darting from the mirror to the road ahead and back again.

"That makes you a mountain girl," he said.

"My sister misses home," Uri added cheerfully. "I do not. I love America; it is so easy to make money here."

An hour later they dropped Viktor off at the Hyatt Regency where a room had been reserved for him.

*   *   *

THE NEXT MORNING there was a knock at the door.

"Yes?" he called. He had just showered and was lounging in his robe watching *Top Chef* on television, his hair uncombed.

"It is Tatyana," came the voice from the other side.

He switched off the TV and let her in. She was carrying two small aluminum suitcases.

"These are the things you requested," she said in Russian as she walked over and placed them on the round table that stood between the bed and the sliding glass door to the balcony.

Viktor examined her closely. She was tall for a woman, nearly his own height, and strikingly beautiful. Her face was European, long and narrow with high cheekbones, but her dark penetrating eyes had something of Asia in them. This was not surprising; Russia was an enormous country that stretched across eleven time zones and encompassed many exotic peoples and lands. He also took note of her clothes, a pair of tight-fitting black jeans and a cobalt blue silk blouse with short sleeves. Her black hair, cut very short on the sides, but longer in back, gave her a slightly androgynous persona which only added to her sexual attraction. He imagined she could have any man she wanted.

He stepped over to the cases and snapped the latches to examine the contents. Inside one was a nine-millimeter Glock with two extra clips, a roll of three-inch tape, a pair of night-vision goggles, and a thin plastic box containing a syringe and a vial of clear liquid. The other case contained a tan-colored vest with Velcro straps and a set of ceramic plates. The vest was designed to be worn under a shirt and guaranteed by the manufacturer, *Bulletproof Me* of Austin, Texas, to stop small arms' fire at close range.

"When will my helper arrive?" he asked.

"I am to be your helper," she said. Under the Communists in the old days, women had been regarded, at least officially, as equals. Viktor, however, had little experience working with women and was annoyed with the arrangement. He needed to talk to Uri. He turned without speaking and gazed at the city through the glass door, his mind weighing the options. Tatyana wasn't young enough to be his daughter but there was a gulf of years between them. Could he rely on her? After a minute, he turned back to Tatyana.

"We will speak English," he said. "Do you have a car?"

"Yes, the one we used yesterday."

"We may also need a cargo van. Not now, later."

"Of course."

"Are you married?"

"No."

"I am surprised."

She looked down and Viktor realized he had embarrassed her. He felt an unexpected impulse to touch her, to comfort her. Instead he called upon his training as a officer—detachment and analysis.

"Do you own fashionable clothes? Can you dress with class and distinction?"

"Like a rich American woman?" The question had confused her.

He made up his mind. He would adapt to circumstances; that was the most important lesson he had learned during his years in Special Forces. Make the best use of available resources, material and human. He had expected a male assistant, but had been provided with a female instead. She was obviously strong, intelligent, and attractive. He would find uses for such qualities.

"Never mind," he said with a wave of his hand. "We will go today and buy you some clothes. Come back in one hour."

THE RACKS, SHELVES, and display cases inside Neiman Marcus were so crammed full of merchandise that Viktor was surprised the clerks weren't begging customers to take some of it away for free, just to make room. He was woozy with jet lag which he knew added a splash of absurdity to his perceptions. America was a land of contradictions, so wealthy and yet so immature. He felt as if he were in a dream.

Tatyana came out of the dressing room wearing a smart, steel-gray suit that worked perfectly to accentuate her figure and minimize her height. She would make a good impression on the people at EnerTex.

"You like it?" she asked.

"Very much," Viktor said.

"Then we will take it?"

"Yes. We will take it. The shoes also. Then we must do something to your hair."

"You act like my father."

"Did he buy you expensive clothes?"

"No, I did not mean that."

Viktor flinched. He was increasingly touchy about his age. He was fit. He performed his three dozen push-ups and eighty sit-ups every morning before breakfast. He could still run six miles without getting winded. And yet, despite all this effort, his stomach had grown flabby and his blue eyes appeared tired and washed out when he looked at them in the mirror. And small injuries took longer to heal. But it was when he was around young women that he became acutely aware of the toll that time was taking on his body and Tatyana's remark angered him. It was stupid, he knew, but he was not yet ready to slide mutely into old age. He thought about the girl at the party in Moscow with the tattoo around her neck. He had trotted after her like a hungry calf. They had danced and drank vodka together. They went outside into the alley with others of her group and smoked marijuana and then went inside and danced some more. The music was loud and he felt self-conscious. He asked her to go home with him but she only laughed and walked away. Then she began dancing with a teenager with long oily hair and a ring in his nose. Viktor felt a loathing for himself such as he had never known; there seemed to be no place in the new Russia for him. That was when he decided to go and see Gromonov. Finding people was Viktor Degtyar's specialty.

*   *   *

THAT NIGHT HE made love to Tatyana. It happened effortlessly. She drove him back to the hotel and he offered to buy her a drink. She had only one and then asked him to take her up to his room. He was surprised but agreed. And then she was in his arms. It had been a long time and he was grateful. Afterwards, as she was drifting off to sleep, doubts assailed him. Could they work together now? Would she follow orders? He thought about telling Uri to find him someone else, but realized if he did he might never see her again. He reached his hand over and gently stroked her dark hair. His heart felt like a frozen river cracking and breaking apart in the spring thaw. It was a physical pain inside his chest. He rolled over onto his side away from her. He would not call Uri. He would trust luck's good hand and his own intuition for both had served him well in Afghanistan and brought him out again safely. Tatyana was nobody's fool. She would do what was asked of her skillfully and without question. And if not, well, what did it matter? He suspected he was dead already.

23

To compare the offices of the EnerTex Corporation with those of CLEAN, the Citizens' Law and Energy Action Network, would be akin to comparing the Waldorf Astoria Hotel in New York City to the Moonglow Motel in Sioux Falls, Iowa. To Reb, they belonged to different universes.

"We have an appointment to see Sheila Kennedy," Reb said to the young woman in the outer office, a college intern was his guess.

"Sheila's not back from lunch yet but you can wait for her in her office, if you want. It's down the hall, third door on the right."

The Thurston Building had been constructed in 1926 and the windows of the director's office looked out onto a metal fire escape. A score or more of framed photographs covered the remaining walls, many of them featuring the smiling likeness of a short woman with bushy red hair standing next to some of the better known political progressives of recent memory. These included Ralph Nader, Bella Abzug, Barry Commoner, Dennis Kucinich, and Lyle Workman. One photograph particularly caught Reb's eye. It was a black-and-white 5 X 7 of a little girl, ten or so years old, standing on a dock hand-in hand with John F. Kennedy, a thicket of sailboat masts behind them. Reb was peering closely at the photograph when the director walked in and dropped her canvas briefcase onto her desk.

"We're related, but only distantly," she said. "That was taken two years before he was murdered. I remember him as a very funny and lively man."

"I'm Alice Carpenter," Alice said extending her hand.

"I'm Reb Morgan; we talked on the phone."

"I'm sorry I'm late,' the director said, "please, be seated."

"We appreciate you taking the time to talk to us, Ms. Kennedy," Reb said.

"Please, call me Sheila. Any friend of Lyle Workman is a friend of mine. Now what can I do for you?"

"As I mentioned when we spoke on the telephone, we're investigating a power plant in west Texas that's owned by the EnerTex Corporation. Several of the workers claim that something at the plant is making them sick."

"EnerTex is something of a mystery if you haven't figured that out already," Sheila said.

Would it be okay if I record our discussion?" Reb asked and the director gave her consent.

"Did you grow up in Texas?" Alice asked as Reb set up the equipment.

"No, I was raised mostly in Italy. After college I worked in the Middle East for a couple of years and then came here."

"Do you like Texas?" Alice knew the questions were off topic, but given her own recent experiences, she was curious.

"Texas is an enigma, a mixture of the very good and the very bad. Some days I love it to death, but then there are days when I wish I was as far away from here as possible, especially Houston." She gave a slight lift to her shoulders. "But I guess if you want to keep an eye on the foxes, it's best to stay near the hen house. And when it comes to energy, Houston's the biggest hen house on the planet."

"We can start now," Reb said—his practice was to wear headphones at the start of the interview to make the sure the levels were set correctly but then take them off in case they might intimidate the person he was interviewing. "Perhaps you could give us an overview of current energy policy in the United

States," he said. "It might help us understand what's going on with EnerTex."

"Do you want the short form or the long form?"

Reb considered his answer. The short form, as she called it, would make his job a lot easier when he was back in the studio—the proportion between raw interview tape and a ready-for-broadcast program could run as high as a hundred-to-one. But there was also the risk with the truncated version that he might miss some crucial piece of information. He looked at Alice who shrugged as if to say, "we've come this far, we might as well get it all." And if the EnerTex story didn't pan out, at least they'd have enough material for a general purpose story about the energy industry.

"Is there a medium form?" he asked and the director smiled.

"Just stop me if I get long-winded; part of my job is testifying before regulatory boards and the state assembly."

She made herself comfortable by rotating her chair so that she addressed the microphone at an angle rather than speaking directly into it.

"The first thing most people think about when someone mentions energy is oil. But oil is about transportation and manufacturing, and to a lesser extent home heating. But our work here at CLEAN is primarily focused on electricity, how it's generated, transmitted, and sold to the consumer. We spend a great deal of time dealing with 'the gang of four,' coal, natural gas, hydro, and nuclear."

"What about alternatives such as solar and wind?" Alice asked.

"We'll talk about them later, but for a highly centralized electrical power system to work, the kind of system we have in this country, you have to have what is called 'baseload generation.' That means a certain number of power plants have to be making electricity all the time. With wind, when the wind blows a little, the blades turn a little; when the wind blows a lot, the blades turn a lot. The same goes for solar panels which generate power only during the daytime and when it isn't raining or cloudy."

"So what you need is baseload generation?" Reb said.

"Yes, and baseload plants are at the bottom of what an electric utility calls its 'resource stack.' If they have nuclear, coal, hydro, and natural gas plants in their resource stack then nuclear, which must run all the time, is dispatched first to meet demand, then coal, then hydro and gas."

"Why in that order?" Reb asked.

"Because of something called 'ramp rates' which is how long it takes a particular plant to begin or stop producing power. Nukes have a long ramp rate; the fuel rods have to be inserted into the reactor and the water heated up before the turbine begins turning. Coal takes a long time also. It has to heat up to the point where it's burning efficiently. In comparison, gas ramps up very quickly, and hydro begins generating electricity almost immediately. The same processes take place when taking a plant off-line."

"What do you do with surplus electricity if it's suddenly not needed?" Alice asked.

"That's a good question because the thing about electricity is that you can't store it. You have to run it on the grid, minimize it, open switches, schedule it out, relay it along. You shut down every other kind of generation you can and switch plants to what's called 'spinning reserve,' because the nukes have to keep running; you can't ramp them down at a moment's notice. The real trick then is coming up with a way to accurately predict energy consumption in advance so the power plants that take longer to ramp up or down can do so without causing the system to fail."

"How's that done?" Reb asked.

"By looking at weather forecasts, time of day, day of the week, seasons of the year, anything that will influence how much electricity people might want. The terms used are 'high-load hours' and 'low-load hours.' A low-load hour, for example, would be three o'clock in the morning on a Sunday in June. Almost everybody is at home and in bed. They don't have to go to work. They haven't begun taking showers. They're not running their heaters or air conditioners; they're not sitting at their computers or watching television."

"Who does all this predicting?" Alice asked.

"The grid operators. They work on what's called 'day-ahead schedules' and 'hour-ahead schedules.' Those are the main ones. Sometimes they work on 'ten minute-ahead schedules.' It happens like this. I'm a utility. I call a generator and say, 'In the next hour I'll need twenty megawatts of power.' Now the generator knows an hour ahead how much electricity to produce and ramps his power plants up or down accordingly. It's all done with computers."

"It sounds incredibly complicated," Alice said.

"It is."

"Could you talk more about baseload generation?" Reb asked. It felt a bit like sitting in class but he found the topic fascinating and hoped KVMR listeners would agree.

"Well as I said, that's where the gang of four comes in. But there are problems with each. Some of the biggest problems, for example, come from burning coal. Putting aside all the environmental damage and worker health and safety issues that come with mining it, burning coal produces high levels of CO_2 which contributes to global warming. Coal also spews a variety of toxic pollutants into the air and water including sulfuric acid and mercury. A third of our country's lakes, and nearly a quarter of our rivers, are contaminated with so much mercury that the fish are not safe to eat. That's 100,000 lakes and 800,000 miles of rivers currently under advisory."

"I heard that something like 30,000 people a year die prematurely because of power plant pollution." Alice said. "Is that true?"

"That's true," Sheila said, "and given the policies of the current administration the problem promises to only get worse."

She swung about to reach a filing cabinet from which she pulled out a printed booklet.

"Here's a copy of the study; it was funded by the Pew Charitable Trusts. You can have it, I have more." She passed the study to Alice.

"So that's coal. And then there's nuclear power. It generates highly radioactive waste that's unbelievably dangerous and that no one is quite sure what to do with. Natural gas, on the other hand, is a more desirable fuel than either coal or nuclear. It burns cleaner but it still contributes to global warming. There's been a real 'dash for gas' in recent years because gas-powered plants are relatively cheap to construct, and until recently, gas prices were low in comparison with other fuels. Unfortunately, domestic gas reserves are in decline and prices for natural gas have shot way up. Still, they have to supply all these new power plants, which will require drilling hundreds of thousands of new gas wells."

"Why so many wells?" Alice asked.

"Gas wells are not like oil wells because a typical natural gas well gives up half its capacity in just two years. So the only way to get more gas is to drill more wells. But there just isn't that much gas underground in North America. We're running out and yet our energy consumption continues to climb.

That leaves hydro, which is a relatively clean technology for generating electricity, but there are problems such as endangering salmon runs by damming rivers. Besides, hydro supplies only a fraction of our current energy needs."

"Aren't utilities in the process of retiring many of their older coal and nuke plants?" Reb asked.

"Not nearly enough of them," Sheila said, her expression grave.

"Why not?"

"Vested interests. Ignorance. Public indifference. Flawed legislation," she shook her head. "It's cheaper operating a polluting, depreciated asset than it is to build a new, cleaner burning power plant. But there's also a psychological component to all this, especially among many old-school politicians and utility managers. It's the belief that real men *burn* things. It would be laughable if the consequences weren't so dire.

"Let me tell you an interesting story. In the mid to late nineties, the Texas Public Utilities Commission was wrestling with how best to bring market forces to bear on the electric system. They adopted a process called IRP, which is short for 'Integrated Resource Planning.' Under IRP, when a utility is faced with growing demand for electricity, the utility and rate payers decide together whether promoting conservation would be preferable to, say, building a new power plant. In other words, it might be cheaper to go out and switch everybody's light bulbs to compact florescents and save the equivalent of a power plant. There are environmental externalities to consider in building a new power plant as well. What do emissions cost society as a whole? Those sorts of questions. And to help do this, a professor at the University of Texas came up with a concept called 'deliberative polling,' because by law an IRP requires public participation.

"So this professor developed a process to scientifically select a cross-section of people within a community, several hundred people, much the same way they pick people for polling in politics; bring them in on a Friday night and give them an extensive poll with questions like, 'Where does your electricity come from?' 'Do you know what the impacts of a coal plant are?' 'Would you rather have cheaper energy or a clean environment?' I have copies of the polls I can show you. Then all day Saturday, they bring in speakers and specialists from the coal industry, the nuclear industry, the air emissions' folks, economists, and renewable energy experts and environmentalists, to educate these selected people on the electricity system, on the economics, the environmental impacts, all of it. Then on Sunday, they poll them again. That's what deliberative polling means: bring them in, teach them, let them think about it, then poll them again."

"And did their opinions change?" Reb asked.

"There was a huge change. I talked to some of the executives from one of the big utilities later and they admitted, rather sheepishly, that they picked Abilene, Corpus Christi, and a town in Arkansas because they knew they were conservative communities and would give them the answer they wanted, which was to build another big coal or gas plant. They said they had ranchers banging on the table saying, "I want clean air for my grandkids, and you better build renewables, and you better spend money on energy efficiency." This is a true story. And the executives got these results in all three towns. Then other utilities went forward with their own IRPs and got similar results: in Beaumont, Texas, with blue collar dock workers; in El Paso, with low-income and minority rate payers; in San Antonio, Houston, and Dallas, across income levels, party lines, and demographics people were saying the same thing: do we want efficient, renewable energy. By consistent margins of sixty plus percent they were saying, "I'll pay more money to conserve the environment. I'll pay five, eight, ten dollars more a month on my electric bill if that's what it takes." It blew previous assumptions out of the water, especially those of the politicians, regulators, and utility managers. They thought people wanted the lowest rates and that was that. In fact, the chairman of the commission, a die-hard market based Republican if ever there was one, said he had a religious conversion to renewable wind energy because of what happened."

"Was there any tangible follow-up?" Reb asked.

"Here in Texas, in 1999, we passed a restructuring law to bring more market forces to the electricity industry with a requirement to build two thousand megawatts of renewable energy. Texas now has more wind power generation than any other state in the union, except for California, which began building its system in 1980."

"Did Republicans support it?" Reb asked.

"Republicans and Democrats both; it didn't fall along party lines," Sheila said.

"But why are the utilities so committed to fossil fuels if their rate payers want renewables?" Reb said.

"They have a huge amount of money invested in these existing technologies and it's what they know how to do."

"And real men burn things," Alice said and Sheila nodded.

"The big problem on the horizon when it comes to dirty coal plants," the director continued, "is what's going on in China and India right now. At least some of our newer plants have scrubbers and bag houses to clean up the emissions, although not the CO_2. But in China and India, because they want to electrify their countries, they burn poor quality, high-sulfur coal in their power plants, and they don't have the capital to put all the pollution control bells and whistles on them. So in a real sense, if we,

meaning the United States, don't come up with baseload generating technology that is viable—that is competitive on a capital
basis with coal—or develop new affordable technologies to clean
up coal emissions and reduce CO_2, then we're going to see China
and India building many more inefficient, dirty coal-fired plants.

"And that's where the argument about global warming and
the Kyoto Treaty comes in. The legislators who opposed it say
countries in the developing world should comply with the same
CO_2 emission standards as the United States, and if they don't get
that, they're not going to sign on. In other words, why should the
United States make sacrifices if China and India aren't willing to
do the same? It's a logical argument, but it's woefully nearsighted
because it ignores the fact that we're responsible for fifty percent
of the anthropomorphic CO_2 in the atmosphere today. And they
don't see that by developing new technologies to control our own
emissions we will have a huge market for those same technologies in China, India, and other third world countries. The United
States should step up to the plate and create the technology we
need and which we can then export to these huge global markets.
It's a win-win proposition for everybody."

"Didn't Enron build a big power plant in India?" Reb asked.

"Yes, the Dabhol project," Sheila said.

"Was it a coal-fired plant?" Reb said.

"No, it was fueled by LNG, liquefied natural gas."

"Do they have a lot of natural gas in India?" Alice said.

"The plan was to bring it in on ships. Part of the project—I
think the budget was right around a billion dollars—was to
construct elaborate docking and storage facilities as well as build
the power plant."

"Is LNG a viable fuel alternative for generating electricity?"
Reb asked.

"Not for the United States. You see, until now we have
generated the electricity in this country from domestic fuels, if
you include fuels that come in from Canada. But if you look at
factors like the depletion and replacement rates for gas wells,
you'll see that our gas reserves are topped off. And yet ninety-

five percent or more of the proposed generation being built in this country is gas fired. These plants literally drink the stuff. I'll give you an example. The State of Washington recently permitted three thousand megawatts of new gas-fired generation. This will increase overall natural gas consumption in the state by one hundred and forty-seven percent—that's two and a half times what it is now. So where are they going to get the gas? That's the big question."

The director leaned forward.

"Thirty years ago, the United States found itself facing the same dilemma concerning its transportation system. We didn't have sufficient domestic oil reserves to keep pace with the growing demand for gasoline and diesel fuel so we either had to re-engineer our transportation system for greater efficiency or begin importing oil. Well, you know what we decided and it wasn't very long until we found ourselves in bed with some pretty unsavory governments. The war in Iraq is just another tragic example of this failed energy policy.

There was an abrupt silence which Reb noticed happened more and more in conversations when the Iraq War was mentioned. Each held his dark thoughts inside but those thoughts were very much the same. A failed oil man from Texas, with the tacit and at times enthusiastic support of big media, had led the nation into a senseless war that left hundreds of thousands of men, women, and children dead or wounded, gutted domestic social and educational programs, fostered corporate corruption and war profiteering on an unimaginable scale, and gravely damaged the international reputation of the United States for years to come. Had there been more to this Greek tragedy than an unquenchable thirst for oil? Reb didn't buy the bogus "spreading democracy" rationale. So what was it then? Were the Gods angry with the people of the United States and determined to punish them? Were they angry with the people of Iraq also? Reb didn't think so. Then it had to be oil. Oil and the stupidly of arrogance.

As if sensing Reb's mood, the director asked, "Would you like me to continue?"

"Yes, please," he said checking the time display on the recorder to make sure there was enough remaining disk space.

"Well as I said, when it comes to generating electricity, the United States until now has been relatively self-sufficient. But that is about to change. We can't keeping burning coal for all kinds of reasons, we're running out of natural gas, and people don't want nuclear. So we either learn how to conserve and develop renewables, or we begin importing fuel for our power plants.

"What about 'clean coal' technology?" Alice asked. "A lot of politicians are talking about it."

"The industry believes it can come up a way to eliminate harmful pollutants, such as mercury and sulfuric acid, while sequestering the CO_2 at the same time. But that's a tall order and still very much in the future."

"So what kind of fuel will be import?' Reb asked.

"Liquefied natural gas. And this LNG won't be coming from nice peaceful places like Japan or western Europe but from political hotspots like the Middle East, Nigeria, and Siberia."

She paused again to allow in the import of what she was saying to sink in.

"Can you explain how natural gas is liquefied?" Reb asked.

"Sure. After the gas comes out of the ground, it has to be cooled to minus two hundred and seventy-three degrees Fahrenheit. Last June I visited an LNG plant on the Kenai Peninsula in Alaska that ships LNG to Japan. You walk up to these massive compression turbines and they're encrusted with a mantle of ice that's eight inches thick because they've got to keep the gas so cold. It's unbelievable. Then to ship it, they have to use special cryogenic tankers. It takes ten percent of the load of LNG on the ship just to keep the rest of the gas cold enough to get it to wherever it's going. Now can you imagine the security concerns having these large ships filled with LNG sailing the open seas and massive storage tanks on shore? Each tank holds anywhere from two to six billion gallons of LNG. What would it take for a terrorist to blow one of them up? Or if there was an accident?"

"It's a good plot for a Tom Clancy novel," Reb said.

"If one of these facilities went up, the fireball would be absolutely horrific."

"How many of these facilities are there?" Alice asked.

"There are presently three in the United States, two on the Atlantic Coast, and one on the Gulf Coast. But as we import more LNG, we will need additional facilities for converting the LNG back into vapor and putting it into our gas pipelines. They'll have to be built in underdeveloped shoreline areas because they require extensive infrastructure. Sadly, most of this is happening now, under the radar screen as far as the average citizen is concerned. There are currently thirty to forty proposals for new LNG facilities in the United States. So in the last couple of years, instead of learning our lessons from the transportation sector and planning for continuation of our energy independence in the electric sector, we're blithely going about becoming dependent on foreign fuel sources for our electricity. The political and economic implications are profound. And yet there are alternatives like wind and solar, geothermal and bio-fuels just waiting to be developed and used. Not to mention conservation. In fact, we have so much wind in this country, there's no reason whatsoever that we need to become net importers to meet our electrical needs."

"Wind is that big?" Reb asked. He had always thought solar was the most promising new energy source.

"We have enough wind in North and South Dakota, Montana, and Texas alone to power our electrical needs many times over. Many times over!"

"So why isn't wind happening?" Alice asked.

"It's not happening because wind power has been more expensive than other sources. It still is, but only slightly so, unless you factor in what's called 'environmental externalities.'"

"What are environmental externalities? Alice asked.

"The price of disposing of nuclear waste or the costs that come with burning dirty coal, such as health problems, acid rain, and global warming. These are *external* to your utility bill and yet they are subsidized by all of us, through the government and higher insurance premiums. The concept of environmental externalities has been a hot topic in the electric industry for the last twenty years."

"It's generational too," Reb said, "because we're passing these costs onto our children, and to their children."

"The problem is we externalize the true cost of these technologies. But if we *internalized* that cost, then wind and other renewables would easily become competitive in the market place."

Reb recalled his earlier meeting with Charles Hathaway at EnerTex and Hathaway's assertion that solar was a non-starter. "What about the claim that it takes more energy to produce a solar panel than it produces?"

"It's bandied about by industry insiders all time, but it's not true. And there are some good numbers on it. One company's new solar wafer, for instance, gets an energy payback in two to three years so that over the lifetime of the solar cell, you come out way ahead."

"What are other countries doing about renewables?" Alice asked.

"Germany, Spain, Denmark,—even Ireland, are building wind as fast as they can. And there's been some progress here in the states. General Electric bought out Enron Wind, and when GE gets into the wind business, you can bet it's a viable technology."

"Can you talk about hydrogen?" Alice said. "Isn't that a viable fuel?"

"A lot of people seem to think so but the question remains, where do you get the hydrogen? Do you get it from fossil fuels? If so, then you're still exhausting CO_2 into the atmosphere; you haven't changed a thing. They talk about hydrogen, how clean it is. They say you can burn it in a car engine and drink the water that comes out the tail pipe and that's true, but the hydrogen has to come from somewhere. Until you find another source for hydrogen, you're still creating an emission by-product, a disordered product out of an ordered energy source." Sheila Kennedy suddenly laughed. "So there's my sermon."

"What do you see happening with global warming?" Reb said. "How serious is it?"

"I was in New Mexico two weeks ago with my husband. His brother just sold his house and we helped him move. We were in a piñon-juniper forest and thirty to forty percent of the forest around the house is now dead because of beetle kill. The winters apparently have not been cold enough in recent years to kill the bark beetles that get into the trees and destroy them. Around Santa Fe there's an eighty to ninety percent kill rate in the forest. I don't claim to know all the impacts, or potential impacts of global warming, but we could lose the Gulf Stream and other major circulating currents in the oceans, and we have no idea what that would do to weather patterns around the world."

"Why would we lose these currents?" Alice asked.

"Because the big currents are driven by the temperature differentials between the atmosphere and the water, from the polar caps to the equatorial belt."

"Which means," Reb added, "that if the cold isn't as cold, then you have less differential, thus less current."

"There's some good speculative science that predicts doom for the ocean currents. Europe is kept warm by the Gulf Stream, so most of Europe could turn into a one huge icebox. Other predictions say there will be more temperature extremes rather than just a massive heating effect. You could have hotter and colder spots, therefore more temperature differentials in the atmosphere. That means more unpredictable and volatile storms, what some scientists call "super storms." What happened to New Orleans and the Gulf Coast may be a harbinger of things to come. Do you want me to go on?"

"If you want to," Reb said.

"Okay, then what about the crops we need? Will a shift of only a few degrees, let's say, destroy the wheat and corn belt in this country? What makes this country strong is our ability to grow enough food to feed our population, and if we lose that ability, we become, what, the next Rome?

"There are two things to keep in mind. One, electricity is the most capital intensive industry on the planet, and, two, it's the most polluting. It's responsible for a third of all CO_2 emissions and seventy percent of sulfur emissions. And then you have the mercury, which I've already mentioned. At least half of the mercury emissions in this country are linked to making electricity, but the utility operators, who know full well what's going on, still won't put mercury scrubbers on their plants. They don't want to spend the money."

"What about EnerTex?" Reb asked. "What's their story?"

"EnerTex is a mystery, as I said. They claim their ATG process is entirely non-polluting—no radioactive waste, no mercury or sulfuric acid, and perhaps most importantly as far as global warming goes, zero CO_2 emissions."

"So that's good?" Alice said.

"Very good if it's true. The trouble is they hide behind the veil of national security and won't reveal what kind of fuel they're using. As far as anyone can tell, it's not nuclear or geothermal."

"Hydrogen?" Alice asked.

Sheila shrugged. "Then where are they getting the hydrogen? It might be a new kind of cold fusion process—that's what the smart money believes—but I have a hard time going there."

"So what *is* your theory?" Reb asked.

"I don't have one. Whatever they're doing just doesn't make sense, given what we know about the physics of generating electricity."

"But if it works?" Reb said.

"If their technology is as good as it's rumored to be, then all bets are off. Coal, nuclear, gas, even renewables, might all go the way of the buggy whip. But EnerTex won't let anyone have a close look. We've been trying to get them to give us something, anything. We even sued the government under the Freedom of Information Act." She shook her head. "That was a joke. What files we did manage to get were so blacked out we could have used them for roofing paper."

"Have you heard anything about worker health issues at the Ranger 1 power plant?" Reb asked.

"Just what you told me when you called. Have you had any luck identifying what's making them ill?"

Reb shook his head. "It doesn't appear to be a known toxin."

They sat looking at each other, no one sure what to say next. Reb switched off the recorder.

"I'm sorry I couldn't be of more help with EnerTex," Sheila said with a sigh, "but at least now you know a little more about the electrical energy industry."

"A lot more," Reb said. "Thank you."

While Alice talked with Sheila about her childhood in Italy Reb broke down the equipment. So much of modern life was about electricity, he mused. The lights, the air-conditioning, even the mini-recorder he was packing away was powered by batteries that he had recharged the night before in a Houston hotel room—with electricity from the Ranger 1 plant as far as he knew. How strange and different the modern world was from that of his forebears. His grandfather, his mother's father, had come into the world in 1892 in a room that was illuminated by an oil lamp. Water was pumped by hand from a well in the backyard and entertainment was provided by an upright parlor piano. Outside on the dirt street of the small farming town where they lived, horse-drawn wagons lumbered by. Now, little more than a hundred years later, a span in the fabric of human time no wider than a single thread, his grandson went to bed surrounded by dozens of little green lights that glowed unwinking in the dark. They came from his Sony 900 MHz wireless telephone, his Sharp fax/answering machine, his I-Mac computer, his D-Link ethernet router, his GE microwave, his Panasonic clock radio, and, hiding like some shy animal under his desk, his APS surge protector with battery-power back up. And all because of electricity. How different his life would be without it.

24

AVERY PUSHED THE call button on the intercom.

"Brenda, call Hathaway and find out how it went with the activists from California." He used of the word "activists" instead of "journalists" intentionally. He saw no reason to elevate their importance, if only slightly.

"You're meeting with the Russians in ten minutes," she said.

"Where?"

"Conference room H."

"Who will be there?"

"Harricks, McBride, and Bruckmeister. Mr. Tannerwith will be on video link. I also invited Linda Orana in case we need a translator."

The Russians were punctual to the minute, which Avery took as a good sign. The man introduced himself as retired Colonel Viktor Degtyar. There was a military-bred precision to his posture and mannerisms that Avery liked. The colonel was accompanied by an exceptionally attractive woman.

"This is my executive assistant, Miss Kreshenko," Viktor said.

Tatyana acknowledged the introduction with a demure smile and a slight nod that left the men in the room captivated—a simple but effective strategy, Viktor knew. Distract your enemy and you reduce his concentration; reduce his concentration and you lessen his caution.

"Mr. Valentin Gromonov, president of Kamal Oil and Gas Corporation," Viktor launched into his presentation, "has authorized me to explore opportunities that may prove beneficial to both our companies. I am speaking, of course, about your new process for electrical generation. Russia is a vast country with a rich history. . ."

Avery leaned back in his chair. Russians were much like Indians in that they enjoyed making grand speeches. That was not his style; he preferred to get to the point. Still, he would let the colonel get the speechifying out of his system.

". . . the Russian people are industrious and clever. We have entered upon a new era. The political mistakes of the past are behind us and as free market capitalism grows in Russia, so will the economy and the demand for electrical energy. We have significant oil and gas reserves but no resource can last forever—"

"Excuse me, Colonel, but how large a stake does Kamal have in the Caspian oil fields?" The interrupter was Guy Tannerwith, head of EuroTex, an EnerTex subsidiary with headquarters in Brussels, whose larger-than-life-size face was displayed on the flat screen at the end of the conference room.

"It is estimated that the Kurmangazy field contains five billion barrels of oil," Viktor recited from memory. "Kamal has a thirty-five per cent stake in the Kurmangazy field."

"What about the nearby Khvalynskoe field?" Tannerwith continued.

Viktor turned to Tatyana who handed him a sheet of paper.

"Eleven point three per cent," he said, "but Kamal's share will grow to nearly twenty percent within the next six months."

There was a stirring of quickened interest around the table.

"How will Kamal acquire this bigger share?" Tannerwith again. The fact that Kamal owned thirty-five per cent of the Kurmangazy field and roughly eleven percent of the Khvalynskoe field was common knowledge. That Kamal was about to acquire additional holdings was *big* news. There would be a flurry of hurried phone calls from EnerTex executives to their stockbrokers as soon as the meeting ended.

"We have been in negotiations with GUK to transfer its holdings in the Khvalynskoe field to us in the near future," Viktor said. Extortion would be a more honest description for what was going on between Gromonov and GUK's management, but Viktor assumed EnerTex knew who they were dealing with, and the less said about means the better.

Ron McBride, vice president of marketing, spoke up. "What is the state of relations between Kamal and the other countries that border the Caspian Sea? I am speaking about Iran in particular. How will their claims upon the oil reserves effect Kamal's future operations?"

"I cannot go into political considerations in detail," Viktor said, "but what I *can* say is that we've reached agreements that will enable Kamal to expand its activities in the region without interference from Iran."

Avery jotted some figures down on the note pad in front of him. Just taking the Kurmangazy field alone, a thirty-five percent stake amounted to one billion, seven hundred million barrels of oil. This told him all he needed to know. He slid the pad in front of McBride who scanned the figures and nodded. They were thinking the same thing. Kamal was the real deal. They possessed the financial resources, and more importantly, the political clout, to partner with EnerTex. In pursuing his business interests, Avery followed a simple dictum that he had learned from his father. It went: *pigs get fat, hogs get slaughtered*. If EnerTex wanted to expand its operations into other countries, the best way to do so was to seek out partnerships with local companies rather than trying to go it alone. Let the partners have a taste of the profits, so long as they shouldered a substantial portion of the risk. At the end of the day, there would be more than enough profit to go around.

There was, however, one major drawback to this approach. The United States government had classified EnerTex's ATG technology ultra top-secret which meant it could not be shared with any country, not even a close ally. That was the deal Avery had struck with Ron Jarrell back when Ron was working out of the White House for the new president's father.

"EnerTex will get exclusive access to the technology," Jarrell told him, "even before the military. EnerTex, however, must not, under any circumstances, reveal details of the technological process to any other party."

Secrecy wasn't a problem when it came to expanding out of Texas into other states. It became more complicated when other countries were involved. The solution eventually decided upon was that EnerTex would build and maintain the ATG reactor and containment building for each new overseas power plant, while a company from the host country would be given the contract to construct the rest of the facility. Furthermore, the host country was required to extend to each EnerTex plant the same diplomatic status enjoyed by American embassies around the world. Under this special arrangement, any and all attempts to enter an EnerTex facility without permission by officials of the host country would be viewed as an invasion of the sovereign territory of the United States, prompting a vigorous military response by said country.

Predictably, this did not sit well with several European countries and in time the European Union was drawn into the fray. The EnerTex Corporation, however, backed up by the United States government held firm: no special status, no power plants. Stalemate. Inaction. Letters of clarification. Back channel negotiations. Requests from delegations from France and Spain to visit the Ranger 1 plant in Texas taken under advisement. Volatility in the energy sector of the equity markets. But Avery Axton knew the Europeans would come around in the end. They had to. Electricity was the most valuable and essential commodity on earth. And until they did, here were the Russians offering friendship and cooperation. The idea appealed to Avery. Kamal wasn't an electric utility; they were an oil and gas company. But they came with capital and the right connections. There was also the odd twist that what EnerTex was offering them had been discovered by one of their own. Avery's appreciation of the irony, however, was cut short.

"We understand that Anatoly Kryuchkov is an employee of the EnerTex Corporation," Viktor said matter-of-factly. "Is that true?"

Avery's exterior facade held, but inside alarms clanged away.

"I'm sorry," Avery adopted a look of pleasant if slightly muddled surprise. "Who did you say?" He would have to get on to Jarrell immediately. As far as he had been told, no one, and Jarrell had emphasized the words *no one*, knew of Kryuchkov's defection to the United States. The KGB ruled his death a suicide. They had the body; the dental records checked out. Jarrell bragged that it was one of the most successful operations in the Company's history—by *Company*, he meant CIA, not EnerTex.

"Anatoly Kryuchkov," Viktor repeated.

"Bob," Avery said turning to McBride, "do we have anyone working for us by that name?"

McBride shook his head. "Not that I know of, Mr. Axton, but I'll check into it." He then asked Viktor to spell the last name so he could write it down. His part was utterly convincing. It should be. Senior as he was, McBride had never heard the name Kryuchkov before, nor had he any reason to connect the name to Dr. Walter Easler, someone he had only met a half-dozen times at most.

"It is not important," Viktor said, with a brush of his hand, "we can discuss him later. I have papers here that detail Kamal holdings, its corporate officers, and recent financial statements." Again he looked to Tatyana who removed a thin folder from her briefcase that she handed to Viktor who then passed it to Avery.

"He is my uncle," Tatyana said to everyone's surprise except Viktor's.

"Who is your uncle?" Avery asked, looking up from the documents, genuinely confused.

"Dr. Kryuchkov. He is my mother's brother. I was hoping I might see him while I was here in Texas."

Avery was not big on surprises and this one had the acid taste of a bad practical joke. The most important person at EnerTex, except for himself, was this young woman's uncle? Unbelievable.

He fought to maintain his composure but his thoughts, and with them his emotions, momentarily slipped their halter.

"As I said, I've never heard of your uncle, Miss. . ." Shit! I've forgotten her name—

"Miss Kreshenko," Brenda to the rescue, "if your uncle works for our company, we'll make sure that he gives you a call. Are you staying at the Hyatt?"

"Yes. In room 1423."

The brief exchange allowed Avery time to regain his balance and he deftly steered the conversation away from Kryuchkov to how Kamal and EnerTex might work together. It was a complex and interesting conversation, but irrelevant for Viktor now that he had the answer he came for. Avery Axton might be an experienced and skilled negotiator but Tatyana's comment had clearly unsettled him, a worrisome shadow passing over his eyes like a cloud across a sunlit landscape. The hunter in Viktor was aroused; game was in the field and he would pursue it. Tatyana's performance was flawless. He looked forward to expressing his gratitude later that evening.

25

SOMETIME DURING THE dark hours of the morning, the Porsche's tires singing their monotonous song to the asphalt of Interstate 10, Marty's efforts to formulate a plan B took on the character of a straw fire inside his cocaine-addled brain, bursting forth in a flash of brilliance and enthusiasm but then quickly sputtering away into irrelevance and absurdity. Phase one of the plan went like this: the morning rush hour would be getting underway by the time he reached Houston. He knew Morgan and the girl were meeting with Hathaway at EnerTex's corporate headquarters on Smith Street at ten-thirty. It would be difficult trying to pick them up there. There would be downtown traffic to contend with and they might recognize his car. So instead he would go straight to his apartment and spend the morning calling hotels and motels in the city. He was confident Morgan would register using his real name, or the girl would. All Marty had to do was ask to speak to Mr. Paul Morgan or Ms. Alice Carpenter.

The hard part would be learning their room number; hotel switchboard operators were schooled not to divulge such information. That's where phase two came in. He would order a large pizza with extra pepperoni from the pizza joint down the street from his apartment—he was familiar with most of the Pizza Time delivery drivers since pizza was a mainstay of his bachelor diet—and when it showed up, he would buy the driver's red and white striped shirt for fifty dollars—or a hundred dollars. Price didn't matter. He would then go to the hotel wearing the shirt. At the front desk he would make a scene of going through his pockets—damn, he'd lost the order slip.

"The name is Morgan—or Carpenter," he would tell the desk clerk, "Can you give me the room number?" The ruse was sure to work.

That left coming up with a viable phase three, the culmination of all his superior detective work. If Morgan were on his own, Marty could send a prostitute up to his room and get a little blackmail action going, as he had done with Nichols. But it wouldn't work with the Carpenter woman there. He could try and plant dope on them again and get them arrested. But how? He didn't know anyone on the Houston police force, and he sure as shit couldn't call Brewer again. Drug the pizza, that might work. He thought this possibility over for the next fifteen miles. He had heard stories about people traveling in Central America who were given drugs that made them lose their minds for several days. Jimson weed was one. Unfortunately, he didn't have any Jimson weed, nor could he get any on such short notice. And they would be suspicious; they hadn't ordered a pizza with extra pepperoni. Or Morgan might answer the door and recognize him. Or, given how his luck was running, they would both be vegetarians!

Marty reluctantly discarded the drugged pizza idea. Physical threats? What about bribery? He could offer them a thousand dollars each to just go away. They could probably use the money.

His radar sensor began beeping and he moved his foot to the brake pedal; he was going ninety-two. A mile later he passed a Texas highway patrol car lurking beneath an overpass.

He returned to the idea of offering Morgan and the girl money but couldn't muster the necessary enthusiasm. They would be too high minded to take it, a pair of certified idealists. He hated dealing with people over whom money had so little power. It removed the motivation, the leverage.

By the time he reached Columbus, eighty miles east of Houston, he was depressed to discover that his thoughts had fallen into a

rut, repeating themselves inside his skull like a steel ball banging
back and forth in a pinball machine: sex, drugs, violence, bribery,
sex, drugs, violence, bribery, sex, drugs, violence, bribery. . . Too
much cocaine!

He rubbed his eyes and swiveled his head from side to side
to take out the cricks. He checked the time. Four-ten in the
morning. A final decision on phase three would have to wait. He'd
go home first, take a shower, grab an hour or two of sleep and
then pull out the yellow pages and get to work. He switched on
the radio to clear his head. Golden Oldies. He hit the scan button,
searching for a call-in talk show—something along the lines of,
"Doctor Linda, my husband got up this morning and his penis
fell off. I put it in the freezer. Now what should I do?" He found
the endless idiocy of America sorting out its petty problems over
the public airwaves seductively entertaining, especially alone at
night on the highway. But instead of a talk show, he found himself
listening to a high-octane Christian evangelist with a thick East
Texas drawl telling the story of Jonah.

"And God gave Jonah a job to do," the preacher said. "He
told Jonah to go and preach to the people of Nineveh. But Jonah
was afraid. He knew the people of Nineveh; they were a rough
bunch. The Bible says they were full of *wickedness*. They lived
sinful lives and persecuted God's servants. Jonah didn't want to
go there. So he turned away from doing what God wanted and
instead took passage aboard a ship bound for the resort town of
Tarshish, which was about as far away from Nineveh as he could
get. It was spring break and all Jonah wanted to do was hang out
on the beach, drink Margaritas, and watch the pretty girls walk by
in their bikinis."

The church audience laughed. "It doesn't say that in the
Bible," the preacher added, "but that's what was going on." More
laughter.

Corny as hell, Marty thought, but he appreciated the effort to
give the old tale modern legs and he kept listening.

"But God wasn't done with Jonah. No, sir. Not by a long shot.
He needed Jonah. He needed Jonah to preach to the people of

Nineveh. So He called up a mighty storm. It was so bad even the Coast Guard refused to go out in it."

As the preacher related the part about Jonah being thrown overboard and swallowed by the whale, Marty's attention strayed to his own story. Avery sent him to do a job. He agreed to go; he hadn't tried to get out of it like Jonah. But still he failed. Now he was going home hoping to make things right. He hated failure. He tried to focus on what he was going to do when he got back to Houston, but he got caught up in the radio preacher's sermon again.

"Now you might be asking yourself, Why did God need Jonah to go to Nineveh? Why didn't God just go there Himself? The people of Nineveh wouldn't dare give God a hard time. They'd fall down on their knees and repent. Well, my friends, it just don't work that way with God. He's got more important things to do than mess around with some no-account little town. He's got new solar systems to make, whole new galaxies on the drawing board. That's why He needs people like Jonah.

"A couple of years ago I was walking past a Catholic school in a run-down section of Dallas. It was an old school and in front was a statue of Jesus standing with his arms outstretched. Only the hands were missing; some vandals had broken them off. I realized the school was probably struggling just to keep its doors open and maybe they couldn't afford to get the statue repaired. A custodian was sweeping the steps nearby and I went over to him. 'Excuse me,' I said, 'but I'd like to make a contribution to fix the statue of Jesus.' I opened up my wallet and started pulling out some bills but the custodian shook his head and said, 'I don't think the sisters want the statue fixed.' I was baffled. 'Why not?' I asked and he said, 'Because the statue reminds us that *we* need to be the hands of God.'

"Well brothers and sisters, I want to tell you I went away from that place with a new understanding of our relationship to God. And that understanding is this: we need God. No doubt about it. Without God, we're lost. But He also *needs* us. That's right and I know some of you good Christian people out there are saying,

'Brother Emmett, what are you talking about? God doesn't need me; I'm nothing but a worthless sinner.' But God *does* need you. He needs you to do the important work in the world, His work—to be His hands. That's a powerful idea when you think about it. God needs you to feed the hungry, to clothe the naked, to visit the prisoner, and comfort the widow. He doesn't want us wasting our time running after money, sex, or drugs. And he sure as heck doesn't want us building big mega-churches with suspended television screens and rock bands and parking lot attendants." More laughter with some 'amens' thrown in. "And He doesn't want his preachers a-sportin' custom-tailored suits and expensive gold watches. Take a good look at this suit I'm wearing, brothers and sisters. It's three years old and it came off the clearance rack at Sears—and my watch is a twenty dollar Timex."

More hoots and hollers from the congregation.

"God wants us to help where help is needed. To stop thinking about ourselves all the time and start thinking about others who are less fortunate, like them poor people in New Orleans. Of course, we can try and hide from His call to service like Brother Jonah, but it won't do us any good. He'll find us, even at the bottom of the ocean. He knows who we are, each and every one of us, and what potential for good lies within us, even if we don't. All we have to do is *call out* to Him. That's right. It says so in the Bible. 'And then, from inside the belly of the whale, his life ebbing away, Jonah remembered the Lord.'"

Organ music swelled up under the preacher's words signaling the end of the sermon and Marty suddenly felt stupid and switched off the radio. He had no use for preachers, especially the big-time televangelists with their "just send in your money to post office box number so-and-so and we'll pray for you—the more money you send, the harder we'll pray." By the sound of him, Marty didn't think Brother Emmett was in their league, but he couldn't see that it made much difference. They were all peddling the same pie in-the-sky-when-you-die bullshit.

He thought about his grandfather. After his second wife died, the old man became a sucker for such pitches. It was all he talked about. The 700 club. Jimmy Swaggart. Jim and Tammy Faye Bakker. When the family cleaned his house out after the funeral, they couldn't believe the stash of study guides, cassette tapes of sermons, and glow-in-the-dark figurines of Jesus he had sent in for over the years. He fully expected the world to end any day and had waited and prayed for it faithfully. Then when it failed to show up as advertised, he died alone and unmourned, just one more insignificant life despite all the religious hocus-pocus.

To Marty's way of thinking the "end of the world" wasn't a host of angels shattering the earth to pieces with divine thunderbolts. It was the moment of his death when the electrons, protons, and neutrons that had been Martin Hamilton flew off in every direction to become parts of rocks, insects, and baseballs. Total extinction. And as for heaven and hell, celestial rewards and fiery punishments, these were nothing but the concocted fantasies of an imagination terrified by the realization of its own eventual demise. He shook his head. If the shabby, stumbling, pathetic procession called human history taught any lesson at all, it was this: enjoy yourself as much as you can while you can because this is the best it's ever going to get.

As was so often the case with Marty, however, his philosophical meanderings were soon drowned out by the clamor of more immediate concerns: such as his need for a warm shower and sleep. And he wouldn't mind a little sex too, once the Morgan problem was taken care of. Hopefully Brenda was available. If not, a hooker would have to do. Imagining these pleasures, he drove toward the silhouette of the Houston skyline backlit by a vermilion sunrise.

THE PHONE RANG as he was stepping out of the shower and he hurried naked and dripping into the bedroom to answer it.

"Avery wants to see you," Brenda said.

"When?"

"At three."

"I can get there earlier."

"No need; he has an important meeting at one."

"What does he want?"

"A report."

"I'm still working on it."

"You better come in all the same."

"What about Morgan and his girlfriend?"

"He said to forget about them. He's trusting Hathaway to handle it."

Just like that? Marty wondered. Then why have me go all the way to hell and back if you're going to suddenly drop the whole thing? Marty was more convinced than ever that it was a test to see how he would perform under pressure. He frowned; he knew he'd made few positive marks in that department.

Toweling off, he threw on his azure silk robe with embossed Oriental dragons and went into the kitchen. The tile cooled the soles of his feet as he opened the refrigerator and pulled out a half-gallon container of two-percent milk. He took several long swallows to settle his stomach. He wasn't hungry, but he scrambled three eggs and did his best to get them down.

"BRENDA SAYS YOU took some photographs?" Avery sat behind his desk with his hands folded together, tapping the tips of his index fingers against his lower lip as if weighing a decision.

Marty handed a large envelope to his boss. He had printed the photos using his computer before coming in. Avery slid the photographs out and spread them out on the desk.

"My guess is the two men work at the power plant and the women are their wives," Marty explained. "They met with Morgan and Carpenter in Lubbock at the—"

"Who's this woman?" Avery held up one of the photos.

"She's a doctor. She works in Lubbock. I think she's given the workers some kind of medical exam."

Avery nodded and went back to studying the photographs.

Marty waited.

"I heard there was some kind of screw-up in Dalton County," Avery said his eyes still on the photographs. "Brenda said Agent Brewer was pretty steamed."

The little prick had called his boss; Marty wasn't surprised. "You said to be creative," he said and forced a smile.

"Best not to alienate the hired help, though," Avery said as he slid the photos back into the envelope and looked up.

"It doesn't matter," Avery appeared to have made his decision. "Morgan and Carpenter met with Hathaway and he's convinced they have nothing. Now that the workers' identities are known, or soon will be, thanks to these photographs, they can be dealt with appropriately."

Avery paused to study his young protégé. He looked a little crazed but Avery wasn't quite ready to give up on him yet, he might still make the grade if given half a chance.

"We have a new problem," Avery said and Marty was relieved to note the use of the collective "we." Apparently he was still part of the EnerTex family. "His name is Colonel Viktor Degtyar. He's a Russian who works for Valentin Gromonov. Do you know who Gromonov is?"

"Russian Mafia," Marty said and Avery nodded.

"The colonel is his man. He arrived in Houston yesterday and we had a meeting this afternoon. He's here to negotiate a deal on behalf of Kamal."

"What do they want?" Marty asked.

"To be our partner in Russia."

This was familiar territory for the Tin Man and he smelled a deal in the air. Despite his fatigue, his juices began to flow.

"We have an employee, a very special employee," Avery went on. "His name is Dr. Walter Easler. I don't believe you would have met him."

"Head of research?"

"Yes. He played a key role in designing the Ranger 1 power plant."

Marty sensed that Avery was sharing confidential information with him, something the CEO would not be doing if his star was indeed falling.

"What does this have to do with the colonel?"

"The Russians would like nothing better than to get their hands on Dr. Easler. They have it in their heads that he can design power plants for them, and they would then no longer need us."

"But why would Dr. Easler help them?"

"Because he's Russian," Avery said. "Easler's not his real name. I hope you realize that what I'm telling you must be kept in the strictest confidence?"

Marty nodded.

"Well, I heard something at today's meeting that worried me. I made some calls, but what I would like you to do is look after Dr. Easler for the next little while."

Marty heard the words "look after" as in "baby-sit" and was not pleased. He was hoping his boss was about to assign him to the team that would negotiate with Kamal.

"For how long?" he asked.

"A couple of weeks," Avery said, "maybe longer—until we feel the danger is passed. I think the Russians may try to do something."

"Like what?"

"Hard to say. They might try to kidnap Easler."

Marty struggled to reconfigure his thoughts to this new reality, but the cocaine had left him a little daffy.

"Do they know where Dr. Easler lives?"

"We don't think they are aware of his new identity."

Marty began to suspect the collective "we" included officials in the government, and that Easler was enrolled in something akin to the Federal Witness Protection Program, like in the movies.

"Why doesn't the FBI or CIA take charge of Dr. Easler's security?" he offered.

"Let's just say at this point, the risks outweigh the benefits."

Translation: Avery Axton doesn't trust the likes of Agent Brewer to keep his mouth shut. Marty liked that and he warmed to the idea.

"Colonel Degtyar will be returning to Russia," Avery continued. "I've contracted with a private security firm for the services

of two bodyguards. They'll take shifts around the clock protecting Dr. Easler at his home."

"Then why do you need me?"

"I need someone to see to Dr. Easler's day-to-day needs. Make
sure he has groceries. Walk his dog. Do whatever is necessary."

"Does he have a dog?" Marty asked.

"How should I know?" Avery said with a flicker of annoyance. "Look, Marty, Dr. Easler is very important to us. I want him
taken care of, do you understand?"

Marty was fed up with special assignments. All he wanted to
do was get back to what he did best, making deals. But he appreciated the opportunity Avery was offering him. Out of the whole
EnerTex organization, he, Marty Hamilton, was being entrusted
with protecting someone who might be the company's most
valuable asset. He had already made the mental leap that Dr.
Easler was *the* inventor of the ATG technology. Perhaps it would
be useful to get to know the man. Wheels were already spinning
inside the Tin Man's head.

"When should I start?"

"Immediately. Brenda will follow you home so you can get
whatever you need. You can then follow her to Dr. Easler's house;
it's not far from where she lives. I must impress upon you the
importance of this assignment. Make sure that someone is with
Dr. Easler at all times, either yourself or one of the bodyguards.
And if you need anything, let Brenda know. I may stop in now and
again to check on Dr. Easler, and as soon as the colonel is out of
the way and we think it's safe again, we'll get you back to the Sales
Department. Ron McBride is looking for a new department head;
he has his eye on you."

26

As a child, Viktor was unsurpassed at games of hide and seek. He could find anyone and after awhile the other children refused to let him play. So he hunted small animals with a sling shot and sometimes helped neighbors locate misplaced objects. He had a special intuition for finding things and it stayed with him into adulthood.

It was early morning and Tatyana lay asleep next him, tall and slender. He considered waking her up, caressing her. Instead he turned his thoughts to the task at hand. He had seen a visual puzzle in a newspaper once that showed a man standing over a pile of ashes holding a magnet. The caption read: "what is this man doing?" It took Viktor only a moment to figure it out. The pile of ashes had been a haystack and the man was looking for a needle. Well Anatoly Kryuchkov, if the physicist still existed, was the needle in the enormous haystack of America. And since EnerTex was the most likely section of the haystack in which he might be hiding, then perhaps Viktor should consider setting a small fire.

When Tatyana awoke she found Viktor sitting in a chair by the window. The heavy curtain was pulled back just far enough to allow a shaft of sunlight to fall upon a map he was reading. That way he could make out the names of the smaller towns without having to put on his reading glasses, which he would not wear in Tatyana's company.

"Are we going somewhere?"

"I must go to the power plant tomorrow," he said. "It is here, near this town called Birdstar." He placed his finger on the map and held it out for her to see. "I will charter an airplane."

"Will you take me with you?"

"No, I need you to stay here and look for Kryuchkov. I believe he lives here in Houston."

"Then why are you going to the power plant?"

"I have reasons."

Such a strange man, Tatyana thought as she dressed. He could be considerate and tender one moment, then secretive and sharp-edged the next. She was conflicted. He was older, perhaps too old, but she was drawn to strong willed men who made her feel safe.

She sat on the edge of the bed and took a cigarette from her purse and lit it. Through the smoke she continued regarding him as he folded the map and slipped it into the outer pocket of a small duffel bag. He was fit. She found him attractive. And his lovemaking was generous. But most importantly, he would take her home. To Russia. A woman needed a protector in Russia. She had no one. No father or mother. No relatives. All gone except for Uri, who loved America too much to leave. Only once had they argued about going home.

"The Soviet Union is dead," he said. "Russia is dead. My future is in America. Here I can become rich. Why do you want to go back there?" She wanted to cry. She didn't have the words to explain why she longed so much to return to her native land. Always she felt out-of-place in America, in Texas. The way people did things, the way they talked. American men desired her but they did not understand her, and so her flirtations were little more than playacting. She didn't want to tell Uri this she hated his lectures. He would tell her to stop thinking so much and enjoy herself. He had many girlfriends but no one serious. He liked freedom. She stubbed out the cigarette. Viktor could give her what she wanted. He would take her home.

"What do you want me to do?" she asked.

"Go among the Russian émigrés. Visit their organizations, their clubs. Ask questions."

"What kind of questions?"

He handed her the photograph Gromonov had given him.

"This is the man we are looking for. He walks with a cane on his right side. See?"

She studied the photograph.

"He will have a new name."

"Do you know this name?"

"No. You will need to make up a story. Be casual. Don't alarm anyone. We don't want Kryuchkov to know we are looking for him."

She knew he trusted her discretion and felt the compliment.

"Yes, I will do this," she said. "When will you return?"

"The day after tomorrow. I am going only to look. You can stay here in my room, if you want."

She laughed. "I am not homeless. I have a life that misses me very much."

What kind of life, Viktor wondered. She must have a boyfriend; she is so beautiful. Maybe more than one. He did not enjoy thinking about this life of hers.

"Visit the chess clubs also," he said. "Someone might remember seeing him. It is said he likes to play chess although he is not very good."

"I thought he was brilliant."

"I am brilliant but I cannot play the cello."

She smiled. "I cannot do all this in two days."

"You will have more time. I may need to return to the power plant again. Do what you can."

"Yes, Colonel."

He opened up his wallet and took out four one hundred dollar bills and handed them to her.

"For your expenses," he said.

"You buy me clothes and give me money," she said folding the bills and slipping them into her pocketbook. She was wearing a black pencil skirt with pink pinstripes, something extra he had bought her. She stood up and stepped past him and gazed out the window, the warmth of the sun on her face.

"Why are you doing this?" she asked. "Why are you looking for this scientist?"

"It is a job," he said.

"Gromonov is an evil man," she said. "You know this?"

Viktor was surprised. "Your brother works for him."

She turned around and her eyes flashed with anger. "Do not speak about Uri. You do not know him, what he has been through. If he works for a gangster, he has his reasons."

Viktor remained silent. He often had trouble predicting what women would say or do and reproached himself for becoming her lover so quickly. They must work together. But Tatyana's anger ebbed away quickly and she sat down in one of the chairs next to the table. The quiet rasp of black nylons as she crossed her legs filled Viktor with lust. She was gaining power over him. He must reassert his mastery. Turning his back to her, he stepped over to the dresser and began gathering up a few of his belongings for the trip.

"Why did you leave the military?" she asked.

"You would not understand," he said, stuffing a long-sleeve silk shirt into his duffel bag.

"You are not a cruel man," she said.

"All men are cruel when there is need." She waited. He turned to look at her. "The stupidity made me angry. The way they used us in Afghanistan was short-sighted and wasteful. And I was angry about what they did to my brother."

He had not mentioned his family before and she was curious. In Russia every family had a troubled story to tell.

"Tell me about your brother," she said.

Viktor paused and then sat down on the edge of the bed facing her.

"His name is Gregory. He is dying because of them."

"Because of who?" she asked.

"The bastards in the Kremlin, who else?" It was the first time he had spoken to anyone about what had happened to his brother. It was his own private grief, shut away from the rest of his world behind a thorn hedge inside his heart. Now he was sharing this grief with a woman with many boyfriends. And yet he could not keep silent.

"Gregory, he is softer than I am, more like our mother. He is Alyosha Karamozov. Kind, gentle, truthful Alyosha. But he is dying, my brother."

Viktor began to rise but Tatyana touched his arm. He looked into her eyes for the span of several heartbeats before surrendering to her silent request and sitting back down.

"Gregory was seventeen years old when they conscripted him to go to Chernobyl to clean up the mess," he said looking down at the carpet. "A truck load of seventeen-year-olds, many who could not yet grow hair on their faces. They did not volunteer for this hazardous duty. They were just children following orders."

"What happened?"

He looked up at her, the heat of anger in his expression.

"They were given no protective garments, just a pair of makeshift metal plates strapped to their bodies, in front and behind, like sandwich boards used to advertise a traveling circus. Inside the reactor building, fragments of radioactive graphite fuel rods lay scattered about amid the rubble like broken toys. The experts said that two minutes was the maximum exposure time—two minutes to receive enough radiation for a lifetime. But they made my brother work inside for more than five minutes and now he is dying of cancer. They murdered him."

Tatyana thought of Uri and what she would do if someone tried to harm him. She moved over and sat next to Viktor on the bed, and took him in her arms.

THE NEXT DAY a small twin engine Cessna set down at the Dalton County airport. "Here's our number," the pilot said, handing Viktor a business card. "Call us when you want to be picked up."

A rental car from Enterprise was waiting for him and he drove into Birdstar. The place reminded him of the nothing sort of towns spread out over the Steppe east of Moscow. The terrain and buildings were different but the aura of bleak pointlessness was the same. Why would people choose to live and die in such places?

Fifteen miles west of Birdstar on county road 645 he came to a crossroads and a store. He pulled up in front of the store and got out. It was three o'clock and the heat was ferocious.

"Afternoon," an elderly man said from the shade of the porch. He was drinking a soda as he reclined comfortably on a cracked red vinyl seat that had been removed from a wrecked pickup truck some years before. "Reckon it's hot enough to suck sweat out of a fence post."

Viktor mounted the porch. The man was ancient, as was his hat, a dilapidated old Stetson that had been stepped on, sat on, and slapped around so many times it had given up even trying to be a hat.

"Are you open?" Viktor asked.

The man set his soda down and stood up. He walked over and pulled open the screen door for his customer to go in first. The interior was dark and cool; the only illumination came through two front windows that looked out onto the porch and the flatlands beyond.

"It's running lights and electric motors that heats a place up," the store owner said, coming around him and stepping behind the counter.

Viktor took in the scene with a trained eye. There were shelves stocked with canned goods and loaves of bread but no coolers or refrigerators.

"They're out back," the man said as if reading his thoughts. "Tell me what you want and I'll go get it."

"Do you sell cigarettes?" Viktor asked.

"What brand do you smoke?"

Viktor didn't smoke but he wanted to talk to the man. "Marlboros."

The man reached underneath the counter. On the wall behind him was a bank of mailboxes, each with a combination lock.

"Need matches?" he said as he placed the cigarettes on the counter top.

"No. How much for the cigarettes?"

"That'll be $2.90. Don't blame me. It's government taxes makes 'em so high."

Viktor pulled out his wallet and paid for the cigarettes.

"I'm going to start carrying them Indian cigarettes soon," the man said. "They're cheaper 'cause the Indians don't have to pay as many taxes. A tribe in Washington State manufacturers 'em. Nothing like Indians to take care of the white man's vices, don't you think?"

Viktor looked at him uncomprehendingly.

"Cigarettes and gambling," the man said. "They ever make drugs legal, the Indians will want in on that too."

"How much farther is it to the EnerTex power plant?" Viktor asked.

"You work out there?" the man said scratching the side of his face.

"No, I just want to see it."

"Can't. They don't let people near the place anymore."

"I don't understand."

"Security. Tight as a nun's ass. Used to be you could get up near the buildings and all like that. Now they've got the whole area blocked off. Why do you want to see the plant anyway?"

"What kind of security do they have?" Viktor asked.

"You're not a terrorist are you?" Viktor could tell the man wasn't serious; he was just lonely and eager for conversation.

"Do you sell gum?" Viktor asked.

"Got spearmint. You want a pack?"

Viktor placed a ten dollar bill on the counter. The man gave him a pack of Wrigley's and picked up the bill to make change and Viktor said, "Never mind, just keep it."

The man looked puzzled but then grinned. "You must be one of them reporter fellas. That's how they get information in the movies. Well, that's okay with me; I've got nothing against reporters." He slipped the bill into his shirt pocket.

"So you want to know about the security they've got out there," he said. "Well, they've got it all. Cameras, armed guards, specially-trained attack dogs, the works. You'd think they was protecting Fort Knox." The man laughed.

"Instead of horses," he said, "the guards patrol the plant on Honda ATVs. Day and night. A gnat couldn't slip into that place even if he greased hisself."

"How do you know all this?" Viktor asked.

"People talk. There's not much else to do around these parts. They talk and I listen."

Viktor couldn't imagine the old man listening to anyone for very long. He took out a stick of gum and slowly unwrapped it.

"Did you ever see a man who works for EnerTex with a cane?" he said.

"What kind of cane?"

"For walking. He had polio."

"Polio? My wife's brother died from polio back in '52. Her parents were afraid she'd come down with it, but she never did. She's gone now. Bad heart."

"I am sorry."

"Ain't your fault."

"Do you know this man with a cane?" Viktor asked again.

"Can't say I do."

"Nobody with a cane works at the power plant?"

"I didn't say that. What I *said* was that nobody using a cane ever stopped in here, not that I can remember." The store owner stepped out from behind the counter. "But if you want to find out what goes on inside the plant, you should talk to someone who works there. There's a beer joint in Birdstar called Knillings. It's just as you're going back into town on 645. A gang of plant workers usually stops there on their way home after the day shift."

Viktor was glad he'd given the old man money. "What time do they go to this Knillings, the workers?"

"Right around five-thirty. Ask for Bernie Niles. He's my nephew. Buy him a beer and he'll tell you whatever you want to know, even if he has to make it up."

Viktor thanked the man and walked to the door. He squinted as he opened it and said back over his shoulder, "Where does this other road go?"

"Take it south and you'll come to Centralia. Go north and you'll run out of gas."

"What's in Centralia?"

The old man came forward and they both moved out onto the porch.

"A couple of stores, a church, and a school. The Sundial Oil storage facility is on the east side of town. I worked there after I gave up ranching. Then I retired and bought this place and they made me postmaster. It's kind of odd, though. When I was working everyday, working hard, seems like I had lots of get-up-and-go. Now I just feel old and played out most of the time. Some mornings it takes all I got just to quit the bed."

Viktor walked across the dry, sun-baked ground to his car, the crunching of the grit under the soles of his shoes pushing back the prairie quiet. With the engine idling and the air conditioning on, he contemplated his options. One idea was to infiltrate the plant and disable a portion of it with explosives. EnerTex would then bring in its top engineers to assess the damage and make the necessary repairs. Hopefully those experts would include Kryuchkov. How then to kidnap the scientist was another matter. Maybe EnerTex would put the engineers up in a motel in Birdstar; it should be easy to snatch Kryuchkov from there.

He needed a first-rate team and a quantity of RDX explosive. That would be Uri's responsibility. He hoped the young man was up to the job. But first he must reconnoiter the power plant. If the security was as thorough as the old man said it was, then he was wasting his time. After surviving the uncertainties and dangers of Afghanistan he had no wish to get his guts shot out by an overly zealous power plant guard in Dalton County, Texas—not for the kind of money Gromonov was paying him.

He put the car into drive and pulled back onto the road. The countryside was flat, cheerless, and empty. A barbed wire fence ran along the north side of the road but Viktor saw no livestock, only scrub brush and lots of tumbleweeds; the latter crowded up against the fence, held in place by the unrelenting wind. Viktor remembered what the store owner said about feeling old. He felt old himself. Old and tired. This is my last search, he told himself. You catch a rabbit and the next day two more have moved into his hole. The mid-afternoon sunshine streaming through the front windshield bounced around inside the car and made him sleepy. He fought to keep the car from drifting across the broken center stripe and even considered pulling over for a short nap, but that wasn't like him. He had a job to do. A phrase he heard somewhere came back to him: old is old. It summed up perfectly how he felt. There was nothing desirable or redemptive about getting old. Old is old. That's all there was to it.

Ten minutes later County Route 645 ended at the security entrance of the power plant. Due to a slight rise in the ground, none of the plant buildings were visible from the entrance except the guard house, which was located inside the vehicle entrance enclosure. Viktor estimated the narrow enclosure, called a sally port, to be forty feet long. A twelve-foot high chain link fence ran along each side. At the far end of the sally port, the fence extended at ninety-degree angles in both directions, providing the power plant with the first of two perimeter barriers. The second was another chain link fence, also twelve-feet high, that ran parallel to the first. The distance that separated the two fences served as a graveled security patrol road. Half way up each fence spiraled a continuous roll of razor wire. The top of each fence was similarly adorned.

As Viktor approached the security entrance, the exterior gate rolled aside. He drove into the enclosure and stopped at a red light as the gate closed behind him. In front of him, a three-foot high steel beam ran the width of the enclosure to prevent vehicles from entering the plant. It was painted red with white letters that spelled the word STOP! Beyond the beam—which could be raised and lowered into the concrete roadway by a guard in the guardhouse—there was another automated chain link gate. Past that, the road wound a serpentine course between a series of asymmetrically-placed concrete Jersey Barriers. Viktor judged it would be impossible for a speeding vehicle to crash its way into the plant given the number of obstructions and other safeguards.

Three guards emerged from the guardhouse. Each wore a helmet, Kevlar body armor, and a side arm. The first came up to the window of his car, while the second walked around the car with a bomb-sniffing German Shepherd. The third remained near the door of the guardhouse. He was holding a M-16.

"State your business, sir," the first guard said.

Viktor feigned confusion.

"I'm sorry, I. . . I must be lost." He picked up the map that lay spread out on the passenger seat next to him and looked at it. "I'm a geologist. Is this the Sundial Oil Storage Facility?"

"No, this is not Sundial. I need to see your license and registration," the guard said.

"Where am I?"

"Please, your license and registration."

"But I have no wish to enter this place," Viktor said but then noticed the guard with the M-16 hitch his weapon into a ready position.

"These are the regulations, sir. We are required to determine the identity of any vehicle that approaches this facility." The guard held out his hand.

Viktor judged it prudent to cooperate. He pulled out his wallet and removed the forged international driver's license Gromonov's people had given him in Moscow. They had provided him with three full sets of false identification to use as needed. Each included a passport, an international drivers' license, and a set of credit cards. Altogether they must have cost a great deal of money and reinforced in Viktor's mind the importance Gromonov placed upon the mission. He only hoped the license he'd chosen in the name of Makar Goshkov from Sevastapol would pass the test of official scrutiny.

The guard examined the document only long enough to compare the photograph with the man inside the car. He then took a small device from a holster on his belt and scanned the license with one swipe. He handed it back to Viktor and waited without speaking while Viktor retrieved the registration for the rental car from the glove compartment and handed it to him. This, too, the guard swiped and returned.

Meanwhile Viktor did his own scanning. His work for the Swiss had kept him current on the latest security technology, and he began by marking the number and location of video cameras within the sally port. He next calculated the distance between the perimeter fences and noted the number of security light poles located along the interior fence. Stacked configurations of sensors on short posts positioned at regular intervals between the fences also drew his attention. These he identified as the newest generation of clear zone overlap microwave sensors that could detect not only walking and running intruders, but, as the manufacturer's promotional materials promised, "commando crawling" intruders as well. And there was more. Woven in and out of the exterior chain link fence he saw a black wire the thickness of a coaxial video cable. It was part of an elaborate motion sensing system developed by an American university that mimicked the ability of a spider to precisely locate where prey has fallen into its web. Touch the fence at any point along its entire length and the computer-based system would immediately inform the security operator where the intrusion was occurring. Other cables he saw led Viktor to believe there was also a system of underground sensors to prevent tunneling. He realized few nuclear weapon facilities in Russia were protected as well as this civilian power plant and he had no hope of entering the plant by stealth.

"What kind of place is this?" Viktor asked with a pleasant smile.

The guard ignored the question. "You have missed your turn, sir," he said. "Centralia is to the south on County Road 612."

Viktor picked up the map again and pushed it toward the guard. "Could you please show me?" he said.

The guard's manner softened as he took the map and folded down one side. He pointed at a tiny blue circle. "This is Centralia. Go back the way you came until you come to a crossroads. There is a store—"

"Yes, I stopped there to buy gum."

"Turn right onto County Road 612. Centralia is twenty-eight miles."

"Thank you, officer. Should I reverse?" he asked. The guard nodded and turned to the guard holding the M-16, who lowered his rifle and stepped back into the guardhouse. The gate moved out of the way and Viktor backed out of the sally port. He maneuvered the car through a three point turn and drove down the road the way he'd come.

He then noticed his sweaty palms against the steering wheel. His heart was racing as well. He had been in situations a hundred times more dangerous over the years and was angry at himself—angry also at the guard with the M-16. He realized this reaction was irrational. The guard was only doing his job. Would he really have opened fire if Viktor had refused to turn over his driver's license and instead attempted to back out of the sally port through the gate? Yes, without question. His weapon would be on full automatic. Two seconds to riddle the car and his body with 5.56 millimeter bullets.

KNILLINGS WAS A single-story cinder block building surrounded by a gravel parking lot. Two narrow horizontal windows bracketed the front door and were illuminated from inside by neon beer signs. Viktor parked next to a black Ford F-250 pickup with a 30-30 Winchester in a gun rack mounted across the rear window and went inside. It took a moment for his eyes to adjust to the indoor lighting. There were two rooms for customers. In front was a bar and a collection of different size tables; the back room contained built-in booths along the side walls and a pool table in the center. Two men were playing pool and the smoke from their cigarettes clouded the beam of light shining down on the table. Viktor went over to the bar and ordered a beer.

"Is the owner here?" he asked.

"That's me," the bartender said, "Jack Knillings."

Viktor smiled. "I'm looking for Bernie Niles."

"He comes in with the EnerTex crowd. They should be along in the next little while."

Ten minutes later a group of six men wearing jeans and cowboy boots entered the bar. They pushed a couple of the tables together and sat down. Viktor watched them in the large mirror behind the bar. He was relieved to see that none of the security guards were part of the group. One of the men came up to the bar and ordered two pitchers of beer. He was wearing a ball cap that said, "Don't Force It, Get a Larger Hammer."

"If you're looking for Bernie, here he is," the bar owner said before going off to fill the pitchers.

Bernie was a thin, angular young man, with the dark shadow of a day-old beard. His nose had a hump in the middle, a souvenir from his days playing high school football. His eyes, Viktor noticed, looked flat and tired.

"Your uncle said I could find you here," Viktor said. "My name is Makar Goshkov. I'm looking for information about EnerTex employee."

"You a friend of my uncle's?" Bernie said with caution in his voice; Viktor's accent was throwing him.

"No, I met your uncle today. This is first time I visit Texas." He knew dropping articles made him sound more Russian.

"Where you from?"

"Russia."

"Russia? No shit," Bernie relaxed and his mood brightened. "Well, you best come on over and join us."

The bar owner placed the pitchers down on the bar next to a tray of frosted beer mugs but before Bernie could pay Viktor handed the bartender a twenty. "Please, I wish to buy for you your beer."

Bernie grinned, grabbed the pitchers, and started back to his friends. Viktor received his change, picked up the tray, and followed.

"I found me a Russian up at the bar, boys," Bernie said with a smile as Viktor came up behind him. "His name is Mike Goshkov."

Viktor said, "I am looking for relative who works for EnerTex."

"Pull up a chair," a man named Junior said. "What's his name, this relative of yours?"

"Anatoly Kryuchkov."

"Never heard of him," Junior said shaking his head. "It's not a name you'd be likely to forget,"

"It is possible he might have changed name," Viktor said quickly.

"Now why would he do that?" another man said in a red plaid shirt.

"It is. . . complicated. He left Russia for political reasons."

No one at the table knew what to say. International politics wasn't their strong suit.

"What kind of relative is he of yours?" Bernie broke the silence.

"My cousin. I've come long way to find him."

"I'd say you have," Bernie said.

"Why do you think he works for EnerTex?" asked the man in the red shirt.

"He is scientist, noted physicist."

Bernie laughed. "We don't hang around with those kind of folks, do you we boys?"

"We're on the maintenance crew," Junior said pouring himself a mug of beer. "The people with the brains are back in Houston. They don't work out here anymore."

"He uses cane," Viktor said. "He once had polio."

There was an evident change in the attitude of the men. He waited. The sharp crack of billiard balls came from the back room. The man in the red shirt was first to speak.

"There was a guy who used to work at the plant who used a cane. He spoke with a foreign accent too, but it didn't sound like yours. More German."

"He was somebody important, I can tell you that," Junior jumped in. "Had his own house trailer on site while they were building the plant."

"This man, what was his name?" Viktor said. He could feel his pulse quicken.

"Can't say," Bernie said. "What about you Mike, you remember his name?"

The man in the red shirt shrugged. "Everybody called him Dr. Strangelove," he said.

"So his name is Strangelove?" Viktor said.

Junior laughed. "No, that was just a nickname. You know, from the movie."

"He's from Russia, you idiot," Bernie said. "He doesn't know about no movie."

Of course Viktor knew the movie but he saw no reason to say so.

"He used to talk to himself," Bernie said. "And he was always taking measurements, you know, and stuff like that."

Mike suddenly decided to change the topic; they'd been warned repeatedly not to talk to strangers about what went on inside the plant. They didn't know who this Goshkov guy was. Shouldn't he know more about his cousin's whereabouts than any of them? And ever since the interview with the reporters from California, he had been on edge. He felt certain EnerTex would find out and can his ass or worse. It was all Hazel's fault but he hadn't told her that.

"The Russians tried to stop us from going to war in Iraq," Mike said to Viktor. "What do you think of that?"

Viktor wasn't going to be drawn into that kind of conversation, especially in a beer joint in west Texas. He judged he had all the information he was likely to get about Kryuchkov. The scientist was still alive and working for EnerTex. That much was certain. Now all Viktor had to do was find him and talk him into coming home. And if Kryuchkov refused? . . . Well, Viktor didn't want to think about that yet.

*   *   *

VIKTOR SLID THE entry key card into the lock and heard a click as the little green light winked. The internal digital lock mechanism encoded the date and time on the electromagnetic strip on the back of the card: 1:34 AM. The room was dark. Was it also empty or was she there? Where did she live? He knew nothing about her other than the small sounds she made deep in her throat when they came together.

He moved across the soft carpet toward the bed where he could make out a shape under the covers in the faint glow from the clock radio. He sat down on the edge of the bed and took off his shoes. She rolled over toward him.

"Did you have a good trip?" she asked, her voice thick with sleep.

"Yes. Did you have success?"

She brushed the hair from her eyes. "No. I went to six places. No one has seen a man with a cane."

"I have thought of a way to find him."

"How?"

"He has polio. He will be receiving medical treatment for his illness."

Tatyana thought about this for a moment. She was still half asleep.

"But there are so many doctors in the city," she said. "How can we ask each one?"

"Only a few see polio patients, I am sure. And EnerTex will pay for the very best. Anatoly is very valuable to them. We will start there. With the very best."

She put her hand gently on his back. "Come to bed, you are tired."

He began to unbutton his shirt. It had been a long day.

"I will need you to be my actress again," he said.

"Will I get an Oscar this time?"

"But I do not call him Oscar," he said.

She laughed. "What do you call him, Ivan the Terrible?"

An hour later Viktor Degtyar and Tatyana fell asleep.

27

"IF MORGAN DOESN'T have a story, I don't see what all the fucking discussion's about." The gravelly voice belonged to Jack Dunnel, who had served on the KVMR board for the last three years. A self-styled "bull in a china shop," he was the kind of person who thought his enthusiastic and predictable use of foul language imparted an earthy realism to his remarks, as though his ravenous intellect could only be satisfied with the red meat of substance; tofu-like obfuscation might suit his fellow board members, but never Jack Dunnel.

He was also the chief reason Alice hated attending KVMR board meetings. She glanced over at Reb who only shrugged and smiled.

"What I'm saying," Jack continued, "is that we've wasted a shitload of money on a bunch of rumors. It's what I said would happen when we got into this news business. It's not part of our mission. Not before, and sure as hell it shouldn't be now."

Reb was tempted to say, "Do you eat with that mouth, Jack?" but decided the board could duke it out well enough without his help. Besides, another board member named Rickie Cousins was already responding.

"It wasn't our money, Jack. Lyle Workman's organization paid all the expenses."

"And who pays Morgan's salary?" Jack said looking around for encouragement. "And Alice's? We do, the station, that's who."

Maryann Babcock, a school counselor and the board's treasurer, felt it was her responsibility to clarify matters. "We cut the checks, Jack, but the money for their salaries isn't drawn from the general fund. It comes from a special account that's dedicated solely to building up the news department."

"Well, that's great," Jack snorted. "Just to get his money, we allow a single contributor to dictate to the board which programs get expanded and which ones don't."

The "single contributor" was sitting across the table from Jack and he wore a pleasant smile. As CEO of his own company in Santa Clara, Brent Abrams had survived his share of contentious board meetings and was more amused by Jack's comments than offended.

Phil Cook, on the other hand, looked as if he had consumed a batch of bad oysters. He arrived at the meeting hoping for a raise—it was long overdue—and Kevin had assured him it would come up for a vote. But now the board was running late and absorbed in a more pressing issue—the EnerTex story.

"Let's get back on track, folks." Skip Mathune was a custom furniture maker and board president. "Reb and Alice have made their report. They interviewed employees of the power plant and their spouses and you have the photos of the power plant in front of you. They also interviewed a doctor, a newspaper publisher, the public relations VP at EnerTex, and the director of an energy advocacy organization..." He turned to Reb to make sure he hadn't left anyone out and Reb nodded. "It is Reb and Alice's conclusion that something very strange is going on in west Texas."

"Everything coming out of Texas these days is fucking strange," Jack said. "I could have told them that and saved them the trip."

Skip had reached the point—usually half-way through a board meeting—where it was either ignore Jack or hit him over the head with a chair.

"It also appears," Skip continued, "that someone working for EnerTex used drugs in an attempt to get Reb and Alice arrested."

"There's no proof EnerTex had anything to do with that," Jack said.

"If Reb and Alice don't have a story, then why did the station receive this?" Maryann said, holding up a single page letter. It was printed on expensive watermarked linen paper, and not only had the station received a copy, but one had been mailed to each individual board member at home. The room grew quiet as several of the board members pulled the letter out of their board packet and began rereading it again for the third or fourth time. It was from the law firm of Clayne-Dancer with offices in Houston, New York, Miami, and Los Angeles. One of the firm's senior partners was a former cabinet secretary, and it was through his efforts and influence that the firm had acquired an impressive list of clients including foreign governments and multinational corporations. The letter stated that the employees of EnerTex had signed a strict confidentiality agreement which prohibited them from speaking to the press about any matter related to EnerTex, its management, policies, or operations. Any attempt, therefore, by individuals associated with KVMR to induce said employees into violating this agreement would constitute grounds for legal action.

"Look, Skip," Jack said adopting a more conciliatory tone. "You know I don't go along with corporate America threatening people. They're just a bunch of sons-of-bitches, we all know that. And I'll admit that something must be wrong at the power plant for EnerTex to sic their lawyers on us. But we can't be expected to go up against a company like EnerTex and survive. It'd be like having a pissing contest with a fire truck. Even if we won in court, the cost of the litigation alone would bankrupt us. That's why I was against this idea of expanding the news department from the beginning. I knew it would get us into trouble. Let's just stick to what we do best, great music and local public affairs."

Jack might be a blowhard, Alice thought, but he was only echoing the murmur of fear in the back of each board member's mind. She looked around the table and most of them looked as if they'd shared in the oysters too.

Then Brent Abrams spoke up for the first time. "Very few of the major media outlets are willing to take on corporate power in this country in a serious way. There are lots of reasons for this failure: advertising revenues, corporate underwriting, and a lack of imagination to name just a few. So you see, it's up to us. That's why Lyle Workman agreed to help. He believes the media should listen to what ordinary citizens have to say about what they experience in their own communities. Concerned citizens are not stupid; they just don't have a voice. I think Reb and Alice should continue with their investigation of EnerTex and I'll pick up any expenses that Mr. Workman doesn't."

"You'll pay for the litigation if it comes to that?" Maryann asked.

"Not alone, but I'll help." The qualification was not lost on the other board members.

"That's what I thought," Jack said, rolling his eyes.

"I believe our members will come forward, if necessary," Maryann said. "And other organizations will help as well—like the ACLU."

"The ACLU's up to its ass in alligators already, dealing with the Patriot Act and all the other crazy shit coming out of Washington," Jack said. "Look, I've been around here a long time and I wouldn't count on our members to bail the station out if we go hundreds of thousands of dollars in the hole. It's not that they wouldn't *want* to, it's just that most of them have their own money problems to deal with."

Alice glanced at Brent Abrams in his Italian twill sport shirt and designer jeans and reminded herself that he was far from the typical KVMR supporter. Most of them were living a lot closer to the edge financially, and yet they still managed to scrap together sixty dollars each year to cover membership dues. She turned to Reb, who was examining one of the power plant photographs Kaye Spooner had given them. He suddenly pushed the photo aside and addressed the board.

"I agree with Mr. Abrams," he said. "There's an urgent need for news organizations to tell it straight to the American people, to let them know what's really going on in this country. I also believe it won't come from the mainstream press; it's got to come from the grassroots, from organizations like KVMR. And as for expanding the news department, we've got to look beyond the borders of Nevada County, even beyond the Sacramento valley, because the problems in other places will show up here sooner or later."

Maryann and Skip both nodded in agreement.

"But we've also got to pick our fights carefully," he went on, his voice softening. "We're waging a guerrilla war and the big corporations have all the power. That means we need to choose where, when, and how to fight. A head-on confrontation with EnerTex could destroy what people have worked so hard to build over the years here at KVMR. I know I don't want to be responsible for seeing the station go under."

He glanced briefly at Alice and then continued. "All we have now is *part* of a story and that's simply not good enough. If we air it we will expose the station to an expensive lawsuit without helping the power plant workers very much. Therefore, I think the prudent course is to retreat for the time being so we can fight again another day. Maybe if they think they can bully anybody they want into silence they'll get careless and make a mistake."

There was silence and then Jack spoke.

"So you're willing to give up the EnerTex investigation?"

"Yes," Reb said.

Alice was suddenly furious with Reb for allowing Jack Dunnel and his supporters on the board get their way. The station could hire a private investigator. Or maybe they could convince the State of California to look into the matter if they went ahead and aired what they had. Why give up so easily?

She looked at Kevin who had said very little during the meeting. He was the station manager; why hadn't he come to their support? She had been involved with KVMR for years. Besides hosting her own weekly show, she had served as the volunteer coordinator and chaired the Program Committee. Now she was the station's news director. She loved the KVMR community. They were as important to her as her own family, and like family, they could drive her nuts.

But she also knew that Reb was dealing with his own problems. His last appointment with Dr. Yoon had not gone well. Tests indicated more damage to the optic nerves, a further loss of his peripheral vision. And his left eye was constantly bloodshot and no one was sure why. The doctor had taken him off his old medication and put him on a new drug that had been recently approved by the FDA. It would take several weeks to see if it helped. More waiting, and she knew how difficult the waiting was for Reb.

"Alice, do you agree with Reb?" Skip asked. The president's voice startled her.

"As far as I'm concerned, he's the producer; it's his story" she said. "If he says it's over, then it's over." And that was that. The last nail in the coffin. It made her blue even though part of her was secretly glad. Enough of Texas already.

"I move that KVMR send a letter to EnerTex's lawyers saying we will drop the investigation," Jack said. "Do I have a second?"

Alice picked up a power plant photo and threw it back onto the table without looking at it. She couldn't bear what was happening. Abrams' expression was sour but he said nothing.

"I second the proposal," another board member said.

"Any further discussion?" Skip asked.

No one said a word. The specter of frustration that had attended most of the meeting was replaced by the silence of resignation. This is where the rubber hits the road, Alice thought. It's one thing to talk about challenging the establishment and quite another to be willing to do the deed and pay the price.

"All in favor of Jack's proposal?"

A rustle of uneasiness; hands lifted listlessly into the air.

"Objections?"

"The proposal passes."

"I propose we adjourn the meeting." Jack again.

"Second."

"All in favor?"

A chorus of tired ayes.

Phil shook his head—no raise this month.

Chairs were pushed away from the table, backs stretched, eyes averted. Reb came over to Alice. "Let's go get a drink."

Abrams, who hadn't raised his hand during the vote, came over to them. "You're both doing great work. I hope you keep it up."

Alice tried to read the man. His words said "keep fighting the good fight," but she thought she detected a vaguely disgusted look in his eyes that betrayed a turning point and she doubted his support for the news department would last long now. Tonight he was disappointed; a week from now, two months from now, he would tire of KVMR and turn his attention to local politics, throw his support behind a liberal candidate for County Supervisor, or perhaps run for office himself. She didn't believe he would place his trust in the radio station again. She wanted to cry.

"WHAT NOW?" ALICE asked Reb after they snagged a table near the bar at Scanno's.

"Hell if I know. I'll call Lyle Workman in the morning. Maybe he can find another journalist willing to take up where we left off." Reb knew this wasn't likely. He took a pull on his Sierra Nevada Pale Ale and thought about Sandra and Ernesto Valdez and Mike Pendergast. He thought about Hazel too and her zebra-striped pants, and the memory made him smile. If a man had to live in Texas, he could do worse than hook up with a woman like Hazel.

"What are you thinking about?" Alice asked.

"Hazel."

"What about her?"

"What she would have said tonight if she'd been at the board meeting."

"Raised some Cain."

"Told them the truth. It's now or never, boys and girls. Time to walk your talk."

"Then why did you volunteer to give up? You didn't have to help them."

"I owe them, Alice. They gave me a job and a new start in life when I needed it most."

"I gave you the job, not the board."

"But the members of the board are the owners of the station. They were elected to represent the interests of the listeners, the broadcasters, and the community. That's how it should be."

"But you think it stinks?"

"Not really."

"Why not? I do."

"Good will win out in the end."

"Do you really believe that?"

"Don't you?"

"I'm not sure. The evidence hasn't been all that compelling lately."

"Do you know what somebody once asked Einstein?"

"What?"

"He was asked, 'What is the big question?'"

"And what did Einstein say?"

"Is the universe *friendly*?"

"It's a great answer. It's so simple. Is the universe friendly? That's what everyone really wants to know."

"So what do you think?" Alice asked.

"I believe it is."

She looked at him skeptically.

"No, really, I do," he said. "Love is the power that turns the great wheel of existence. Love moves the planets and the stars. Love keeps our hearts beating. All those other bitter, hurtful emotions, hate, envy, greed, cruelty, they're nothing but the negation of love. By themselves, they are mere shadows with no substance or energy of their own. Only love is real. That's why it will always win out in the end."

"So you're not depressed with what happened tonight, with the way the board flaked out on us?" she said.

"I'm depressed. I'm angry too."

"Then what about love winning out in the end? If you're so sure it will, then why be depressed or angry?"

"It depends on whether I'm *looking* at the world or *seeing* the world."

Alice waited.

"Remember Carlos Castaneda and what Don Juan said? When you *look* at the world, you experience the duality and drama of life. It makes you happy or sad, hopeful or angry. But when you *see* the world, then you're taking in the big picture, a universe unbounded by time or space, where human concepts such as gain and loss are essentially meaningless. So the trick then is to learn how to switch from *looking* to *seeing* and back again when necessary."

"It must be getting late, you're sounding way too new-agey for me."

"Do you know the story of Lazarus?" he asked.

She nodded.

"Well, Lazarus is Jesus' best friend. He gets sick and they send for Jesus to heal him. But Lazarus dies, and when Jesus shows up, they tell him that his friend is dead. And what does Jesus do? He breaks down and weeps. He's devastated that his best friend is gone. But then Jesus goes to the tomb and calls Lazarus forth. And out comes Lazarus, alive and well again."

"And?"

"When I was a kid and heard that story at school, it never made any sense. I mean, if Jesus was God, and God knew every-thing, even before it happened, then He must have known from the moment He arrived that He could bring his friend back to life. So why all the tears?"

"Don't ask me."

"Because Jesus needed to *look* at life first. He needed to know what it was like to be human to the very core of his being and to experience the wrenching sorrow of losing someone you love. It's only later that He switches from *looking* to *seeing* so that he can perform the miracle of restoring Lazarus to life."

"So are you *looking* or *seeing* now? Alice said.

"Drinking. It's a way station somewhere between the two."

"You're full of shit," Alice laughed.

"Yes, and that too, Brother Jack."

28

THE FINANCE COMMITTEE meeting lasted most of the morning. It left Dr. David Hasenglad exhausted and irritable. As he entered his outer office, he noticed a young woman waiting for him.

"This is Tatyana Ashkenazy, Dr. Hasenglad," his secretary said, "she was hoping she could talk to you."

The director of the Texas Polio Institute hated when people dropped in on him unexpectedly. Lord knows, he had remonstrated with his secretary enough times about it.

"Don't let them camp out in my office, Hilda," he told her. "Ask them to call first and make an appointment. You know I'm a very busy man."

After eleven years, Hilda took these reprimands and the exchange that invariably followed in stride. There were like the comically predictable routine of an old married couple.

"It's awkward asking them to leave," she said.

"Then tell them I'm out of town or something."

"I really cannot do that if at any moment you might walk in. It would create bad feelings."

Hasenglad would then change the subject and nothing more would be said about the matter until the next unscheduled visitor showed up on his doorstep.

David invited the woman into his office, not knowing what else to do. She was most likely the relative of a patient but the generosity of her smile held out the chance of a surprise.

"I was born in Russia, in Moscow," she said with a light accent, "but I now live here, in Houston. My husband is a most wealthy man and I do not need to work. I have no children. So I am thinking, I should do something to help others, yes?"

David smiled and nodded; he was enchanted by the young well-dressed woman with her dark eyes and hair.

"Perhaps I should help feed the homeless. I could teach people to read, but maybe my English is not so good. Then I think about my father." She lowered her voice as if confiding a secret. "He died from polio when I was little girl. It was very hard for my mother and sisters. So I will do what I can to help those suffering from polio. This I know is what I should do."

To the director's ears, these were magic words. A wealthy husband, a father who had died from polio, a desire to serve—clearly Mrs. Ashkenazy was a prime candidate for major donor status. And best of all she was young. He guessed late twenties, early thirties. Ninety percent of his donor base was sixty-years-old or older. Polio was not an issue that generated much passion in the United States since it had been all but eradicated. Images of rooms filled with iron lungs and little children being fitted for leg braces were a vague and distant memory to most Americans, if a memory at all. But here, remarkably, was a woman who could reach out to other young women. And he would enjoy spending time with her.

"What help did you have in mind?" he asked.

"I want to work with patients," she said. "I understand that many are getting sick again from polio they had as children. Is that true?"

"The condition is called post-polio syndrome."

"Do you treat these patients here at your center?"

"Yes, we provide medical treatment and physical therapy."

"And the patients come for this *physical therapy* on a regular basis?"

"Most do. It varies. Some come every week. Others, once a month. It all depends."

"Then this is something I would like to do very much," she said. "I am strong and learn quickly. I could help the therapists in some way?"

"I'm sure something can be arranged. An extra pair of hands"—and such beautiful hands, he thought—"would be most welcome. When would you like to start?"

"Tomorrow if that is possible. If not tomorrow, then next week. I can come in every day. My husband is away often on business. I want you to meet him. He is a very generous man."

I'm glad to hear it, David thought to himself. "I'll have my secretary take you over to Grace Bollinger's office," he said. "She's our volunteer coordinator. She'll get you situated."

Tatyana stood up to leave. "Perhaps I could make a small donation to the Institute now?" She unsnapped her purse.

"No, please," David said getting up so he could walk her to the door. "Get to know us first and observe the work we do. Then we can talk."

Better a large donation later than a small one now. He would take her to Eduardo's for lunch in a month or so. They would get to know each other, share stories. Afterwards, they would discuss money.

As she left the office, the director noted that his mood had improved and he felt a surge of gratitude for Hilda, thankful this once that his secretary was so self-willed.

OVER THE NEXT three weeks Tatyana made every effort to ingratiate herself to Dr. Rachel Posner, head of the Physical Therapy department. Dr. Posner was older and unmarried and a bond quickly formed between the two women. In some ways Dr. Posner began to regard the young Russian as the daughter she never had. Tatyana, however, was far from satisfied because no one even remotely resembling Kryuchkov showed up at the Institute for treatment. Victor was becoming impatient. He continued the rounds of Russian organizations and attended local chess competitions without success. For hours he sat at a table by the window at the Starbucks on Smith Street, watching the entrance to the EnerTex Building for a man with a cane. Other than giving his bladder a serious workout, this too proved a waste of time. Uri had provided him with a couple of voice-activated recording devices, which Viktor used to tap the home telephones of Avery Axton and Ron McBride. But he heard nothing, not a whisper, concerning the whereabouts of Kryuchkov.

"Today will be your last day at the Institute," he announced to Tatyana one morning. "There is another physical therapy facility. I am told that it is highly respected and they treat patients with post-polio syndrome also."

"Where is this facility?" Tatyana said.

"It is in the northern sector of the city. I will take you there tomorrow. Today you will work at the Institute."

She lit a cigarette. She knew Viktor didn't like her smoking but he never complained.

"What will you do today?" she asked.

"I have another meeting with EnerTex. They are serious. They want to be partners with Gromonov."

"That is good?"

"Gromonov thinks so. He is sending other people here next week. They will take over negotiations."

"Does Gromonov still want you to find Kryuchkov?"

"For now."

"What is wrong?" she asked.

He looked at her for a moment without speaking. The ashtray was across the room so she knocked the ash from her cigarette into the palm of her hand.

"Even though I am certain Kryuchkov is alive," Viktor said, "I have not told Gromonov yet."

"Why not?"

"I will find Kryuchkov first. That is what matters."

Tatyana suddenly realized that Viktor was worried that Gromonov might hire someone else to find Kryuchkov. The colonel was afraid of failure. She wanted to say, "Don't worry. Whatever happens, I will stay with you. We will go back to Russia together." She wasn't sure she believed this herself. A protector must be strong and confident. Perhaps Viktor was too old; he was beginning to doubt himself.

THE CAFETERIA WAS always crowded during the lunch hour but Dr. Posner and Tatyana managed to find an empty table. It was Tatyana's last chance to find out if the older woman knew anything that might help her.

"Do any Russians come to the Institute for treatment?" she asked.

"Russians? No. None that come through my department."

"What about other foreigners, people who were born in other countries, but who now live here in Houston?"

"There are a few. Why do you ask?"

"I am myself a newcomer to America. I am interested in people who have come here to live."

"There's a woman from Buenos Aires. Her name is Dorbeta. She was here for her treatment two days ago."

"Yes," Tatyana said, "she has such lovely hair."

"She sings in the opera. She's very talented from what I hear. Another woman who comes every Friday is Swiss. Here name is Adele. I love that name."

"Any men?"

"There's a man who was born in Germany, but he came to the United States when he was very young. He is a nice man."

"What does he do, this nice man?" Tatyana did her best to mask her interest under a veil of innocent curiosity.

"He's a scientist. He's exceptionally bright. We've become quite good friends."

Tatyana sensed something special in the way the older woman talked about this man. Perhaps there was a romantic interest.

"What do you talk about?"

"All kinds of things: philosophy, literature, the arts. He's fascinated with quantum mechanics," she chuckled. "Not my best subject, I must admit, but he seems to enjoy having someone to talk to about it. I think he's a bit lonely."

"It is good that he has you for a friend," Tatyana said and watched as Dr. Posner's cheeks reddened.

"What is his name?"

"Walter."

"How old is he?"

"Sixty-three."

Tatyana felt a rush of excitement and anticipation. According to Viktor's information, Kryuchkov would be in his early sixties.

"You said he was born in Germany?" she asked.

A flicker of concern showed itself in Dr. Posner's eyes and Tatyana feared she was growing suspicious. Perhaps she was asking too many questions but she hoped the older woman would welcome any excuse to talk about a man she had feelings for. So far this had appeared to be the case.

"He was born in Dusseldorf but he came to the United States when he was six."

The look of concern persisted, stronger now if anything. Tatyana suspected that it had nothing to do with her. Something else was troubling Dr. Posner, something she wanted to talk about.

"What is he like?"

"I'd have to say he's something of a mystery."

"Why?"

Dr. Posner leaned forward and lowered her voice.

"He says he grew up in the United States, in Cleveland, but he knows so little about American culture."

"What do you mean?"

"Televisions shows. Movies. Root beer floats. Stuff people used to enjoy doing. I think Walter must have led a very sheltered life."

"Does his polio cause him much pain?"

"I believe it does, but he never complains."

Dr. Posner glanced at her watch and stood up. It was time to return to work; she had eaten only half of her tarragon chicken salad.

"When does Walter come in for his treatment?" Tatyana asked, also standing and picking up her tray. "I would like to meet him."

"Twice a month, on Thursdays. He canceled his last appointment. That's why you haven't met him. He will be here tomorrow."

Tatyana wanted to ask, "Does he walk with a cane?" but stopped herself. She could wait twenty-four hours. So could Viktor. She smiled as she rode the elevator back up to the fourth floor.

29

"MAY I PLEASE speak with Reb Morgan?"

Mattie recognized the voice; it gave her an unexpected thrill.

"I'm sorry, but he's not come in yet," she said.

"Well, please tell him that Lyle Workman called. Ask him to call me as soon as he can. It's important." He gave her his office and home phone numbers.

Reb walked in two hours later and Mattie told him about the call.

"What did he want?"

"He didn't say."

"Is Kevin still out of town?"

"He won't be back until Monday."

"Thanks. I'll use his office to make the call," Reb said. He got through to Workman on the second ring.

"Lyle, this is Reb Morgan."

"Great, I'm glad you called back. I realize you and Alice are laying off the EnerTex story, but I did a little digging on my own and I think I came up with something. I couldn't get to it right away because I had to finish up a book tour." A month had passed since Reb and Alice returned from Texas.

"What did you find out?" Reb asked.

"I called Sandra Valdez to ask her how the interviews went and she told me her husband was fired. So was her friend's husband, Mike Pendergast."

Once as a kid at the beach, Reb had been knocked down by a sneaker wave. One moment he was stomping around in the water enjoying himself, and the next, his world was in a jumble. Workman's news had the same effect on him now. ~~This was the effect Workman's news had on him now.~~ How the hell did EnerTex found out about the interview? Was it the electronic bug in the car? Had he or Alice said their names aloud? He couldn't recall. . .

"You still there?" Lyle said.

"Yeah, I was just thinking about those poor people; I betrayed their trust."

"That's not how they see it."

"But I had—"

"Sandra said it was bound to come out one way or another that they talked to the press. In fact she's actually relieved that her husband no longer works for EnerTex."

"What about the Pendergasts?"

"We build 'em tough down here in Texas, Reb. I wouldn't worry too much about it."

"How do you think EnerTex found out?"

"Hard to say."

"I never told you this, Lyle, but somebody planted marijuana in our rental car to get us arrested. And there was a guy in a Porsche who followed us."

"What guy?"

"I think he was working for EnerTex," Reb said and filled Workman in on the details.

"Well, you must have done something to get their hackles up," Lyle said. "I say we keep the heat on."

What *we* are we talking about? Reb thought to himself. He appreciated the fact that the Texan had paid for a couple of airline tickets and hotel rooms, but it was Reb and Alice who would take the heat if they weren't careful. And KVMR.

"I hope you don't feel as if we wasted your money," Reb said.

"No, not at all, but there's more work to be done. What do you know about Avery Axton?"

"He's the CEO of EnerTex."

"And the president. I've known the family for years. Avery has a younger brother who's a doctor. His name is Elliot. Runs a non-profit clinic in Houston for low income families. He's a real likable guy, not at all like his brother."

Reb stood up and paced, the portable phone held against his ear. Something was coming; he could feel it, a change that would shatter the weird half-life he had been living for the last month.

"So here's the thing," Lyle continued. "I happened to remember the other day that Elliot knows a scientist at EnerTex. His name is Dr. Easler and he and Elliot play chess together. So I called Elliot and told him about you and Alice and the trouble you were having with the EnerTex story. As I said, he's a doctor and he was genuinely concerned about what might be happening to the plant workers. I asked him if his friend Dr. Easler might know something. It was a long shot, but even a cross-eyed fiddler can win top prize now and again."

"What did he say, your friend Elliot?"

"That he'd get back to me."

"And did he?"

"This morning. He said Dr. Easler is very eager to meet with you. He claims he can explain everything. If you're still game."

"I'll have to talk to some people on this end first."

"Well, I wouldn't dally, Reb. I got the impression that Dr. Easler is in a bit of a hurry."

"I'll get back to you by tomorrow, Lyle."

"Here's something else to think about. Elliot has another friend named Marion Harless. I served on a committee with Marion once; he's an oil man and something of a character. Anyway, he owns a spread not far from Houston called Chancewater Ranch and Elliot says Marion offered to let you interview Dr. Easler there."

"And you said Easler is willing to go on the record with what he knows?"

"That's what Elliot says. Easler claims he designed the Ranger 1 power plant single-handedly from the ground up."

Reb wasn't sure he believed what he was hearing. It was the break he had been hoping for. He could see Workman on the other end of the line, his pearl gray Stetson pushed back on his head, his boots up on his desk, smiling like some kind of bizarre Texan wizard whose words possessed magical powers, capable of conjuring Reb's enthusiasm back to life. Or perhaps Lyle was a trickster, like Old Man Coyote, who would lead Reb and the radio station to destruction in the end.

He said goodbye and put down the phone. He had a lot to think about. He also needed to talk to Kevin and Alice. Unfortunately, the station manager was out of town. Even if he wasn't, Kevin wasn't likely to give the go-ahead without board approval, and that would require calling a special meeting which would add several more days to the process. And there was no telling what the board might do. He left Kevin's office and went looking for Phil.

"So that's the deal," Reb finished relating the particulars of Workman's call to the program director. "If I decide to go back to Texas, I'll need to leave soon, by tomorrow if possible.

"What about Alice?"

"I haven't talked to her yet."

"Do you believe him?"

"Workman? Yes, I do."

"It's a big risk."

Reb nodded.

Phil leaned back in his chair. The voice of Woody Guthrie drifted out of the wall speaker in the adjoining room. Dan Donaldson's folk music show was in its second hour. Scully, the station engineer, sauntered in with a stack of mail addressed to the program director and dropped it unceremoniously on the table next to Phil's desk. It was impossible to keep up, Phil thought. Demos for new radio shows arrived every day from all over the country. It was his job to audition them. He was also responsible for finding replacements for broadcasters who were out sick or on vacation, designing innovative pledge drives, scheduling tests of the emergency alert system, attending program committee meetings, and helping train new broadcasters. All the while he made sure the FCC and CPB reporting requirements were met and regulations followed, no small task in itself. It was therefore was understandable that his crowded days often extended into crowded nights. And now the EnerTex story was back again, like one of those chainsaw-wielding villains in a slocker-shocker movie who after being clubbed, stabbed, run over by a truck, shot, thrown off a cliff, and blown-up still manages one last attack upon the hapless hero.

He swiveled his chair around and looked out the window at the Miner's Foundry Cultural Center across the street. The phone rang but he ignored it. Kevin was off hiking in the mountains with his family and couldn't be reached. That made him, Phil Cook, acting manager. According to Workman, the sooner a decision was made, the better. Should he call a special meeting of the board? Maybe just the executive committee? They were running scared, as well they should. If the government could put reporters from the New York *Times* and *Time Magazine* behind bars, what was to keep them from jailing the likes of Reb Morgan? Alice too, if she went with him. What protection could KVMR give them? None. Not without a national shield law, and that wasn't coming down the pike anytime soon.

He turned back and began scrolling through his Rolodex looking for Skip Mathune's number. But then he heard the haranguing, self-important voice of Jack Dunnel in his head, which effectively drove out any idea of consulting the board.

"I don't know what to tell you, Reb," he said, pushing away the Rolodex. "When I got into radio a hundred years ago it was because I wanted to make a difference, you know, change the world." He shrugged. "Maybe some days I do. It's hard to say."

"I have an idea," Reb said in an effort to overcome the impasse. "What if I write a letter of resignation and give it to you. I'll date it for yesterday and you can keep it in your desk, just in case."

"In case of what?"

"In case the bad guys come after us. You can then say I no longer work for KVMR and that I'm pursuing the story on my own."

"They'll probably still sue us."

"I imagine they'll sue everybody," Reb said. "Me, you, the board, even Kevin's dog. It's how they do things in the corporate world. But the letter should give the station some legal cover."

"And if you and you and Alice break the biggest story of the century and win all kinds of awards, what then?" Phil asked.

Reb smiled. "Then KVMR shares in the credit. Because—"

"Because you still work here, you never quit."

"Not unless you show Jack Dunnel the letter."

Phil rubbed his chin and also smiled but his eyes were tinged with sadness.

"You know if trouble comes, Reb, you'll be on your own. It can be a cold lonely world out there."

These words clarified exactly what was at stake for Reb. He could lose his job. They could also haul him off to some secret detention center in the Caribbean or eastern Europe. The glaucoma put his future in jeopardy; going after EnerTex could smash it to pieces.

"I'll talk to Alice and get back to you," he said and got up to leave.

"I've heard it said that God watches over fools and drunks," Phil said.

"Let's hope that includes citizen journalists as well."

PUTTING DOWN THE phone, Alice realized her relationship with Reb had reached a turning point. He was coming over to talk about the EnerTex story. Since their return from Texas and the ill-fated board meeting, things had been different between them. They had gone to dinner a couple of times and once to a movie, but Reb no longer stayed the night at her house. The cooling had more to do with her than him. She told herself she needed some time on her own. And then Vicki quit the news department, giving only a week's notice to move to Hawaii with her boyfriend. That meant Alice had to advertise the intern position all over again, conduct interviews, and train her replacement. Only her heart didn't seem to be in the work anymore. Little things about KVMR wore on her—the way the DJs squabbled with each other over who got the best on-air slots in the schedule, or who had walked off with the newest Neil Young CD. More than once she considered quitting as news director. Too many changes in too short a time—the divorce, expanding the news department, Reb and his glaucoma, and then EnerTex. How could she seriously consider going back to Texas after what Wayne told her?

The conversation took place several days earlier, when Wayne stopped by to pick up some power tools stored in the garage.

"This isn't about jealousy or anything like that," he said, "but from what you tell me, this boyfriend of yours is determined to hunt up trouble one way or another."

"What are you talking about?" She made no attempt to hide her annoyance. Now that she was free of the marriage, she resented having her judgment questioned. And just because Wayne said he wasn't jealous didn't make it so; men were possessive creatures when it came to the women in their lives.

"All I'm saying is that he should think twice before taking on the energy industry."

"He's not *taking on* the energy industry as you put it. He is investigating one company."

"EnerTex."

"Yes, and if you need to know, he's decided to drop the story."

"Good. I won't pretend that I care all that much what happens to him but I don't want you getting hurt because you're associated with him."

Words had specific meanings for her and she loathed euphemisms. As director of the news department, she wasn't *associated* with Reb Morgan. She was his supervisor. They were also lovers. And what's more, how did Wayne know about EnerTex? As far as she could remember, she had never mentioned the company to him. He had always kept his distance from her work at KVMR. If in his mind there had been a rival, it was the radio station, not Reb, so it wasn't likely he would have heard about EnerTex from that source.

"They contacted me," he said.

"Who did?"

"A lawyer from EnerTex—or that's who I took him to be. He claimed he was with an electric utilities association, but when I checked later, I found out there is no such group."

Alice was clearly having trouble following him.

"I met him at a conference in Phoenix last week," Wayne continued. "I'd just finished a presentation on criminal procedure and I was in the hotel lobby bar having a drink and he came up and sat down next to me. He said his name was Russell Hargrave. He looked and talked like John Wayne."

"So what did he say?"

"He said, 'I understand you live in Nevada City. Well, there's a radio station in your town that's got some important people down my way a little upset.' It wasn't hard to tell he was from Texas."

"How's that?"

"Texans have a unique way of talking, a mixture of Deep South and Appalachia, with sprinkling of Mexican thrown in." This was a revelation for Alice; she had never thought of her ex-husband as a linguist.

"Okay, go on," she said.

"Well, this guy Hargrave said, 'I wouldn't want to be them if they keep pushing their noses into places they don't belong.'"

"He really said that?"

"Word for word," Wayne said. "And so I asked him what he was getting at and he said that you and Morgan were investigating a company called EnerTex."

"Why was he talking to you?"

"I guess he somehow knew you and I were once married. He was using me as a messenger."

"And you're delivering the message."

"It's best to know these things, Alice. This isn't a game. These people play for keeps."

"Oh, don't be so melodramatic!" She didn't want to appear frightened but she was. She ran a hand through her hair and then folded her arms, pulling them tightly around her body. Wayne turned toward the door.

"EnerTex threatened to sue the station if we continue with the investigation," she said. "The board met last month to talk over what they should do about it."

"And?"

"As I said, Reb offered to drop the investigation. He really doesn't have a story, just accusations from a couple of workers at the EnerTex power plant. They say there's something at the plant that is making them sick."

"Well, I don't think this guy Hargrave was talking about a lawsuit. It was more serious than that."

"Did you get your tools?" she asked, changing the subject.

"Whatever you do, Alice, take care of yourself," he said and left.

Alice began preparing dinner. She looked at the clock; Reb would arrive in ten minutes or so. As she diced the tomatoes, she recalled how the police in Dalton County pulled them over and searched their car. The memory was still vivid, the flashing lights, police eyes hidden behind dark sunglasses, her feeling of powerlessness. She pushed the tomatoes off the cutting board into a cast iron skillet and added two cloves of crushed garlic and other seasonings. She then opened a bottle of Sonoma County Cabernet and poured herself a glass. A car drove past, the thumping the base line song assaulting every ear for blocks around. It drove her crazy how inconsiderate people could be. She sipped her wine and tried to calm down. The door bell rang. She stirred the sauce, adjusted the heat, and went to let Reb in.

"Why didn't you come into work today?" he said as he dropped his hat on the arm of the couch. "Are you not feeling well?"

"Just a little tired and out of sorts. Come into the kitchen and tell me about Lyle's call."

She poured him some wine as he related the details of the conversation and the meeting with Phil and his offer to write a letter of resignation.

"So will you go back to Texas with me?" he asked.

"Have you already made up your mind to go?" she asked.

"It depends."

"On what?"

"All kinds of things, but mostly on you."

"You can't put this on me," she said.

"It's just that we've worked on this story together so far."

"Then why did you tell the board you were dropping it without asking me how I felt?"

"You're right," he said, "I should have."

"A fine time to admit it." She picked up the wooden spoon and stirred the sauce so that the sweet simmering aroma filled the kitchen. Reb's mother loved to cook Italian food and the scent of basil and oregano always brought her memory back to him.

"You know by rights it's my call whether you go back or not," she said. "I'm the news director, not Phil."

"Will you fire me if I go?" he asked.

"I thought that's what the letter of resignation was for."

"Look," he said, stepping closer and taking her hand. "Let's not fight over this, okay? I understand if you don't want to go. It's probably a foolhardy thing to do."

"Have you talked to your son about this?" she asked pulling her hand away.

"No, it's my decision."

"I wouldn't want to unduly worry my children," she said.

"Then don't go," he said.

"Don't tell me what to do."

Reb suddenly laughed. "I'm famished. How's that sauce coming along?"

She pushed a wooden bowl at him and a head of lettuce. "Here, work on the salad."

Nothing more was said about EnerTex until they finished their meal.

What weighed most on Alice's heart and mind was the thought of Reb's nightmare in the hotel room in Lubbock. In the dream, Death had appeared at the door. She could picture Death so clearly, a tall gaunt figure dressed in black, silent and waiting. She was convinced the dream was an omen. Something terrible was going to happen to Reb. The ringing telephone, was that the call from Lyle Workman? And the Victorian house. She wondered what kind of house this Marion Harless owned?

"I thought you hated Texas," she said placing her napkin next to her plate.

"Not any more," he said.

"And why's that?" she said.

"Because we met some really great people who live there," he said, "And, well, because we were there together."

"What is it with you?" she almost yelled at him, but managed to stop herself.

Reb began to gather up the plates to take them back to the kitchen.

"Wait," she said. He looked at her and sat down again.

"Are you going to Texas? Just tell me the truth."

"I don't think I have a choice," he said and he suddenly knew that this was true. It was a debt he owed Ernesto and Mike. They had lost their jobs because of him.

"There's no law that says you've got to be a hero."

He shrugged and drained his glass. The clock chimed eight on the mantle in the living room.

"It comes down to the people's right to know, Alice," he said, "That's what being a journalist is all about."

"Don't lecture me on the responsibilities of the Fourth Estate. I've gone to jail for my beliefs. You haven't."

This was news to Reb. "When?" he asked.

"It doesn't matter," the wine was fueling her anger, that and the pent-up frustration of the last month.

"No really," Reb said. "When were you arrested?"

"Three years ago, in Washington State, for blocking access to a nuclear submarine base. I was part of a group of protesters."

"Well I'll be damned!" he said, adoration illuminating his features. "KVMR's own Ida Tarbell." He looked so child-like that the fight drained out of her. She loved him and had missed having him around more than she cared to admit. Tears welled up in her eyes and her limbs began to tremble.

"What's wrong?" he said coming over to her. "Are you all right?"

She stood up and put her arms around him. The gesture surprised him.

"I'll go with you," she said, her voice almost a whisper.

"Are you sure?"

"Yes."

Reb stroked her hair. " I love you," he said.

"I know," she said.

"Look, if you don't want me to go—"

"We'll see this through to the end and we'll do it together," she said.

"And if you lose your job?"

She lifted her head and looked into his eyes. "I have my own reasons for doing this," she said. "I'll take my chances."

Those reasons had to do with EnerTex. She no longer saw them as just another conniving amoral corporation motivated by self-interest; they were for her the very incarnation of everything she abhorred in the new social order—the increasing centralization of economic and political power, the corruption of democratic institutions by shameless cronyism and bribery masking as campaign contributions, the privatization of the commons by individuals bent on satisfying their greed at the expense of the public good, and the pervasive and growing influence of machines in every aspect of human existence. At some point these forces had to be challenged and defeated. The hill called EnerTex was as good as any upon which to make her stand.

"Let's go get 'em, partner," she said and Reb nodded. No more discussion. The decision was made, their fates sealed. They were going back to the Lone Star State.

30

FOR WALTER, THE last four weeks had felt more like four years. A naturally shy man, he cherished his privacy and solitude and resented the intrusion. He had important work to do. Ever since returning to Houston, after overseeing the construction of the power plant, he had spent nearly every waking hour immersed in complex mathematical equations, trying to solve the one problem that rendered the great discovery of his lifetime meaningless. And this effort had exhausted and nearly broken his mind. Then came the arrival of the brash young man. He disliked everything about Marty Hamilton, his brusque manners, his restless, anxious boredom, the constant drone of the television set—the young man was addicted to sporting events and shows involving billionaires—even the scent of his aftershave offended him. Avery Axton had sent the two men who frightened him—large, humorless men trained in the arts of intimidation and murder.

Marty was not frightening, just annoying—a talker who talked about himself, even when he was talking about others. He was a man whose soul was being consumed by the ravenous tapeworm of ambition. Walter saw this but felt no pity. He suspected Avery Axton saw it too and was making full use of it.

"Hey, Walter, want some coffee?" It was late morning and Marty stood at the door to the older man's office holding a coffee pot.

"No," the physicist said, not looking up from work.

"Suit yourself. When is your appointment at the Institute?"

"Two o'clock."

"Be ready by twelve-thirty."

"I can drive myself."

"Not today, Doctor. I'm taking you."

Numerous times each day Walter recalled the moment at the airport when he had almost left. A short walk down the jet way into the Boeing 737, and Texas and the Ranger 1 power plant would have been behind him forever. But he had allowed his resolve to slip, had turned back, chosen security, the safe harbor, over a future of uncertainty and perceived uselessness. It was a decision he now bitterly regretted. He also feared that his masters at EnerTex had sensed that something was wrong. Perhaps he was spotted at the airport. For a month he had endured this private hell. But no more. He had a plan. All it required was outside help and he had that now.

"I'll be taking Easler to the Institute after lunch," Marty said to the on-duty bodyguard as he came back into the kitchen and placed the coffee pot down on the counter next to the unwashed dishes from breakfast. "You stay here and keep an eye on the house."

The bodyguards spelled each other every twelve hours so there was always one around at any given time. Marty's task was to keep the EnerTex scientist company 24/7, or until his boss decided that the threat to Dr. Easler was over.

"I'm to stay with the client at all times," the bodyguard replied.

"You are to follow my directives," Marty said. "I'm in charge here."

The man nodded.

"I don't intend to leave the house empty and unguarded," Marty expanded. "Dr. Easler has many valuable papers that EnerTex does not want to fall into the wrong hands. Savvy?"

The guard nodded again but was ill at ease. He would talk to Mr. Axton the next time the CEO stopped by. Nothing had been said about what to do if the client left the house.

Marty, on the other hand, was happiness itself. He had been angling for some serious one-on-one with the Russian physicist and now he would have it. Dr. Easler was the brains behind the Ranger 1 power plant. Avery had implied as much and Marty had been selling the new power plants without anyone knowing how they worked, including himself. It irked him that he was as much in the dark as Maggie Greer and everyone else outside the Department of Energy. Even inside the agency, only the nine members of SEPOC, the Special Energy Production Oversight Committee, really knew what was going on. Add to that the president of the United States, the vice-president, the national security advisor, the Senate Majority leader, and the Speaker of the House—all in all two to three dozen individuals on a planet with a population topping six billion. Incredible. Power in the information age was all about possessing the right information and Marty yearned for that kind of power. The money was secondary; to gain admittance into the Inner Circle was his true goal—to "be in the loop." He decided to work on Easler and win his confidence. He knew the old man disliked him but that didn't matter. Marty was a trader, a deal maker. Walter didn't need to like him, he just needed to want what Marty was offering. It was certainly worth a try but he couldn't do it with the muscle tagging along.

The drive into the city, however, proved less productive than Marty had hoped despite his efforts to trowel on the flattery.

"You're a clever man, Doctor," Marty said, "a genius, from what I hear. But sometimes clever men fail to attend to their own long term interests. I'm sure EnerTex pays you good money but it can't be that good, judging by the house they gave you to live in." Marty couldn't stand the place, a standard issue split-level at the end of a cul-de-sac. The neighborhood was populated by junior accountant executives, department store managers, emergency room nurses, and airline pilots. The fact that Brenda lived only five blocks away only made it worse—being chained hand and foot to Easler as he was, a quickie was simply out of the question.

"Sometime soon Mr. Axton will need to raise a substantial amount of capital if he intends to start building power plants all around the world," Marty continued. "To do this, he'll have to take EnerTex public, but there's no telling when that might happen. Could be a year, maybe two. So buying EnerTex stock isn't an option right now."

Marty took his eyes off the road briefly to glance over at Easler. The fucking guy was unreadable. He forged ahead.

"The good news is that *other* companies will be supplying the materials to build and fuel the new power plants, and they are publicly-traded companies. Now, if someone knew exactly which companies these were, and if he was able to purchase a chunk of their stock, well, he'd become a very wealthy man once the ball gets rolling, if you see what I mean. Of course, he'd have to avoid any suspicion of insider trading. Do you know what 'insider trading' is?"

Walter said nothing.

"Yeah, well, it means you can't profit from buying and selling stock if you have special knowledge that investor Joe Blow doesn't have. It's illegal and they can throw your sorry ass in jail." He made a mental note to watch his language. He wanted to win Easler over, not offend his Old World sensibilities.

"What you need, Dr. Easler, are a few discreet, well-placed friends. Agents who know how to purchase and sell stock so that the paper trail doesn't lead back to you. The money you make then gets shipped off-shore to the Cayman Islands, or Switzerland, or anywhere you want so that when you decide to retire, you can do it in style."

"What do you want in exchange?" Walter said. The traffic was lighter than usual and they were already approaching their freeway exit. Marty picked up the pace of his pitch.

"I need to know how the electric generation process works at the Ranger 1 plant. That way I can—we can—predict which companies EnerTex will purchase their supplies from. I don't need to know the exact details, you understand; I'm not trying to steal company secrets. Just give me the general outline. What is the power source? Who has it and how does EnerTex buy it?"

"You ask for much."

"But I'm offering you much, doctor. You don't know how to structure a deal like this, but I do. It's complicated. Income and expenses have to be accurately projected out ten to fifteen years. There are sophisticated models to predict all that."

They were now four blocks from the Texas Polio Institute, sitting at a red light.

"I will consider what you are saying," Walter said, "but I do not think your employer would be pleased to hear that you are offering me a *deal*, as you call it."

A current of fear made the Tin Man's scalp tingle. He could deny the conversation ever took place, but his boss would see through him in a heartbeat. Perhaps Avery would appreciate his initiative. Not likely. Marty should have predicted this kind of response but he hadn't. He was blind that way.

"Do not worry, young man," Walter said. "I will not tell on you." The light changed and they moved forward with the traffic along Montclair Avenue.

"Then you will think over my offer?" Marty said, his hopes only momentarily derailed by Walter's comments.

"Yes, I will think about what you propose. I may need more money soon. My health is not so good. It's expensive to get old and sick in America."

Marty smiled broadly. "You can say that again."

They turned into the entrance of the Texas Polio Institute. The building was an elegant structure of brushed aluminum and aqua green glass, a testament to the soul's ability to rise above the pain and difficulties of life.

Marty parked in a handicap slot and walked Walter to the front door. He had no reason to notice the white Ford cargo van parked at the far end of the lot. They crossed the lobby and Walter leaned on his cane as they rode the elevator up to the fourth floor. Stepping out, they turned right down a corridor that opened up at the end into a well-appointed waiting room. On the far side of the room was a reception window next to a door marked "Physical Therapy Department." Walter went to the window and signed himself in.

"You can go right in, Dr. Easler," the receptionist said.

Walter turned to Marty. "Wait here for me. I will be two hours."

"No-can-do, Doc. I've got to stick with you. Orders."

Walter frowned and his eyes narrowed. "Physical therapy for my condition is difficult and painful. It is not something I wish to share with anyone, not even a family member."

The message in the old man's eyes was unmistakable. The message read: "this far and no further." Marty was under instructions to baby-sit the Russian scientist. Still, he thought, I don't go to the bathroom with the guy. Why embarrass him? Besides, nothing will be gained by alienating Walter now that he's considering a partnership. Play nice and I might find out what the big secret is, and make a few million bucks for myself and Walter to boot.

"Okay, I'll wait out here," Marty said and Walter went through the door into the treatment area. Marty ignored the half dozen people in the waiting room as he half-heartedly worked his way through a stack of magazines on a small table—*Redbook, Better Homes and Gardens, Family Circle*—it was as if the only people who got polio were women. He sat down and took out his cell phone. He ran through the numbers on the liquid crystal display, pushed the call button, and began talking. An elderly woman nearby looked up from her reading with a pained expression. The Tin Man's voice was anything but discreet.

"Hey Dean, it's Marty. Yeah, I'm in Houston. Look, I've been thinking about that real estate deal you mentioned, you know, the one with the church group in Colorado Springs. . ."

TEN MINUTES BEFORE Walter's appointment, Tatyana made an excuse and went out and to sit in the waiting room. She watched as an older man approached using a cane to steady himself. She recognized him from the photograph. What she hadn't anticipated was that he would have a companion with him, a younger man. The two men talked and then Kryuchkov went into the treatment area. Tatyana waited a minute, got up, and went back into the department. She saw Dr. Posner lead Kryuchkov into one of the private treatment rooms, closing the door behind them. Another patient approached her from the direction of the whirlpool and gym. Tatyana waited until she passed before pulling out a small walkie-talkie from the side pocket of her coat.

"Uri?" she whispered. "Uri, are you there?"

"Yes." Her brother's voice was too loud and she quickly turned the volume down as she stepped into an empty treatment room across the hallway and closed the door.

"It is him. Kryuchkov. I am sure of it. But he is not alone. There is another man with him."

Down in the parking lot in the white van, Uri looked over at Viktor. "There is someone with him," he said.

"I can hear."

"Listen," Tatyana said. "I have an idea."

"Go on," said her brother.

"There is a room on this floor, examination room 16. It is down the hallway beyond the elevators. I will bring the other man there. In ten minutes."

Viktor reached over and took the walkie-talkie from Uri. The plan had been simple up until now: wait outside the Institute in the van, find out from Tatyana if Dr. Easler was Kryuchkov and, if so, wait for him to come out, and then force him into the van, drug him, and drive away. Now they must improvise. His heart rate quickened; he welcomed the challenge, the added complexity.

"Is the man armed?" he asked.

"He has no jacket," Tatyana said. "I do not think so."

Viktor wasn't convinced. He could be wearing an ankle holster.

He asked Tatyana to repeat the directions to room 16, which she did.

"I will bring him there in ten minutes," she said and dropped the walkie-talkie back into her pocket. She turned and looked at herself in the mirror above the sink. She pulled a loose strand of hair back into place and then used the tips of her fingers to smooth the lipstick at the corners of her mouth. She looked at her watch.

Coming out, she glanced over at the door to the treatment room Dr. Posner and Kryuchkov had entered. It was closed. Good. She knew the treatment would last an hour. Afterwards Kryuchkov would go to the whirlpool. There was ample time to deal with the scientist's companion.

"EXCUSE ME, ARE you Dr. Easler's friend?"

Marty looked up at the young woman in the long white coat. "I'll call you back, Dean. Gotta go," he said and snapped the phone closed. "What's wrong? Is Dr. Easler okay?"

Tatyana smiled pleasantly, "Oh yes. He is receiving his treatment now. I've been asked to tell you that Dr. Hasenglad, the director of the Institute, wishes to have a word with you. It's about Dr. Easler."

Marty stared at the woman stupidly. She was gorgeous, every part of her. She had the face, the hair, the legs, the whole package.

"He's just down the hallway," she said softly, considerate of the others in the room.

"Who is?"

"Dr. Hasenglad. It will only take a moment of your time. I will take you to him."

"But I need to be here when Dr. Easler comes out," he said.

She looked at her watch. "That will not be for at least ninety minutes. This will only take a moment. Please." She stepped back, and some invisible force emanated from her smile and young body that drew Marty up out of his chair without his conscious intent. She then turned and he followed her down the hallway toward the elevators, hurrying to catch up.

"Are you a nurse here?" he asked. He couldn't think of anything else to say.

"I'm a therapist. I work with the children."

"I didn't know children got polio anymore."

She had made a mistake and was angry with herself.

"We deal with a variety of medical conditions here at the Institute," she said.

There was something familiar about the girl, Marty thought. He might have met her at a nightclub or a party. He tried to think. She wasn't the kind of woman he would easily forget. They passed the elevators and came to a door.

He turned to her uncertainly. He was trying to figure out the best way to ask her for a date. The deal with Easler wasn't going to last forever and he was starved for female attention. He thought about giving her one of his cards and asking her to call him when she was free. But before he could reach for his wallet she opened the door and motioned for him to go in. He stepped into the room and the door closed smartly behind him. He had expected an office, not an examination room. He then noticed two men. One was quite a bit older than the other, and like the girl, he looked familiar. Then it came to him. He was a Russian, Colonel somebody or other. The girl was his assistant. Every meeting at EnerTex was covertly video-taped and Avery had shown him the tape of the meeting with the Russians. Avery told him her name. What was it? But while he was trying to remember, the older man stepped toward him and took hold of his arm. Adrenaline flooded Marty's system and he managed to yank his arm free and throw the colonel off balance. He turned toward the door but the other man kicked his feet out from under him and Marty went down in a crazy, spiraling motion, smashing his nose and the side of his face against a cabinet next to the sink. Blood gushed from his shattered nose and left a long red streak on the white melamine surface as a rough, strong hand grabbed his shirt collar just before he hit the floor. He was yanked upward as a knee came crashing up into his stomach. His senses were in chaos, his gravitational orientation obliterated. All the same, a part of his mind was hyper-aware and this inner observer understood that the second blow had missed its mark. The man had been aiming for his solar plexus. With a burst of effort, Marty pushed off the side of the counter with his hands, backwards, pulling his attacker with him. The momentum put them both on the floor. Despite his blurred vision, Marty successfully reached out and grabbed the other man by both ears, and head butted him. He heard and felt the cartilage of the man's nose give way under the force of the blow but the thrill of revenge was short-lived. His hair was grabbed from behind and his head jerked back violently. Marty was suddenly sick and vomit spewed out of him. He then felt a stab of pain in the muscle of his right arm. He stared down in disbelief as a syringe was pulled out. "You son-of-a-bitch. . ." he tried to yell but his mouth was awash in vomit, and the effect of the drug was already stealing away his consciousness. A single thought kept repeating itself over and over inside his brain. I'm being murdered. I'm being murdered. His limbs grew heavy and unresponsive. He was slipping away. He wanted to cry out. Then came the blackness.

Viktor strode quickly to the door, opened it, and looked around to see if anyone overheard the scuffle. The hallway was empty. He closed and locked the door. He had not expected the confrontation to turn so violent. Clearly the man had recognized him. It was there in his eyes. And now Uri was injured, sitting on the floor holding his hands over a broken nose, blood seeping through his fingers. Viktor took him by the elbow, helped him to stand, and walked him over to a chair in the corner next to a set of scales. Luckily the room contained medical supplies and he soon found gauze and tape. He had dealt with broken noses before. Hazing in the Russian army was a cherished tradition visited upon new conscripts by their alcoholic non-commissioned officers, who liked nothing better than to come into the barracks drunk late at night and start beating up anybody they could get their hands on. In recent years, the practice had gotten worse; conscripts were regularly killed. It was another reason Viktor quit the service.

He pulled a handful of paper towels from a wall dispenser and ran water over them. These he used to clean away the blood. Uri sat and made no sound, even though Viktor knew it must be very painful. He then bandaged the nose. There was a light knock on the door just as he finished.

"Yes?" he said.

"It is Tatyana," she whispered. "Is everything all right?"

Viktor let her in and locked the door again. He was going to ask about Kryuchkov but Tatyana didn't give him the chance. The room reeked of vomit and her eyes went quickly from the bloody smear on the side of the counter to the man she brought from the waiting room, lying in a heap on the floor. She then caught sight of her brother sitting in the chair with a white bandage across much of his face. A strange animal-like sound issued from her throat and she ran over to him, dropping down onto her knees and looking up at him, her face tortured with concern.

"Uri, my darling," she crooned, "what have they done to you?"

Her brother made no attempt to respond, imagining how foolish he would sound speaking with a crushed septum.

"He fought well," Viktor said.

"My brother is very brave," she said, glancing back at Viktor, her eyes filling with tears.

Viktor was surprised. He had not meant Uri. He was talking about the man on the floor. He nodded his head in the man's direction and she understood.

"Who is he?" Viktor said. "I do not think he is a bodyguard."

"Is he dead?" Tatyana asked indifferently as she turned back to her brother. She held one of his hands with both of hers.

"No, I gave him a strong sedative. He will sleep a long time; we must hide the body."

The room had another door. Viktor went over and opened it. It was a closet with shelves along the back and one side. Supplies and test equipment lined the shelves.

"There is just enough room in here I think," he said. He walked back to the unconscious man and searched him for weapons. Finding none, he removed the man's wallet and cell phone. He shoved the wallet into the front pocket of his trousers. He then dropped the cell phone on the floor and crushed it with the heel of his shoe; he didn't want it to suddenly come alive and begin playing some stupid song.

"Come help me," he said and Tatyana turned toward him again.

"No, not you," he said. "You will foul your clothes. Go back to Kryuchkov. Uri and I will move the body."

"Kryuchkov will be some time yet receiving his treatment," Tatyana said coldly. "I must stay here and help my brother."

"Do as I say," Viktor ordered.

She glared at him and refused to move. Uri had his head down and seemed not to hear what was going on. Viktor was suddenly struck by the image before him. It was like a painting; Tatyana on her knees in front of her injured brother soothing him like a frightened mother. No, he thought, not a mother, a sister, a sister who was still a child herself. And Uri, a child also. That was the image. Two abandoned children alone in the world clinging to each other. The sad tenderness of it made Viktor want to turn away.

He decided to move the body on his own. Dragging it across the floor by the feet, he could feel the anger and jealousy churning inside him—the defiance in her eyes, the devotion to her brother. Reaching the closet, he found he could not get the body inside and shut the door by himself; there wasn't enough floor space. He needed to stand the body up and this required two people.

"Uri, come now and help me," he said.

Uri stood up, pulling his hand away from his sister.

"Go back and make sure Kryuchkov does not leave until we are ready for him," Viktor told her sternly. It was vital for the mission that he reestablish team discipline.

She went to the door without a word.

"We will return to the van," Viktor said. "Call us on the walkie-talkie when Kryuchkov is about to leave."

She stared at him briefly, her eyes hard as stones, and left the room. Uri now had hold of the body and the two men managed to position it so Viktor could shut the door. It took them several minutes to wipe up the blood and vomit with paper towels.

As they walked to the elevator, Viktor tried to adjust his plans to the evolving situation. "I have more sedative in the van," he said to Uri. "We will wait there until your sister calls. Kryuchkov will be confused. He will not know where his companion has gone."

They reached the elevator and pushed the call button. Viktor turned to Uri. The area around the young man's eyes were already turning black. They were fortunate to be in a medical facility, he thought. A freshly bandaged man would not appear out of place.

He looked at the lighted numbers above the elevator, his impatience growing. "Come, we'll take the stairs," he said.

Meanwhile, Tatyana hurried back to the physical therapy department, seething. The man on the floor had hurt her brother and it was Viktor's fault. It had been two against one. He was the commander. How could he have allowed such a disaster to happen? When they first came to Houston, Uri was fifteen, and he got beat up all the time. He was a thin boy with thin bones and the bullies took advantage of him. They later paid dearly for their cruelty. When Uri was hurt, it was as if someone had injured her own body. She felt the pain of it. Uri, Tatyana called out with her soul, why did we trust this Colonel? He is old and stupid.

These thoughts, however, were abruptly driven from her mind as she entered the physical therapy department. The door to Kryuchkov's treatment room stood open. She glanced at her watch. It was too early, thirty minutes more, at least. She went and looked inside. Empty. No Dr. Posner. No Kryuchkov. She ran through the gym to the whirlpool, but he wasn't there. She began to panic. She hurried to Dr. Posner's office and entered without knocking.

"What is going on?" she said. "Where is Dr. Easler?" Her voice was hard edged and direct. It was a voice Dr. Posner, who sat behind her desk, had not heard before.

"What do you mean? What are you talking about?"

"Dr. Easler. Why are you not with him?"

"He had to leave early today."

"But I did not see him leave."

"He went down the rear stairway—" she stopped herself, confusion giving way to indignation.

"Why are you so interested in Dr. Easler?

"You must tell me where he has gone."

"What is this about, Tatyana? You have no right to talk to me this way."

Tatyana moved with cat-like quickness around the side of Dr. Posner's desk. The doctor started to rise, but Tatyana grabbed her shoulder and shoved her back down into the chair.

On the desk lay an antique letter opener with a mother of pearl handle. Tatyana grabbed it and held it up against Dr. Posner's throat, while taking hold of her hair with the other hand.

"You're hurting me," the older woman simpered.

"Call out and I will kill you," Tatyana said and Dr. Posner felt the point of the letter opener push against the skin on the side of her neck. She nodded her acquiescence.

"This is very serious," Tatyana said. "You will tell me where the doctor has gone. There are people waiting to talk to him."

Dr. Posner stammered, "Dr. Easler didn't want to see anyone, especially the man who brought him here today. You're hurting me. "

"Tell me more!" she gave the hair a sharp tug.

"He asked me to help him leave by the rear employee entrance and that's what I did. But I don't—"

"How long. How long ago did he leave?"

"Just now. A couple of minutes ago."

Tatyana released the older woman's hair but kept the letter opener against her neck. She then withdrew the walkie-talkie from her coat pocket.

"Uri, something has happened."

The two men were nearing the bottom of the stairway and they stopped as Uri pulled the walkie-talkie from his pocket. He handed it to Viktor.

"What is the problem?" Viktor demanded.

"Kryuchkov is gone. He went down the back stairway several minutes ago. He will go out the employee entrance at the back of the building. If you hurry, you can still catch him."

"Leave the building. We will see to Kryuchkov."

"What is this about, Tatyana?" Dr. Posner said in a soft and troubled voice. "Who is Kryuchkov?"

"Where is the bandage tape?" Tatyana snapped.

"There's some in the cabinet."

"Get it for me." Tatyana walked Dr. Posner over to the cabinet, ready to use the letter opener if necessary.

It took only a moment for Tatyana to run tape across Dr. Posner's mouth and bind her hands together behind her back. She then sat the older woman in the chair and bound her feet. She finished by running the tape around Dr. Posner's chest and the chair several times so the therapist couldn't move.

"I am sorry to do this to you," Tatyana said, "you have been nice to me."

She left the room and closed the door behind her. Dr. Posner started to sob, the salt tears streaming down her face to soak the tape that was drawn tightly across her mouth.

As they reached the fire door for first floor, Viktor paused.

"Get the van and bring it around to the rear entrance. I will go through the lobby in case Kryuchkov doubles back." He pushed the door open. "Hurry," he said.

Uri sprinted for the entranceway and nearly knocked down an elderly woman with a walker as he exited. The startled, offended woman yelled after him, which drew the attention of John Howard, the security guard, who manned a post at the far end of the lobby. Between the information desk and the security post, a corridor led down to the Institute's administrative offices. The rear employee entrance was at the far end of the corridor, beyond which lay the auxiliary parking lot. Viktor started down the hallway despite protests from the woman behind the information desk.

"Sir, this is a restricted area," she called. "You must have a pass."

Viktor ignored her and quickened his pace. In the distance, through the automatic sliding glass door of the employee entrance, he saw a man with a cane. A blue Honda Civic stood next to the curb and someone got out and opened the rear door. Kryuchkov was bending down to get in. Viktor realized he had only seconds to reach him.

"Stop!" a baritone voice boomed out behind him. Doing nothing to check his pace, Viktor swung his head around to ascertain the nature of the threat.

A six-foot-four, two hundred and thirty pound African-American, John Howard was an impressive figure. He had recently retired from the Houston city police office and now worked as a security guard at the Institute. In his twenty-one years on the force he had never once drawn his service revolver in earnest, but as Viktor turned toward him, he noticed the man's hand dart in under his jacket. He was certain the man had a weapon and he pulled his own Smith and Wesson automatic from its holster and chambered a .45 caliber round.

Both guns went off simultaneously. Viktor had an extra second to aim and his nine-millimeter slug entered Howard's body, shattering his pelvis above the right leg and dropping the large man to the floor with a groan. The bullet then continued its journey downwards, deflected by its impact with the bone. It struck the hard surface of the Terrazzo floor and ricocheted up and to the left. Having just entered his office, Dr. David Hasenglad, the director of the Texas Polio Institute, heard the guard's shouted command and stepped back into the hallway to see what was going on. As he did, the projectile struck him in the face. It had already lost much of its energy and was stopped by the cheekbone. The force, however, was enough to knock Hasenglad off balance and he stumbled backwards into the office, where he landed flat on his back with a thud that drove the air from his lungs. Hilda, sitting at her desk, saw the blood splattered across her boss' face and let out a scream that could be heard throughout the first floor of the building.

Howard's bullet flew past Viktor's ear with the sound of a hornet, missing the Russian by less than an inch. It continued its course down the corridor and punched a neat hole through the safety glass of the sliding door that led outside.

Viktor already regretted pulling his weapon but he had no time for remorse. He looked for Kryuchkov and saw that he was already in the car while the man who had been helping him staggered sideways. Viktor broke into a run. It was less than forty feet to the door; he must reach Kryuchkov. He glanced over his shoulder to see if the security guard would shoot again, but when he turned back, the blue car was gone. The rear entrance doors slid open as he emerged from the building, the bitter taste of frustration in his mouth. The Honda was already exiting the parking lot. He turned and saw the white van as it careened around the corner of the building and sped toward him. It pulled up and he jumped in.

"The blue car, over there, the one leaving the parking lot," Viktor ordered. "Kryuchkov is with them."

Uri looked at the automatic in Viktor's hand.

"A guard. I had to shoot him," Viktor answered.

Uri gunned the engine, and when he reached the end of the parking lot, he turned so sharply that two of the van's wheels came up off the pavement.

"Do not worry," Uri said, almost laughing, "I will not kill you."

Viktor said nothing; his entire mind was on capturing Kryuchkov.

They turned out of the driveway six cars behind the blue Honda. Viktor tried to work out in his mind what had happened. Kryuchkov must have somehow anticipated the kidnap scheme and had accomplices ready to whisk him away to safety. But how did he know? If only Tatyana had gone back sooner to the therapy room, as he had ordered her to, she might have been able to stop him.

Again he felt the sting of betrayal but suppressed the emotion. He would deal with it later. Up ahead the Honda came to a stop at a traffic light along with the cars that followed. Viktor flung his door open and jumped out, with his automatic still in hand. He sprinted forward past the stopped cars, but before he could reach Kryuchkov, the Honda lurched forward into the intersection against the light. Horns blared as cars swerved to avoid a collision. Viktor stopped, uncertain what to do next. Helplessly he watched the Honda make it safely through the intersection and accelerate away. He turned back and saw that Uri had pulled the van into the oncoming lane. He was blowing his horn and flashing his lights at a red Subaru station wagon that had just made the turn and was driving right toward him. At the last moment the Subaru pulled aside, riding up onto the sidewalk. The van jerked to a stop and Viktor got in.

"Don't lose them," Viktor gasped as he struggled for breath. Uri pushed the van into the intersection against the traffic. A green pickup truck, the driver talking on his cell phone, barreled through the intersection straight in front of them and Uri slammed on the brakes, barely stopping in time. At the same moment, a silver SUV skidded to a stop on their right and another car struck it in the rear. This drove the SUV into the side of the van just behind the rear wheel, and it spun around to face the oncoming traffic like a gale-tossed ship turning into the wind. The SUV's stuck horn only added to the confusion and disorientation.

"They are getting away," Viktor barked. "Hurry!"

The intersection was tangled with vehicles and some of the drivers were getting out of their cars.

Viktor reached over and began pushing the steering wheel to the left. "We must go. Now!" he said.

Uri recovered his senses and knocked Viktor's hand away and turned the wheel himself. As he stepped on the gas, the 305 horsepower V-10 engine propelled the van through a sharp ninety-degree turn and they gained the far side of the intersection. The blue Honda carrying Dr. Kryuchkov, meanwhile, was now five blocks away and as the van picked up speed a high-pitch screeching sound filled the vehicle. This was quickly followed by the stench of burning rubber.

"What is that?" Viktor yelled.

"It is the metal pushing against the rear tire. It will scrape through the rubber and blow the tire."

"Do not stop or they will escape." Viktor was beginning to lose sight of the Honda in traffic and he knew his chances of capturing Kryuchkov were slipping away with each passing second.

"Soon the police will come," Uri said. "There were many witnesses. We will be arrested. We must get rid of the van."

"Do as you are told," Viktor said, motioning with the automatic. "I must have Kryuchkov."

"It is impossible to stop the car and take him by force. Can't you see that?"

"Then I shall kill him. Just get me close enough and I will do the rest."

"Kill him? But why?"

"I have my orders."

"From Gromonov?"

Viktor didn't answer, the incessant screeching frayed both their nerves.

"Then let me tell you this, Colonel. Gromonov can no longer give orders to anyone."

Viktor had trained his gaze on the traffic in front of them. He now turned to look at the younger man.

"What are you talking about?"

"Gromonov was arrested last night in Moscow."

Viktor did not trust his hearing over the metallic racket.

Uri repeated the information.

"Gromonov was charged with tax evasion and fraud," Uri said. "The government seized his assets, including Kamal Oil."

Viktor felt like a parachutist dropping blindly into a blanket of fog. The botched kidnapping. Tatyana. Shooting the guard. And now Gromonov.

"How do you know this?" he demanded.

"An associate of mine in Moscow emailed me early this morning," Uri said.

"Why didn't you tell me?"

"I thought it best to wait until after we had Kryuchkov. With Gromonov out of the picture, it is about us now. You and me and my people here in Houston. If we cannot kidnap the old man today, we will do so tomorrow. Then we will sell him to the highest bidder, and they will extract from him the information they require."

"But who will buy him?"

"Anyone, everyone. The Germans, the Saudis, the Chinese. Do you not know something of the great secret he possesses?"

Viktor was surprised Uri knew why Kryuchkov was so important. Looking at the young Russian with the white bandage across his nose, Viktor was reminded of a clown. Why would Valentin Gromonov confide in such a man? Perhaps he hadn't. Perhaps the story about Gromonov's arrest was a lie. Viktor did not like Uri Gryaznov. He was jealous because of Tatyana. Why should he trust the young man now? Fumes from the burning rubber filled his lungs and he began to cough.

"The tire will go, we cannot continue chasing this car now," Uri said and he abruptly turned the van onto a northbound street. "We must dispose of the van. I do not want to go to jail."

In the span of a heartbeat, Viktor had made his decision. If they were arrested for leaving the scene of the accident, the police would have no trouble linking him to the shooting at the institute. Uri was right. They must get rid of the van. He slipped the automatic back into its holster and rolled down the window—he needed fresh air—but this only made the screeching louder. Suddenly there was a terrific bang and the van rocked and swerved like a punch-drunk fighter. Viktor realized the metal had cut through the tire and they were riding on the rim. Uri looked about intently and swung the van into an alley that ran between a pair of two-story buildings. Just before the alley opened out onto another street, Uri brought the van to a stop. He reached behind his seat and grabbed a nylon bag with the NIKE logo printed on it. With the bag on his lap, he unzipped it and reached inside but Viktor could not see what the bag contained.

"Out!" Uri said and Viktor obeyed. As he did, Uri tossed the bag into the back of the van. The young man hurried away with Viktor close on his heels. They turned left and started up the street. Uri pulled out his cell phone. He pushed a button, held the device up to his ear, and began speaking. They had traveled a block when Viktor heard the boom and felt the concussion from the explosion. He turned around to see shattered glass and pieces of metal spray out of the alley onto the street. Cars stopped and people ran out of buildings as a cloud of black and gray smoke billowed up into the sky. Uri didn't appear to notice; he was talking to someone, giving directions. There would be no evidence now, Viktor understood. No fingerprints. No hair follicles. Nothing to tie them to the van or the shooting at the Polio Institute.

Ten minutes later a car pulled up next to them as they walked down the street. Uri opened the rear door jumped in. Viktor followed and the car pulled away from the curb.

Kryuchkov had escaped; Viktor accepted the fact. Finding him again would be much more difficult. He tried to focus his mind on the task but all he could do was recall the look of bitter reproach Tatyana had given him. He wondered if she had gotten away safely from the Institute.

Uri spoke. "Can you find him again?"

"Kryuchkov?"

"Who else?"

"Yes, but it will take time."

"Shall we take you to the hotel?"

"No, I think they know who I am."

"What do you mean?" A note of concern.

"The man at the hospital, the one we fought with," Viktor said, "I'm sure he recognized me. He must work for EnerTex. They must have shown him my photograph."

"But how? How would they have your photograph?"

"From their security cameras. I went there for a meeting with your sister."

"So they will have Tatyana's photograph as well?"

"Yes, I would think so."

Uri was silent for several blocks.

"Take us to the ship canal," he said at last to the large bald man driving the car. A smaller man with coarse black hair sat next to him in the front seat. Neither man spoke.

"Let me have your weapon," Uri said to Viktor.

"Why?"

"If we are to take care of you, you must trust us." He held out his hand.

The automatic could be traced to the shooting and Viktor realized that Uri meant to throw it in the canal. All the same, he was reluctant to surrender it.

"I will dispose of it myself."

Uri continued holding out his hand. His meaning was clear. These are my men, Colonel; you are no longer in charge and will do as I say.

Viktor had no choice. Without Uri, he was lost. He handed the gun over.

"Take care of this, Mikhail," Uri said as he passed the gun to the black-haired man in the front seat.

They drove on in silence.

31

ELLIOT MET REB and Alice at the airport and drove them to the medical district in his recently purchased Honda Civic hybrid. Elliot was a tall and slender man graced with an attractive, open face and intelligent blue eyes. Reb and Alice took to him immediately.

They arrived at the Texas Polio Institute and parked two rows down from the rear employee entrance. Ten minutes later Dr. Easler emerged as planned from the building and Elliot pulled the Honda up to the entrance. Reb, who was in the front passenger seat, jumped out and introduced himself. The two men shook hands and Reb opened the rear door and held the older man's cane as he climbed in. At that moment something struck Reb on the right side, just below his armpit. He lurched forward against the car, the cane slipping from his hand and clattering onto the asphalt, his mind blinded by pain and surprise. Inside the car, Alice heard a metallic thwack as the lead bullet, finished with living tissue, embedded itself in the C-pillar behind the rear door. She heard the muffled report of a gunshot.

"What's happening?" she called as Reb fell against the car, rocking the suspension.

"You friend is hurt!" Walter exclaimed. "I think someone shot him."

Alice scrambled frantically toward the door, trying to push past Walter to get to Reb. She listened intently for more gunshots.

Walter also was reaching out and together they managed to pull Reb into the car and close the door.

"We have to get out of here!" she yelled, and Elliot shot away from the curb. A moment later a man appeared outside the entrance of the Institute with a gun in his hand. Alice tried to make out his features without luck given the distance and the motion of the car. She turned her attention to Reb instead. His shirt was soaked with blood. The nightmare was coming true and she fought to hold back the tears.

"There's a hospital not far from here," Elliot said as they stopped at a traffic light. "We'll take him there."

"Yes, hurry," Alice said.

"No." Reb said.

"What are you talking about?" Alice said. "You've been shot. We've got to get you to the hospital."

"I don't. . . I don't think it's that serious." It burned like blazes but he somehow knew he wasn't in mortal danger.

"I'm afraid we're being followed." Elliot said, his eyes on the rear view mirror.

Again Alice turned and looked out the rear window.

"Six cars back, Elliot said. "A white van."

"I see them," Alice said.

"Who are they?" Reb asked.

"Your guess is as good as mine," Elliot said.

"Someone is getting out," Alice said, her voice rising again. "It's the man with the gun; he's running this way."

"Right," Elliot said. "Hang on, everyone."

He gave the horn a long blast and eased the car forward into the intersection. Other horns sounded followed by the screech of brakes and swerving of tires.

Alice held her breath. The crossing traffic was heavy and she expected a car to slam into them any moment. In that instant she realized she didn't have her seat belt on. Neither did Reb. She took hold of his left arm, closed her eyes, and said a prayer. Suddenly they were free of the intersection and picking up speed. She opened her eyes and began looking around for a police car.

She heard another series of horn blasts and a crash some distance behind them.

"They're determined, I'll give them that," Elliot said.

"Did they get through?" Alice asked. She hoped for a cement truck to smash them.

Elliot kept his eyes on the mirror and his foot on the gas pedal. Alice could just make out the sound of a prolonged horn blast.

They traveled a block before Elliot spoke again. "Well, they're still following us."

"The white van?"

"None other."

Meanwhile, Reb was attempting to unbutton his shirt and Alice tried to help. She wanted to say something encouraging but the words wouldn't come. When the last button was undone, Reb held up his right arm and gingerly pulled the blood-soaked cloth away from the wound. There was so much blood it was difficult to assess the damage.

"We need something to stop the bleeding," Alice called anxiously to Elliot.

"I have a medical bag in the trunk."

"Can we get to it through the back seat?" She owned a Honda and knew this was possible but Elliot shook his head.

"This is hybrid; the batteries are between the seat and the trunk. We have to pull over."

"You can't," Reb said, "not while they're following us."

"Here, use this," Walter said quietly as he handed Alice a clean, starched handkerchief. "I am sorry to be the cause of all this trouble."

The gesture made Alice grateful beyond words. She pushed the white cloth firmly against Reb's side, just under his armpit. He winced and caught his breath but did nothing to stop her.

"I got a badge in First-Aid when I was a Girl Scout," she said, forcing a smile. "I bet you didn't know that."

A delivery truck pulled out of a driveway and Elliot hit the brakes. The abrupt motion jerked Reb forward and he let out a dry yelp.

Alice put her other hand on his shoulder and eased him back against the seat. She wanted Elliot to slow down but she knew he was doing his best to get away from their pursuers.

"Are they still following us?" Reb asked.

"Yes."

"We could call the police," Alice said, "I have a cell phone."

"Not yet," Reb said.

"No hospital. No police. Why are you being so difficult?"

He didn't answer. The buildings swept past, Hollywood Video, Office Depot, Beck's Prime Steakhouse. Besides the steakhouse, Alice thought, they could be anywhere in America. Except that they were being chased by murderers. After several more blocks, Elliot said, "I think they've given up."

"Are you sure?" Reb said.

"They turned north; they're no longer following us."

"Can they come around at us some other way?" Alice asked.

"I don't think so," Elliot said, "but I'll turn left at the next intersection just to be safe. My guess is they're gone."

"Then let's get Reb to the hospital," Alice said.

"If we go to the hospital," Reb said, "they'll get Dr. Easler and that'll be the end of everything. They might even try to kill him."

"Kill Dr. Easler?" Alice said. "But you were the one who was shot."

"I don't think the bullet was intended for me."

She turned to Dr. Easler who nodded.

"What do you want to do?" Elliot said from the front seat. "The hospital's close by."

"You're a doctor," Reb said. "Maybe you could look at it first and see if it's serious."

"Yes, of course." Thanks to his work at the clinic, he had seen his share of gunshot wounds over the years. "Are you still bleeding?"

Reb looked down to where Alice held the cloth against his side. He felt slightly nauseous but he attributed this to an overdose of adrenaline, not a loss of blood. "No, I think it's stopped."

"What if another car is following us?" Alice said.

"I don't see any," Elliot said.

"Go a couple more miles and then see if there's a place we can pull over," Reb said.

"I know this neighborhood," Elliot said. "Leave it to me."

He made several turns and drove a dozen blocks before coming to a vacant lot with an old sign that indicated it was once the site of a used car dealership. Elliot pulled into the lot behind an abandoned garage and turned off the engine. He popped the trunk and went back to retrieve his medical bag. He then opened the rear door and squatted down next to Reb. If Elliot was upset about the bullet hole in his new car or the blood stains all over the upholstery, he never showed it. He removed a pair of surgical gloves from his bag and slipped them on. Next he withdrew a packet of sterilized gauze and a bottle of hydrogen peroxide.

"This is going to hurt a little," he said.

"Do what you have to," Reb said.

Elliot pulled away the handkerchief and saw that the bullet had cut a shallow trough through the soft flesh of Reb's side an inch and a half below the armpit. He probed the wound with a gloved finger, feeling the rib bone underneath. The pain was excruciating but Reb did his best not to pull away.

"You were lucky," Elliot said, "it's a surface wound." Reb didn't feel lucky but said nothing as Elliot affixed a large bandage to his side. Elliot then removed a stethoscope from his bag, and placed it on different locations on Reb's back, carefully comparing the breath sounds from side to side to make sure air wasn't leaking into the pleural cavity and deflating the lung.

Alice suddenly saw a large bearded man looming up behind Elliot. She almost screamed she was so startled, and Elliot, catching her expression, turned around. The man smiled revealing a row of discolored teeth. His clothes were ragged, his sneakers full of holes, and he held a soiled sleeping bag under one arm. He was intensely interested in Reb's injury.

"Had a buddy in 'Nam took one under the armpit like that. Never could use his arm again."

"Look friend, we're kind of busy here," Elliot said with some gentleness.

But instead of backing away, the man drew closer and leaned over Elliot, his expression one of childlike curiosity. He smelled awful.

Elliot stuffed the stethoscope back into his bag and handed the bag to the newcomer. "Can you put that in the trunk for me?" he said. "And keep an eye out for a white van. If you see one lurking around, tell us quick."

"Yes sir," the man answered brightly, apparently relishing the unexpected elevation in status.

"I think you'll be okay," Elliot said to Reb. "The bullet tore away some the muscle and glanced off one of your ribs but I don't think there's any pulmonary contusion."

"What's that?" Reb asked.

"The shock wave from the bullet could have bruised the lung and caused internal bleeding," Elliot said. "I can't be sure without an x-ray, but the lungs sound good."

"So we don't need to go to the hospital?" Reb asked. It was all he wanted to know for the moment.

"I'll take a closer look when we get to Marion's ranch, and if we need an x-ray, I can arrange for one then. But there's no immediate danger."

"Great, then let's get out of here," Reb said. "I'm feeling kind of exposed."

Elliot turned to the homeless man and thanked him for his help. Alice was impressed at how deftly Elliot had changed the dynamics of the situation from one of apprehension and irritation to one of shared responsibility.

Elliot asked Walter to move up to the front seat and they were soon on their way again. He then handed a plastic bottle of water over the seat to Alice.

"Make sure he drinks plenty of water. He's lost a considerable amount of blood and we need to keep him hydrated."

It was a long seventy-two miles on the freeway to their exit, from which point they followed a two-lane county road for an

additional thirty miles. Reb fell asleep with his head on Alice's
shoulder but she felt him wince every time the car went over a
bump.

Walter, meanwhile, kept company with his own thoughts. The
last thing he wanted was to put other peoples' lives at risk. Mr.
Morgan could have been killed, or the woman, or his friend Elliot.
Was EnerTex chasing them? The CIA? Did it really matter? He
stared blankly out the window. Whoever it was, they did not want
him talking to the press and were prepared to commit murder if
necessary. Guns. He detested guns. He hated all the weapons of
mankind—the laser-guided bombs and the chemical nerve agents,
the tank shells made of depleted uranium and the ubiquitous land
mines. Why did the human animal so willingly, even gleefully,
dedicate such a large portion of his ingenuity and strength to his
own destruction? It puzzled and saddened him. He recalled the
night he said goodbye to his old life next to the Moscow River.
The silhouettes of men carrying a corpse against a burgundy sky,
illuminated by the distant lights of the city, was an image etched
forever upon his memory. They drove passed an Embassy Suites
Hotel and he thought about Samantha and their days together in
the Lisbon hotel by the sea. The warm, salt-laden breezes wafted
in through the open French doors and mingled with the scent
of her perfume, filling him with desire. Yet he said nothing to
her and now he regretted his shyness. He imagined she expected
his advances and would have been willing. He was a big prize
for the Americans; he must be rewarded. All the same, she did
seem to care for him. Samantha. She wore a wedding ring. She
told him her husband worked for the State Department, a trade
attaché assigned to the embassy in Copenhagen. What must this
husband think of her clandestine work, of her meeting with lonely
men in seaside hotels? Perhaps he did not care. Perhaps he was
a homosexual. Yes, that was it. She would marry a homosexual,
a career diplomat. For cover. Walter laughed at his foolishness.
What did he know about the secret world of espionage?

Still his thoughts clung to Lisbon.

"You will like America," Samantha had assured him.

"Why?" he asked.

"Because it is a new country. America worships everything new."

And after half a century of life, she helped him become new again. He was reborn as Dr. Walter Easler. At first it made his head hurt, there were so many details to memorize about his new made-up life. Born in Dusseldorf, Germany, during the War. Arriving in America with his family in 1950 where his father found work as a pipe fitter in Cleveland, Ohio. The two-story house at 316 Oak Street with the tire swing in the backyard. His made-up mother, Geisla, and how she suffered from diabetes and mourned the loss of his younger brother, Frederick, when he was killed in Vietnam. His own bout with polio, the treatments at the hospital and his recovery. Captain of his high school chess club—a private joke; he was a mediocre player but he couldn't expect them to know that. His engineering studies at the Rochester Institute of Technology. All the little corners, crevices, and pockets filled up with packets of information to make a believable story, a story of a life lived, and yet not lived. He liked to imagine a frustrated novelist in some cubicle in Langley, Virginia, day after day typing out the story of his life. Dr. Walter Easler. Brilliant physicist, obedient and dutiful son, loyal American.

And now he was running away, He felt like Frankenstein's monster, stealing away from those who so carefully brought him into the world and who now sought to destroy him.

32

THE CAR BUMPED over the cracked and broken asphalt of the abandoned oil depot until they came to a gate secured by a chain and padlock. Mikhail got out, unlocked the gate, and held it open as the car passed through. It drove a short distance and stopped. Two hundred yards away was the blue expanse of the ship canal. Mikhail was not sure why they had come to this place. In the past they had used it for only one purpose.

As he walked back toward the car, Uri got out and came to meet him. The driver, a Georgian named Mgelika, which meant "wolf," remained with the colonel.

"I want you to do this, my friend," Uri said when they met. "Use his gun, not your own."

Mikhail nodded.

"Be careful, he is a dangerous man."

"Is he wearing a vest?"

"Yes."

"Is this necessary?" He never questioned his orders but he felt compelled to do so this time.

Instead of appearing annoyed, Uri look tired and sad.

"He shot a security guard and the authorities have his photograph. They will be looking for him. If he is captured, we will all be in great danger."

Mikhail nodded and slipped a hand into his jacket pocket and felt the scored plastic grips of Viktor's automatic.

He had killed men before but never enjoyed it. Uri was his boss and his friend. They had been together for three years. For a man such as Mikhail, loyalty was everything. He would not let Uri down.

Together the two Russians walked back to the car. The ground was littered with scraps of old paper blown by the wind coming off the canal into the tuffs of grass that poked up through the broken concrete Reaching the car, Uri opened the rear door. A tug boat sounded her horn in the distance; the air was heavy with the scent of salt marshes and industrial pollution.

"Comrade Colonel, please come with me," Uri said. "I have something important to show you."

Mikhail stood three steps behind Uri but he could not make out the colonel's response. His mouth tasted thick and sour.

Mgelika opened his door and got out.

There was a long pause, the tug sounded again, and then the colonel climbed out of the car. Uri moved around to the other side of the vehicle where the older man stood, the younger man's manner friendly and easy.

They talked but again Mikhail could not hear what was said. They were a strange sight. The colonel was somber, very erect; Uri smiled, his nose covered in bandages. Mikhail waited. He could feel sweat forming under his shirt, but he could not remove his jacket. Then Uri gestured to him.

"Come with us, Mikhail," he said and led Viktor toward a low building with a corrugated roof that shimmered in the Texas heat.

Mikhail no longer attempted to overhear the conversation. His attention was fixed on the next four seconds, a seemingly short and insignificant period of time until stretched by the proximity to death. He was glad he did not have to peer into his victim's eyes. Instead he came up from behind, his running shoes moving quietly across the rough ground. Suddenly the colonel's his muscles tightened and his head began to turn and as he sensed the danger from behind. But he was too late. The automatic made a single pop as the bullet tore through the back of older man's skull. Death was immediate and he slumped to the ground without uttering a sound.

Mgelika came up quickly as Uri knelt down to inspect the corpse.

"Have a good journey, Colonel," he said softly. "We may yet meet again in another world."

He straightened up and Mikhail handed him the gun which he slipped into his belt where it warmed his stomach. Before he left he would cast it in the canal along with the corpse.

"Mikhail, take the car and go back to the apartment. Tatyana will be there. I will call you with instructions."

Mgelika already had hold of the colonel's ankles and was dragging the lifeless body toward the building where bags of cement waited inside. Mikhail walked back to the car but didn't get in immediately. Instead, he turned his gaze east to where the blue ribbon of the ship canal made it's way out to the sea. One shot. No warning. No suffering. He felt within him the peace of completion. He had done the unhappy colonel a great service.

LATER THAT EVENING, a redheaded Tatyana wearing dark glasses waited inside the Greyhound bus station. Mikhail sat next to her. Uri could not be with her; he needed to stay out of sight until his nose healed. Two small suitcases sat at her feet. She was exhausted and her eyes stung from the diesel fumes that seeped into the waiting room. She said nothing about Viktor, asked Mikhail no questions. She didn't need to. Uri explained everything to her over the phone. The police had her photograph; it was time to disappear. Already the shooting at the Polio Institute was the top story on all the television newscasts and in the newspapers as well. She wasn't sad. She would stay with friends in San Diego. A year, no longer, he told her, and then it would be safe to return. She would miss her brother terribly, but perhaps it was good to be away from him for awhile. She felt no regret or sorrow for Viktor. She had liked him at first. He appeared strong and decisive. Now he was dead. Unfortunate, yes, but Viktor was careless and made critical mistakes. It was just as well. He didn't want to grow old.

Now he wouldn't have to. Life had a way of taking care of such things.

And it was only a matter of time until her brother found Kryuchkov. Then they would auction the physicist off to the highest bidder and return to Russia and their home in the mountains. They would build a large house on the outskirts of Magnitogorsk. Uri would be restless but he would find things to do. Russia was changing. He would take over Gromonov's organization. And she would take care of him.

The announcement for her bus came over the loudspeaker. Mikhail stood and helped her with her suitcases.

"Take care of my brother," she said before kissing him on the cheek and climbing up into the bus.

THREE DAYS AFTER the incident at the Polio Institute—it was five o'clock in the morning, and Mikhail was asleep on the couch in the apartment—the front door crashed inwards and two concussion grenades detonated within a second of each other in the hallway. Mikhail's senses reeled as he rolled off the couch and onto the floor. A black metal tear gas canister bounced along the carpet past him spewing its noxious contents. Moving about clumsily on his hands and knees, coughing and looking for his AK-47, he knocked over a lamp. He saw a muzzle flash to his right but heard nothing; the explosions had deafened him. Then he saw Uri through the whitish gas. He was in his underwear and firing his Uzi. Short quick bursts. Suddenly the side of his friend's face tore away in a splash of red and he went down. Dark shapes in masks poured into the apartment from every direction. The bright narrow beams of light gleaming from the tops of their helmets made them look like strange, one-eyed aliens from a dark and gassy planet. More muzzle flashes from the direction of the bedrooms. Then a knee to his back slammed him to the floor. His right arm was yanked back so roughly it dislocated his shoulder, flooding his mind with pain.

It was over in less than forty seconds. The FBI counter-terrorism assault team killed two and captured three. Special Agent

Arnold Brewer had directed the operation, but he was reluctant to make the call to his superiors. They had failed to find Dr. Walter Easler and the leader of the cell was dead.

FIFTEEN HUNDRED MILES away, Tatyana turned fitfully in bed. She opened her eyes and peered into the dark. She had the impression that someone was in the room with her.

"Who is there?" she said. There was no answer and she switched on the lamp. The room was empty and suddenly an inexplicable sadness washed over her.

"Is that you, Uri?" she said. "Is something wrong?"

She waited but received no reply.

She picked up her cigarettes but laid them down again.

"Uri, we must leave this crazy country and go home to Russia," she said. "We must leave soon."

She switched off the light but lay open-eyed in the dark for a long time before at last falling back asleep.

33

THE GLISTENING EYE of a security camera peered in at them through the front windshield as Elliot punched the code into a keypad that operated the wrought-iron gate.

"Your friend Mr. Harless lives well," Alice said as they drove under a sign made from a twenty-foot pine slab upon which were painted the words "Chancewater Ranch."

"As Lyle likes to say, Marion has enough money to burn a wet mule," Elliot said and the expression made her smile for the first time since the episode at the Polio Institute. They followed a road lined on both sides with live oaks beyond which stretched lush irrigated pastures filled with cattle. Alice half expected to see Roy Rogers and Trigger come galloping up to greet them.

"We're almost there," she said gently to Reb, who lifted his head groggily and looked around.

"How are you feeling?" she asked.

"Like I've been kicked down a flight of stairs. It hurts all over." Which was true; his side throbbed and he felt the first stabs of a major headache.

"How big is the ranch?" he asked Elliot, just to change the subject.

"Twelve hundred acres. Marion has a twenty-thousand acre spread in Montana so he calls this his 'town' ranch."

"What's Marion like?" Alice asked.

"You wouldn't believe it to look at him now, but he used to wildcat with my father all around Texas and Oklahoma just after the war. From what I hear, they had some rough and rowdy times together."

"What's his interest in EnerTex?" Reb asked. "I mean, why is he willing to let us stay at his house and do the interview here?" It was a question he'd been meaning to ask since his last talk with Lyle Workman, but the opportunity hadn't presented itself.

"My brother treated Marion poorly," Elliot said.

"How?" Alice asked.

"Marion wanted to invest in EnerTex back when my brother needed capital to keep the company afloat. Avery turned him down. It hurt Marion's feelings."

"Why did it hurt his feelings?" Alice asked.

"Marion's practically part of the family. We used called him Uncle Marion when we were growing up. So I guess it's payback time."

"Do you like your brother?" Alice said. Normally she wouldn't ask such a personal question of someone she had just met, but she felt justified after what they'd been through together.

"With family, it's not about liking or disliking," Elliot answered.

"Do you get along?"

"Let's just say my brother *tolerates* me."

"Does that bother you?" she asked.

"Not really. Avery tolerates everybody. That's just the way he is. You see he's incredibly smart when it comes to making money. A mixture of Silas Marner and Ebenezer Scrooge, with a little Albert Einstein thrown in, if you know what I mean."

They pulled up in front of a huge white house with faux-Hellenistic columns along the front. It looked like a set piece from *Gone With the Wind*. As the Honda came to a stop, a slight elderly man came trotting out the front door and down the steps. He was dressed in neatly pressed black slacks, a billowy white silk shirt, and a braided-leather string tie. His silver belt buckle was encrusted with turquoise, and he wore black cowboy boots with embossed red leather toes. He made to open the rear car door with all the courtesy of a butler but, recoiled when he beheld Reb in the backseat, half-naked and stained with blood.

"Appleyard, there's been an accident," Elliot said coming around the front of the car. "This is Reb Morgan and Alice Carpenter. They're radio journalists; they're here to see Marion."

The manservant quickly regained his composure and nodded to Reb and Alice formally. Walter climbed out of the car and stood next to Elliot, his right hand on the front fender for support.

"We also need a walking cane," Elliot said noticing Walter. "My friend lost his. Do you think you could find us one?"

"I'm sure Mr. Harless has a cane someplace. Do y'all you have any luggage?"

"Our bags are in the trunk," Alice said and moved to help Reb out of the car.

Elliot walked over and opened the trunk and retrieved his medical bag. He gave Walter his arm and they all climbed the broad steps into the house, leaving Appleyard to bring the luggage and then find a cane.

The front hallway was a massive expanse of cool, polished marble and white painted wood. A split stairway curved up on either side to a second floor landing, that was illuminated by a ten-by-twelve-foot stained glass window. In the center of the window was the map of Texas, with an image of the Alamo on one side and a patch of oil well derricks on the other.

"So here you are at last," a booming voice greeted them from a hallway to their left. "I expected you an hour ago—"

There was a pause of half a second. "What in Sam Hill *happened*?"

Moving across the hallway toward them was a corpulent man in his seventies, wearing a navy blue jacket and red silk ascot. Alice was in no doubt that the elderly man was their host, Marion Harless, oil baron extraordinaire and master of Chancewater Ranch.

"It looks worse than it is," Elliot said. "There was a shooting."

"You were attacked?"

"Something like that. We were at the Polio Institute—"

"Never mind. Have you called the police?"

"No. We don't want to involve the police."

Marion starred at his friend for a moment.

"Well, I guess you know best." He turned to Reb.

"How are you feeling, young man?"

"A bit woozy but otherwise all right."

The large man leaned down to examine Reb's bandaged side more closely filling Reb's nostrils with the scent of expensive cologne.

"Elliot is an exceptional doctor; you're in good hands," he said straightening up and looking satisfied.

"I'll need to redress the wound," Elliot said.

"Do it right away. I'll have my cook hold dinner."

There was an awkward silence.

"I'm Alice Carpenter." She offered her hand.

"Of course you are, my dear," Marion said taking it with such care that she was afraid he was about to bend over and kiss it.

"Elliot and Lyle told me about you both and I must apologize on behalf of my fellow Texans for giving you such a disgraceful welcome to our great state."

"I wouldn't worry about it," Reb said forcing a smile. "We have our share of shootings in California." It was the best he could come up with.

Elliot then introduced the physicist.

"This is my friend, Dr. Walter Easler."

Marion turned and the two men shook hands.

Appleyard appeared with a silver-handled walking cane for Walter.

"Thank you," Walter said

"You can use the downstairs lavatory," Marion said to Elliot. "I will show Miss Carpenter and Dr. Easler to their rooms."

With that, the party went their separate ways.

Elliot and Reb walked along a hallway where the mounted heads of large wild animals looked down at them from walls.

They eventually came to a set of stairs that led down to a long, low-ceilinged room. In the middle of the room stood a matching set of billiards tables. One table was for straight billiards and the other for pocket billiards. As they walked passed the tables, Reb saw that their felt surfaces of had been specially dyed so that the state of Texas appeared in the center, surrounded by a ring of stars.

Reaching the end of the room, they turned down a hallway and entered another large room with a built-in bar and a three-lane, automated bowling alley. Again, the state of Texas had been inlaid in dark walnut in the blond maple of each lane. Reb speculated that if the oil business went bust, Marion could rent out the house to his fellow Texans for weddings, bar mitzvahs, and meetings of the Sons and Daughters of Texas, if such an organization existed.

"In here," Elliot said, opening a door into a spacious spa. He directed Reb to lie down on a massage table in front of the Swedish sauna and then removed the gauze covering the wound.

"Marion seems to be a very considerate man," Reb said, trying to keep his mind off the pain.

"He is. He's helped support my clinic in Houston for years."

"What else does he do with his money?"

"Travels and collects vintage Ferrari and Maserati racing cars. He has the largest collection outside of Italy."

"Where does he keep them?"

"This will hurt a little," Elliot said. He pulled the last of the bandage away from the injured tissue.

"He keeps them here at Chancewater in a large warehouse. He enters races all over the world. Last month he won the Pittsburgh Vintage Grand Prix driving a 1934 Maserati."

Reb was going to ask how Marion, given his size, managed to fit himself into a race car but he suddenly felt faint.

"What's wrong?" Elliot said.

"Just a bit dizzy."

"You lost a lot of blood."

"It's really starting to hurt."

Elliot walked over to a sink and wet several washcloths which he used to cleanse the wound. He opened up his medical bag and took out a tube of antibacterial ointment.

"It's not like it is in the movies," Reb sighed.

"Getting shot?"

"Yeah."

"As far as I can tell, the bullet didn't carry any fabric into the wound."

"Is that good?"

"That's good."

"Does it need stitches?"

"There's not enough tissue left to hold a stitch. We'll just keep it bandaged and it should heal all right."

"Will it leave a scar?"

"Most likely but fortunately it's under your arm."

Elliot gently rebandaged the wound.

"Can you give me something for the pain?" Reb asked when Elliot was finished.

"I have some Vicodin, but you shouldn't take it on an empty stomach."

"I don't think I could eat a meal right now. Maybe a glass of milk and I'll go to bed."

"Okay. We'll see how you feel tomorrow. If you develop a fever, I'm taking you to the hospital."

Upstairs Marion had finished showing his guests to their rooms. Alice's was at the rear of the house on the second floor. It had its own balcony overlooking a courtyard and the swimming pool. The room was painted pink with lime green accents. Had someone warned her beforehand about the color scheme, she would have mounted the stairs with less enthusiasm. Pink was one of her least favorite hues, but once inside the room, she found the effect soothing and restorative. A large vase of fresh-cut flowers stood on the dresser, and the white satin sheets on the bed were turned down. Sure beats Motel Six, she thought to herself and walked out onto the balcony.

*   *   *

AN HOUR LATER, Marion, Elliot, and Alice were in the dinning room seated at one end of an enormous table finishing their soup as Appleyard brought in the main course. Ten milligrams of hydrocodone bitartrate had worked its magic on Reb and he was wrapped in the warm arms of Morpheus. Dr. Easler was also absent. He pleaded exhaustion and shuffled off to bed. Alice wondered if he could be planning to escape. After what had happened, she wouldn't blame him.

"Miss Carpenter," Marion said, "I'll show you my horses tomorrow, if you like."

Alice was a sucker for horses. "I would be delighted, Mr. Harless."

"Please, call me Marion. We don't stand on formalities here at Chancewater, do we Elliot?"

"Then you must call me Alice. And while we're on the subject of names, where does the name 'Chancewater' come from?"

A satisfied grin took command of the large man's features.

"From a gambling debt. Legend has it that a professional gambler from Tennessee came to Texas with Davy Crockett. They parted company before the Alamo."

"Lucky for the gambler," Alice said.

Marion smiled. "That it was. And then there was that unfortunate disagreement between the states, and not long afterwards, the gambler got into a poker game with a fellow named Druggins, who owned this land and a lot more besides."

"What was the gambler's name?" Alice asked.

"Trimble. Stark Trimble. The story goes that they played late into the night, and at one point, the pot on the table got as high as a thousand dollars. Druggins had three aces and he was sure he could win, but he was out of cash. So he put up the ranch as collateral and raised the bet. A one-eyed Indian and a doctor were also in the game but they folded. That left Trimble to keep Druggins honest and it would take every cent he had, along with his horse, his saddle, and his Remington revolver, to see the bet. If he lost, he'd be flat-ass broke, excuse the expression." Here Marion paused for effect and took a sip from his crystal wine glass.

"What happened?" Alice said.

"Well, Trimble asked Druggins, 'how's the water taste on that ranch of yours?' He didn't ask about the grass, the timber, or anything else. All he cared about was the water, and Druggins smiled and said, 'it's the sweetest water this side of paradise.' And he wasn't lying; it is. So Trimble took his chance on the water and saw the bet."

"Did he win?" Alice asked.

Marion features fell in mock despair. "Alas, all Trimble had was two-pair, jacks over sixes."

"So he didn't get the ranch?" Alice was confused.

"No, he got the ranch," Marion said with a wry grin. "You see Druggins had dealt the cards and Trimble accused him of cheating. He claimed one of Druggin's three aces, the ace of clubs, was the very ace he had discarded on the draw, and when Druggins got mad and went for his gun, Trimble shot him through the heart in self-defense. He then split the pot with the Indian and the doctor and kept the ranch for himself."

Alice realized that she wasn't the first visitor to be taken in by the poker game story, nor would she be the last. All the same, she wished Reb had been there to hear it with her.

34

MARTY AWOKE IN total darkness and confusion. He was in a painful half-standing, half-sitting position with his left shoulder jammed between two sharp-edged surfaces, his knees pressed against another. He couldn't move his arms, his wrists were bound together behind his back, and his ankles were secured as well. Surgical tape was stretched so tightly across his mouth that his cheeks were pushed back against his ears. And the taste inside his mouth was revolting. He wanted to spit but couldn't, and when he swallowed, his throat burned. He tried to maneuver himself into an upright position as scraps of memory flitted about inside his head like bats in the moonlight. After what felt like an eternity the face of a woman came into focus, a woman with almond-shaped eyes and dark hair. Then came the image of two men that conjured up a witch's brew of fear and rage. The men ambushed him, but he hurt one, broke the man's nose. Then the memory of the hypodermic syringe in his arm and the long fall into blackness.

He directed his bound hands to his back pocket and searched for the familiar bulge with his fingers. It was gone; they had his wallet. He tried to curse them out loud but couldn't open his mouth. Worse still, his nasal passageways were clogged and he was having trouble breathing. He felt panic seize him. With a violent tug he tried to free his hands, but all he did was speed up his heart and make his head throb. It wasn't just a robbery, the beating of bats' wings whispered as he pushed open the attic window of his mind to coax them in. One of the men was familiar. Yes. The older man. So was the girl. Marty fought against the drugs in his system as one by one the memories returned. The man and the girl were Russians. Avery had shown him their photographs. They were looking for Dr. Easler, and Marty's job was to do, what?. . . keep Dr. Easler safe from them. Yes, that was it. And he had failed. He had ordered the bodyguard to stay back at the house so he could have Easler to himself. And now the Russians had him. They wanted the secret of the ATG technology. The full realization of his failure washed over him. His career was over, vaporized. He would have to move to Nepal to find a job! He fought to steady his nerves. He was in some kind of closet, and the sooner he got out, the sooner he could chase down Easler and the Russians. Perhaps they were still in the building. How long had he been out? He needed a plan. Maybe if he thrust his shoulder against the door, he could break it down. But in the pitch black, he wasn't sure where the door was. He made a guess and shoved with his legs. There was a sharp pain as his head struck something hard, and he sank into oblivion again.

Time passed and once more he regained consciousness. The darkness surrounded and pressed in upon him like a phantom, hateful and implacable. He knew Easler was gone for good. His job now was to survive. He was still having trouble breathing and he attempted to clear his nose with a powerful snort. This only made matters worse. Now he could barely breathe at all. He suspected his nose was broken and full of dried blood. He had to calm down but his gurgling septum was driving him crazy. The real danger he knew was not getting enough air into his lungs, it was getting the CO_2 out of them. He'd learned this from his health teacher, Mrs. McKinney, back in middle school. The class was doing a unit on the effects of tobacco use, and she wanted her students to experience what it was like to have emphysema. So she had them breathe through a cocktail straw. The passage in the straw was extremely thin but Marty was able to draw in enough air. It was while exhaling through the tiny straw that difficulties arose; he couldn't empty his lungs fast enough and he got dizzy. His lungs felt as if they would burst. At the time, his Aunt Gloria had emphysema. She lugged an oxygen tank around with her everywhere she went. At family gatherings she sat in a chair in the corner of the room with a plastic mask over her mouth, which she pushed aside every time she took a sip of her Manhattan. It depressed Marty to see her so helpless. Before her illness she had been the spirited hell-raiser in the family, not like his parents whose blood ran tepidity in their veins at the best of times. Thanks to Mrs. McKinney and the cocktail straw exercise, he gained an appreciation for what his aunt was going through and he promised himself he would never to take up smoking—he wasn't going to wind up like his poor Aunt Gloria. Only now, here he was, his mouth taped shut and his nose broken, fighting to breathe with every fiber of his being.

The torturous minutes wore on as he listened for anything, passing footsteps, a doctor's page, but the silence was as complete as the darkness. And the pressure inside his lungs was steadily increasing; it was only a matter of time before he suffocated to death. It was then he began to hear a voice, very faint at first, but slowly growing louder. It was vaguely familiar but he couldn't place it. A male voice. Not Avery. Not his father. It rang in his ears and then he remembered: the preacher called Brother Emmett, whose voice had come to him out of the vast Texas night through the speakers of his car radio. Brother Emmett telling the story of Jonah. . .

"And then, from down inside the belly of the fish, his life ebbing away, Jonah remembered the Lord," the voice said.

The words broke upon Marty like a tidal wave breaching the dikes of his self-delusion and pride. In the raging water's aftermath, he suddenly saw his life for what it was—a blighted country governed by mindless currents of ambition and lust. Martin Hamilton. The Tin Man. The nickname, suddenly shorn of its comedic appeal, aptly described who he was, a two-bit con man, a hustler, who was about to have his sorry ass thrown into the dumpster of history. He was the rotting banana peel whose

sole purpose in life was to trip up those with nobler callings. Bert
Nichols, the crusading journalism student at Vanderbilt. Reb
Morgan and Alice Carpenter, aging hippies still committed to
truth, justice, and the American Way. Marty Hamilton. Garbage.
An immense sadness descended upon him as he contemplated this
pitiful self-portrait. He had wasted the most precious gift of all,
the gift of life, and hot tears coursed down his cheeks. He thought
about praying but didn't know how. Who would he pray to? Was
there a higher power, a Supreme Father who ruled over heaven
and earth? His own father had taught him precious little about
such things. William Camden Hamilton III had done the bidding
of the NRA for so long he couldn't tell the difference between the
voice of God and the voice of Charlton Heston.

Marty then noticed that his hands and feet were tingling and
very cold and knew that the CO_2, unable to escape his lungs, was
poisoning him. The end was close and his personality was beginning to break apart, to fragment and fly off into the darkness
like shards of broken glass. He also knew why the voice of the
Brother Emmett had come back to him. Inside the closet, *he* was
Jonah, Jonah in the belly of the whale. This dark claustrophobic
place would be his tomb—and as he thought this, something in
the word arrested his attention. How close it was in sound and
meaning to another word. Womb. Tomb and womb. He began
repeating the two words over and over again in his mind like an
incantation until slowly their meaning penetrated his heart with
the power of discovered truth. Death wasn't just an ending; it was
also a beginning. Time was the road *and* the journey, and he saw
it stretched out in front of him forever. And with this vision came
a change of heart so profound that his tears of remorse turned to
tears of joy. He would get it *right* the next time around, he told
himself. He would learn to be kind and selfless. He would make
amends. He would reach for the best in himself. And the time
after that, one lifetime after another. For all eternity. He closed
his eyes as the vital force, like a departing visitor, stole away and
he surrendered to death's embrace.

Then came the dazzling white light. An explosion of light. A riot of light. God Almighty's light, shooting through every atom of his body setting his soul free. He felt weightless and there was a sensation of falling. Falling. . . He *was* falling. Out of the closet, expelled from the belly of the whale into the painful light of life and hope.

He crashed to the floor and heard a yelp of surprise. His shoulder throbbed with pain; his head swam. He blinked his eyes as the pupils rushed to limit the surfeit of photons pouring into them. A face appeared above him. A woman's face. Blurry. A nurse. Pretty. Blond. With a button nose. Her expression? Very surprised. Very concerned.

"Are. . . are you all right?" she stammered.

Mumbled words and feminine fingernails smelling of antiseptic soap pulling the tape away. Cheeks and lips burning as the stale, poisoned air rushed up his throat and out of his mouth. Then the glorious sensation of sweet air being sucked down deep into lungs that quivered in celebration. Marty Hamilton was resurrected, restored to life! He wept, and shook, and wept some more. With joy and gratitude. The nurse, completely freaked out, ran off to get help.

THE NEXT MORNING in a private room at Methodist Hospital, Brenda and an unknown man came to see Marty. The man wore an expensive suit, had sweeping gray hair, and never smiled. Marty pegged him right off as a lawyer.

"Mr. Axton is anxious to talk to you," Brenda said. "Did you give a statement to the police yet?"

"I described the men who attacked me," Marty rasped. His throat was raw and talking came hard. "One of the men was the Russian with Kamal Oil. I recognized him." He reached for a glass of water on the moveable tray nearby.

"His name is Colonel Degtyar," the man with gray hair said. "What about the girl? Was she there?"

"Yes."

"And you didn't recognize her?" the man said.

"Not until later. When it was too late."

The man surveyed Marty with the cold, stern expression of the headmaster of an exclusive boarding school reprimanding a wayward student caught peddling dirty pictures. Clearly, Marty had let the old school down, betrayed a sacred trust.

This thought started Marty laughing, great peels of laughter that made his bruised stomach and throat hurt.

"Oh for God's sake, Marty, stop it," Brenda scolded him.

Her mention of God, however, only added to his hilarity. He couldn't stop laughing even if he wanted to. Their absurd lives were filled with petty concerns: the ambitious, adulterous secretary and the high-priced corporate attorney. The new Marty Hamilton didn't give a tinker's damn what happened to Dr. Easler or the Russians. Or what they, as agents of the all-powerful EnerTex Corporation, might do to him. Take away his Porsche 911? His Cartier *tank* watch? He no longer needed them, no longer desired them. All he wanted to do was to tell them that it was okay; everything was A-okay.

LATER THAT AFTERNOON, after her anger ran its course, Brenda found herself thinking about Marty. He was a world-class jerk who had seriously fucked up. But maybe, given enough time, he could work his way back up from the mail room—that is if Avery could be persuaded to keep him on. She had never known her boss to be so stressed out. After that first meeting with the Russian, Avery holed himself up in his office for hours talking long distance on the telephone. Usually she placed his calls, but not that day. Then suddenly the California-Nevada deal was on the front burner. Ron McBride stopped her in the hallway one afternoon to ask what was going on.

"Why the big push to get Ranger 2 and 3 under contract all of a sudden?" he asked. "I'm driving my team as hard as I can, but these projects take time."

"I know they do, Ron," she said with a weak smile, "but Avery has his reasons. He's leaving tomorrow for three days of

meetings in Washington. It has something to do with SEPOC."
She touched his arm. "You know Avery, he'll handle it."

"Yeah, well, keep me informed if you hear anything."

Brenda nodded and Ron, less than satisfied, turned and continued down the hallway toward his office.

Her position was difficult. She had to watch carefully what she said—rumors were beginning to circulate and the troops were jumpy. What she hadn't told Ron was that she was making the trip to Washington with Avery. She had never traveled with him before and had a pretty good hunch it wasn't going to be all business. It was the look in his eyes when he asked her. Say what you want about the evils of stress, how bad it is on the heart and other organs, nothing beats it for firing up the old libido. What surprised her was her husband's reaction when she mentioned the trip.

"I'd rather you didn't go," he said.

"I have to," she said, "it's my job."

"I've got next week off and I was hoping we could maybe go fishing together."

She was brushing her hair and she stopped and turned around. "Fishing? What are you talking about?"

"I heard of a place in Arkansas, up in the Ozarks. A resort on a private lake. It's very secluded and rustic."

She wanted to laugh; it was such a lame-brained idea. A weekend of sun-bathing and snorkeling in the Bahamas, she could get with that, but fishing? No fucking way

"Sorry, baby," she said returning to her brushing, "duty calls. Why don't you ask one of your buddies to go with you?"

The only fish she was after was Avery Jordan Axton. Land him and she might just give up angling altogether. Larry could go his own way. It had been fun, but all things come to an end.

Which, in Larry's case, happened sooner than she expected. While she was rolling around in her boss' arms in the executive suite of the Four Seasons Hotel, Larry was using a pocket knife to cut an X in the muscle of his right leg just above his boot, where the rattlesnake bit him. His heart was going all flippity-flop and he knew that wasn't good. He was also alone and that wasn't good either. He should have taken Brenda's advice and invited a friend. Too late now. He thought about sucking the poison out with his mouth but his body wouldn't bend that far. Instead, he began fumbling with his boot laces with the idea of making a tourniquet but the tips of his fingers were numb and wouldn't work. And something weird was going on with his eyesight; there was a sharp taste on his tongue and a hammering in his chest. His leg was swelling up and he tried to stand but couldn't keep his balance. He decided the best thing to do was to lie down and let nature take her course. He soon fell into a deep sleep from which he never awoke.

35

REB CONSIDERED PUTTING off the interview for a few days because he wanted to be at his best and feared the pain pills would dull his concentration. But if he did he ran the risk of Dr. Easler getting cold feet and refusing to talk—or the cops showing up to haul the good doctor away. Alice, on the other hand, was all for getting on with the interview.

"Look, if you're just not up to it, I understand," she said, "but the sooner we can get this over with, the sooner we can go home."

It was early afternoon and they were lounging next to the pool under the shade of a blue canopy. Elliot had just finished redressing Reb's wound and was inside using the phone. He told them he would stay another night—he wanted to attend the interview—but then he needed to return to Houston and his work at the clinic.

"What about Marion?" Reb asked.

"What do you mean?" Alice said.

"Do you think he'll want to at the interview too?"

Alice shrugged. "Let him. It's his spread."

"But why's he being so helpful?"

"He's Elliot's friend."

"He's also in the energy business. Maybe he just wants to get the skinny on a major competitor."

"So what? It's not our job to look after EnerTex's interests. We're here to find out what's happening to Ernesto and Mike and the others. That's all." The rude way Charles Hathaway had shown them the door still vexed her when she thought about it.

For several minutes neither spoke and Alice was beginning to doze when she heard an odd tapping sound. She opened her eyes to see Dr. Easler coming toward them with his cane.

"May I join you?" he said as he came up to them.

"Yes, of course," Alice said, jumping up and pulling a nearby chair over next to hers.

"Thank you," he said and sat down. He turned to Reb. "How are you feeling today?"

"Not too bad," Reb said. "We were just talking about you. I thought we might conduct the interview this evening, after supper."

"If that works for you, Dr. Easler," Alice added.

"Please, my name is Walter. I hope we shall become friends."

Reb and Alice glanced at each other and reached a quick decision; it was going to be "Walter" from now on.

"And you can call me Reb."

"And please, call me Alice."

They speculated about the weather and then talked about California and Nevada City. Walter and Alice discovered they shared a passion for gardening and were soon discussing the relative perils and benefits of earwigs and fish meal. It was a court-ship dance of sorts, knocking off the awkward edges with small talk. As if by unspoken consent, the subject of EnerTex could wait until later.

"Tell me about this radio station where you work," Walter said. "What is it called?"

"KVMR," Alice said.

"Where do you get your money? From the government?"

"We receive a small amount of funding from the CPB," Alice said.

"What is this CPB?"

"Government money," Reb said. "The Corporation for Public Broadcasting."

"But it's a very small part," Alice said. "The bulk of our support comes from our listeners and business underwriters."

"So you are free to do what you want? The government cannot tell you what to broadcast?"

"We have a board of directors; they're the ones in charge," Alice said. "People apply to become board members and we hold an election."

"So you are a collective then, like Communism?"

"We've been called communists," Reb laughed.

"And this is good? This board that is elected?"

Now Alice laughed. "Not always. Depends on who gets elected." Whenever she thought about Jack Dunnel, she doubted the wisdom of the process.

"There are no perfect systems for organizing society," Walter said. "I was born in Russia and lived under Communism all my life. I saw what that system did to people, how it killed the imagination and imprisoned the spirit. But what I find in the West I am not sure is much better. Here there is such competition and greed."

Reb had assumed, given the name, that Walter was German, or maybe Swiss. He suddenly realized he knew nothing about the man. "Can you tell us what it was like growing up in Russia?" he asked.

"I will tell you about my father. He also was scientist. His name was Lev Kryuchkov. He was—"

"But I thought your last name was *Easler*." Reb said.

"Easler is not my true name," Walter said.

"Please go on," Reb said, embarrassed for interrupting the older man.

"My grandfather was Russian, but my father's mother was from Latvia. She was Jewish and a member of the Assars. Do you know of the Assars?"

"Weren't they socialist rivals of Lenin and the Bolsheviks?" Reb asked.

"Yes, many were murdered or imprisoned during the Red Terror. My grandmother was sent to a prison camp in Siberia. Eventually, through my grandfather's efforts, she was released and he brought her to Moscow. That is where my father was born and grew up—in Moscow. He studied at the Bawman Institute and helped design weapons that were used against the Germans during the war. He was a young man and very intelligent, and after the war, Stalin put him to work on the hydrogen bomb. He agreed to do this, but the work ruined him."

Walter shifted painfully in his chair.

"How did the work ruin him?" Alice asked.

"He drank very much and began to go with low women. It was difficult for my mother. She did not want me to become a scientist but I am much like my father. He used to take me for walks and show me things about the natural world. In my heart he planted the love of science and it became my religion. But I made a promise to myself: I would never use my intelligence to make weapons to kill people."

"What happened to your father?" Reb said.

"Because of his drinking, he lost control of his mind; he began seeing things."

"What kind of things?" Alice asked.

"Ghosts. The ghosts of dead German soldiers and little babies blown apart by the Katyusha rockets he helped build. They put my father in an asylum. A dreadful stone building that reeked of disinfectant and despair. He died there, a tormented man."

"What about your mother?" Reb asked.

"She died in 1988, two years before I came to the United States. She had a life of sorrow. She was infected with polio when she was twenty-eight years old and had to walk with crutches and leg braces. I contracted polio from her but I was young and threw it off easily. It was only later that the disease returned." And Walter touched his cane and gave strange smile.

"Perhaps you'd be more comfortable in the recliner," Alice said and began to get up.

"No, no, this is fine," he said, "please."

Reb was eager to ask Walter how he came to the United States to work for EnerTex but decided to wait until the interview, when the digital recorder was turned on. There was more to the elderly physicist than met the eye. But that was how it was with most people. If he could get them telling their story, sooner or later they would say something that kindled his interest. That was the part of being a radio man he enjoyed most.

"Elliot says Marion is going to give you a tour of his automobiles in a little while," Reb said.

"Yes," Walter said brightening like a child. "Will you also come?"

"No, I'm feeling tired," Reb said. "I think I should rest."

"Then perhaps you will join us, Alice?"

"I would be happy to," she said.

"We'll talk more tonight," Reb said and reclined his chair and closed his eyes.

AFTER SUPPER EVERYONE made their way to the study while Marion talked about Elliot as if he wasn't there.

"Elliot's a fine man. I love him like a son. I only wish he would find a girl and settle down. He works too much. He's married to that clinic of his."

"I'm not married to the clinic," Elliot said good-naturedly, and Reb could tell this was a well-worn topic between the two men.

"I heard you're in a band," Alice said. "What kind of music do you play?"

"Old-time Texas swing," Elliot said.

"It's his only form of amusement as far as I can tell," Marion reasserted his ownership of the conversation. "It's dangerous work Elliot does at that clinic. One day he'll contract a deadly disease, you mark my words."

The study was given over to dark wood and muted lighting, the kind of room that embraced its inhabitants in the familiar and reassuring way a favorite uncle might hug a child; danger and insecurity had no place in such a room.

Reb directed Elliot and Marion as they rearranged the furniture while Alice unpacked the recording equipment and Appleyard went for a pitcher of water and some glasses. Alice offered
to run the recorder and monitor levels so Reb could give his full
attention to the interview.

Reb asked Walter to make himself comfortable in a leather
Stevenson chair and Alice placed the microphone on a stand in
front of him.

"Shall I call you Dr. Easler for the sake of the interview?" Reb
asked.

"Yes, that is the name I am known by here in America."

"Good, then let's get started." Reb nodded to Alice who
started the recorder.

"This interview is taking place at a ranch not far from Houston,
Texas, and I am interviewing Dr. Walter Easler. Dr. Easler, how
long have you worked for the EnerTex Corporation?"

"Since 1990."

"What is your position with the company?"

"I am their chief research scientist."

"What can you tell us about what is happening to the workers
at the Ranger 1 power plant in west Texas?"

"For you to understand, I must first talk about the nature of
time," Walter said. "Other scientists seek to understand the physics
of light, or gravity. A colleague of mine at the Institute refused
to work on anything but electro-magnetism. But I am fascinated
with time. A person can not see or hear time. You cannot smell
time with your nose, taste it with your tongue, or touch it with
your finger, and yet it enters into everything we do."

He looked at Reb, who nodded in agreement even though he
was wondering where this was all going.

"There is an concept in physics called 'the arrow of time.' It
means that time is asymmetrical; it flows in only one direction,
from what we call the *past* into the *future*. Theoretically, time
should flow in the opposite direction as well, from the future into
the past. Mass can be turned into energy and energy can be turned
into mass. Why then should not time move in both directions?

"There is another concept that we physicists call entropy, which comes from the Second Law of Thermodynamics. Entropy means that everything in the universe moves from an ordered state to a disordered state.

"Imagine I am holding a brand-new deck of cards." Walter began a pantomime with his hands. "I break the seal and remove the cards from the box, so. . . I discard the jokers . . . and I inspect the remaining cards and see that they are arranged in suits in an orderly sequence, from ace to king. Now I begin to shuffle the cards. . . and I fan them out and discover that they are no longer in an ordered state. They are randomly arranged, disordered. I shuffle again. And again. And again, but no matter how many times I shuffle the cards, I can never return them to their original ordered state. It is a statistical impossibility. So you see, the arrow of time and entropy describe the same phenomena, which is that time flows in one direction only, and that direction is always from an ordered state to a disordered state."

"But how does this relate to EnerTex, Dr. Easler?" Reb asked.

"People talk about there being an energy shortage but that is not exactly true. Energy is abundant. It is everywhere. Energy is in every atom in this room but human beings can only make use of *highly ordered* energy. What we do is take out the order and leave disordered energy in its place. Coal, for instance, is a form of highly ordered energy. It was created many hundreds of thousands of years ago from the remains of organic matter that trapped light and heat from the sun. The highly ordered structure of its molecules captured the energy. So when we burn coal, we take the order out of the coal. What remains is still energy but it has become disordered, and as such, is of no further use to us. It is the same with petroleum and natural gas, even uranium."

Reb pictured a handful of multinational companies sucking the ordered energy of oil from beneath the sands of the Middle East, leaving political and economic disorder on the surface. He knew this wasn't what Walter was talking about but the analogy had a strange logic to it all the same.

"Now I want you to consider something," Walter said. "What if one could find a way to *reverse* the arrow of time? If this could be done, then entropy would also be reversed, and disordered energy would become ordered energy."

"And this ordered energy could be used to light cities, heat homes, and power vehicles?" Alice asked.

"Yes." Walter said.

"Would reversing the arrow of time be like reversing the orbit of an electron around a proton inside an atom?" Reb asked.

Walter shook his head with an air of gentle forbearance. "No, atoms are particles; they are mass," he said. "Time is very different. It is a dimension. To change the direction of time would be like. . . turning your left shoe into your right shoe."

Without thinking Reb glanced down at his shoes. He then noticed Alice doing the same thing.

"In the early 1980s," Walter went on, "I was doing my research at the Landau Institute of Theoretical Physics in Moscow. One day something very remarkable happened. It was the middle of the day and I was suddenly very tired; I could not keep my eyes open. We kept a cot in the laboratory and I went and laid down on it. I don't know if I was awake or dreaming but suddenly I understood that the arrow of time *could* be reversed. The revelation was so simple and elegant, it took my breath away."

"Well, shoot a bug!" Marion blurted out. "Don't that beat all."

Reb and Alice were both speechless.

"You see," Walter said, "the universe has many dimensions and time is only one of them. Physicists try to understand these dimensions, but because they are human beings, they retain their space-bias perspective. This means they see themselves living in conventional three-dimensional space and moving *through* time. Look around you." Walter motioned with his hand. "What you see are the well-defined dimensions of space. They are familiar and reassuring, yes? Time, on the other hand, is this strange *other* dimension. It is invisible and yet you sense that it is there. When you watch a child with a jump rope, you see the jiggles of the rope in space and sense time happening to them. But if you were able to switch from your space-bias perspective to a time-bias perspective, then you would see the jiggles lined up in time and *space* happening to them. This shift in perspective is what happened to me. I cannot explain how or why but it changed my life forever."

"What did you do with this discovery?" Reb asked.

"I built a reactor that could reverse the direction of time. It was quite small and capable of generating only sixty kilowatts of electricity. But it worked and I was elated. I also saw that a much larger reactor could be built that would be capable of transforming significant quantities of disordered energy into ordered energy. Ambient temperature water could be pumped into this reactor so that it came out as very hot and very cold water. This water—"

"Highly ordered water," Reb said.

"Yes. This highly ordered water could be used to both *power* and *cool* a turbine and thus produce electricity. Afterwards, the resultant disordered water could be pumped back into the reactor, where it would again be turned into highly ordered water, and so on."

A closed system, Reb thought and remembered the way Mike Pendergast had described the large pipes that ran through the reactor at the power plant.

"What happened next?" Alice asked.

"Chernobyl was a horrible tragedy for my country. We desperately needed a safer source of electricity and I told my superiors that I had found one. But they handed me over to the military and ordered me to develop a working reactor to power a submarine called the *Tigron*. I objected strongly to this; I had not forgotten what had become of my father. I told them that I only wished to use my discovery for peaceful purposes. But my mother was still alive and they threatened to send her to prison if I did not cooperate. At last I agreed, but I was determined that they should not learn the secret."

"You were able to do that?" Alice asked.

"Yes. I built the reactor without revealing the core concepts that made it work. They provided me with all the engineers I wanted, even an American. But I refused to cooperate with other physicists for fear that they would steal my ideas."

"Was the submarine project successful?" Reb asked.

"No, there was an accident and the *Tigron* was lost at sea."

"Why? What happened?" Reb said.

"To function properly, the time reversal process taking place inside the reactor must be isolated from the outside world and so I developed a very powerful electromagnetic containment force field that performed flawlessly at first. But then, without warning, the field collapsed. I shall never forget the photographs taken by the rescue team. In those few seconds between the collapse of the force field and the reactor shutting down, the sailors onboard the *Tigron* aged hundreds of years."

"My God," Marion said, "those poor men."

"But I thought you said the reactor reversed the direction of time," Reb said, deeply confused. "How could it age people?"

"I will try to explain. A wave moves across a body of water but the remaining surface of the water appears flat, yes?"

Reb nodded.

"So where does the extra water come from that makes the wave? It comes from the troughs that run along just before and after the wave. There the level of the water is depressed to make up for the difference in the water level. It is difficult to see this, of course, because waves move so quickly. Well, inside the reactor, time moves backwards, but immediately *outside* reactor, in the space between the reactor and the containment force field, time moves forward with greater velocity. This time acceleration effect must be kept from the outside world. Despite all my efforts, however, this is where I have failed."

Like the deft fingers of an experienced safecracker, Walter's words had at last coaxed the tumblers of Reb's understanding into place. He had been expecting to hear that some insidious unpronounceable chemical compound like phenazopyridine hydrochloride was making the workers sick, but that wasn't the case. Nor was radiation the culprit. Instead, it was time.

"So what you're saying is that the Ranger 1 power plant uses the arrow of time to make electricity and that somehow this time acceleration effect is getting outside the containment force field, and the workers aren't getting sick, they are just getting *old*?"

"Yes," Walter said.

"And that is why the plant workers present different symptoms," Elliot said, giving voice to his thoughts.

"Their ailments are genetically determined," Walter said. "For one, his eyesight begins to fail, while for another, his heart wears out more quickly. As the reactor generates electrical energy, it simultaneously accelerates the aging process."

"So that is why EnerTex shuts down the reactor whenever their top people visit the plant," Alice said. "They know what's going on and they don't want to be effected?"

Walter nodded.

"That's so wrong!" she said. She could hardly take in the magnitude of what Walter was telling them. Those unfortunate workers. She saw their faces—Ernesto and Mike and their wives—and it made her sad and angry beyond words.

Reb had yet to react emotionally; he was still trying to work out the science in his head.

"How far does this time acceleration effect extend geographically?" he asked, "What I mean is, how far away from the reactor does it still effect people?"

"That is difficult to say. The effect is also much like a wave. When you drop a pebble into water, the waves spread out evenly in every direction. But as they radiate outward they dissipate, until at some distance, the surface of water is undisturbed. The time acceleration effect is strongest nearest the reactor but quickly diminishes as it travels outward."

"What about in Birdstar?" Alice said. "The town can't be more than thirty miles away."

"Twenty-three miles and yes, the effect is less in Birdstar than inside the plant itself."

"How much less?" Reb asked.

"I cannot say with certainty. EnerTex claims they conducted tests in the area and that the time acceleration effect is negligible."

"Negligible, what's that supposed to mean?" Alice's agitation was such that she had to keep herself from jumping up out of her chair.

"Do you think EnerTex is lying about the impact, Walter?" Elliot asked.

"Yes."

Reb's thoughts were already racing ahead. If what Walter said was true, then the EnerTex Corporation was generating electricity not from coal, gas, or uranium, nor from the wind, sun, or ocean currents, but from time itself. Incredible! But what would the impact of such a technology be on the environment? On the global balance of power? On the future of humankind? Reb looked over at Alice and their eyes met. They had either stumbled onto the biggest story of the century, of the millennium, or Walter was the biggest bullshitter since P.T. Barnum. Doubt was already pushing itself forward inside his mind like someone fighting to get off a crowded elevator.

"If time is speeding up outside the reactor, as you say," Reb asked, "then wouldn't clocks and everything else run faster?"

"That's what I was wondering," Marion said. "You'd notice pretty quick if your watch was speeding up; I know I would."

Walter nodded as if anticipating the question.

"To explain this behavior I must talk about fractals," Walter said. "A fractal is an infinite length packed into what seems like a finite distance. Imagine a zigzag line running between two points." He traced an imaginary zig zag line in the air in front of him. "Now if you zoom in, you discover that every zig and every zag in that distance is itself a zigzag line. Zoom in again, and each zig and zag is another zigzag line. And so on, all the way to infinity. That is why you can have systems that appear to have a finite distance between two points, but if you tried to walk the line, making sure to follow every little every zig and zag, it would take forever—you would never get there."

He took a sip of water before continuing.

"Fractals are common in nature. A snowflake is a good example. When you look at the periphery of a snowflake at large scale, it seems to have a discreet border, yes? But it also has little projections, and if you look more closely at these projections, you discover that they too have projections. And if you look closer still, even those projections have projections. For this reason, a snowflake is said to have a fractal quality."

"But what do fractals have to do with your discovery about time?" Reb asked.

"So far I have been talking about fractals as they relate to space, to objects in space. What I discovered when I reversed the direction of time was that I had created a fractal in the fabric of time. I realize this is difficult to understand but please be patient with me."

Again he shifted in his chair.

"Normally, between the moment *now* and the moment one second from now, there lies a straight line. I'm not talking about a line in *space* but a line in *time*. Think of the line as a single thread and it takes one second to walk along this thread. Now consider what happens if time develops fractal character. At longer time lengths it continues to look like a straight thread and it should take only a second to walk along it. But as you zoom in and begin looking at shorter and shorter times lengths, you see that the thread is all bunched up. And if you were to walk along it, in baby steps, it would take you much, much longer. However, if you took bigger steps, you would be stepping over the bunched up parts, and it would take you only a second.

"Another way to understand what I am saying is to imagine an old rubber band. When I stretch time backwards inside my reactor, it is like stretching the rubber band. Do you see? But just outside the reactor, time compensates by snapping back—remember the wave; if you have crests, you must also have troughs."

"The piper must be paid," Reb added.

"Yes." Walter smiled. "But because it's an old rubber band and has lost some of its elasticity, it does not fully recover its original shape when it snaps back. There are very small wrinkles in it now. You can see these wrinkles only if you look very closely at the rubber band. From a few feet away, or from across the room, the rubber band looks perfectly normal."

Alice thought of the book *A Wrinkle in Time* that she had read to her children when they were young. Reb, however, had something else on his mind.

"What about the force field?" he said. "From what one of the workers told us, the reactor containment building at the power plant projects a powerful force field."

"With a real rubber band," Walter said, "when I stretch it and then let it go, it needs *time* to recover. Yes? Well, when time is stretched and let go, it needs *space* to recover. The purpose of the force field is to compress the space so that time can recover in a packed region. But this is where my technology failed. The field does not fully contain the compensating effect produced by the reactor; a portion of the accelerated time leaks out into the surrounding space. Even several miles away from the power plant, time is still recovering; it is still bunched up at very short time lengths. And it is what happens at these very short time lengths that effects aging in humans and other living organisms."

"How? I don't understand," Reb asked.

"Because, you see, chemical and biological reactions take place at these very short time lengths and the molecules must traverse all the little meanders of time, the bunched up thread of time. To the individual molecule, the amount of time it experiences going from, say, *midnight* to *midnight plus one second* is more like *ten* seconds than one second."

"How small are the time lengths where this bunching up takes place?" Elliot asked.

"Oh, very, very small," Walter waved his hand. "Pico and femtosecond time lengths; those are the time lengths of molecular vibrations and electronic transitions in atomic-molecular systems."

"Don't quartz clocks operate at small time lengths?" Reb asked.

"A quartz tuner oscillates once every thirty-three thousandths of a second, but that is still quite long compared to pico and femto-second time lengths where the molecular reactions associated with aging take place. Those times lengths are much shorter."

"So what you are telling us," Elliot said, "is that clocks don't show time going faster even though the molecules inside the body have to walk along the extra thread of time."

"Yes, that is correct."

"Can people notice this acceleration of time?" Alice asked.

"No, because consciousness, and specific conscious thoughts such as looking at your watch—even the internal behavior of the watch itself—all of these activities experience time at relatively long time lengths. They take large steps across the distorted, bunched up, but not fully recovered time. So midnight to midnight and one second still seems like one second. Almost."

"Why do you say *almost*?" Reb asked.

"Because a small amount of time-noise has been introduced into some of the longer time lengths. It emanates out from the bunched up, much shorter time lengths like static that degrades the sound of a radio. But now it's static in *time* that degrades the order in everything it encounters."

"Can people sense time noise?" Alice asked.

"I do not know. The sensation would be so very subtle."

"Would they feel ill at ease?" Reb said. "Hurried or anxious?" He recalled how much he and Alice had wanted to get out of Birdstar.

Walter shrugged. "This phenomenon has never existed before, as far as I know. My calculations indicate that the time noise should cause longer time length devices to lose their order more quickly."

"So clocks *would* run faster?" Reb said wondering if they might be going in circles.

"No," Walter said shaking his head, "clocks would lose their accuracy. Sometimes they would run fast and sometimes slow."

"Remember the trouble I was having with my watch in Birdstar?" Alice said, turning to Reb. "I thought I needed a new battery but by the time we got to Houston it was running perfectly again."

"What other things would act up?" Marion said.

"Certain kinds of electronic devices."

"What about laser printers?" Reb asked.

Walter thought a moment and said, "Yes. The dot patterns might randomize."

Marvin Spooner's trouble with laser printers, Reb thought.

"Then what about birds?" Alice said.

"I don't understand."

"You said that biological systems are effected at the short times lengths. Would this include birds?"

"Yes, certainly."

"Could they then suddenly all decide to fly away?" she asked.

Again Walter paused to consider the question. "Like any living organism, birds would age faster," he said. "They would hatch their young earlier, all their biological processes would accelerate. But I cannot say if they would be conscious of this change. If they were, if they somehow sensed this bunching up of time, then it is possible that they would fly away."

The individual parts were all adding up. The complaints of the plant workers, the missing birds in Birdstar, even what the waitress said about the fruit going bad. It all made sense now, which meant Walter's story was the real deal.

"How potentially dangerous is this?" Reb asked. "If the time acceleration effect is aging the workers at the power plant, and perhaps people as far away as Birdstar, might there not be other hazards?"

"I am particularly concerned about insects and bacteria," Walter said.

"Why?" Alice asked.

"Because both will replicate more rapidly and this will speed up the rate of mutation."

"That means they could develop immunity to pesticides and antibiotics more quickly," Elliot finished.

"That is something I worry about. These resistant strains will eventually migrate out into the world, far from the Ranger 1 power plant."

They were silent as each considered this possibility. Reb went back in his thoughts to their meeting with Sheila Kennedy. Given the serious and seemingly intractable problems associated with traditional ways of generating electricity—global warming, mercury contamination of the air and water, and how to safely store nuclear waste for the next several hundred thousand years— Walter's discovery was a godsend. But looking at what might happen to bacteria and insects if time on earth sped up was enough to induce nightmares. And there were the plant workers to think about, and anybody else who lived near an EnerTex power plant. Hathaway had bragged about how they would soon be building power plants all around the world. How many of these plants would be built near large population centers? How could any kind of rational policy regarding these plants be developed when no one knew the truth of what was happening? National security was being used as an excuse to cover up what was potentially a monstrous crime against humanity. The greedy bastards.

He took a long, slow breath to calm down and then filled a glass with water and drank. Get as much of the story as you can, the voice of the inner journalist cautioned him, so you don't have to come back again later.

"Can you tell us how you came to the United States to work for EnerTex?" he asked the physicist.

For the next ten minutes Walter talked about the counterfeit suicide and how the CIA provided him with a new identity and brought him to Texas. He told how for nearly fifteen years since coming to the United States he had worked to fully contain the time acceleration effect. He convinced himself that he had succeeded, only to find, once Ranger 1 began operations, that the effect, though greatly reduced, still existed. It was a crushing disappointment and he went to see Avery Axton to urge him to close the plant. But all Axton did was deny there was a problem.

"He claimed they had done extensive tests," Walter said, "and that there was nothing to worry about. But I know the face of the official lie and I knew that nothing would be done. This time, however, I had given away the secret of my discovery. EnerTex now owns it and they can build their power plants without me. So I tried to convince myself that I might yet solve the time acceleration problem. Is this not sad? But then my good friend Elliot called. He said that journalists wanted to talk to me about the workers and the power plant. That is when I decided to do what I could to rectify my mistakes. I am trusting you, Reb and Alice, to warn the people about this new technology. If EnerTex builds more plants, then each will contribute to the time acceleration effect. It will be cumulative and there may be harmonic effects of which we are ignorant; no one can predict the outcome."

Like genetically engineered food crops, Alice thought. It all sounds great on paper; let's feed the starving of the earth through better science. But what happens when the genetically engineered plants commingle with native plants? No one really knows.

Reb realized he was both mentally and physically spent.

"Let's stop for tonight and continue again tomorrow morning," he said. "Is that okay with you, Walter?"

The older man nodded.

Alice switched off the recorder and Reb stood up. He was incredibly stiff and all he wanted to do was go outside for some air. He had a ton on his mind. Walter meanwhile reached for his cane and stood up. Watching him, Reb tried to switch his space-bias to a time-bias frame of reference, to perceive Walter's movements in *time* with *space* happening to them. He gave up the exercise with a shake of his head; he was just too much a space-bias kind of guy.

Reb stretched his arms to ease the tension in his back and a quick stab of pain reminded him of his recent injury. EnerTex was willing to kill to keep Walter's story from getting out which was just one more piece of evidence that confirmed that what the Russian said was true. Fear, rather than doubt, now tried to push itself forward in Reb's mind. Getting the story was only the beginning. What to *do* with it was by far the greater challenge. He wanted to be alone with Alice so they could talk.

"Well, I've heard some whoppers in my time," Marion said coming up to Reb and Alice, "but nothing to top that. Imagine using time to make electricity. Do you reckon I should unload my oil wells while I still have the chance?"

"Thanks for letting us use your home for the interview," Reb said.

"My pleasure," Marion said and he turned to Elliot. "You know, your brother Avery's got a tiger by the tail. I just hope it don't bite him too hard."

Elliot looked troubled and said nothing.

Marion then turned back to Reb, Alice, and Walter. "Apple-yard has prepared the screening room. I thought you all might like to see the newest creation from Mr. Scorsese. It won't be released to the theaters until next month, but he's a friend of mine and he sends me his latest work when he's finished with the editing."

There was an awkward pause and Marion said, "Well, I guess we all have more important things to think about. I'll say good night then."

IN BED TOGETHER later that night neither Reb or Alice could sleep.

"Remember when you talked about there being two kinds of time?" Alice said. "You called them *mythos* time and *logos* time. Well, which kind do you think is influenced by the Walter's reactor?"

"Good question. I guess they both are."

"Why?"

"Mythos and logos time might go forward at different rates, like in the fairy tales, but they *do* go forward. I've never heard of time, any kind of time, going backwards."

"But what about time travel?"

"I think of time travel as traveling *through* time while time continues to flows in one direction."

"Until now."

"Yep, until now."

Far off a dog began barking.

"How do you think this will effect mythos time?" Alice asked. "Will messing with time trouble the spirit world?"

"That's a Nevada City kind of question," Reb said. "You'd have to go to a shaman with that one."

It was a feeble attempt at humor, but the idea that the unseen world of sprites, gnomes, and banshees might experience the effects of the Walter's reactor was unsettling and not all that far-fetched. People might scoff at the notion that such entities existed but not him. It was true he never saw one, but he had felt their presence. Even his mother had come to him on several occasions, or so he believed. And what about string theory, the latest attempt by physicists to come up with a unified theory to explain the universe? From what he understood of the theory, the universe was supposedly made up of multiple dimensions, not just the three experienced through the five senses. Something happening in one dimension ought to effect the other dimensions as well. The fact that humans can't observe the effect doesn't negate its importance. A gang of men with chain saws screaming their way through a grove of old-growth Redwoods, a diesel-belching bulldozer filling in an ancient wetland for a housing development, a herd of monster dump trucks hauling away uranium and coal from the scarred, sacred lands of the Navaho. . . And now man's machines were invading the realm of time. It was madness.

While Reb imagined troubled spirits fleeing the ravages of human ambition, Alice was thinking about the birds that came to the feeder by her back door in Nevada City. She had a special affection for birds. With their hollow bones and paper-thin skulls, they were among the least substantial of all creatures, some of the smaller song birds little more than beautiful thoughts. How she would miss them if they one day all flew away.

36

THE Y WERE SITTING with Elliot by the pool in the swelter of mid-day heat and humidity. Reb interviewed Walter for the second time earlier that morning but he had learned little that was new. Elliot had stayed for lunch and was getting ready to return to Houston.

"But you *know* who these people are," Alice was saying to Reb, her voice laced with irritation. "They nearly killed you. I just don't see what you hope to gain by going to them for *their side of the story*. You already know their side of the story."

"Strictly speaking, I don't," Reb said. "I only have Dr. Easler's word for what's going on at the power plant." He didn't want to get into an argument, not in this heat, but he wasn't sure he could avoid one.

"But what Walter says squares with what the workers say," Alice said, "and it's consistent with how EnerTex tried to stop Walter from escaping."

"We don't know for sure if EnerTex was behind what happened at the Polio Institute," Reb said.

"Who else could it be?"

Reb didn't have an answer.

"You know what your problem is?" Alice went on. "You think a corporation should have the same rights as you and me and Elliot here. But a corporation isn't a person. It's just a machine for making money."

Reb knew corporations were a hot-button topic with Alice, and for good reason. In the eyes of the law, a corporation enjoyed the same rights as a living person, and yet it was spared the attendant responsibilities. This meant it could buy and sell property and sue individuals in the courts. And if along the way, it happened to screw up the environment or manufacture products that harmed people, well then, tough cookies. You couldn't put a corporation in jail; it was only a piece of paper, after all.

"I think what Alice is trying to say," Elliot said, "is that under normal conditions you'd be right to offer EnerTex the opportunity to respond to Dr. Easler's allegations, to give them a chance to go on the record. But EnerTex isn't some little mom and pop outfit, Reb. They have the full weight of the federal government behind them. That means the CIA, FBI, ATF, the whole alphabet soup that's supposed to protect the homeland. And thanks to the Patriot Act, the government can lock up anyone they want to and throw away the key."

"So are you suggesting I just walk away from the story?" Reb said. "Pretend that the workers aren't in danger and that Walter's just batty old eccentric?"

"That's not what Elliot's saying," Alice said.

"What other choice is there? If I run with the story, if I somehow manage to get it out to the public, then should I expect to be arrested in the middle of the night and whisked off to Guantanamo Bay? KVMR already has my letter of resignation, so they can deny any involvement. I'd be completely on my own. Is that what I should do?"

Before either Alice or Elliot could respond he went on, his own frustration getting the better of him.

"Let me tell you what I think will happen. Despite the danger, I go ahead and broadcast the story, and guess what? No one believes it, not a word of it. Electricity made from time? Who's kidding who? Even with Walter's interview, you have to admit it's a pretty hard pill to swallow. EnerTex will know it's true, of course, and they'll come after me with everything they've got—the government too. So I'll have to go into hiding, find some lonely

cabin in the wilds of Montana, like the Unabomber. Or I go to jail
and pray the ACLU sends me a lawyer. Then, if I'm exceptionally
lucky, there'll be a trial. Witnesses will be called and Walter will
have to testify. Oh yeah, I forgot to mention Walter. He'll have
to go underground too, because everybody and his brother will
be looking for him—EnerTex, the government, Larry King, hell,
there won't be a hole deep enough for him to hide in."

"I think Walter knows what he's getting himself into," Alice
said, her voice quieter now.

"Don't bet on it," Reb said. "This is unknown country we've
stumbled into here, folks. Terra Incognito. A bunch of monkeys
throwing rocks at King Kong—or is it Godzilla?"

"Goliath," Alice said, her voice now little more than a whisper.
"And you're not in this alone."

This brought him up short. He was such a knucklehead; Alice
was as committed to the story as he was.

"You're right," he said, "I'm sorry. I'm a little stressed out."

"We both are," she said.

"Make that three," said Elliot with a smile.

"Okay, let's apply some order to this process," Reb said.
"Question number one, putting aside for the moment what
happens to Walter, what can Alice and I expect if we broadcast
EnerTex story?"

"You both become famous," Elliot said matter-of-factly.

It wasn't the answer Reb expected.

"You mean like Woodward and Bernstein?"

"Bigger," Elliot said. "Energy is a global issue of enormous
importance. It effects everybody."

"And if we get sued and lose everything we have in the world
and have to go to prison?"

"You will still be heroes to most of the people on the planet,
and your names will go down in history as the journalists who
uncovered the truth about what happens when you make electricity out of time. Not a bad legacy, when you think about it."

"So we either continue living safe lives in relative obscurity or
we become famous and risk going to jail."

"The latter worked for Martha Stewart," Alice added.

"What about getting killed then?" Reb said. "Is that a possible outcome?"

"Who would do the killing?" Alice asked.

"That's part of the problem, we don't know," Reb said. "But it's naive to think that corporations don't have people murdered when it serves their interests."

"You're talking about EnerTex," Alice said.

Reb turned to Elliot. "Is your brother capable of doing something along that line?"

"Along what line?" Elliot said.

"Having someone killed? I'm sorry to ask this, but you know him a lot better than either of us."

Reb sensed Elliot stiffen and feared he'd gone too far.

"I wish I could say no, absolutely not," Elliot said, measuring his words carefully. "But I honestly don't know, and that troubles me. Avery's not a cruel man; he's just extremely ambitious. I should think you have as much to fear from the government as from EnerTex. I'm sure there are agencies that act outside the law when deemed necessary."

It wouldn't have to look like murder, Reb reflected. It might be a car accident or an airplane crash—the suspicious death of a Minnesota senator came to mind. Or they might suddenly contract an exotic deadly disease or die in an elevator with a cut cable. He realized his imagination was feeding off a grab bag of old movie plots. It wasn't always easy in today's world to distinguish where fiction left off and reality began. Unconsciously he touched his bandaged side with his left hand.

"You could move to another country," Elliot said.

"What country?" Reb said.

"That's up to you. Europe, South America. It might be safer for you."

"I don't know if another country would take us. And how would we live?"

"With enough money, anything is possible," Elliot said. "I had a talk this morning with Marion and he has offered his help."

"What kind of help?" Alice asked surprised at the direction the conversation was taking.

"Money to live on, to hire lawyers, for whatever you have to do. He knows what you're up against and he thinks you're both quite brave."

"Well, I don't feel particularly brave right now," Reb said.

"Nor do I," Alice said, "but this country is my home, and I'm not going let EnerTex or anyone else force me to leave. "

Reb knew she was thinking about her children. He had a son as well and a number of close friends. Besides he had no desire to go blind in a foreign land amongst strangers.

"I'm with Alice," he said, "we're staying."

"Then maybe you should turn the story over to NPR," Elliot suggested. "They're a much bigger outfit."

This was a solution Reb hadn't considered, although a part of him wanted to reject it out of hand. Why should NPR get the glory? It was reporters from a community radio station who had dogged the story from the beginning and uncovered the truth. And what's more, Hathaway claimed the information about the ATG technology was classified. That would put NPR on a collision course with the president and Congress. Would they buck that kind of pressure? It was hard to tell.

Alice had her own ideas. "There's *Democracy Now* and the folks at *Free Speech Radio News*," she said. "We could also contact *Mother Jones Magazine*."

"If you go with print journalism," Elliot said, "then I recommend the New York *Times* or the Washington *Post*; they have a larger readership."

Back to big media again, Reb thought.

"Maybe we're exaggerating the danger," he said. "I mean, once the story is out there, then we're no longer a threat to anyone, right? They could harm us out of spite, but would they really do that?"

"They would use us to get to Walter," Alice said.

"How?"

"Force us to tell them where he is."

"But what if we don't know where he is?"

Neither Elliot or Alice responded.

Reb took a long breath. "I say we proceed one step at a time. If we need to go to NPR or somebody else, then we'll do it. Maybe I should give Lyle Workman a call and see what he thinks. Are we agreed that simply dropping the story is just not an option?"

Alice nodded.

"Okay then, let's do it by the book."

"Which means?" Alice said.

"Which means we handle it like any other story; corporation or not, EnerTex gets an opportunity to comment before the story goes public."

"You're really committed to this, aren't you?" Elliot said.

"Call it taking care of karma," Reb said. "When it comes to our journalistic ethics, we have to be impeccable. At a higher level, it's our only protection."

"But you can't just waltz into EnerTex headquarters and ask to talk to Avery Axton," Alice said. "You'd never come out again."

"You could do it by telephone," Elliot said.

"Do you think your brother would agree to that?" Reb asked.

Elliot thought it over and shook his head.

"No, Avery's very careful with telephones. And if he *did* agree to a telephone interview, it would only be so that the FBI or someone else could trace the call. That's the way he operates, and I suspect he's extremely eager to get his hands on Walter again."

They sat in silence and hoped for the hint of a breeze. Reb had a tall glass of lemonade next to him. The ice had already melted. He took a long swallow and watched a lone buzzard circling in the distance. He felt a sudden, unexpected kinship for whatever poor creature was drawing the bird's attention. Texas can feel so God damn lonely, he thought to himself.

"I have an idea," Elliot said, breaking the silence. "Perhaps I can set up a meeting with my brother in a neutral setting."

"What kind of *neutral* setting?" Alice said.

"I'll tell you if I can work it out. Give me an hour or so to see what I can do."

"But I thought you had to return to Houston," Reb said.

Elliot glanced at his watch. "The clinic will be closed by the time I get back as it is. Why don't you take Reb for a walk, Alice. He needs the exercise."

She wanted to say, "In this heat?" but instead she stood up. "Come on, Reb," she said, "I'll show you around the stables."

"Meet me back here in an hour," Elliot said and walked off toward the house.

Reb got up and noticed that his side was causing him less pain.

"Where thou shalt lead, there shall I follow," he said to her, "but let's keep to the shade."

THE MEETING WAS on, Elliot informed them. It would take place in two days time. Avery Axton and Reb alone—no cops, no Charles Hathaway, just the two of them discussing the future of mankind. And what's more, Avery didn't know about the meeting.

"Think of it as a surprise party," Elliot said with a grin.

"But you're sure he'll show up?" Reb said.

"As sure as I can be."

"What about Alice?" Reb said.

Elliot turned to Alice. "I suggest you go back to California and do what you can to build support with the people at the radio station. When Avery figures out what's happening, he'll come on like gang-busters—lawyers, private investigators, law enforcement. It could get ugly."

"Women and children first into the lifeboats," Alice said. "Is that what this is?"

Neither man replied.

"And if I decide to stay?"

"Then you stay," said Reb.

"Appleyard said he can take you to the airport in the morning," Elliot said.

"I'll let you know," she said and was angry with herself for being so emotional. Reb and Elliot were only watching out for her; they knew she was aching to go home. She also realized that this was just the beginning. The days and months ahead would be extremely difficult for all of them. She hoped she was up to it; she didn't do well with uncertainty.

"What about Walter?" she asked. "What's going to happen to him?"

"That's the sixty-four thousand dollar question," Elliot said.

"He's dead-set against going back to EnerTex," Reb said.

"Who can blame him?" Elliot said, "Marion owns a jet. Perhaps he can arrange to get Walter out of the country."

"Where will he go?" Reb said.

Elliot shrugged. "That's up to Walter, but I'll miss him."

Reb was surprised to discover that he too shared this emotion. Walter's courage and determination were inspiring. Perhaps also it was because they both risked becoming outcasts. Yes, he would miss Walter as well.

37

AVERY SPENT THE morning alone in his office going over the Houston Police Department crime report and similar reports from the FBI and his own security unit. Over the last week he had read them so often he could recite their contents verbatim. The security officer at the Polio Institute had survived the shooting; he would require an artificial hip and months of physical therapy. The Institute's director recovered as well but had been so traumatized by the event that he decided to retire—soon afterwards he announced his engagement to his secretary, Hilda Montgomery, this according to the FBI report.

A local Russian "terrorist cell" had been dismantled and their leader, Uri Gryaznov, killed. Unfortunately, Colonel Degtyar had not been captured although one of the cell members claimed that Degtyar had been executed and his body dumped into the ship canal. Agent Brewer was still pursuing Gryaznov's sister, Tatyana. She was believed to be in San Diego and an arrest was imminent.

This left only Anatoly Kryuchkov at large although he clearly had accomplices. Whether they were agents of a foreign government or a rival energy company, no one could say.

Avery pushed the reports to the side and picked up a letter. It was from the director of the New Orleans Chapter of Habitat for Humanity. The letter stated that Mr. Martin Hamilton had applied for the position of Volunteer Coordinator and that he had listed EnerTex as a reference. Avery could feel his temperature rise; to think he had put his trust in that dimwit. He stood up, walked over to the bar, and poured himself a drink. He seldom touched alcohol during working hours but he had a lot on his mind. Brenda was one of them; great sex, but she was already dropping hints about how he should divorce Bea. As for EnerTex, the company was poised for a surge of growth that would put the early days of AT&T and GE to shame. Within the next six months, the company was set to begin simultaneous construction on four one-thousand-plus megawatt power plants: two in Nevada; one in Arkansas and one in Wyoming. Partnership papers were also being prepared for joint ventures with a half-dozen European utilities. Luckily, Kryuchkov wasn't necessary for any of that to happen. All the same, Avery regarded the physicist's sudden disappearance as a bad omen. He needed to find the Russian whatever the cost—or some assurance that the man was dead. He could live with either.

"It's better to wear out than rust out," Avery muttered. It was one of Archibald Axton's pet sayings, which he had passed on to his oldest son along with the company he had built up over the years.

"Well, I'm not worn out yet," Avery said and sipped his whiskey. He moved to the window and gazed out. Smith Street was bustling as always and he began picking out the headquarters of some of the world's leading energy companies. They had done very well over the last handful of years. Several had posted profits in excess of sixty-percent per annum. All that, however, was about to change. By the time Archie Axton's son was done, EnerTex would wield more power over the lives of more people on the planet than ever did the likes of Caesar, Ghengis Khan, or Exxon-Mobil.

Avery stepped back to his desk, finished his whiskey with a long swallow, and pushed the intercom button.

"Brenda, come in here."

*   *   *

THE CLUB WAS crowded and smoky and Avery regretted his decision to come. He had never seen his brother's band perform. Texas Swing was, next to rap, his least favorite style of music, even though his paternal grandfather had been a fiddler back in the hills of Tennessee. Avery met the old man only once and never heard him play. The fiddle eventually turned up among his father's possessions when he and Elliot got together to parcel out the family heirlooms. Avery's first choice was his father's gold ring, the one he purchased the day his first oil well came in. It was a massive piece of jewelry that showed off his father's initials—AA—as a pair of overlapping oil derricks inset with diamonds. Elliot's first choice, to Avery's surprise, was the fiddle. It wasn't much of an instrument; Avery believed his grandfather had purchased it for six dollars from a Sears and Roebuck catalog back around 1910. "Well, each to his own," was Avery's only comment.

"Come hear us play, big brother," Elliot had said on the phone. "It'll be a hoot."

"Bea's out of town; I don't think I can make it," he told Elliot. This was called *wifeing* someone, a term coined by car salesmen. Just when a man was about to write the check, he would get cold feet and say, "I need to talk it over with my wife first." Such men hardly ever returned to complete the transaction.

"Come on your own then," Elliot said. "We'll have some drinks afterwards; it'll be like old times."

What old times? Avery wondered. As kids they seldom played with each other and they sure as hell didn't go out carousing together when they got older. All the same, Elliot asked for little, not even a donation for his precious clinic. Marion Harless supported the clinic, Avery knew, and had even served on the board. But what did that matter to him? The old fart could spend his money any damn way he wanted.

"All right, Elliot, I'll be there," he told his brother. Maybe the distraction would do him good. He didn't even know what instrument his brother played in the band. Maybe it was the old fiddle; he was curious to find out.

Hanging up the telephone, Avery found himself thinking about Marion again. He knew his brother and Marion were close friends, which seemed odd given the difference in their ages and the sorts of people they were. Marion loved money almost as much as Avery did. He loved jet-setting around the world buying vintage racing cars and generally playing the bon vivant. Sometimes Avery compared Texas with the ancient land of India. As America's sub-continent, the two regions shared more than a geographical similarity. Both had been colonized by outsiders at the end of a gun and had known a rigid caste system—on the lowest rung in India was the "untouchable," while in Texas it had been the Indian and the African slave, and later the Mexican "wetback." So why would a Raj like Marion be such bosom buddies with his idealistic brother? Maybe it was a Mother Teresa thing.

It bothered him to think about Marion. He had known the man all his life but they'd fallen out when Marion asked to invest in EnerTex and Avery turned him down—angry words and injured feelings all around. Instead, Avery mortgaged the house and yacht, sold the timeshares in Hawaii and St. Moritz, and hocked every gas well he owned just so he could keep the company going. This was during the mid-eighties when California was booming and Texas was struggling for air.

A table had been reserved for him up close to the stage, and as they snaked their way through the crowded room, he was glad he brought Brenda along. Straight after work they had gone to a little Thai restaurant he was fond of and over plates of roast duck curry she had talked about her family. It was, as she told it, a short and not very edifying tale of growing up in Texarkana with an alcoholic father and an over-worked mother. He asked about her husband's recent death but she changed the subject to what Avery liked to do when he wasn't being captain of the *Starship EnerTex*.

"I enjoy skiing and scuba diving," he said and her spirits sank. That's what everybody who has money and isn't ambulatory wants to do, she almost said. She expected rock climbing next but he surprised her. "I want to take a journey on the *Orient Express* someday."

Now you're talking, she thought. His wealth and power were aphrodisiac enough, but a romantic trip on the *Orient Express*—

"Why are you smiling?" he asked her. She was saved from answering by the arrival of the check. As they stepped out onto the sidewalk, he acted on impulse and invited her to go with him to the club.

"Come listen to some Texas Swing," he said.

"My, you are full of surprises," she said and laughed.

"What do you mean?"

"I just didn't figure you for Texas swing."

"It's my brother's band. He asked me to come hear them play tonight. The club is in Old Town."

The patrons of the club were mostly white middle-aged pseudo-cowboys and cowgirls in Dustin boots and brightly colored western shirts with snaps instead of buttons. Avery stood out in his three-piece tailored suit, but his native-born "I don't really give a shit what anyone thinks" attitude insulated him against such petty concerns.

A few minutes passed and the band ambled out onto the stage and began tuning their instruments. Avery got the attention of a waitress who was wearing a skin-tight tee-shirt with the words "McGee's Roadhouse" in red, white, and blue letters blazoned across her ample breasts. Brenda noted Avery's look of approval and was pleased. She wanted Avery hungry; she had great hopes for the evening.

"What's the band's name?" she said above the clamor of hoots and whistles that greeted the musicians.

"The *Texas Wonderboys*," Avery said.

"I've heard of them. They're supposed to be quite good."

"Really?"

She was in high spirits; she'd have to watch her drinking. When she felt good, that's when she liked to feel even better. But she couldn't risk a thoughtless remark. As the soon-to-be Mrs. Avery Axton, she had her reputation to think about, after all.

38

TIGHT HARMONIES AND driving rhythm were the *Wonderboys'* hallmark and tonight was no exception. Jerry Ray Wilson on the pedal steel was in particularly fine form. He sat hunched over his shining chrome instrument with the intense concentration of a Mongolian shaman communing with the spirit world. And the audience loved it and expressed their appreciation with wild abandon. Meanwhile Elliot, thumping away on the upright bass, watched his brother closely to see if he was enjoying himself. It was impossible to tell. Avery had ordered a whiskey but barely touched it while his female companion had thrown back three margaritas and was on her fourth when the band started in on their last number of the first set, the Bob Wills' classic "Faded Love."

"Well, what did you think?" Elliot asked as he came up to their table. "Time to quit my day job?"

"Why do you call yourselves the *Wonderboys*?" Avery asked. "You've got a girl playing fiddle."

Typical Avery, Elliot thought. Not a word about the music. "When we started out six years ago, the fiddler was a man. But then he went off to play with Willie Nelson and that's when Joanna joined us. We didn't think *Wonderpersons* had quite the same ring to it."

"And *Wonderboys* makes me think of the *Playboys*," Brenda added.

Elliot was surprised she knew about the band they modeled themselves after. He would have bet the farm Avery didn't know Bob Wills from a hole in the ground.

"Aren't you going to introduce me?" he said to his brother.

"You've already met," Avery said. "This is Brenda; she works for me." Brenda held out her hand and her eyes sparkled with delight. Whether it was the music, the thrill of illicit romance— the fact his brother was having an affair was obvious—or the three margaritas she had knocked back, Elliot couldn't tell. But now that Avery had mentioned it, he did recall her face. It had been two years or more since he had last visited his brother at his office.

"There's someone backstage I want you to meet," Elliot said.

"Who is it?" his brother asked.

"Just somebody I think you'll want to meet."

Brenda was spinning celebrity fantasies in her head. It had to be somebody famous; she'd heard they often showed up at clubs unannounced to hear a local band play. It could be Emmy Lou Harris or Garth Brooks. Maybe it was Justin Timberlake or Eminem. This was Houston, not Texarkana. Anything was possible.

No harmless celebrity worship, however, was going through Avery's head. He was suspicious.

"Is it Marion?" he asked. "I really don't want to see him right now."

"It's not Marion and Marion's not all that fond of you these days either."

"Then who is it?"

"Trust me. It'll take all of fifteen minutes. He's in the green room. I can walk you back."

"Can I come?" Brenda asked.

Both men gave her a puzzled look. Elliot didn't want the girl tagging along but he couldn't come up with a plausible reason to exclude her. Avery solved the problem.

"I'll go and see who it is. You stay here. I'll be right back."

They walked down a narrow hallway into a room filled with a dozen people, most of them band members. On a long table against one wall, next to a plastic bowl filled lime slices, sat a dwindling bottle of *Jose Cuervo* tequila. Further along the table was a platter of cold cuts with slices of cheese and strips of celery arranged neatly along the edge. Avery's nose detected the scent of marijuana as he scanned the room with a meticulous efficiency born of years of attending corporate conferences. Few men could size up a room full of people as quickly or accurately as Avery Axton.

Elliot led him toward a couch where a man was seated by himself. Avery judged him to be in his fifties. He was in need of a haircut and his skin had a sallow cast to it. Probably the sound guy, Avery thought. The man was thumbing through a year-old copy of *Entertainment Weekly*. Suddenly it dawned on Avery that this was the person his brother wanted him to meet and he regarded the stranger more closely. The man put down the magazine and looked up. His face was vaguely familiar but Avery was sure they had never met. Maybe he had seen the man's face on television—most likely an environmental or anti-globalism activist. Such people often glommed onto popular musical groups as a way to prop up their pathetic "save the world" agendas. But then it came to him with a jolt that nearly ripped his head off. Of course he recognized the face. Hamilton had given him the surveillance photographs he had snapped in west Texas. This was the son-of-a-bitch from California, the radio guy, who was poking around trying to stir up trouble. Well, Avery would be damned if he would be maneuvered into an interview this way. He wanted to pound the crap out of his brother then and there for pulling such a stunt, but instead he turned on his heel without a word, fuming, and started for the door.

Reb called after him. "I've been talking to your buddy Dr. Easler. You know, Anatoly Kryuchkov."

Avery checked himself and turned around.

"What are you talking about?"

"We're working on a story about what's happening to the workers at the Ranger 1 power plant," Reb said, "and I wanted to give you an opportunity to respond before we air it."

How the hell did he know about Kryuchkov? Avery wondered. Didn't the Russians have him? How could he be talking to the press? None of it made sense. He needed time to sort it out in his head, to consider the implications.

"I suggest you call my office and schedule an interview."

"That wouldn't be very smart of me, would it?" Reb said.

"Look, I'll not be manipulated this way," and there was real heat in his voice.

"Well, it's your choice. It's now or never," Reb said matter-of-factly.

Elliot stood to the side and regarded the two men. They reminded him of two fighting cocks facing off, each scratching the dirt and extending his neck feathers. He even had names picked out; his brother was "General Chang" and Reb was "Morning Fire." Perhaps it was time to intervene.

"Mr. Morgan is understandably concerned for his safety given the nature of what's going on. That's why he's reluctant to come your office, Avery."

"And what *exactly* is going on?" Avery's voice was full of acid as he glared at his brother.

"I'll let him explain but I think you have a pretty good idea."

"So you're in this with him?"

"Dr. Easler and I are friends, you know that."

In a flash Avery put the pieces together. Elliot met Easler at the opening reception in Houston celebrating the Ranger 1 plant. It was the only EnerTex corporate event Easler ever attended; showing his face in public was too risky. But the plant was his baby, and Avery believed he had a right to be there. Elliot and Easler talked about chess most of the evening. Elliot bragged about seeing the great Bobby Fischer play; Easler mentioned meeting the Russian grandmaster Anatoly Karpov on several occasions. It pleased Avery that the scientist had found someone like his brother to talk to—less chance of drawing undue attention from any of the other guests. But it was news to him that they had continued their friendship. Avery found his anger reined in by curiosity.

"What has Easler been telling you?" he directed the question at Reb.

"Everything."

"Where is he?"

"Safe."

"Is he coming back to EnerTex?"

"What do you think?"

"Don't get cute."

"Or what? You'll have me arrested for cocaine this time. Or will it be heroin?"

Avery didn't know what Reb was talking about, but he suspected Hamilton was somehow responsible. The ignoramus must have tried to frame the guy. He remembered Brenda telling him that Agent Brewer had called and raised hell about something. He now realized Brenda hadn't told him the whole story. He had an uneasy feeling that she was covering up for the golden boy.

The ambient noise in the room—Jerry Ray and another musician laughing at a joke, the pedal steel player refilling his glass with tequila, the drummer in a red satin shirt on the other side of the room talking to a leggy woman about how he needed to find a new agent—all belonged to an alternate universe as far as Avery was concerned. It was time for serious damage control.

"Why don't you two stay here and talk while we perform our next set," Elliot said. He motioned to his band mates and the room began to empty.

"Tell Brenda I won't be long," Avery said as an afterthought.

Elliot left feeling oddly lighthearted despite the likelihood that Avery would never speak to him again. He had betrayed a brother's trust, an act of primal import, but he was also a doctor and he knew that it was sometimes necessary to administer poison to cure a more serious malady. In Avery's case, that malady was conceit, one of the deadliest on the planet. He only hoped Reb could hold his own with his angry and manipulative brother.

Avery *was* furious on one level, but also grateful for the opportunity to find out what had become of his Russian. And as Reb made no effort to get up, Avery pulled up a chair and sat down. They were now alone.

"We thought the Russians had Kryuchkov," Avery said.

"What Russians?" Reb said, confused.

"The Russians who were looking for him. That's why we provided Dr. Easler with extra security."

"Was it a Russian who shot me?" Reb asked.

Avery eyes widened and Reb realized what he had just said was news to the CEO.

"At the Polio Institute," Reb said. "I was shot while I was helping Dr. Easler into the car. Your brother patched me up. I read in the newspaper that a security guard was also wounded."

"My brother was involved in all of this?" Avery asked.

"He was driving the car. Were the Russians trying to kill Easler?" Reb asked.

"It must have been the guard's bullet that hit you," Avery said. "He was trying to shoot the Russian but missed."

"So it was the Russians who were chasing us." Reb was telling the story to himself as a way of making sense of it. "They were the ones in the white van. We thought they were trying to kill Dr. Easler and assumed they were with the government or EnerTex; that's why we didn't call the police."

Avery just looked at him.

"Well," Reb said, "is it true?"

"Is what true?"

"What Dr. Easler says about time? How it's the fuel source for the ATG process?"

Avery's face betrayed nothing. "And how could that be?"

"By reversing the arrow of time. According to Dr. Easler."

"Are we talking reality or science fiction?"

"You tell me."

"Look, I don't know what nonsense Dr. Easler has been peddling. He works for EnerTex; that's true. But he's only a mid-level engineer. A technician. He wanted more money and we refused. I expect that's why he came to you. But the idea that he can speak authoritatively about our new generation technology is frankly absurd. I'm afraid you've been taken in, Mr. Morgan."

"Okay, then let me record your comments." Reb patted a black equipment bag on the couch next to him.

"I don't conduct interviews on the spur of the moment. If you wish to set up an appointment with our Corporate Communications department, I'm sure something can be arranged."

"We've already had a little talk with Mr. Hathaway," Reb said shaking his head dissmissively. "Here's the thing. We're going to produce and air our story within the next couple of days, a week at the outside. We have several hours of taped interviews with Dr. Easler that I'm sure people will find very interesting. So if you want to comment, as I said, it's now or never."

Avery's pulse quickened and his palms slickened with sweat. A couple of days, he thought to himself. Not much time to stop or discredit Morgan. But as for having his comments recorded, only a numskull spoke to the media without being fully prepared.

"Your schedule, Mr. Morgan, is irrelevant as far as I'm concerned. You can contact my office. Here's my card."

He handed his card to Reb.

"Well, I'm sorry I wasted your time," Reb said pleasantly and dropped the card carelessly onto the sofa cushion next to him. He picked up the magazine again, leafed to an article, and began reading.

His nonchalance infuriated Avery. He inspected the room for any sign that he was being secretly filmed. He hoped to see a the telltale hole in one of the walls or the glint of a lens poking out from under the cold cuts. He had a sudden irrational impulse to arrest the little prick. A citizen's arrest. The charge? Kidnapping. Perfect. That would make it a federal crime.

"Your honor, I had reason to believe that Mr. Morgan was responsible for the criminal abduction of Dr. Walter Easler, who is a Russian national and in the employ of the EnerTex Corporation. May I also point out that Dr. Easler is a brilliant scientist whose significant discoveries in the fields of physics and electrical engineering are vital to the maintenance of our national security."

But he dropped the citizen arrest idea as counter-productive; it was much too public. Then maybe he should just knock the shit out of Morgan, throw him over a shoulder, and take him out the back door to his car. Brenda would figure out that something had happened and find her own way home. His security people back at EnerTex, the head of which was former NSA, would make Morgan divulge the doctor's whereabouts. But there were too many uncertainties to guarantee the plan's success. Morgan might be stronger than he looked. Or he might be armed. Avery evaluated his own position with mounting frustration. He had no weapon, short of his bare hands, and no back-up. This was Elliot's fault. He had been led like a lamb to slaughter by his own brother. The thought galled him and he gave up the idea overcoming his opponent with physical force. His only hope of finding Easler was to use his wits. It was going to be a cat and mouse game, and Avery entertained no doubts as to who was going to be the cat and who the mouse.

"I will talk to you," he said sitting down again, "but no tape recorder."

"I can go with that," Reb said with a shrug, setting the magazine down. He pulled out a small spiral note pad and a pen out of his shirt pocket. He flipped the notebook open. "Let's begin. Tell me about the time acceleration effect."

"What do you want out of all this?" Avery asked.

"The truth."

"Why?"

"The truth will set you free."

"It may get you killed."

"Are you threatening me?"

"No, I'm just being realistic. You have no idea what you are dealing with here."

"Perhaps not, but neither do the workers at your power plant, or the general public."

"Have you always suffered from this exaggerated sense of heroic self-importance?"

"It's a mid-life crisis sort of thing. That's not to say, of course, that I wasn't an idealist in my youth. But what about you?"

"What do you mean?"

"Didn't you go through any of the hippie, war protester, times are a-changin' thing when you were a teenager? You're the right age. Rock concerts? Smoked a little reefer? You know, got down?"

Avery had been guilty of a few of these indiscretions during his youth but they left no more of a trace on his personality than morning dew on a window pane.

"I am very different from my brother," he said.

Reb wondered why he was bringing up his brother all of a sudden.

"Elliot's a great guy," Reb said. "You're lucky to have him as a brother."

"So you say."

"He's a doctor; he's concerned with what's happening to the workers at your power plant."

"And what *exactly* is that?" Avery asked. He was eager to steer the conversation away from his personal life.

"They're getting old."

"We're all getting old."

Reb smiled and nodded. "But they're getting old a whole lot faster than the rest of us and you know it."

"We conducted studies—"

"Hold on," Reb said, holding up his hand. "I believe we're beginning to understand each other so I'll make you a deal. I won't treat you like an idiot if you'll do the same for me."

Again Avery took a quick glance around the room to make sure he wasn't being filmed.

"We're alone," Reb said. "It's just the two of us."

"Okay, let's just say for argument's sake, that the ATG process creates some kind of time acceleration effect. I am not saying it does; my researchers do not believe it does."

"Dr. Easler does," Reb said.

"Yes, I know." Avery sighed. "Dr. Easler thinks it is a serious problem. It is also a problem he has convinced himself that cannot be solved."

"Go on."

"For the sake of argument, let's take Dr. Easler's side for the moment. The power plant is speeding time up, not a huge amount, but enough to present symptoms of aging in the men who work at the plant."

"It's extends beyond the plant as well," Reb added.

"That's Dr. Easler's assertion, but let's stick with the power plant for now. What you are asking me is this: is it right to harm the health of a handful of workers for the sake of increasing the supply of affordable clean electricity? According to Dr. Easler, EnerTex is not harming their health so much as facilitating a set of natural changes to occur more quickly."

"You do have a way with words, Mr. Axton, but please, continue."

"Then this harm must be weighed against the benefits."

"We're talking about human beings, not cubic feet of natural gas or kilowatts of electricity," Reb said.

"But if human beings are central to the cost-benefit analysis then such considerations are appropriate."

Reb wasn't sure where Avery was going with his argument, but he decided to let him have his head.

"What I want you to see, Mr. Morgan—or may I call you Reb?"

"Let's stick with Mr. Morgan."

"What I want you to see, Mr. Morgan, is that the welfare of human beings and the availability of affordable, clean energy are inextricably linked. You cannot consider one without the other. Imagine a hospital with no electricity to run it. No electricity for x-rays, MRIs, or kidney dialysis. No electricity to run emergency response centers or power the surgeon's laser scalpel. For that matter, how could a modern hospital even function without the basic necessities of light, heat, and air conditioning?"

"New Orleans in other words," Reb put in.

"Exactly. And what about food storage? What would happen if crops were left in the fields to rot because there was no electricity for refrigeration or to operate canning factories? No electricity for milking machines and irrigation systems. We have a huge population in this country that needs to be fed. People need water too, but without electricity to pump it, how would the water get to them? Cities wouldn't be able to operate their waste treatment plants, and typhoid and cholera would once again become the scourges of mankind. You see, Mr. Morgan, these concerns about worker safety pale in comparison with what would happen if society ran out of electricity. And that is precisely what is happening right now. We are rapidly running out of electricity because we are dependent upon a set of traditional fuels that helped create the modern technological world."

"I'm aware of the big picture," Reb said. "Every time corporate America gets ready to perpetrate a new outrage, they haul out the old *big picture* argument to justify it. What I want to know is, what's the bottom line? Not the bottom line in terms of company profits but in how far you will go to achieve those profits? Are there any ethical or moral limits that you are willing to place upon your actions, Mr. Axton?"

"Are you speaking to me as an individual or as the CEO of EnerTex?"

"I fail to see how that makes a difference," Reb said. He had yet to make a single note on his pad. "The workers at your power plant are aging at an alarming rate and yet you continue to operate the facility. Have you at least considered informing them? Don't they have a right to decide for themselves if what they're paid is worth the years of their lives they're giving up?"

"We are talking theoretically, you understand," Avery said, "but why do you think the plant employees would refuse to work if they knew about the time acceleration effect?"

"Common sense."

"I wouldn't be so sure of that. If the money was good enough, I'm sure we could find all the workers we need. It's always been that way. In the 1800s, most of the fourteen-year-old girls who left their parents' farms to come to work in the textile mills of New England died before they reached thirty. And yet they still came. Miners willingly went underground to dig coal even though they knew their lives would most likely be cut short by accidents or black lung."

"But they had no choice," Reb said. "They were forced by economic necessity."

"There's always a choice. They could have looked for work elsewhere."

Reb closed his note pad with a shrug. There was no winning the social conditions versus personal initiative debate with someone like Avery. He could hear the band working its way through its second set.

"Okay, forget about yesterday," Avery said, "let's look at today. Did you know that a deep sea diver who works on the North Sea pipelines spends, on average, five months out of each year sitting in a decompression chamber no bigger than this room? Don't you think that's a lot of time to throw away for a job? And yet they're highly skilled professionals. They could find plenty of other work that pays enough to put food on the table and a roof over their heads. But that other work doesn't pay *one hundred thousand dollars* a year, which is what they earn working on the pipelines. The truth is, Mr. Morgan, some people don't value their time as highly as you think they should. If a man with nothing but a high school education can make enough money to live in a nice house, take his wife and kiddies to Disneyland a couple of times a year, buy a new boat, and pay for his aging mother's prescription drugs, he's going do it. Most people would make that kind of deal."

"But you don't pay your people a lot of money."

"That's beside the point," Avery answered with a grimace of impatience. "We could pay them a hundred thousand dollars a year and the cost would add only pennies a day to our customers' electric bills. Remember, the energy source for our electrical generation is essentially limitless and free. Once an EnerTex plant is built, the only hard costs are maintenance and security."

"And corporate salaries," Reb said.

"Yes, and corporate salaries. I fully intend to get rich building power plants and selling electricity. So what? The people will love me for it, because by building those plants, I will be helping solve problems that have made life on this planet a miserable affair for a very long time. Look at the Middle East. What are the big problems there? Oil is one. Well, what happens when cars don't need oil to drive down the highway because they're being powered by batteries or hydrogen? Both can become viable technologies given a stable supply of abundant, cheap electricity. And what's the other big problem in that part of the world? Water. There's simply not enough of it to go around. Either the Jews get it, or their Arab neighbors do. But with sufficient electricity, sea water can be desalinated and pumped to wherever it's needed. Everyone comes out a winner with our ATG technology and the implacable issues that now compel a young Palestinian woman to strap explosives around her body and blow herself up suddenly don't seem so implacable anymore. What does North Korea want? Cheap power. If they can have it—and they can now, thanks to EnerTex—then they can stop building nuclear bombs with which to blackmail the rest of the developed world. The same goes for Iran."

"But every time you build another power plant, you speed time up for everyone. Dr. Easler has done the calculations. Down the road people could lose as much as ten years of their lives."

"That's a gross exaggeration," Avery said sitting back in his chair and shaking his head. "I know what I'm talking about. Worst case scenario, three years."

"So EnerTex *has* done its own calculations," Reb said arching his eyes in mock wonderment. "I thought you said there was no time acceleration effect."

Avery knew he was being sloppy and revealing more than he should. Strangely, he didn't much care.

"What do you think will happen when you broadcast your story?" Avery asked. "Do you honestly believe that people will rise up in protest and demand that these power plants not be built?

Don't be simple. Americans love their electricity and they're not going to live without it, no matter what the cost. And as for your contention that they won't sacrifice a portion of their lives for it, well, just look around you. That's what they're doing now or I'm very much mistaken. And I'm not just talking about the workers at the Ranger 1 plant. I'm talking about the citizens of this great nation, all three hundred million of them. They're more than willing, eager even, to swap substantial chunks of their time for all the marvels the Electric Age has to offer. Did you know the average American spends over four hours a day sitting in front of a box that uses electricity to flicker images at him, and that the average American household has the TV on eight hours a day?"

"But what if some people don't want to be part of the bargain?" Reb said. "Let's say Sharon doesn't want to give up a year of her life, not a day of her life, not even a second of it, in exchange for the electricity you offer? If you keep building power plants, then she will age like everybody else. Her time on this earth will be stolen away too. Doesn't she have a right to object?"

"Of course she does," Avery said, "but don't start bandying words around like *stolen away*. Nobody will be *stealing* her time. You believe in democracy, don't you?"

"What's democracy got to do with it?"

"Everything. Put it to a vote. Let the people decide what they want. We can have polluted air and water. We can have global warming and no one knows where that's taking us—we could go out like the dinosaurs. And let's not forget more wars to control oil and natural gas reserves, runaway inflation—you name it. Or everyone, including your Sharon, gives up a few years of life. How do you think the people will vote given that choice? Just look at how they voted the last fifty years and you have your answer. The desires of the present moment *always* win out over what will happen next year, or even next month."

Again Reb was forced to agree. Did he honestly think that some baby-boomer willing to plop down $53,000 for a three-ton, three hundred horsepower Lincoln Navigator with all the goodies—movies in the back seat for little Britney and Jared to watch, climate controlled air conditioning for the wife so she doesn't have to put down the window and muss her hair—really give a rat's ass about the fact that he's using up energy resources that took the sun and earth a millennia to create and store? No, he was raised to believe that everything on God's green earth was created with the sole purpose of satisfying his slightest whim. And should the thought ever penetrate his consciousness that he is not alone on the planet, that the gallon of gasoline he burns driving twelve miles to Baskin Robbins for an ice cream might be better used by a struggling family in Ethiopia or Costa Rica so they can run a generator for an hour each day to pump fresh water, Mr. American consumer has only to turn on a Christian radio station to receive assurances that it doesn't really matter what he does because according to the Book of Revelations he's living in the "End Times." That was what was really going on inside a good many American heads, Reb suspected. How else to explain the startling popularity of the *Left Behind* books, or the beliefs of the country's own top elected officials? If they honestly thought that there was going to be a tomorrow, say fifty or a hundred years down the line, would they really allow widespread destruction of the environment?

Avery had stopped talking and looked at him with a knowing smile. Reb realized the conversation was making him crazy.

"So what's this got to do with whether or not I believe in democracy?" he said.

"In a democracy, the majority rules," Avery said. "If over fifty percent of the people would rather have cheap, clean energy than time, then they get what they want. That's democracy. My dad had a saying about antiques. He said they were not all they were cracked up to be. Well, that's how most people feel about time, Mr. Morgan. It's an overrated commodity, and if given half a chance, most Americans would be happy to cash in some of their time for a dash more pizzazz in their humdrum lives. That's what electricity does. It adds the pizzazz. Look at the popularity of Las Vegas and Times Square. And if the minority doesn't like it, well, they can lump it."

Reb looked at Avery and tried to imagine him as a precocious little boy climbing trees or laying on his back looking up into the sky to find pictures among the clouds. Sadly, that person, if he ever existed, had long ago been reduced to ashes in the furnace of the marketplace. In Avery's world everything was a commodity to be bought and sold. Air. Water. Even the mysterious invisible airwaves that Maxwell and Hertz discovered could be auctioned off as *bandwidth* to media moguls like Rupert Murdoch and Lowry Mays. All God's sacred gifts neatly divvied up, priced, and thrown on the shelf for sale to the highest bidder. And now thanks to Avery Jordan Axton, *time* was being commodified, converted into electricity, and sold back to an unsuspecting public by the kilowatt. It made Reb sick at heart.

"What about other countries?" Reb asked. "If they vote democratically not to trade time for electricity, it won't matter if you continue building your power plants. Dr. Easler says there's no way to isolate the acceleration effect; time will speed up for entire planet."

"Last time I looked, we were on top of the heap," Avery said. "Do you have a *problem* with that. Mr. Morgan?" He flicked an imagined speck from the sleeve of his jacket and continued. "Rome had its day. France had Napoleon. The British Empire enjoyed its supremacy. Well, now it's America's turn. No one seriously cares what Bangladesh wants, or even New Zealand, do they? It's the evolutionary imperative. Let someone try and stop us from building our power plants and see what that gets them."

"What about China?"

"What about China?"

"They're the rising power, not us."

"My point exactly," Avery beamed, "ATG is the next big thing and the United States has it. Not China. Not Russia. Not the E.U. We do, and I say thank God for that. They'll have to come to us for the technology or watch their people choke to death on their own automobile exhaust and high-sulfur coal emissions. Or maybe you'd rather have them in charge, the Chinese, I mean. They aren't as sensitive about labor conditions as the big bad

....

corporations here at home are, you know. Do you want to see us building prison labor camps in Iowa and New Jersey just so we can compete with them economically? Somebody's got to be a grown-up, Mr. Morgan. If it hadn't been for America's incredible industrial strength and technical know-how during World War II, we'd all now be speaking German and hailing the Fuhrer."

Avery stood up and walked over to the table and poured himself a glass of tequila. He held the bottle up as if asking Reb if he wanted some. Reb shook his head and Avery came back to his chair.

"So where does that leave us?" Avery asked as he sat down. He took a sip of his drink. "Do you know what the life span of a white male in the United States was in 1800? Forty-one. Well, today it's seventy-seven. That's a net gain of thirty-six years. And do you know what was responsible for this remarkable improvement? Technology. Technology, all made possible by electricity, led to increased food production, the elimination of many deadly diseases, and the mechanization of labor so that people simply stopped wearing themselves out. But the future of that technology is now very much in question. Without a sufficient, reliable supply of energy, mankind could find itself sliding backwards into another Dark Age where existence once more will become mean, short, and pointless. So even if we collectively trade in a decade of our lives, shorten the span of each person's life by ten years, which far exceeds our most liberal predictions, then we'd still have a net gain of *twenty-six years*—and that's before factoring in an increase in longevity from having cleaner air and water."

Avery nodded and smiled as if agreeing with his own logic. "Also consider for a moment the breakthroughs in medical science that will occur in the not too distant future, when stem cells and genetic mapping are used to cure diseases and prolong life. It won't be long until people are living well into their hundreds. And yet none of this will happen without electricity."

"You act as if there's no alternative," Reb said. "What about wind and solar power? These and other renewable technologies could make a huge difference."

"I was wondering when you'd get around to renewables. It's true solar and wind could change the energy equation in a big way. But it won't happen. And you know why? Because if there's anything in shorter supply in this country now than oil and natural gas, it's imagination and political will. You can't just drive over to Wal-Mart and buy them; they have to be encouraged and nurtured. Dumbing down the culture and playing off petty internecine rivalries is not the way to do it."

He looked at Reb, his eyes shining with mischief. Knowing the enemy was a strategy that served Avery well, Reb realized.

"You know what the trouble with you and people like you is, Mr. Morgan? You're afraid of the future."

"That's not true, Mr. Axton. I'm not afraid of the future. It's just that I'm not particularly interested in the kind of future you're proposing. It's too much about making money."

"The future has always been about making money," Avery said, "and only a fool would believe otherwise."

Reb felt as if Avery had cast a spell over him. His mouth was dry, his brain numb, and he was taking in air in short shallow breaths. He thought about Walter and the technology he had invented. How could such a discovery have fallen into the hands of a man like Avery Axton? He tried to think of what to say next but there really wasn't anything to say. Parsed out point by point, comparison by comparison, Avery's logic was unassailable. If human ingenuity had evolved to the point where it could control and manipulate time, then it was only right and proper that it should do so. The will of nature had ordained it.

Reb missed having Alice with him. He trusted her instincts. Would she buy Avery's arguments? He didn't think so. He didn't buy them himself. Some voice, not from his intellect but from his heart, a voice older than the ages of humankind whispered in his ear, "this far, gentle traveler, but no farther." It was a voice to remind him that time was sacred and must never be violated. He would trust the voice. He would do what he could to stop Avery Axton and EnerTex and the entire United States government if he had to. He would start by sounding the alarm.

All this while, Avery gently tapped the side of his glass with the tip of his index finger. He was undergoing an unexpected transformation. Since the day Anatoly Kryuchkov showed up on his doorstep, it had been secrecy, secrecy, and more secrecy.

"The Russians must never find out that we have him," Ron Jarrell had told him. "This comes down directly from the president."

"What about the ATG technology? Is that to be kept secret as well?" Avery asked.

"Yes."

"But what if we need help to make it work?"

"What kind of help?"

"We could partner with one of the research universities."

"Absolutely not, too risky. A foreign exchange student might pass the secret on to one of our enemies."

"What about our allies then?"

"We're going solo on this, Avery. No outside involvement. Just you and the president."

"And Kryuchkov."

"Yes, and Kryuchkov. He either makes it work or he doesn't. Agreed?"

"And if he does?"

"Then we take another look and figure out where to go from there."

"And what if the Democrats are in charge by then?"

Ron smiled. "That's one reason we're bypassing the government, Avery. Too many cooks spoil the broth. As far as the Democrats or anyone else is concerned, EnerTex is responsible for discovering the ATG process and that's why it's vital we keep everything about it secret. The president likes you, Avery. And he trusts you. Don't let us down."

Avery, however, was not by nature an evasive or devious man. Over the intervening years these strictures grew increasingly distasteful, though he accepted them as sensible precautions. Even inside his own organization he had to be extremely careful to make sure that only those with a compelling need-to-know were privy to the truth about ATG. He had been entrusted with a monumental responsibility and played by the rules. But now, thanks to Kryuchkov and Morgan, the cat was out of the proverbial bag. The defector had defected again, this time to the media. The New York *Times* wasn't about to break the story. Or *CNN*. Instead, it was a two-bit radio station from God knows where California. Well maybe that wasn't such a bad thing after all. He took a sip of his drink. "Go with the flow," the mediation tapes told him each day as he drove to work. "Change obstructions into opportunities." Okay, he would go with the flow; he would let the story get out. He wouldn't call Jarrell or the president or any of the others. It would solve a mountain of problems for EnerTex. No more pussy-footing around state regulators and stonewalling reporters, and there would be full disclosure when EnerTex went public. Of course, he would keep the nuts and bolts of the ATG technology under wraps—no Linux open-source bullshit there. ATG was EnerTex's gravy train and Avery planned to ride it all the way into the station. He took another sip of Tequila and felt the burden of secrecy lift from his shoulders. He realized there would be a grand hullabaloo at first. The philosophers and moralists on the left would weigh in with their predictable condemnations, but he wasn't worried. What had they accomplished trying to stop the invasion of Iraq? Nothing. He remembered seeing a bumper sticker at the time that made him laugh. "How did *our* oil get under *their* sand?"

"Is there anything else you wish to say?" The sound of Reb's voice called Avery out of his reverie. He put his glass down on the floor next to him and smiled.

"Mr. Morgan, I have decided to let you broadcast your story. In fact, I encourage you to do so."

Reb just stared at him, not knowing what to say.

"Again, this is off the record and I will deny that this meeting ever took place," Avery said, "Furthermore, EnerTex will not help you in any way, but neither will we do anything to *hinder* you. We will be evasive, we'll spin the hell out of it, but essentially, we will not refute the facts."

Reb had trouble taking this in. Now, all of sudden, after overcoming one roadblock after another, EnerTex was saying, go ahead, broadcast your story and have a nice day?

"Okay," Reb said, "what gives?"

"You're journalistic ship just came in," Avery answered leaning back and smiling. "You have the scoop of the century, and this century is not very old yet. But let me give you a piece of advice. I would make myself scarce after the story airs. I mean it. There will be a lot of people wanting to talk to you and there are some you really should avoid."

"What kind of people?"

Avery shrugged. "A cadre of federal and state officials I would think, but there will be others too, some in the employ of foreign governments and multi-nationals. I trust you have plans. Well, go ahead with them. It was a courageous thing you did, by the way, arranging to talk to me this way. Why risk it?"

"To give you a chance to tell your side of the story."

Avery nodded and smiled. "Very noble. But unless I'm much mistaken, you're in the wrong line of work."

"Why do you say that?"

"Because if you hope to get ahead in journalism with ethical fair dealing, you'll be gravely disappointed. Most of the big media players aren't in that business anymore."

"What about Dr. Easler?"

"The smart thing for him to do would be to come back to EnerTex. We'll protect him. If he doesn't, then he's on his own."

"Does he have anything to fear from EnerTex?"

"Let's just say we don't want him on the loose. He's got too much knowledge crammed inside that oversized brain of his; all it can do is cause us trouble."

"What harm would you do to him?"

"That's not for me to say, but according to the Russian government, he is dead already."

The brutal indifference of this last remark spoke volumes. Reb was tempted to plead for Walter, beg that the poor man be left alone, but he knew it would be a wasted effort. He and Walter were both now out in the cold. And possibly Alice too.

"So you don't care if the story gets out?" Reb said.

"I *do* care," Avery said, "but not in the way you suppose. You see, Mr. Morgan," he leaned forward and Reb smelled the Tequila on his breath, "nothing will change. The people will not cry out. They will not prevent us from building our power plants. No, they will welcome us into their communities with open arms. You'll see."

"I think you're selling the American people short," Reb said.

"Do you really?" he leaned back again. "Well, perhaps I am. Only time will tell."

39

THE ROAD OUT of Hayfork wound its wet, lazy way deep into a moss-clad forest of Ponderosa pine and Douglas fir. The green '49 Chevy pickup rattled along pleasantly with Reb in the passenger seat by the window and Alice in the middle. The air was heavy with moisture, the temperature in the mid-forties, a typical February day in the Trinity Mountains of northern California. Behind the wheel Stretch talked away with the enthusiasm of Neil Cassady driving the bus for Ken Kesey. Stretch had dropped out thirty-five years earlier after being discharged from the army to become a "misfit in these nervous, bustling, trivial times," a line he'd borrowed from a book by Thoreau that he read one day while guarding an ammunition dump in Quang Tri province on the border with North Vietnam. Hiding out in the mountains around Hayfork were others of his clan, combat veterans traumatized to the point of social alienation by their experiences in the jungles of southeast Asia. They supported themselves in a variety of ways, chief among them the illegal cultivation of marijuana. Only growing pot wasn't as profitable as it used to be because a huge share of their business was being steadily siphoned off by hitherto political conservative farmers in the Midwest, who found they could pay the taxes and upkeep on the family farm by planting the desirable weed in among their rows of field corn and soybeans. America was about change, if it was about anything.

"The Dutchman's got the shop up and running on all cylinders," Stretch said. "Tommy De Franco and Augie are helping him out. You remember Augie? You guys met last time you were up here."

"How's he doing?" Reb asked.

"His girlfriend is pregnant. She moved up here from San Francisco a couple of months ago. Her name is Raven. You know it used to be you couldn't hardly get a word out of that boy. Then he hooks up with Raven and he's a regular chatter factory."

They came around a bend and a small doe bounded across the road. Stretch hit the brakes, throwing Reb and Alice forward against the dashboard.

"It's getting dangerous around here," he said as the truck picked up speed again. "Some folks got it in their heads that the deer have that wasting disease, so they don't hunt 'em as much as they used to. That means less venison going into the freezer and more accidents on the roads. Me, my brain's pretty much wasted already; I can relate to them poor deer."

Reb met Stretch years ago at a rock concert. Two half-loaded bikers in black leather vests with oily pony tails spilling out from under red bandannas were hassling a girl out in front of the porta-johns. One stood in front of her, blocking her way, while the other moved around behind her. The concert grounds were packed and a crowd quickly formed but no one did anything. The girl looked frightened and Reb looked around for festival security. Suddenly a very tall, lean man stepped out the crowd and went up to the girl, ramrod straight and very gallant. The bikers, who weighed in the neighborhood of two hundred and forty pounds apiece, with tattooed forearms the size of Christmas hams, closed ranks and advanced on the interloper. Then a very peculiar thing happened. The bikers hesitated and stopped less than four feet from Stretch, as if rooted to the ground. Their features, so full of mischief and aggression just moments before, were transformed into maps of doubt and anxiety. It seemed as if the whole of creation had abruptly stopped on its axis to catch its breath. The seconds ticked by and no one moved. Reb sensed an invisible energized sphere surrounding Stretch. He also thought he detected the distinct aroma of burning sulfur in the air—the stench of brimstone that was said to accompany the devil wherever he went. As he got to know the man better, Reb theorized that Stretch, in his efforts to survive, had taken into himself a portion of the hell that was Vietnam, had swallowed it like a sin-eater, so that nothing in the middle realms frightened him anymore. The bikers with all their crude strength and bravado sensed this also, saw the death skull staring out at them from Stretch's eyes and felt the eternal dank cold of the grave awaiting them. Whatever it was, the bikers clearly had no interest in going any place Stretch had been and turned around and shanked it out through the crowd without a backward glance. Stretch then turned to the girl who gave him a weak smile of gratitude and promptly melted away with the rest of the crowd. Reb then stepped forward and introduced himself and it wasn't long until they were friends. And that was the thing about Stretch, the essential paradox of his nature. On the one hand, he was the most dangerous of men and yet he could be exceedingly gentle and considerate. Never once during the years of their friendship did Reb ever hear Stretch raise his voice in anger or take pleasure in cruelty of any kind. A remarkable person in every way and the first person Reb thought of when it came time to recruit someone to be Chief of Security for their new organization.

"What's Tommy doing now?" Reb asked.

"He's taken over procurement so Eddie can direct manufacturing full time. Augie's job is getting the RTG devices out the door to the folks who want them."

"How much are we charging now per unit?" Alice asked.

"We adopted a sliding scale: from free to four hundred dollars for those who can afford it."

"And Mr. Dark is still picking up the tab?" Reb asked. The code-name belonged to Simon Westgard, who lived in the Bay Area. Simon inherited a bundle from his family. The name came from *Cooger & Dark's Pandemonium Shadow Show* in the Ray

Bradbury novel *Something Wicked This Way Comes*, a story about a calliope that turns backward to carry its riders into the past.

"He deposited 200K in the bank account last week and he's trying to get some of his rich friends to kick in some more, but baby-boomers can be a tight-assed bunch."

Stretch made the financial part sound simple. Truly, it was a masterpiece of misdirection and misrepresentation involving banks in the Cayman Islands and eastern Europe and a variety of convoluted currency-trading schemes. Stretch developed and refined the procedures during his marijuana production and distribution days.

"How many units have been shipped out?" Alice asked.

"Eighty so far. Walter's delighted."

"And how is the Dutchman?" Reb said.

"He's doing good. Raven is teaching him how to read palms and Tarot cards."

"He's into that stuff?" Reb asked.

Stretch gave a conspiratorial grin. "I think he's a got a thing for Raven. He says he wants to teach her how to play chess. She and Augie plan to make him an official granddaddy."

They skirted a small creek for several miles and then turned off the blacktop onto a narrow gravel road. Stretch pushed Peter Rowan's *The Walls of Time* into the truck's CD player and they banged along with Stretch singing loudly out of key. Meanwhile Reb reflected on the events of the last year since he first met Walter. It had been a trying time but also exhilarating. To their credit, KVMR went ahead and broadcast the EnerTex story after a lengthy and highly contentious board meeting during which Jack Dunnel and two other board members resigned. Two days later Amy Goodman aired the story on *Democracy Now* and this was followed by a flurry of calls from news organizations. Reb had taken Avery Axton's advice and already gone into hiding, as had Alice, so it fell to Phil—with Mattie serving as the station's temporary Public Information Officer—to handle the flood of interview requests. It was a complicated process involving public pay phones and several VoIP internet phone services. Land-line and cell phones were too easily traceable. All in all he and Alice did two dozen interviews, mostly with reporters from public and community radio stations including interviews with Terry Gross at WHYY in Philadelphia and Warren Olney at KCRW Santa Monica. Charlie Rose also invited them to come on his television show, but while they were trying to think through the security risks of such an appearance, the show's producer called and withdrew the invitation without giving a reason. As for *FOX News*, not only did they refuse to report on the story, they went out of their way to paint Reb and Alice as untrustworthy liberal opportunists, aligning them with their favorite whipping boy, Michael Moore.

But it was thanks mainly to the blogosphere that the story reached a broad international audience and in time editorials began appearing in newspapers such as the *Guardian, Der Spiegel*, and the *Times of India* calling for the United Nations to launch a full scale investigation. These efforts, however, were successfully blocked by the United States in the Security Council and by the fact that most countries in the world wanted the ATG technology and had no wish to alienate the nation who possessed it.

In Congress, a representative from New Jersey called for hearings to look into allegations that the CIA had turned over a valuable defector to a private company in Texas. Among the subpoenas issued, one summoned Jane Doe, alias Samantha Haverling, and another John Doe, alias Paulson "Pauli" Algren. Both failed to appear. The White House and the CIA, meanwhile, staunchly denied any involvement in the matter, and in time the investigation died from want of hard evidence.

Not surprisingly, EnerTex's fortunes rose on the tide of publicity and soon utility managers from across the country and around the globe were lining up to sign contracts. The increase in business, in fact, forced EnerTex to hire dozens of additional deal originators who gleefully racked up frequent flyer miles, padded expense accounts, and helped make Avery Axton one of the richest men in the world. Neither EnerTex or the government would discuss the particulars of the ATG process, nor whether *time* was being used as the fuel source.

"People are free to believe whatever they want," the president's press secretary said during a news conference, "it's freedom and democracy that makes our nation great. Now can we move on to more important matters. . ."

What EnerTex and the government did deny, repeatedly and vociferously, was that the ATG process was harming the plant workers or those who lived nearby.

"Absolutely not," Charles Hathaway insisted when questioned by reporters. "We've conducted numerous tests and the results are irrefutable; the ATG process is completely safe. Now I'd like to talk about our upcoming IPO. I have a prospectus here that I think you will find interesting. . ."

As for Reb and Alice, surviving outside officialdom was daunting at first. They had to acquire forged documents, open bank accounts under false names, and learn to deal exclusively in cash. This would have been impossible without Marion's generous financial support and Stretch's underworld connections. Reb likened the process to learning to live off the electric grid, difficult in the early going, but once you got the hang of it, it was a life that bestowed a marked degree of freedom. And there were other benefits, such as the wonderful people they met while helping grassroots organizations in places like Sheboygan and Bangor oppose construction of EnerTex power plants in their communities. Having endured the long, dreary, unimaginative years of America's decline, the members of these groups met in living rooms and church basements, at teach-ins and music festivals. They were ready and eager to strike a blow against the machinations of the corporate empire. Reb found the travel exhausting, one day in Boulder, Colorado, and a week later in Charlottesville, Virginia—security concerns prevented them from flying so they had to drive everywhere or take the train. All the same, he felt he was making a difference. That, along with Alice's love, sustained him. His code-name was "Captain Chronos" and Alice's was the "Duchess" from *Alice in Wonderland*.

It was the unexpected improvement in his eyesight, however, that most cheered Reb during this time. Dr. Moon called it a miracle, for not only did the glaucoma go away, but Reb soon regained most of his peripheral vision. In reality, it was all Walter's doing. The physicist built a special goggle-like contraption that strapped around Reb's head. It looked externally like a virtual reality gaming device but the resemblance ended there. He had started work on it soon after it was decided that the three of them would go into hiding together. For two years he toiled away inside his secret laboratory—again thanks to Marion—hidden away in the mountains of northern California. Never had his creative intelligence been more stimulated and productive. It was all part of a larger plan and the device he invented for Reb's eyes was only the beginning.

Reb, Alice, and Stretch traveled four miles to the end of the gravel road. Stretch jumped out and moved several strategically-placed fallen pines to reveal an abandoned logging road that disappeared into the forest. The truck's tires spun in the loose dirt a few times before finding sufficient traction and a mile and a half later they came to a small clearing. Several dozen fir saplings grew on top of a low earthen mound in the center of the clearing. The site was the headquarters of the Time Liberation Front.

As they climbed out of the truck, a door suddenly materialized on the near side of the earthen mound and Walter emerged, having been informed of their arrival by an array of hidden surveillance cameras and other sensors. He smiled broadly.

"Reb and Alice, how good it is to see you," he said, giving Reb a very Russian bear hug as Stretch began unloading boxes from the back of the pickup truck.

"And how are you, dear?" Walter said, taking Alice's hands in his own and looking into her eyes.

"I'm fine, Walter. And you?"

"It has been too long, but I too am fine."

"The modifications you suggested for the wind turbines made a big difference," Reb said. "Marion is very grateful."

"You have seen him recently?"

"We traveled through Texas last month and visited his new wind farm. It's outside Centralia and is already generating 250 megawatts of electricity. They hope to double their output by next year."

"That is very good."

"Do you remember Ernesto Valdez and Mike Pendergast?" Alice said. "They were the workers at the Ranger 1 plant who got fired because they talked to us."

"Yes, of course; they were very brave."

"Well, they're now working for Marion at the wind farm. Mike is the maintenance foreman, and Ernesto is in charge of security and education. He gives tours to school groups and others who are interested in wind energy."

"I think the decision to build the wind farm so near the EnerTex plant was Marion's way of getting back at Avery," Reb said. "But tell me, how are the RTG devices working?"

Walter smiled, "I will show you. Please, come inside."

They clambered down a flight of metal stairs into a cavernous underground complex. A work bench ran down the center of the main room and metal shelves filled with boxes of parts ran along two walls. Against another wall stood a huge generator which was vented outside with a muffled two-inch pipe.

"The others have gone for a hike," Walter said, "I called them on the mobile radio and they will be back soon."

He walked over to the generator, pushed a switch, and the starter engaged the propane-fueled engine. The room filled with noise and Walter picked up a square black box that looked like a laptop computer.

"I thought it best not to make them stand out," Walter said, grinning like a child.

He picked up a power cable and connected one end to the black box; the other he plugged into a 110-volt receptacle on the generator. He pushed a button on the side of the box and the generator came under load.

"Using the generator isn't the same as hooking up to the grid but it will show you how well my device works."

This was Walter's big invention, the one he'd worked on with nearly superhuman determination since coming to California from

Texas. Now instead of making electricity by effectively speeding
time up, he had developed a process that used electric current to
expand time, to slow it down. Walter referred to his new RTG
process as "mirror image" technology, with one essential difference. Whereas ATG was a centralized technology requiring huge
amounts of capital for plant construction and equipment, RTG
was small and decentralized. Some RTG devices weighed less
than three pounds and yet could transform substantial quantities
of electrical power into time at the flick of a switch. And they were
inexpensive to build. Walter's vision, one shared by Reb, Alice,
and the rest of the members of the *TLF*, was to get as many of
the new devices as possible into the hands of people around the
country so they could begin counteracting the cumulative time
acceleration effect caused by the new EnerTex plants. It promised
to be a Herculean effort but Walter was confident they were at
last on their way.

Reb looked around to see if he could detect any difference
now that the device was turned on. Nothing seemed to have
changed and yet he felt decidedly different. The sense of hurry
that seemed to accompany him everywhere was gone, and in its
place was something that was difficult to describe. He looked over
at Stretch.

"Like when you were a kid, right?" the director of security
said with a huge grin.

It was an apt description, Reb thought, just like when he was
a kid and the afternoons of summer seemed to go on forever, a
leisurely sensation that made him feel . . . he had to search for the
right word . . . rich. Yes, that was it. He felt rich. Not with money,
but with something infinitely more valuable. With time. He could
now attend to all those activities that had, by the modern world's
standards, become mere eccentric delights, such as writing a letter
with a fountain pen or having a conversation with a friend about
philosophy and the meaning of life. He could build a boat, brew
his own beer, or even learn to play the clarinet, something he'd
always wanted to do. He could remember when such activities
were commonplace but that seemed like a very long time ago.

Now, thanks to Walter and this ragtag band of social misfits, he could reclaim his place in a universe full of stories, marvels, and possibilities.

"Give us a year, maybe two," Stretch said, "and we'll have enough of these puppies around the country to give the bigwigs a real run for their money."

"When they figure out what we're up to," Reb said, "they'll come after us with a vengeance."

Stretch shrugged and smiled. "We'll stay a step ahead of 'em, don't you worry." He was confidence itself and Reb had a strange thought. Pot farmers used large quantities of electricity to power their grow lights and now a bunch of former pot farmers would use large quantities of electricity to manufacture time. There was a corollary there somewhere.

"What do you say, Walter?" Reb turned to the scientist, "Is this what you hoped for?"

"We may not defeat the *Crocodile*, my friend," Walter said with a note of tragic fatalism peculiar to Russians, "but I feel a great burden of guilt has been lifted from my heart." The practice of using code-names was something of a mania with the *TLF*. *Crocodile* referred to the EnerTex Corporation. It was borrowed from the name of the creature who "ate time" in the story of *Peter Pan*.

"At least now I can help undo the evil I helped bring into the world," Walter said, gesturing around him, "And here I have good friends, a home, a family. You cannot know what that means to a man like me after so many years alone."

He reached out to switch off the RTG device but Reb stopped him.

"What's the hurry, Walter? Leave it on. We've got a lot to go over and we can use the extra time."

EPILOGUE

ON THE OUTSKIRTS of Sheboygan, two young men and a woman park their van up the street from the electrical sub-station for Lakewind Industrial Park. It is two o'clock in the morning and they are dressed in black jeans and long sleeve tee-shirts. The area around the sub-station is deserted. From the rear of the van they remove a canvas duffel bag, an army-surplus trenching shovel, and a gray metal box that resembles a 62 quart Coleman picnic cooler. Warren, the team leader, opens the bag and takes out a CO_2 pellet gun and three pairs of night-vision goggles. A single high-pressure sodium light pole illuminates the area. Warren shatters the sodium element using the gun and they are swallowed up in darkness. They wait and listen but the only sounds they hear come from the traffic on the freeway a quarter of a mile away and the sixty-cycle hum of the electric transformers on the other side of the chain link fence. They strap on their goggles, and after twenty minutes of digging, they pass underneath the fence and enter the facility. Rae takes two pairs of insulated rubber gloves out of a pouch slung over her shoulder. She holds each glove up to her mouth and inflates it like a balloon to make sure there are no unseen tears or punctures. She then hands the gloves to her accomplices who put them on. Warren has located his "point of entry," a pair of 7,200 volt conductors leading from the sub-station to the industrial park. Five minutes later the box they brought with them is hot-wired to the conductors and switched on. They fill in the hole under the fence and drive away. Tomorrow night's target will be the substation adjacent to the Bellinger Steel Mill.

DRIVING UP TO the security gate at Stroutman Manufacturing, Tad Kurosaki presents his laminated OSHA identity card that he fabricated the night before on his home computer using the latest version of Adobe Photoshop. The guard gives the card a cursory glance and hands him a green visitor's badge.

"Visitor parking is up on the left," the guard says and he goes back to watching *Days of Our Lives* on the miniature TV inside the kiosk. Tad pulls his car into a space labeled "VISITOR" and gets out. From the trunk he removes a white hard-hat and what appears to be a large tool box. He clips the visitor badge to his shirt pocket even though he knows he doesn't need it; the hard-hat alone gives him the run of the place. Stroutman manufactures mobile homes. Tad enters the main building and finds his way to the electrical control room. The door is unlocked and no one is around. He slips inside and closes the door behind him. Using a battery powered screw driver, he opens up the main distribution panel. He knows his business; for six years he served as an electrician's mate onboard the missile cruiser USS Gettysburg. Now he's working for the other side. Not another country. Just the other side. He removes a device from the toolbox which connects to the "line" side of the current transformer so the increased electrical consumption will not register on the meter. He switches on the device and leaves the plant. Two months later when the device is discovered, federal investigators find a suspicious entry in the security log book. It notes a visit to Stroutman Manufacturing by an OSHA inspector even though the regional office of Occupational Safety and Health Administration in Chicago denies ever dispatching one. By this point, Tad Kurosaki is living in Bangor where the EnerTex Corporation has recently built a new power plant.

*   *   *

OVER THE YEARS, the basement of the Unitarian Church in downtown Olympia, Washington, has provided a venue for a variety of functions, from folk music performances and wedding receptions to independent film festivals and meetings of the Jung Society. Tonight a group of thirty people are meeting to learn and plan. The oldest is seventy-two, the youngest eighteen. They sip cups of free-trade coffee and munch homemade oatmeal cookies as they listen to Tony Doncamari, a retired high school science teacher and track coach, explain a diagram on the dry erase board.

"Only a few of you will need to know this but the "corona effect" means you can tap into a power line without having to break through the insulation—that is if you have the right kind of clamp. The reason you can do it is because the electrons run on the outside of the conductor, just beneath the insulation. In large volume lines, there are multiple currents, one flowing on top of the other, each at a different voltage. This diagram gives you a general idea of what's going on."

He steps over to a table and picks up what looks like a laptop computer. "Our community has been supplied with three kinds of RTG devices. This one you can think of as the "consumer" model.

"What are the others like?" a middle-aged man wearing a ball cap asks.

"They are larger, "industrial grade" devices. Other people are being trained on how to use them but that doesn't concern us here tonight. As you can see, this RTG unit looks like a computer. It's designed to be plugged into an everyday 110-volt receptacle. You can plug it in at home or at work—even at the shopping mall. Then all you do is switch it on and let it run. These devices are not designed to draw large amounts of current because most outlets are fused for fifteen amps. Draw more than fifteen amps and you trip the breaker. But used collectively over time, these RTG units will make a difference. But I should warn you not to tell anyone that you have one. There's currently no law against owning an RTG device but I suspect that will soon change."

"How can they make them illegal?" says a twenty-something girl named Floyd who has green hair and a silver stud in her tongue. "We're not harming anyone."

"They'll come up with some rationale for taking away your rights," says the man with the ball cap. "The war on drugs and the war on terrorism gave 'em plenty of experience."

"But if we're willing to pay for the electricity we consume making more time, than we should be allowed to do it." This from an elderly woman with white hair.

"I'm not going to *pay* for the electricity," says Floyd. "The commons belong to all of us and *time* is part of the commons, like the air we breath and the water we drink. Who gave EnerTex the right to use it up making electricity?" She looks around and heads nod in agreement. "We have the right to take back our lives because that's what time is. I'm going to do like Mr. Doncamari says and take my RTG unit to the mall and to McDonalds and to anyplace there's an unprotected outlet."

Someone one yells out, "Right on, sister," which makes every-one, including the elderly woman, smile.

IN THE CONTROL room of Midwestern Edison the board tells the story. Within the last six hours, the load on the grid has increased seven percent. Something is definitely going on. Dick Grebbins, the chief operator, picks up the handset on the control panel, and twenty minutes later in the south Aegean Sea, the captain of the private yacht *Osprey* receives an urgent call over the SSB radio. He hurries to the stern where Avery Axton is strapping on a fresh air tank for his second dive of the day. His wife of two months, Brenda, in a Rosa Cha bikini, is helping him.

"I'm sorry to bother you, sir, but you have an urgent call."

"Who is it?"

"A Mr. McBride from Houston. He said to tell you that *they're at it again*. This time in Wisconsin."

The truth finally hits home; Avery can no longer deny the obvious. It has to be Kryuchkov. Who else? He has somehow turned the technology around on EnerTex and is out there, probably with that Morgan fellow, making time as fast as EnerTex uses it up. A queer sort of battle. If they were paying for the electricity, he would applaud their efforts. Go ahead, make all the time you want. But increasingly they aren't paying for the current, they're stealing it. He'll discuss it with the president on Friday when they dine together at the White House. He has to find the clever sons-of-bitches and put them out of business. There is no telling how far it might spread; it simply isn't possible to secure every electrical outlet in the country.

"What's wrong, darling?" Brenda asks.

"Just a small problem. We're going in to shore." He lowers the heavy air tank onto the deck and feels a dull ache in his lower back. He thinks, I'm getting too old for this.

REB WONDERS HOW it will end as he drives north through central Massachusetts on his way to Bangor, Maine, where he will meet later that evening with a newly formed chapter of the Time Liberation Front. How long will it be before the authorities catch up with him? The odds are in their favor. They have so many sophisticated machines for finding people, modern-day bloodhounds constructed of silicon and copper wire. Will they come for him in the middle of the night so that no one notices? Will they read him his Miranda rights? Allow him to make a phone call? Perhaps he should escape while he still has the chance. The open airline ticket Marion bought him is folded up inside in his money belt along with the forged passport Stretch gave him. He should forget about the meeting and take the next exit for Boston and Logan International Airport where he can board a flight to Buenos Aires. Marion will wire him enough money to live on and Alice will join him in a month or two. They can buy a place in Patagonia and run a small white-water rafting company. Thanks to Walter he has his eyesight back—no longer the blind boatman.

The rolling hills of New England slip by in the afternoon sunlight, granite-strewn fields and forests of maple and hickory, and suddenly his heart is filled with affection for his native land.

America is so full of fear and trouble—but of promise too. To hell
with it, he decides. He'll not run away. He'll trust the deep magic,
the old magic, to protect him. He passes a billboard with a picture
of an EnerTex power plant on it. He knows it's a fight to the
finish, whatever the outcome. On one side, the organized agents
of corporate power, on the other, a loose affiliation of individuals made up of aging hippies, book readers, twenty-something
anarchists, religious mystics, organic gardeners, artists, golfers,
would-be Luddites, storytellers, hikers, weekend sailors, and tea
drinkers. They have become his people, his clan; individuals who
long for a world in which time is cherished more than money—
and there's more of it.